G R JORDAN

Man Overboard!

A Highlands and Islands Detective Thriller

Just for the sake of amusement, ask each passenger to tell you his story, and if you find a single one who hasn't often cursed his life, who hasn't told himself he's the most miserable man in the world, you can throw me overboard head first.

VOLTAIRE

Contents

Foreword

This novel is set around the highlands and islands of Scotland and while using the area and its people as an inspiration, the specific places and persons in this book are entirely fictitious. The ferry company in this respect is also entirely fictitious.

Acknowledgement

To Ken, Jessica, Jean, Colin, Susan and Rosemary for your work in bringing this novel to completion, your time and effort is deeply appreciated.

Novels by G R Jordan

The Highlands and Islands Detective series (Crime)

1. Water's Edge
2. The Bothy
3. The Horror Weekend
4. The Small Ferry
5. Dead at Third Man
6. The Pirate Club
7. A Personal Agenda
8. A Just Punishment
9. The Numerous Deaths of Santa Claus
10. Our Gated Community
11. The Satchel
12. Culhwch Alpha
13. Fair Market Value
14. The Coach Bomber
15. The Culling at Singing Sands
16. Where Justice Fails
17. The Cortado Club
18. Cleared to Die
19. Man Overboard!
20. Antisocial Behaviour

Kirsten Stewart Thrillers (Thriller)

1. A Shot at Democracy
2. The Hunted Child
3. The Express Wishes of Mr MacIver
4. The Nationalist Express
5. The Hunt for 'Red Anna'
6. The Execution of Celebrity
7. The Man Everyone Wanted

The Contessa Munroe Mysteries (Cozy Mystery)

1. Corpse Reviver
2. Frostbite
3. Cobra's Fang

The Patrick Smythe Series (Crime)

1. The Disappearance of Russell Hadleigh
2. The Graves of Calgary Bay
3. The Fairy Pools Gathering

Austerley & Kirkgordon Series (Fantasy)

1. Crescendo!
2. The Darkness at Dillingham
3. Dagon's Revenge
4. Ship of Doom

Supernatural and Elder Threat Assessment Agency (SETAA) Series (Fantasy)

1. Scarlett O'Meara: Beastmaster

Island Adventures Series (Cosy Fantasy Adventure)

1. Surface Tensions

Dark Wen Series (Horror Fantasy)

1. The Blasphemous Welcome
2. The Demon's Chalice

Chapter 01

Macleod stepped out of the small, green sports car, shaking his head, and stumbled towards the rear door of the Inverness Police Station. He swore to himself that the next time the car was going in for an MOT, he would get a taxi rather than let his sergeant drive him to the station.

'Seoras, you forgot your coat. Do you want me to bring it?'

Macleod didn't answer and simply found his bearings to the hallway of the police station and took the stairs up to his team's office. He ignored the 'Good morning' from Ross and made for his own smaller office at the end of their work area, stepping inside and collapsing in the chair behind his large desk. It took ten seconds before there was a rap at the door, and it opened. Macleod looked up and saw his other sergeant, the red-haired Hope McGrath.

'Are you okay? You're looking a bit peaky this morning.'

'That woman—does she drive like that with you in the car, or is it just me? I felt like I was on some sort of big dipper ride. Tell me, she can see those cars, can't she? She does know they're there?'

'Well, if she didn't hit any of them, I guess she probably does.'

Macleod looked over Hope's shoulder and saw Clarissa Urquhart, the sergeant who had driven him in. She was taking off her trademark large shawl but today was sporting tartan trousers. He couldn't believe the contrast in his sergeants. Young and fresh-faced Hope McGrath was steady, resolute, and efficient. On the other hand, the older Clarissa was a woman who couldn't wait to get things done. She could charge here and there and had earned herself the name of Macleod's Rottweiler for her brisk attitude.

'I take it the coffee's made?'

'Yes,' said Hope, 'as always. You want one?'

'Absolutely and apologise to Ross. I just didn't feel like I could speak to anyone coming in.' There came a shout from outside the office.

'Ask Seoras if he wants a lift home.'

Macleod shook his head at Hope. 'I'll get a taxi,' he said. 'I'll get a taxi if that car is not ready.'

'I'll drop you off,' said Hope.

'But it's not on your way.'

'No, but I'm not having you come in like this every day. You can be grumpy enough at times, without feeling discombobulated.'

Macleod lifted his eyes to Hope, shook his head, and sat back in the seat, closing his eyes again. A minute later, he heard the door open, and a cup was placed in front of him. There was no speech and the person turned away ever so quietly, tiptoeing back to the door.

'Thank you, Ross,' said Macleod.

'Pleasure, sir.'

Detective Constable Ross was the only person on the team who nowadays called him sir. It was a staple from the past, but

2

Ross said he could never get used to calling Macleod Seoras, or even Inspector Macleod. It was always sir. Apart from Hope, Ross had been the longest to serve with him out of his colleagues and was the solid core of the team. Ross made sure everything happened, while Macleod was left free to think long and deep on cases, to make the connections. It had taken him a while, but he felt he had a team now that functioned well together.

Macleod rested his eyelids for another five minutes before opening them and looked down at the paperwork on his desk. There were various things to sign off, reports to read through, and he sat looking at them for an age, before beginning. His coffee had been drunk at this point and almost by magic, Ross appeared to take the cup away and recharge it. In some ways, he felt like a manservant to Macleod, and Seoras sometimes wondered did he take Ross for granted.

He couldn't do that with the other two. If they felt Macleod was overstepping his mark, they'd tell him. Hope, professionally and calmly. Clarissa with the sarkiest of comments.

Picking up the recharged cup, he stared through the glass at his team working in the office outside. Things had been quiet for a week. There had been a couple of routine deaths to look at, but none of them had been suspicious. Times like these he had learnt to enjoy, when there was less cut and thrust, when things were just calm. In his younger days, he'd have been itching for something to happen. Nowadays, he could stay like this for the year, although preferably without the lift in to work.

Macleod watched Clarissa Urquhart pick up the phone and begin to chat to someone on the other end. He was always taken aback by her purple hair. The woman was vivacious and in a lot of ways, he'd grown to like her, but he always felt he had to watch just in case she misbehaved too much. Some people in the force didn't like the sharp comments, but then again, she was like him, edging closer to retirement. She really didn't care less about who she offended anymore. Macleod did, but not from a worry about his job; it was just his nature.

He watched the woman scribble a few notes from her phone call and then stand up and come towards his office. Almost automatically, he put his head down in his work again as the door was knocked and then opened.

'Seoras, I think I'm going to have to give you a lift again.'

Macleod looked up rolling his eyes. 'No.'

'I've just taken a call from Minchlines, the ferry company, stating that they'd sent all of the information to the Coastguard. I think they've called the wrong place.'

'How come?' asked Macleod.

'There seems to have been a number of tragedies on the ferries recently, several passengers who went overboard and whom they were unfortunately unable to rescue. It seems that the Coastguard asked for quite a few details, but somebody at Minchlines has managed to send it to us. I've tried to redirect them. Maybe you should give them a call, because I think Minchlines has got the wrong idea.'

'Will do. They operate all up and down The Minch, don't they? And just south of it.'

The Minch was a stretch of water between the Western Isles and the west coast of Scotland. The islands were served by the ferry company in what was described as a lifeline service. The crossings varied in length, but the water could be rough in the winter. Macleod had used the ferry on many occasions from his time living on the Isle of Lewis.

4

'I'll give them a call,' said Macleod, 'we're not doing anything else at the moment, are we?'

'If you need to get dropped down, I can give you a lift.'

'Dropped down?' queried Macleod. 'The Coastguard's based in Stornoway for that area.'

'All right, out on Lewis? That'll be a fair hike then.'

'No, it won't. We won't need to take the car out for a run either,' said Macleod, 'I'll just ring them.'

'Okay,' said Clarissa, 'but if you need a lift back tonight, just say; okay?'

Macleod didn't even start to argue. He just waved his hand and reached down for his phone. He looked up the number for the Coastguard in Stornoway and gave them a call.

The controller at Stornoway had a name that Macleod thought he recognised from his school days. James MacArthur, as Macleod recalled, was also a quality footballer and a bit of a Romeo in his day. He'd gone to the Nicholson Institute, the same secondary school as Macleod and just about everyone on the Isle of Lewis, and Macleod was sure he would know him.

'Seoras Macleod, long time, I have obviously heard about you, seen you on the news a few times, some bloody business you're involved in.'

'Indeed, James, but I thought you'd left the island. You're back over again?'

'We all return home,' said James, 'except you.'

'You don't want me to visit,' said Macleod. 'I only bring death and destruction and that's why I'm ringing. We took a call today from Minchlines, apparently about sending us all the details on various passengers that had died. Three, they said recently. I don't understand why they're ringing us.'

'Might be enforcement branch that was looking for it,' said James.

'Is something untoward happening?' asked Macleod.

'Is this official? Because I thought enforcement were going to speak to you.'

'Speak to us?' asked Macleod. 'Why would they want to speak to us? I take it these are people who have gone overboard. I thought that was their jurisdiction out there.'

'They've got a theory,' said James, 'nobody else here knows about it but I was advised in case any information came my way, so I could pass it to them.'

'What do you mean, a theory?' asked Macleod.

'Well, I'd better tell you the whole story,' said James. 'Buckle up, it could be a long one.'

'Just hang on a minute,' said Macleod and he placed his phone down and went to the door.

'Hope, come in a minute, sit down, and listen to this.'

His redheaded sergeant stood up, strode over, and took a seat on the opposite side of Macleod's desk.

'James, I've got Hope McGrath here with me to hear this. I just want a second opinion on it because by the sounds of it, this could be quite juicy.'

'Fair enough. Hello, there,' said James, 'nice to meet you, Hope. I was telling Seoras that recently we've had a number of deaths on the ferries, people who have gone overboard. Our investigation branch has been looking into it and they've been asking Minchlines for some of their documentation. We don't think the ferry company has done anything wrong at all. In fact, they reacted splendidly each time in terms of trying to rescue the people who went overboard. We also don't think that any of their equipment or ferries are out of line in any way. In fact, there's a high likelihood of suicide in all three instances, but with them so close together, we decided to take a proper look at it.

'The first one happened on the ferry from Tarbert to Uig, Harris to Skye run. A man by the name of Andrew Culshaw went overboard. No one saw him go in, but he was seen briefly in the water afterwards by a young couple on the other side of the deck, who'd simply walked round and were looking off the back of the ferry when they saw him. There are some rumours that he and his wife were having trouble, but there was nothing to indicate anybody else was with him at the time.

'We don't know the method of entry into the water. We don't know if he knocked himself out or if he simply was deciding to do it, or if it was an accident. A lot is unknown at this time. That obviously was a tragedy, and we went out looking for him, spent several days with lifeboats up and down and the helicopter, but we couldn't recover the body.'

'That's not unusual though, is it? I mean the body will wash up at some point, but it's not unusual not to find them if that happens?' asked Macleod.

'That's correct, Seoras. Once they're in, if you don't get to them quick and they go under, well, it's almost potluck in some ways. He didn't have a life jacket on. Like I say, we don't know the method of entry, could have knocked himself out on the way down.'

'Where was the next one?' asked Hope.

'Sound of Mull, Oban to Mull Ferry. A narrower stretch of water, but Peter Hughes fell off that ferry. Again, he wasn't seen going in, only once he was in the water. They didn't say he was waving or indicating any form of distress. There didn't seem to be any reaction from him in the water, which is one of the reasons why we think these are possibly suicides. However, they spun around, and tried to find him. Again, they didn't succeed.'

'Very similar in some ways,' said Macleod, 'but I guess if somebody's intending to commit suicide, it's pretty reasonable that the circumstances could be similar. Maybe learnt from the first one.'

'Well, yes, because the rescue was all over the news both times. The third one we did manage to pick up the man involved. Unfortunately, we're struggling to get his state of mind.'

'Where did that happen?' asked Hope.

'Leverburgh to Berneray.'

'Where's that?' asked Hope.

Macleod almost tutted. 'That's the Isle of Harris down to North Uist.'

'They're all pretty close, aren't they?' said Hope.

Macleod took a deep intake of breath, 'Pretty close is true,' he said; 'that's interesting. What happened with this one, James?'

'Well, again, we don't know. He was simply seen in the water. It's not that big a ferry, quite hard to go in unnoticed. Although, if people were inside, which most of them were, it is possible. But you don't get a lot of blind spots.'

'Is there any connection between the three ferries?' asked Macleod. 'Passenger names and that?'

'I don't believe they think so. I haven't been running the investigation, I'm just the Controller here at the Operations Centre. It'll be enforcement and investigations that are looking into it, MAIB as well—the Marine Accident Investigation Branch. They're having a look at it, but they seem to be saying suicide.'

'I don't like it,' said Macleod, 'it's all very neat to be suicides that close together, the closeness of water and on three different ferries. How many suicides do you get annually on those ferries?'

'They're not unheard of but maybe one a year around the coast. Most people who commit suicide don't go on a ferry first. They go to Beachy Head, down south. Up here, there's fewer specific places.'

'What's your take on it?' asked Macleod.

'It bothers me, Seoras, to be honest; it really does. One of the things with our team as well is we're not used to investigating deliberate acts of murder. We look at boat infringements. We look at where people have bent the regulations or procedures on the water, and in that sense, the ferry company looks fine. We don't think it's anything to do with the ferry company; it isn't at fault. I mean, they're a professional outfit.'

'But,' said Hope, 'there's a but coming.'

'Yes,' said James, 'the repetitiveness of this is ridiculous. Could we just be unlucky? I don't know.'

'We're not busy at the moment,' said Macleod, 'I could take a look. I don't want to step on your toes. I mean, they all happened in the maritime environment.'

'They did and certainly we can pick up the rescue side of it but to investigate if something is amiss. I mean, to say something is amiss, you're talking about someone murdering people by throwing them off the back of a ferry. How? Why? I don't know where to begin with that. I'm not sure our guys do either.'

'You begin where it always begins,' said Macleod, 'with the people. Give me the phone number of your people, James. I'm going to give them a ring. I think it's worth us taking a look at this, but from the perspective of the people involved, not from whether or not anything's amiss in the maritime environment.'

Macleod took down the number James gave him before putting the phone down. He looked up at Hope.

'It's just a feeling,' he said.

'Yes,' said Hope, 'it's just a feeling but I'm getting it, too.'

Chapter 02

Macleod got the go-ahead for his investigation, both from the Coastguard and his chief inspector. As soon as he was given the case, Macleod dispatched Clarissa down to Mull, figuring if he could get her in the car as far away from him as possible, someone else might have to give him a lift to any ferry he was going to investigate.

Initially, they would speak to the two closest ferries before sending someone down to the Leverburgh ferry, which would be a much more involved trip. Macleod was aware that he was following suspicious circumstances but that he was still responsible for investigating any other deaths and murders that happened in his area, and they may need to return quickly. On that basis, he didn't want his team scattered too far and wide.

Macleod made his way down to the Tarbert-to-Uig ferry, routing with Ross to Skye and the port of Uig where he met up with the current crew during its shuttling back and forth. Macleod had agreed to come on board to spend time with the master and the various crew members.

Macleod was given a small room and advised that the crew would pass through to speak to him, starting with the master of the vessel. Ross was on board as well, taking various photographs and being shown round by the second officer while the first officer oversaw the current passage they were on.

The master of the vessel was a man in his fifties with a serious face, someone Macleod thought wouldn't tolerate many jokes and certainly didn't seem to laugh. Macleod could appreciate a man in this position being like that. Once upon a time, he'd been rather dour himself but the formality with which the man greeted him seemed a little over the top.

'We don't get many inspectors coming out to us.'

'I would think you wouldn't. Mr McGregor, isn't it?'

'Yes, it's McGregor and you're Macleod. Seems everybody knows Macleod these days; been on the news a lot, haven't you?'

'Unfortunately, it seems to more and more be an obsession with people. In the old days, we just went and solved crimes but a lot of them, they weren't on the news or they were reported at least in a half-sensible fashion.'

'Aye,' said the man, 'that's the times we're living in, but I'm a little concerned why you're here.'

Macleod stood up from behind the desk and paced his way round the small cabin. 'I won't lie to you,' said Macleod, 'I'm not here for good reasons, but I want to assure you that one thing we're not looking at is the ferry company, or particularly the employees. We have three different vessels which have suffered a tragedy with a passenger going overboard. The crew's different on each one. The boat's different. The master's different. So far, we're being told that all the passengers are different. However, a run like this, it's—'

'Crazy,' said McGregor. 'It's crazy. It doesn't seem right,

does it?'

'No,' said Macleod, 'that's why I'm here. They said that they weren't able to recover the body from your incident.'

'No,' said McGregor, 'we tried. We turned the ship around and sent out our small rescue vessels. Lifeboats came out from Portree, Leverburgh as well as being bolstered by the Stornoway lifeboat. Later on, the helicopter was out, boats that travel up and down The Minch and from all around, they were everywhere. Coastguard did a good job but looks like he went down pretty quick.'

'But nobody saw him fall overboard, did they?' asked Macleod.

'No,' said McGregor, 'but that's not uncommon. It wasn't a particularly busy run. We believe he fell overboard from the aft of the ship. There's plenty of areas that you can't actually see someone. If he's a jumper, all he's got to do is stand up on the rails and go. You can't barrier in everywhere on a ship. Most of our passengers don't want to get off until they get to the other side. That water is darn cold.'

'How likely would you be to die if you jumped off?' asked Macleod.

'Well, I would say the water's cold and if you don't know what you're doing, learn to relax, and try and float yourself back up to the surface, you're really playing with fire. It's worse than jumping into a river—you'd have much more of a chance. We were halfway over as well; we weren't even close in.'

'What's the run here?'

'About an hour and a half. Like I say, I think we were forty to forty-five minutes after leaving Uig.'

Macleod continued the conversation with the master, but the man seemed to shed very little light on the incident. He hadn't been there but had been summoned to the bridge on discovery of the man being overboard. He could talk about the search in great detail, but that wasn't what Macleod wanted; he needed to understand the deceased passenger, Andrew Culshaw. Who was he? What had happened to him? Had he been seen onboard?

Macleod awaited the rest of the crew coming through. The master had organised the crew starting with the deckhands, the senior officers, but very few of them had even seen the man. He had parked his car down below, seen briefly with his wife. Macleod knew that was where they were heading next, to start talking to the relatives of Andrew Culshaw and see if the man's mind was focused on suicide. Although Macleod knew that wasn't always the case. Sometimes suicidal thoughts come in an instant.

It was well into his stay when the canteen chef came in, and sat down in front of Macleod, wiping his hands on the apron that spread across his lap. His trousers were bold black and white squares, and Macleod wondered why the man wouldn't look him in the eye.

'It says here that you're Anders, Anders Smith. It's a strange combination of names.'

'Yes,' said the man. 'I have a Norwegian mother, a Scottish father.' The man again looked over Macleod's shoulder rather than look at his face.

'You've been the chef here for how long?' asked Macleod.

'Four months,' he said.

'Everything okay? Work going fine?'

'Work is okay.' The man looked at the door. 'I should be getting back. Help them with the service.'

'It's fine,' said Macleod, 'the master's giving you the time.

14

I'm sure they can run without you. You leapt onto one of the rescue vessels, is that correct?'

'Yes. That's what I have to do when something like that happens, but we couldn't find him.'

'Okay. Did you see him while he was on board?' Anders was looking at the door again. 'Is something bothering you, Mr Smith?' asked Macleod. 'You seem to be very distracted, as if—'

'Why are you here?' asked Smith.

'We're just looking into various suicides that have happened on the ferries recently, just making sure that there isn't something more untoward.'

'Why are you really here? You have my record.'

'I actually don't have your record,' said Macleod; 'tell me about it.'

The man on the other side of the table narrowed his eyes and for the first time looked at Macleod. 'I was young. I didn't know any better. I didn't mean to kill him.'

'Okay,' said Macleod, 'but you obviously did kill someone. Who?'

'It was at a boxing club. Things kicked off. I hit him with a punch. He died and they called it manslaughter. I went away for ten years, only got out two years ago. Finally got this job, so I want to keep it. I have a wife and family now and I need this job. Do you understand?'

'Mr Smith, you're not under investigation,' said Macleod. 'I'm here looking at these suicides. Did you see this man on board?' Macleod held up a photo of Andrew Culshaw.

'Yes. I see most people that come on. Most people come for either a coffee or a drink. I was serving that day as we were shorthanded. I prepared a lot of food and then I had to come through. He was getting very agitated.'

'Really?' said Macleod. 'Why was that?'

Macleod watched the man twiddle his thumbs, clearly still nervous. 'I think he was having problems with his wife as they were arguing. I was trying to find out if he wanted the chips or potatoes, and he turned around and told me to piss away off. I said, "Excuse me?" and his wife apologised for him, but then they argued again. I think their home life wasn't particularly good. He called her something—frigid, that was the word. He called her frigid. You don't call your wife that in front of people. Even if it was true, you wouldn't say it, maybe in quiet but—'

'And how did she take it?' asked Macleod.

'She was livid. She went for him, told him this, told him that.'

'She went for him?' said Macleod. 'What? Physically, like hit him?'

'No, but she put her finger right up to his face. She let him know. The whole staff, the canteen staff will tell you. The rest of the crew, they didn't see it. They don't see the passengers the way we do.'

'And what happened after that?'

'You can confirm with the rest of the crew, but we were talking about it afterwards as you do, generally, just conversation. We reckoned that they sat down for the meal but they had another row, and then he disappeared off. She stayed down below. She came back for another coffee and a bit of cake, and then we got the call.'

'Does any of the rest of the crew know where he went?'

'He was seen going upstairs, up on deck, so we believe he was up on top deck.'

'But nobody saw him go into the water?'

'No. There was a couple on the other side of the deck, we believe, from where he was. He was then seen in the water by them as the ferry pulled away from him. They didn't know it was a person at first, but it looked strange so they shouted, and it all got a bit crazy. Then the wife, she couldn't find her husband and we launched the rescue vessels. We called, "Man overboard". It was less than two minutes from him being in the water, I believe. The master, he didn't take a chance and stopped immediately. I think he told the Coastguard it was a possible man overboard, and then we confirmed it.'

'And you know the captain's actions because?'

'As I said, I went on to the rescue vessel, the small vessel at the side of the ship, which we use to go and do these things. I pilot it. That's part of my job, and I listened to all the communications on channel 16 on the radio, the Mayday call, man overboard, all that.'

'Did you see him once he was in the water?'

'We went everywhere. Never saw him.'

'Did the couple say that he was in any way indicating to them that he was in the water?'

'No, that was the thing. It was difficult for them. He didn't seem to be moving at all. He didn't look like someone that had gone in and then thought, 'Ah, help' and start waving his hands, but it's quite a fall from the top of the ferry down. He could have hurt himself on the way in, knocked himself out. The cold could have seized him. The water, you don't want to be in there.'

Macleod thanked the man for his frank discussions and once again told him not to worry, that Macleod was not trying to hunt him down for anything else. As the day wore on and many of the rest of the crew confirmed what Anders Smith had said,

17

Macleod met up with Ross out on deck. As he watched the water pass behind him, the sun reflecting off it, making it sparkle, he thought how delightful it looked, almost as if he could plunge in. Of course, once you got into the water, the truth of how cold it was and how high those waves actually were compared to your head, would soon become apparent.

'So, what do we know, Ross?' asked Macleod.

'Well, sir, from my investigations and the people I've spoken to, it looks like he was up here on the top part of the ferry, over here on the port side. There was a couple on the starboard side. They turned and saw him out the back, but he was on the opposite side. So, it looks like he jumped from over that side.'

'Or was dispatched on that side. It'd be easy enough to get up and down the stairs. There's a couple of ways in and out, is there not?'

'Yes,' said Ross, 'and I'm struggling to get a picture of where everyone was. The timeframe of when he goes in, it's all a little blurred. If someone did this to him, they could be back down in the canteen in no time before the alarm's actually raised.'

'They might have had something with them to do it because they'd had to have forced him up and over those railings. You don't just push someone, and they simply spin over the railings on a ferry. Do they?' asked Macleod.

'No,' said Ross, 'it's too high. It's definitely too high. He'd either have to be forced over them or he'd have to jump or—'

'You'd have to incapacitate him, to then flip him over.'

'How strong would you have to be for that?' said Ross. Macleod pushed Ross up against the railings.

'I knock you out,' said Macleod. 'Your body's lying there. I can just grab your feet and tip you over. I can't rule out suspects of weaker strength based on that.'

'To be honest, sir,' said Ross, 'it's looking like suicide. He's had a terrible row with his wife. The other couple, they didn't see anybody up and about here, and there's nobody on this ferry who was also on the other ferries according to the records.'

'I think we'll wait and see what comes back from the other ferries. I've still got that feeling, Ross. Hope's got it, too. Can't remember the last time that both of us had that tightening of the gut. Let's see how Clarissa gets on.'

Chapter 03

C larissa Urquhart was in a good mood. She had stuck it to Seoras that morning, driving him in when his car was having an MOT and had clearly rattled him. He was so sheepish with the way he drove. After all, what was the point of having a nippy sports car if you didn't use it? After taking the phone call that morning from Minchlines ferry company, Clarissa was now navigating her way down to the Oban Ferry Terminal to speak to the crew that were currently on board.

It had been over three weeks and the crew had turned around again having had some shore leave. Clarissa had to drive from Inverness, past the side of Loch Ness all the way down to Oban, but in truth, she was loving it. This wasn't big open motorways, rather a decent 'A' road with lots of little turns through some villages and towns, and with some great countryside to look at. She was in her open-top sports car, the wind was racing through her hair, and it just felt good to be alive. The only thing that was missing was a good-looking man beside her. Well, in truth he didn't have to be good looking, but he would have to be interesting and certainly a lot of fun. It was only recently she had been to the Isle of Mull when they'd investigated some murders at the airport.

Macleod has suggested that she fly down but Clarissa didn't like the idea. It was a possibility she might have to stay down this way. When they'd been on that last case, there had been a rather interesting fireman at the airport. At the time, Clarissa was part of the investigating team and she certainly couldn't have made any moves towards the man, but maybe this time she might just get a little time away.

The other thing that was delighting Clarissa was the fact that the sun was out and today was going to be warm. Of course, it wasn't summer, but it was going to be warm in the sense that the shawl might even come off at some point. Obviously not for the drive, for the wind rushing around the little car would make you cold unless you were well wrapped up. That was a small price to pay for having the joy and wonder of such a nippy little sports car.

Clarissa had broken her journey on the way down by stopping off at a coffee house and enjoying a rather nice cream tea before jumping back into her car and speeding off. She remembered the days when she didn't have such a car and as she drove past the looks would have been at her and not at the vehicle she was in. Times had changed though. She told herself that these days, men would have to see past the superfluous packaging to the quality that was inside. She told herself a lot of things these days, but in truth, she knew she was lonely.

As she drove along the winding roads, her mind flicked through the men in her life. This fireman was certainly an option and probably the only viable one at the moment. There was that guy at the gym, the workout she went to endure on two occasions a week. After all, she had to keep reasonably fit in her job. The downside to him was he was twenty years younger, and she thought he also had a girlfriend who seemed to be in the gym a lot as well. *The man was a pipe dream but at the end of the day, everybody needed their dreams to hang on to*, thought Clarissa.

Then there was Seoras. She was very fond of him, and not only as a boss, but she also knew he was very firmly attached and so decent a man, there was no way he was ever going to leave someone he had promised himself to. *Still*, she thought as she drove along, *no need to ruin a good day like this. There's a free man in Mull I might be able to get my hands on.*

The port at Oban was looking splendid and Clarissa stood at the dockside noticing the orange RNLI vessel to one side, as well as the small ferry that ran across to the isle of Kerrera. The ferry out to Mull was not the longest run, but certainly could be the most scenic as it channelled down through the Sound of Mull. If the run continued on out to Barra, you would get to see the full delight of the Sound of Mull passing up by Tobermory.

Clarissa thought she should take the car sometime, run round the islands without having to go on work business. That was the problem. In the art investigations, you seemed to get more time off in the evenings; everything wasn't so crucial, so desperate. When a murderer was afoot, you didn't feel that you could hang about; you had to keep going.

Clarissa was aware she was more and more becoming Macleod's go-to girl, the one he would send out long distance, who could operate alone. He seemed to be keeping Hope closer at hand. She reckoned this was because he was trying to train her. It was a little bit unfair in some ways, but Clarissa had no aspirations to make detective inspector, rather she thought it was unfair on Hope because the woman knew what she was doing already. She just came at things differently to Macleod.

Once on board the ferry, Clarissa met the master, a man of maybe thirty-five, who was decidedly clean-shaven. She sat down in his cabin behind a desk as he relayed to her the day of the suicide.

'It's shaken the crew up, it really has. You don't get that sort of thing too often. Sometimes yes, it happens, and you train for it. We have our rescue vessels which we launched. There were a lot of vessels going up and down the Sound anyway. With the patch of water that we were given to search, I really thought that we would be able to find him. He was called Peter Hughes,' said the man, almost as if he'd known the guy personally. 'He'd come on board with another friend, a Gerald, Gerald Lyndhurst, he was called. I remember that because the man was absolutely distraught when it happened.'

'What exactly did happen with him?' asked Clarissa.

'You can talk to the rest of the crew later on, but I've already gone through it with them and patched it together. The story goes a bit like this: Peter and his friend had come on board and after we set off, they were in the canteen. They were seen walking around the ship together. It appears at some point they'd had a bit of a to-do, an argument. In truth, the crew felt they'd seemed very close. It's not often you see two men together and think, they're probably very tight pals. They seemed to complement each other very well.'

'But they argued?'

'Yes,' said the master, 'but not a blazing row; it was very discreet, very quiet, but it was clear that they had very differing opinions. It wasn't a slanging match or anything like that; it was very precise, detailed arguments being made, but they were being made so quietly that no one could hear. One of the crew, Jenny, she was operating the coffee cabin, and she was looking straight at them. She hadn't any customers, so she was doing what a lot of us do, just fixating on the things that are going on around us. She said to me that they had the row. She said it was deep, and she thought she saw a tear on that Lyndhurst guy's face.'

'But what happened with the suicide?' asked Clarissa.

'He went up on deck, and we haven't got a big deck with our vessel, but he disappeared from sight. That's what Lyndhurst said, and we know Lyndhurst was down below. The crew confirmed that he wasn't up with him. Anyway, there wasn't too many up top either, but they saw him walk about briefly. Then the next second somebody is shouting, "The man's in the water".'

'How did the report come to you?'

'I was on the bridge so as soon as one of the crew heard "Man Overboard' Overboard," it got relayed through the comms. We stopped the vessel, turned quickly, launched all our rescue craft, but it was to no avail. A lifeboat came out from Tobermory, also one from Oban, and they were here quick, but you can see the patch of water we've got here. We had just entered the Sound. It's small—I thought we'd get him. The trouble is though, if people go down below, you don't know when they'll surface, or where. It could be miles away. The sea's got him.

'We had people up and down the shoreline, not just the Coastguard, but lots of other searchers trying to see if he'd wash up on a beach, but we haven't seen him yet. He'll probably come at some point. These things tend to happen. He'll scare the living bejesus out of people along the shore. People don't look pretty after they come out of the water, especially several months in.'

'You have experience of that?' asked Clarissa.

'Yes, a Coastguard team member for a number of years. You get sent out to recover the body. Usually it's on rocks and that; you need to have a trained team who can carry someone deceased across and give them to the undertaker or the police pathologist.'

'Did any of your crew know why the two gentlemen were on the ferry?'

'No,' said the master, 'but Jenny spoke to him when he bought a coffee and apparently, they'd won the trip. Somehow somebody was giving away trips and they'd won it and it seemed that they were more than happy to take it.'

Clarissa was brought up onto the top deck and shown by the master exactly where Peter Hughes had fallen in. She stood staring at the water. It looked cold despite the sunlight glinting off it. She looked left and right and saw that there was no road close enough on the shoreline to be able to see the ferry clearly at that point.

'How busy is the water behind us, out of Oban?'

'Well, oh, there's usually a number of boats shooting around. You've got workboats going up and down. There's the Glensanda quarry; large vessels take cargo from there. If it's rough weather, boats come through the Sound. It's a quieter way to route, but also you get a lot of sailing yachts and vessels coming out of Oban.'

'So how easy would it be to spot somebody on your ferry?'

'What? You think that somebody else could have seen what was going on? I would doubt it.'

'What about from that road over there?'

25

'You'd have to have good binoculars and have been watching. There were no reports from the road of him going overboard, from what I understand. You can check with the Coastguard, but I don't think anybody called it in from onshore.'

'What's your feeling about it?' asked Clarissa.

'Well, it's a funny one. I talked to Jenny because she really had the closest view of them, and she talked to them. I think it's suicide, but Jenny would disagree with me.'

'Can I speak to her?'

'Of course,' said the master, 'you can speak to anyone. I'll just go and find her for you. Do you want to do it up here on deck? There's not that many people about. It's a nicer place than stuck down in one of the cabins.'

Clarissa nodded, and she let the wind blow through her hair as she waited for Jenny to arrive. There was a tap on Clarissa's shoulder. She turned around and then looked down at a young girl dressed in black trousers and a crisp white shirt. She had her hair tied up behind her and Clarissa reckoned she could barely have made twenty.

'Are you Detective Inspector Clarissa Urquhart?' the girl asked.

'No, I'm Detective Sergeant. I haven't risen that far yet, but I am Clarissa Urquhart. Please, just call me Clarissa. You must be Jenny?'

'Yes,' she said. 'You wanted to know about the man who died?'

'Yes, about him and his friend, Gerald Lyndhurst. Your boss said that, basically, you were the one who had seen them the most, and probably talked to them.'

'That's true,' said Jenny. 'He doesn't want to admit it, but I think they were gay.'

'I'm sorry?' said Clarissa.

'I think there were partners. I mean, that's the thing nowadays, isn't it? The older generation don't want to talk about stuff like that, but you know, it's the thing nowadays. There's no problem with it. I think that they were partners. I don't know how close they were since they weren't lovey-dovey; they weren't putting arms around each other and kissing in front of people. They seemed to be very quiet about it, but I thought that they were a couple.'

'Right,' said Clarissa, 'but your master seems to think that it's a case of suicide. Did Peter Hughes seem to be in that frame of mind?'

'Far from it,' said Jenny, 'that's why I don't think it's suicide at all. If it was, he must have gone downhill incredibly quickly to go and jump off a ferry. The two of them seemed to be happy together. Yes, they were debating something. It was definitely a case of something that meant a lot to them, but they weren't fighting over it in the sense of being poles apart. It seemed like an ordered discussion. It was intense, very intense, but really, something that they wanted to mutually work through.'

'Do you have any idea what it was about?'

'No,' said Jenny, 'I didn't really. I get the idea, possibly if, as they were older men, or maybe if they were a couple, maybe that was bothering them. Maybe they didn't want to show that. As I say, they weren't very overt about it. It's just a feeling I had looking at them.'

'What sort of feeling?'

'That they were in love. You can see that in everybody, can't you? You can tell when a mum loves her child, you can tell when a man and a woman love each other, two women or men together. It's the same thing, isn't it? The love? That one when

27

you realise that somebody is together? Don't get me wrong, they may have been completely platonic. Maybe they didn't live together. I don't know. Maybe I'm putting a backstory in that's not true,' said Jenny. 'The boss calls me a daydreamer. He says I sit up there in the coffee hut and just make up stories about everybody that comes, but I don't think I'm wrong with this one.'

Clarissa thanked the girl for her input before standing on the aft deck and looking back at the wake behind it. Macleod had said to her before she had left, if there was anything amiss, they'd find it in the detail of the people. They weren't there to talk about the procedures. They weren't there to realise if there was a fault with the ferry company. They were there to see if there was something hidden amongst the people.

Clarissa understood it was a modern age, but these were older men with a very modern issue. She'd need to talk to Gerald Lyndhurst. Maybe Jenny was onto something, or maybe she wasn't. It looked like the fire chief might have to wait.

Chapter 04

Chris sat looking at the lamb chops in front of him and was struggling to decide whether or not they needed gravy. They were surrounded by peas, some mashed potatoes, and some onions he'd whipped up. He'd missed lunch on the way in. Now, starting his shift in the afternoon, he was trying to eat something quickly before they would go out to practice flying.

Having previously been in the military, Chris now flew the Coastguard helicopter based at Stornoway and had enjoyed that morning out in the sunshine at home, playing with the dog. The lively hound seemed to go here, there, and everywhere, chasing a ball that many people would not want to pick up. He had also completed a short run with her. Then, having headed into work, he realised he'd forgotten to eat. As ever there was always food available, some sort of emergency rations stored at the base, and Chris was now sitting down to enjoy them thoroughly. He hated flying on an empty stomach. He knew if they got a call out, it would be even longer until he'd get to eat.

Gravy it was. Chris went over, switched on the kettle and pulled the gravy granules out of the cupboard.

'You all right this afternoon?'

'Of course,' said Chris to his colleague, and watched Dan make his way over to the small office. Chris stood looking out the window at the airport and remembered the weather briefing he'd taken on arrival. At the moment the sky looked good, but it was going to deteriorate. By evening, the weather would clag in. There was always a possibility of a haar at this time of year as well, a thick fog that surrounded the coast, and the trouble with the airport at Stornoway was that that haar tended to sweep in from one side, sometimes occasionally obscuring the base. It just slowed everything down and made flying that little bit more difficult.

Chris heard the kettle click, took the water, and poured it into the small jug with the gravy granules inside. He stirred the mixture with a spoon, realised it was thick enough and made his way back over to the plate sitting on the table. The gravy was splashed first across the chops, then over the mashed potatoes. It looked lovely, absolutely lovely. Chris picked up his knife and fork, cut off a bit of the lamb chop and placed it in his mouth. He rolled it around his tongue before chewing and letting the hot gravy fall down his throat. It wasn't a bad life after all, was it?

Chris heard the phone go. Another of his colleagues went to pick it up, but he knew what the sound meant. They were being tasked and quickly he cut up a couple of bits of chop and threw them into his mouth, followed by several large lumps of potato. He took the glass of water from in front of him, drank from it quickly and then ran through to the office to see what the call was.

'Man overboard from the Stornoway ferry,' said his colleague. 'It's just coming in to Stornoway at the moment. Let's get that chopper on the move. It's about ten miles shy of the harbour.'

30

Chris raced to get his suit on and then to get out to the helicopter to fire it up, while he would wait for the winchman and the rest of the crew to gather. As he did so, he gave out a large burp. Always the same; miss your meal into work, that's the day you're never going to get to catch up.

* * *

The operations room at Stornoway Coastguard was a flurry of activity. Alison had simply put on her headset after coming back from her lunch, and the first words she had heard were 'Mayday, Mayday, Mayday. Man overboard.' The least he could have done was let her get settled in. Regardless, the rest of the team had sprung into action.

The ferry was approximately ten miles from Stornoway Harbour and they'd instantly requested the helicopter and lifeboat at Stornoway to launch towards it. Alison put out a Mayday relay on the radio advising all vessels in the area, to see if any could assist. She was also talking to the ferry, which was turning around, launching its own rescue vessels and routing back to where they thought the person had gone into the water. They didn't know the method of entry and the crew were counting the passengers to ascertain if anyone was definitely in the water, for no one had seen the person enter. Instead, through one of the windows of the ferry, a child had seen someone fall quickly past them and land in the water. At the moment, Alison was also trying to get the vessel to verify that claim, but clearly it was a serious enough one that the master had decided to act on it anyway.

Alison's colleague was quickly constructing a plan of where the lifeboat and the helicopter should search, something they

31

called a rapid response search plan. There would be more plans to draw up if these first ones were unsuccessful, and the forecast for the evening was looking like the weather was going to decline badly.

The Stornoway Coastguard helicopter called on channel 16, the main VHF channel for all maritime traffic, and it was advised to route direct to the point of entry and was given a search plan to work off from that position. It was times like these that being an operator of the Coastguard working Channel 16 became so busy. Normally it was just routine traffic, bumbling through, reporting some minor points that the vessels were passing, but when a job was on, the channel 16 position could become incredibly busy.

Alison always marvelled at how calm the services were in their response. The radio telephony switching back between the helicopter and the station, clean, accurate, precise. Then, when the lifeboat called up, she fired out instructions for it. A glance over her shoulder allowed her to see the lifeboat racing past the station making way out of the harbour towards where the incident had happened. Several other vessels were now converging, and Alison was finding it hard to keep typing up the notes that automatically went into the job record on her computer screen, noting all the information that was flowing through her ears.

Yet with all this, her heart was skipping a beat. Many of the jobs they got were routine; a yacht had broken down and you became something like the AA on the sea. But this was different. Somebody's life was in serious peril. How long could you last in the water? Well, the charts talked about lasting a day sometimes, even with it being a cool eleven degrees, but in reality, the person was unlikely to have a lifejacket on and therefore survival would be less likely.

Some twenty minutes after the fearful words 'Mayday' had come across the radio, Alison found herself finally getting on top of the job. The helicopter was into its first search, the second search was planned, the lifeboat was arriving. Other vessels were hunting, too, following the lifeboat's lead which organised them into a vast line going up and down through the area where the person had hit the water.

The ferry had called in and advised that the person entering the water was believed to be a female by the name of Daphne Walsh. Currently they were searching the vessel for her, seeing if she'd collapsed somewhere else. Maybe what the child had seen had been some bit of debris falling down to the sea, but in truth, with a person missing, and what the child had seen, it was unlikely that the two weren't connected. It was gearing up to be a long shift.

* * *

Chris was beginning to feel the effects of a long search. They'd already been out there three hours and then returned to fuel up again, before heading back out. They could see the lightboat below them, all the other vessels going backwards and forwards, but there had been no sign of Daphne Walsh. Not an item of clothing, a shoe, nothing. It was almost as if she'd gone under the water, never to come back up.

However, because the woman had entered with no life jacket on, it was hardly surprising that they hadn't seen her. The waves had started to build as the wind had picked up over the last couple of hours and they were effectively looking for a head in the water. They took the helicopter down low, trying to match up the height they could be at to the distance they could see, crisscrossing the path that the boats were taking.

In the rear of the cab, Chris's colleagues were looking through cameras, checking the sea as they passed along. They also had the thermal imaging on, given that the water was cold and the body would've been hot, but as time wore on, that would become less of a stark contrast. Chris tried to keep his eyes scanning to and fro, for at this point, his colleague was flying the aircraft and not him. They took it in turns, trying to keep the fatigue away. Chris was currently wolfing down a Mars bar as he looked left and right.

From the rear of a cab, came a shout. 'Let's hold the position. I think there is something.'

'Where?' asked Chris.

'Starboard side, just down from us. Just zooming in with the camera now. Hang on, it looks like a head.'

'Get a position on that. Let's get the lifeboat over to it.'

Chris waited for the position to be relayed from behind and his colleague then took the helicopter over towards where the object in the sea had been seen. His colleagues in the rear also called the Coastguard and contacted the lifeboat so that the orange vessel was making way over to the location.

Chris looked down and could see the crew reaching out with long poles to try and make a grab for whoever it was in the water. In the rear of the cab, the winchman, who was also a paramedic, was getting ready to descend and, if needed, to whisk the unlucky woman up into the cab and off to hospital.

'She doesn't seem to be moving much,' said Chris; 'this doesn't look good.'

'She wasn't moving on the camera either,' said his colleague behind him. The lifeboat crew picked the woman out of the water using long poles. Chris could see them placing her on the deck. Several of them began to work on her while the winchman called to begin his descent down onto the boat. The lifeboat was quite far out now from Stornoway Harbour and to take her back by land and then ambulance to the hospital would take so long that the winchman coming down was an obvious and simple solution to get her quickly to hospital. As Chris focused on the task of getting the winchman down to the deck, he didn't see the Stornoway lifeboat crew fighting hard for the woman's life. However, there seemed to be no reaction from there.

The winchman, having touched down on the lifeboat skirted round to the rear of the vessel and began checking the woman for any signs of life. The crew turned around and said that they thought she was dead, but as a trained paramedic, the winchman was someone who could officially call that life was extinct. After a few checks, he stood up and called it to the lifeboat crew before radioing upstairs to the cab.

Chris tried to focus on bringing his colleague back up and then safely into the helicopter before returning to the airport and touching down. Over the radiotelephony, he heard the Coastguard calling off the search, advising all the vessels that they could go on their way, thanking them for their efforts in a rather dull and sombre tone.

After arriving and doing all their shutdown checks in the helicopter and then leaving it to the ground crew to fuel up, Chris made his way to the shower and stood impassively cleaning himself down. Spending so long in the survival suit up above had caused him to sweat. Now clean, he made his way back up to sit down for a meal. He looked at the half-eaten chops, partly demolished potato and the congealed gravy now lying over the top of it all.

'I take it the ground crew is going out to get us our meal?'

'Yes. Just need to do the reports and the phone-ins,' his colleague said to him; 'make sure the Coastguard are happy, but hopefully, that's us for the day. It wasn't a pretty one.'

Chris nodded and felt a growl in his stomach. The two chocolate bars he'd had while up in the air hadn't satisfied his stomach after the missed lunch. *That's a fourth one overboard,* thought Chris. *It's almost like something's going on at the moment.* But he gave his head a shake, looked down at the meal, and threw it into the microwave. It wasn't going to taste great, but with the way his stomach was growling at him, who cared?

Chapter 05

Macleod stood watching the various officers taking statements from those onboard the Stornoway ferry. When he had arrived after the search, the local officers had cordoned off those coming off the ferry, making sure they'd take statements from everyone, trying to identify what had happened to Daphne Walsh. Her husband was also onboard and Macleod had the man assigned an officer to, first of all, help with his grief, but also then to escort him to a room where Macleod would interview him very shortly.

Macleod had been down in Skye looking to return back when he had got the call about the Stornoway ferry and had managed to jump onboard the Tarbert Ferry going back across and make his way up to Stornoway. Hope had still been back at the station, looking after things, preparing for her trip to Leverburgh, and Macleod had insisted that she continue with that rather than join them in Stornoway for the most recent event. He wanted a full picture, but that same churning feeling in his gut had continued, especially now there were four persons who had gone overboard.

Surely it was too many. Nowhere could be this unlucky. Either that, or there was an epidemic of jumping. Were people like lemmings? Did they see the idea and just simply follow it? Would these people have dispatched themselves anyway, but in a less dramatic fashion?

Macleod was struggling with the idea of it. It was a fact that throughout all his career, he'd seen many grisly murders and, in many ways, he'd begun to understand the mind of the murderer. Suicide was different and something he really did struggle with, the idea that life could get that bad. Of course, for some people it did, and for some people, it was just a medical situation that their mind went off on a tangent. It was still a subject that caused him a degree of bewilderment, despite his wife's own tragic demise in the cold waters off Lewis.

It didn't help that when he was brought up within the Calvinistic church, the idea of suicide was seen as an affront to God, something that meant you could lose your place with your Maker and whatever life was to follow. The idea of that sitting with predestination was something that Macleod always struggled with and nowadays, he just tried not to think about it. He'd seen so much, especially in these latter years, that the earlier teachings that had been given to him at times seemed hollow and certainly incorrect on occasion.

Jona had also been dispatched, looking to pick up the later Uig ferry. She was debating whether or not to send her team over that way while she flew over on the plane to do some initial studies. Macleod had encouraged the latter, but now as he stood watching the various constables under Ross's supervision making notes and pulling together what had actually happened on board, he wished his whole team were here. He found it hard when the team was split up, all in different directions.

38

It could have been worse for he still had Ross with him. The man could organise anything, and if Macleod was ever fortunate enough to have a daughter, though that seemed highly unlikely, Ross would be brought in to organise the wedding. The man's attention to detail was phenomenal in the height of a mountain of work, something that Macleod wasn't good at. He was the muller, the man who sat back looking at the overall picture and finding the details fly out to him. Ross was knee-deep in detail.

Macleod had taken a call from Clarissa, who was now going even further on her travels, and he was surprised when at the end of her call, she almost gave a note of concern. Was he all right without her or Hope? Macleod had said that Ross was here, but he did get the feeling that he was some sort of geriatric to be looked after. He put it down as concern rather than any obvious deterioration in his physical attributes, but that was the conundrum about Clarissa. For all that she turned round and took the mickey out of Macleod, there was a deep underlying concern that worried him, more so when he thought about it, but it made him smile. He really was getting soft.

'Sir, we've gone through just about everyone. I'm still pulling the statements and looking, but you're not going to like it.'

'Let me guess. No one about to see her?'

'That's right. No one saw her between when she went to the stairs to the top deck until she disappeared off it.'

'Do you find that strange?' asked Macleod. 'Somehow, we have four people jump off ferries and nobody sees them until they're in the water. Tell me, Ross, if you were committing suicide, would you be worried about somebody seeing you go in? Would you not be more focused on simply getting on with it?'

'They may not want somebody to see them just in case they get rescued,' offered Ross.

'All four of them? You don't think it's some sort of a club where they actually take notes beforehand how to do it?'

'No, sir. I think you may be stretching it with that one. However, I do have Mr Walsh in the interview room back at the station. I think we should really get to him. The man needs some rest. Heck of a tragedy for him.'

'Indeed,' said Macleod. 'You're going to tell me they were seen rowing, aren't you?'

'Yes, they were,' said Ross. 'Numerous people mentioned her when I showed her picture. Apparently, she was quite loud and vocal, stormed off from them. One person said she slapped him, hard.'

'Do you think Jona's going to come up with something? I mean, when bodies go into the water like this, it must be quite hard to work out sometimes what happened to them.'

'You really need to talk to her about that, sir,' said Ross. 'If you don't mind, I need to get on with these statements, try and pull them together.'

'Do these ferries have any CCTV?' asked Macleod.

'There's occasional bits around the port and that. Do you think we should do a canvas with it? See if the same person turns up?'

'It can't hurt, can it? Although if this was a murderer doing this, I doubt they'll, A, use the same name, or B, look the same each time they come on board.'

'Well, they certainly haven't used the same name. I've been checking through that already. I'll go through the Stornoway incident and see who was on board, but to be quite frank, they don't have to show their ID. You book the ferry. You can go on as a guest and book the ferry, so there's no need. The card might be the one. We'll trace the bank cards. Although, if they're smart about it and they've managed to obtain a bank card in the correct name, well, then I guess they could pay for it. You wouldn't know until it was stolen.'

'All good lines of attack, Ross. Get on to them because at the moment, I feel we're struggling. It may be we just have four unlucky tragic incidents. Four sad people that felt life was no longer worth living, but somehow, I'm beginning to doubt it.'

Ross showed Macleod over to the police car where a constable drove him round to the local station. He made his way quickly to the interview room to see a man sitting with his hands on a table and staring straight ahead, eyes full of tears.

'Sincere apologies for keeping you waiting, if I have,' said Macleod. 'I'm Detective Inspector Seoras Macleod. My sincere condolences, Mr Walsh. It must be quite a shock for you.'

'To a point, yes. You see, it's not been easy with Daphne.'

The man was dressed in a brown leather jacket and a shirt that was looking highly distressed at this time. Macleod noticed there was a coffee stain on one side, but also noted the man had taken his shoes off while waiting.

'Sorry, I hope you don't mind, but it's just that my feet swell when I get agitated. The shoes become tight. I did say to the constable, but he didn't mind.'

'Of course not,' said Macleod. 'But you said it was not much of a surprise. Why is that?'

'Daphne. I think she lost it. I've tried really hard with her. I did. We went to counselling and everything. I came home one day and there she is, some kid.'

'Kid?' said Macleod. 'What do you mean?'

41

'I don't mean a child or in that way. A kid, he must have been maybe nineteen and there's Daphne on top of him in our bed. When I asked her what she was doing, she just laughed, and she went like this all of a sudden. Over four or five years we had this, and then we thought she was getting better, and everything was okay, and then I came home and there's another kid. She'd take herself off to nightclubs. She's forty-six. We don't go to nightclubs at our age. She'd dress herself up and I tell you, Inspector, you didn't want to see your wife like that. Everything just saying, "Here I am. What do you want?" When I'd tackle her on it, she'd get angry, violent, said I didn't love her anymore. Said I couldn't see how she was. She said she was as good now as she was a teen. I think she lost her mind; I really do.'

'Did she give any indication at any point? I'm sorry for asking this, it is delicate, but did she give any indication at any point that she would be potentially looking to take her own life?'

'Nothing,' said the man. 'Nothing. She'd just bought tickets for a concert. She bought two. She told me that she wasn't going with me; she was going to take somebody she'd pick up in a nightclub and she slapped me here, right on the ferry.'

'A row? What was the row about?' asked Macleod.

'She was looking like a complete tart. Skirt was up to wherever, everything else half hanging out. I mean, she looked like a dog's dinner. Don't get me wrong, Inspector. I have no problem when she was that age and wearing that sort of thing. It was great, but now, I don't go back to wearing my tight leather trousers, I don't have my shirt opened with a medallion trying to look like something, some sort of sex symbol. That's gone. I'm older now. Comes to us all. She wouldn't accept it and I told her on the ferry. I lost it. I'd said to her, "Look, you are just an old piece of meat in a glitzy outfit." I know that was harsh, it's cruel, but it gets to you. I know the two I found her with haven't been the only ones she's been with. The doctors, they think she's gone a bit as well, lost it. She certainly wasn't seeing straight.'

'But you were getting help,' said Macleod.

'Yes, and you think it's going well and all of a sudden, out she comes wearing whatever, taking whoever to bed and not giving a toss about me. I just lost it today. Sorry. Then she went and...'

The man's head dropped into his hands, and he began to cry. Macleod held his composure for a moment, giving the man time to let his pain flow out through the tears he cried.

'Can you just enlighten me on the movements of your wife, and of yourself, from when you came on the ferry?'

'We parked down below. Both of us then went up on deck. I went down, got myself a drink and that. She followed and wanted a double whiskey, which I brought her. Anyway, then we're standing in the top lounge watching the boat sail across the Minch. Halfway across . . . , in fact, not even that, earlier than that, she's over to some kid laughing and joking with him. It was embarrassing. You could see people looking, so I told her to get back and to stop it, and that's when it all kicked off and I called her an old bag of meat.

'She stormed out, but not until she'd caught me with a couple of blows across the face, and that was it. I didn't see her again after that. The next I know, I saw the helicopter arrive and they're saying that somebody had gone overboard. The boat's turned round. I didn't think it was her at first, but then they started asking where everybody was, so I went to find her, and she wasn't there. She just wasn't there. I should've kept a tighter rein on her, Inspector. I should've held onto her. I should've . . . ,'

'And what would've happened then? She would've hit you more,' said Macleod. 'We all make our own decisions, choose our own actions. I'm very sorry for your loss, Mr Walsh. I may need to talk to you again, but I think I've got the basic gist of what happened. The best thing for you to do at the moment is to be left to have some time on your own. The constable who's been with you so far will stay as long as you need. I realise you're away from home, so I believe there's been a hotel room booked for you. You need to get some sleep. Then you can decide what you're doing, whether you want to get home. Is there anyone at home for you?'

'My brother will come,' he said. 'It'll take him a day or two to get up from England, but he'll come. Can you thank them, Inspector?'

'Thank who?'

'The lifeboat. The people in the helicopter, everybody that came out. At least they brought her back to me. At least I can say goodbye.'

'I will do,' said Macleod.

He watched as his young constable came in and took the man from the room. He didn't envy the constable's position and Macleod had been uncomfortable for the short time he'd been with Mr Walsh. In his line of work, Macleod was often with people who were bereaved, but he didn't have to stay with them. He simply interviewed them and went. The officers who stayed, they sat through all that pain. He admired them, but it wasn't something he could do himself. Of that, he was sure.

Chapter 06

Hope McGrath had boarded the flight that took her to Stornoway and then down to Benbecula, the middle isle of the Uists. From there, she picked up a hire car taking it from Benbecula in the middle isle to North Uist at the top of the three islands. It was connected to the Isle of Harris and thereby up to Stornoway by a small ferry run by Minchlines that set sail from Bernera, arriving in Leverburgh and crossing Sound of Harris. Hope had managed to find the master who had been on that day. He lived in Borve, right beside where the ferry came in.

When she'd been in Stornoway and in Harris, Hope had driven across many single-track roads, but her journey from Benbecula up to North Uist, although it had taken in some amazingly scenic vistas, was one that frustrated her. Unlike Macleod, Hope was more used to carriageways where cars passed easily, side by side. Here on the trip up, there were many single-track roads, and then causeways, and she found herself having to be alert to watching for traffic coming in the opposite direction.

Hope was also having difficulty finding the house of Ian Angus MacDonald and drove around Borve several times before stopping and asking someone. This made her at least ten minutes late.

The house was set off the road with a small track leading down to an abode that Hope thought could only hold one or two persons comfortably. As she approached, she saw a man inside with welding gloves on, a cylinder behind him, and about to don a mask. Two bits of metal were laid on the table in front and Hope was struggling to work out what he was building.

She stepped out of the car, thought about getting her jacket but decided against it and called over to the man.

'Would you be Ian Angus MacDonald?'

The man put down the mask that he'd been holding up to his face and turned around and looked. 'Aye. Who would you be?'

'Detective Sergeant Hope McGrath. We spoke on the phone.'

'We did, didn't we?' The man was much older than his voice gave away, Hope placing him possibly as someone heading towards retirement.

'Do you work for that Macleod fellow?'

'I do,' said Hope. 'Yes.'

'They want to put you on the telly then, not him. Inside, come on.'

Hope, for a moment, felt she should be offended in what seemed to be quite a sexist remark from an older man, but inside she actually felt quite good about it. She was struggling at times to see herself leading the team, and although the man's intention had obviously been to praise her looks, she allowed herself to take it a different way that she should be in the leadership role. The man, however, did not turn back. He simply left his front door open, meaning Hope should follow.

Once inside, he made his way down a hallway, opened the door to the kitchen, and pointed to the table.

'I don't suppose you ever have a dram, especially if you're on duty.'

'No,' said Hope. 'I can't, but thanks for the offer.'

'Well, just don't stand there, have a seat. I can do you a cup of tea, or a coffee, or something stronger if you really want it.'

'Please,' said Hope, 'that'd be great, just a coffee.'

She sat down at a double-leaf table that only had one side pulled out. There were two chairs, one large and one barely more than a stool with a very faint back on it. She took the stool-type chair and watched as the man pottered about with a kettle before taking a jar of instant coffee out. Hope looked at the brand and nearly spat, but beggars couldn't be choosers, and in truth, she was parched after her trip.

'So, you're the master of the Harris to North Uist ferry,' said Hope. 'How long have you been doing that?'

'Longer than you can imagine,' said the man, 'or maybe not,' laughing. 'It's nearly been thirty-five years though. That's a tricky wee stretch of water. It's got currents going here, there, and everywhere, but once you know it, it's not too bad. I mean our ferry is just a very basic roll-on, roll-off. We don't take that many cars. Enough. The trip's only an hour back and forward. You have to watch the tides. Hence, the sailing times can change. In really rough weather, well, we don't go.'

'Have you had many people go overboard in your time?'

'Well, a couple, but this was a bit different.'

'In what way?'

'Well, I think it's two we've had before. One of them was a kid whose parents should have known better. The kid was climbing up on the rails and fell off. We got him. The other one was a suicide attempt, but she was making such a noise that I think she wanted to be recovered and we got her. This is the first one on this stretch that's died.'

'What happened exactly then, from your point of view?'

'Well,' said the man, placing the coffee in front of Hope, sitting down on his chair, and pulling it close so that Hope felt his knee touch hers, 'it was just a normal run. I was up top piloting the vessel and the first I knew of it, one of the other boys shouts, "Man overboard." Of course, you stop, you put the call out to the Coastguard. We turned around and started our search. We got the new inshore lifeboat over at Leverburgh which came out, various other vessels, but we never saw anything. Not for a while anyway.'

'No? What do you mean "not for a while"?'

'Exactly what I said. For a while, we didn't see anything. Over forty minutes, the helicopter's out, then the lifeboat saw a body briefly come up and then down, and then fifteen minutes later came right past our own boat. Lifeboat got over, picked the corpse out of the water.'

'The name was Fred Martin; is that correct?'

'Yes. It looked like a suicide. The local police guy came up, he did a bit of digging, more than me. I mean, there's nothing we could do but the usual investigation and statements we had to make for the MAIB, the Maritime Accident Investigation Branch people. In truth, there was little to be done. Very sad though.'

'Was there anybody with him at the time? It doesn't say so in any reports.'

'No, he was on his own and we had to take the car off afterwards. That wasn't easy. Eventually, they broke into it, and I managed to free the handbrake. Breakdown guy came and pulled the car off. If you want to know more details about him, you need to go down and talk to Alan, the local constable. I think he's off duty today.'

'You know him well?'

'Well, yes. He came up here once in pursuit of someone. We talked, met, and yes, we share an interest in the boats. I helped him with his. In fact, why don't I take you over there?'

'I'm sure if you give me the address, I can do it,' said Hope.

'No, it'd be no trouble, honestly. I don't get that many visitors. It'd be a delight to take you there.' Hope watched the man stand up, finish the dram he had in his hand, and then stand behind her, taking her stool away as she got up. She wasn't quite sure how to take it because she should have been the authority figure. In some ways, the man was quite charming.

Hope made for her car, and Ian Angus sat down in the passenger seat before pointing her down the road. They travelled all the way back across into North Uist and made their way round to a place called Sollas, which had a long stretch of beach.

'They used to land all the private planes in there when they had a big rally. Some guy out of Stornoway came down; he organised it. I don't think he's around anymore. If you continue along the road past that, we'll get to Constable Alan McNair's.'

Hope continued to drive, and the track got even rougher than normal, but she found a house sitting beside a small inlet where the water flowed close by. She could see a boat sitting on the water, tied to a makeshift pier. As she switched off the car engine, a man appeared from the house. He was younger than Ian Angus, somewhere in his thirties, and over his shoulder she could see a young woman with him. Ian Angus exited from the car, waving towards him.

'Alan, sorry to bother you. This here is a detective. She's called Hope. She's come to talk to me about that suicide we had on the boat. I said you knew more about him than I did.'

'Grand. I did put a report in, the initial one.'

Hope, again leaving her jacket in the car, walked over to Alan McNair and extended her hand. 'Detective Sergeant Hope McGrath. Pleased to meet you.'

'Macleod. You're the one that works with Macleod.'

'I was telling her she should be the front person,' said Ian Angus. 'Better looking than that Macleod.'

Alan shot him a look. 'We don't talk like that anymore, Ian. I told you before you need to be careful.'

'She a good-looking woman. Just letting her know.' The man turned past Alan and gave a wave to the woman standing behind him. 'Hey, Alice, how are you? Another good-looking woman.'

Alan rolled his eyes, staring at Hope. 'Sorry,' he said. 'He doesn't mean anything by it.'

'I don't think he does. It's okay. It's not the worst comment I've ever had.'

Alan turned and showed Hope to the front door, where she shook Alice by the hand. Inside, they sat around the kitchen table. Hope noticed that Alice poured Ian Angus a large dram, whereas Alan joined Hope and his wife with a coffee.

'The guy was called Fred Martin who went in. I've read the report, and you say, Alan, that basically, he seemed to have jumped off.'

'That's correct. No one actually quite saw him. We don't know the method of entry, whether he struck his head or whatever, and knocked himself out. It could've explained why

50

he wasn't waving.'

'Do you know anything else about him—why he would have jumped?'

'After the initial investigation, I sent that report off, but just out of interest, I tried to make some contacts. Turns out that Mrs Martin had actually committed suicide a month previous. The couple had attended counselling and it was Fred Martin's brother who told me all this. Apparently, it seemed that it was a bit of a rough relationship; he cheated a lot with younger women, but she was besotted with him. They'd won a trip to come up here. Apparently, Fred had thought this would be a great chance to get together, but she committed suicide before the trip. That's a month previous, so the man decided to do it anyway. Not surprising then that he jumped.'

'When you say it's not surprising, is there any definitive proof that he did from the persons on board?'

'I spoke to some of them, but nobody actually saw him. He was only reported as overboard. Once he'd gone into the water, he was spotted by a member of the public at the aft of the vessel. So, the answer to your question is no. There's no conclusive proof that he jumped. It's just presumed. Why are you asking?'

'I'm sure you're well aware, Alan, that there's been a number of incidents of people going overboard recently off the Minchlines ferries.'

'One just recently in Stornoway. Do you think there's something untoward going on?'

'We don't know, but the spate of incidents is giving cause for concern. As I understand it, the Maritime Investigation Branch, the Coastguard, they all seem happy with the way the vessels are operating. It just seems a bit crazy to get that many suicides, that close together, all with very similar modus operandi.'

'Well, that's true,' said Alan. 'That's definitely true, but in this case, as far as I'm concerned, it definitely looks like suicide.'

'Quite something though,' said Hope, 'to follow up on a journey he made with the wife and then to go and end it all. Maybe it got too much for him, or maybe he planned it. Yes, well, I better get on. See where the boss wants me to go next. Thank you for your time, everyone.'

'You get off,' said Alan. 'I'll give Ian Angus a lift back over.'

Hope saw Angus' face drop. 'It's fine,' she said. 'I'll run him.'

The trip back over to Berneray was not that long, but the man made three offers of dinner for Hope and then told her that if she was passing by anytime, it wouldn't be a problem to find her somewhere to stay. As she dropped him off at the house, he turned, gave his hand to her, and when she shook it, he leaned forward and kissed her on the cheek.

'I hope you didn't take offense in that,' he said. 'It's just, well, yes. In my day that was normal. It's been an absolute pleasure to meet you.'

As Hope drove away, returning down towards the airport, she realised she needed somewhere to stay that night. In her head, she thought Ian Angus was innocent. She liked the compliment he gave her, but something else in her said there was no way she was staying anywhere in his house. As she continued to drive down towards Benbecula, it set Hope wondering. How these days do you tell the difference between the kind, sweet old man who was a little bit taken with her, and someone who had much darker intent?

Chapter 07

Macleod had spread his teams far and wide and he now wanted to make sure that he could pull together all that they'd found out. In that regard, he had called a conference call for that evening and was sitting in his hotel room with Ross beside him, awaiting Jona's arrival. The woman had made it over earlier that day. Having set up her temporary morgue at the hospital, she was hopefully coming with some news for Macleod. One of the problems they had at the moment was that there was no conclusive proof that anyone had been killed. So far, all they knew was people had entered the water by unknown means and a feeling in Macleod's gut that this number of suicides was too much to be true. He watched as Ross took the kettle and poured himself and the inspector a cup of coffee each. The constable then sat down and started fiddling with Macleod's laptop.

'I don't think you've opened the call up yet, sir.'

'You just do what you have to do,' said Macleod, 'you don't have to tell me I'm rubbish at it in the process.'

'No sir, of course not.' He watched Ross sheepishly begin to work away, then Ross turned around to see Macleod smiling at him.

'I know I'm rubbish at it,' said Macleod, 'I'm just glad you're here.' Macleod sat and watched the screen until a sudden vision of purple hair appeared. There was no face with the hair. Macleod heard Ross tell Clarissa to sort her camera out. For a moment, Clarissa's chin came into view, before finally her full face. Then Hope's image appeared in a small box in the corner.

'Good, you're all here. Just waiting on Jona to arrive. I hope everyone's okay.'

'I had an offer to stay the night at someone's,' said Hope, 'but I turned him down.'

'Wish I'd got an offer,' said Clarissa. 'I didn't even get to see a man who might have made me an offer.'

'That's a bit of a pain,' said Hope.

'Who are we talking about?' asked Macleod. 'You're on work here, not a jolly.'

'Leave her alone,' said Hope. 'I'm sure you'll get back to Mull sometime, Clarissa'

'Mull? What are you talking about, Hope? Why is she going to Mull? Who's in Mull?'

'That's the trouble with you, Seoras. When you're on the case, you see nothing else. It's a wonder that Jane stays with you.'

Macleod went to reply but actually, there was some truth in that statement. He had thought that for a while but Jane was still with him, so he didn't argue.

There came a rap at the door and a rather bedraggled Jona Nakamura made her way into the room. The woman was in a pair of jeans and a t-shirt, and her hair, rather than being tied up, hung around her shoulders. Even Macleod could see the weariness in her face.

'Are you okay?' asked Macleod.

'Let's just get on,' said Jona.

'Only if you're okay. I mean, if you've got the rest of your team here, they can join, take this if you need to go and do something. Take a rest.'

Macleod realised he was rambling at the end of the sentence. It was one of those things. Why was Jona tired? Was there something specific? Was it that time of the month? Oh, of course he can't say that. It was always the way, wasn't it? He always wondered was that it? But if he was saying it, he was somehow implying something. That was never his intention; he just wanted to know if she needed a rest.

'I'm fine, Seoras; let's get on.'

'Right. Well, let's start with Jona then from today. I haven't heard anything, so this is the first report.'

Jona gave a brief wave to Clarissa and Hope on the camera before turning and looking at Macleod. 'Right,' she said, 'I've examined Daphne Walsh and found some interesting things. It appears that she was incapacitated before she went into the water.'

'How do you mean?' asked Macleod.

'Well, her neck broke hitting the water. But then, and this took a while, I discovered she'd been injected; ketamine.'

'That's the stuff they use for date rape, isn't it?'

'Yes, but this is in a serious quantity. Highly likely she'd have been immobilised.'

'Immobilised?' queried Macleod. 'Are you sure?'

'Oh, yes,' said Jona, 'I'm sure, she was immobilised.'

'Then how did she get in the water?'

'Well, that's up to you, detective,' said Jona. 'I'm telling you she was immobilised. She could not have got into that water

55

by herself, but it also explains why, when she goes in, she's not waving for help and why she disappeared down quickly. They won't struggle; if they are lucky, they might float. However, her neck's broken. I think it's from the impact of the water. I can't find any markings indicating the neck was broken by a person. It looks like it was by an impact.'

'Could somebody have struck her?' said Macleod.

'You wouldn't strike somebody and then inject them,' said Jona, 'that would be quite messy. Also, to be hit with a force that broke her neck there was liable to be surface damage if they were using an item. The water being what it is, you don't get the same impact on the skin. You don't get any cut. It's just a simple straightforward break of the neck.'

'So, she was murdered,' said Macleod.

'That's what my judgment would be,' said Jona.

'Okay,' said Macleod. 'Hope, what about your man?'

'Fred Martin? It looks like a case of suicide. His wife died a month before, but they were in counselling. She was a bit put upon. Apparently, he seemed to have a sex addiction with younger women and was doing the sly on her all the time. He was only on the ferry because he'd won a trip. They'd planned to go on it, but she killed herself a month before it. He went anyway and then seemed to jump in the water, too.'

'Any indication he was immobilised?'

'Not from statements I've got but I haven't checked the body.'

'And you won't,' said Jona. 'I had a look for pathology reports on these bodies and Fred Martin was already cremated. They didn't do an investigation on him and in truth, even if they did, to find a needle mark you'd have to be looking. I was extremely thorough because this was the only body we had.'

'Blast,' said Macleod,' and the other two are still in the water somewhere.'

'It does kind of put an awkward spin on it,' said Hope.

'Then we have to do it the other way. We have to go digging
and we have to find out who these people were, all about their
lives. Hope and Clarissa, we're going to need you to dig into
the three previous victims. Andrew Culshaw, where was he
from?' said Macleod, scrabbling through notes.

'Derbyshire,' said Ross without even looking.

Macleod stared across at him. 'Does it just sit in there soon
as you read it?'

'Well, I did think, sir, where people might need to go next.
Derbyshire.'

'Hope, I want you and Clarissa to get down to Derbyshire.
Go and speak to his wife. Find out what was going on within
that relationship. See if there's anything untoward.'

'Okay, I'll get the plane over tomorrow down to Glasgow. If
you could pick me up from there, Clarissa.'

'Not a problem. Just make sure you bring something for your
hair. We're taking the little green machine.' Hope nodded and
then saw Macleod's look of horror.

'I'm quite happy for the pair of you to hire a car to get down.'

'Nonsense, Seoras. I've got the car with me. It'll be nice and
quick. Hope's not as fuddy-duddy about cars as you are.'

There was a silence.

'Fuddy-duddy,' said Macleod, 'just in case I don't feel old
enough; fuddy-duddy.'

Macleod heard a snigger from beside him. He turned to see
Ross looking the other way.

'Can I just remind everyone, we're now in a murder investigation? So down to Derbyshire first. Don't hang about either.
Ross and I will tidy up this one because this is where we can

get the most evidence from. We know we've got a killer on board here, so we'll get into the passenger manifest, see what's going on. We need to run plenty of cross-referencing on this. Four different instances. Let's not be afraid to understand that one of them may even be a suicide but see what we can find out about the others.'

'Once we're in Derbyshire and complete, we'll go and see Gerald Lyndhurst then,' said Hope. 'I doubt there's any point going down to see anyone associated with Fred Martin. I kind of got the lowdown from a Constable Alan McNair. He said that he'd already contacted people down there to get a fuller story, and to be fair, I think he has done. There's no wife to interview. They were in counselling so possible we could find out who the counsellor was, maybe get more information that way.'

'Very good,' said Macleod. 'I know this seems a strange case. We haven't exactly arrived at a body. We've come a roundabout route to get there but this doesn't change things. If we do have a murder, we've always got the idea that they can murder again.'

'Have we thought about putting the ferries on alert?' asked Hope. 'If we reckon there is an actual murderer on the go, maybe we need to advise them, keep people off the decks.'

'That might be the worst way to do it,' said Macleod. 'If there's definitely nobody on deck, our killer might get free licence to lob them overboard. The more eyes you have, the lower the risk of it occurring again.'

'Not sure I agree on that one, Seoras,' said Clarissa.

'Either way, I'll talk to Minchlines,' said Macleod. 'Make them aware they've got a murder with this case. Tell them what we're doing but we'll keep it quiet, talk to their chief exec and their operations manager. It'll probably be the easiest way to run this. We don't want to panic people. These ferries are about to get busy, summer coming in. They're going to be booked out and the last thing we need is a panic on our hands. I'm sick and tired of being on the media,' said Macleod.

'Indeed,' said Hope, 'I had a guy today, say to me, 'Do I work for Macleod?' You really are the pinup boy, Seoras.'

Macleod gave her a stare. 'I was going to feel sorry for you in that car, but do you know what? No.'

'So, shall we run through the plan again, sir?' asked Ross. 'Just to make sure we all understand it.'

'Absolutely,' said Macleod. 'Tomorrow, Hope flies to Glasgow, down to join Clarissa. They make their way to Derbyshire; interview Marie Culshaw to find out everything about the death of Andrew Culshaw. From there, they'll need to go and speak to the friends of Peter Hughes to check out that situation. I guess his friend Gerald Lyndhurst is the person we start with. Meanwhile, Ross is going to go through trying to ID everyone who's come on the ferry to Stornoway and we'll try and match up passenger lists. We'll see what CCTV we've got. There's bound to be some on the ships as well, just to see if we can find a common person.'

'It's going to be quite an effort, Seoras,' said Clarissa. 'If you're going to do four murders like this and you don't want to be associated with being on the passenger list, you're going to have to change your passenger name, you're going to have to book it with a different card. You're also going to have to get a different car each time. If we're quite serious about there being four murders here, and I realise at the moment we can't confirm that, we're talking about someone who's got serious planning abilities. Someone who's possibly got a bit of money, who also understands how to use ketamine properly, how to

59

administer it, and has got the strength to throw somebody overboard.'

'I don't think they're going to have to be that strong,' said Macleod. 'These people are incapacitated.'

'And like a dead weight,' said Jona.

'But if they get them close to the edge,' said Hope, 'these ferries, it's not easy to toss somebody over, is it? And if you're beside them when you've been injected and you collapse, surely, they're going to lean up against the railings. You could grab their feet and tip them. Maybe that's why Daphne went in headfirst, broke her neck.'

'It's a long fall,' said Jona; 'you could rotate. That's not a guarantee.'

'Fair enough,' said Hope.

'Right,' said Macleod, 'we'd better get to it. Ross and I have got a bit more work today. You two get to bed, and, Jona, go get some rest.'

Jona nodded and left Macleod's room and he switched off the conference call. As Ross went to leave, Macleod looked over at him.

'Do you know what's up with Jona?'

'Well, I can't be 100% accurate, sir, and maybe I'm not the best person to look at these things but I think she's pregnant.'

'What?' said Macleod. 'How is Jona pregnant?'

Ross stood and looked at Macleod for a moment. 'Do you want to clarify that question, sir?'

'I know that bit of it,' said Macleod. 'I didn't think she was seeing anyone.'

'No,' said Ross, 'and that's why I'd leave it.' Macleod stood and looked at Ross for a moment, then nodded. This was Jona Nakamura. A mistake in getting pregnant? Jona was thorough, planned, on top of things. Jona was the person who'd taught Macleod how to stay balanced, how to get rid of any negative emotions, and now here she was possibly pregnant and not telling anyone.

'Maybe I should get Hope to speak to her.'

'No,' said Ross, 'maybe you should keep out of it until she tells you.' Then after a long pause, Ross added, 'sir.'

Ross was right. It actually wasn't Macleod's business and tomorrow was another day. He needed to get the work done and then get on with whatever else came his way. What bothered him was Jona's possible pregnancy seemed more of an issue to him than potentially four deaths on the ferries.

Chapter 08

Hope generally didn't spend that much time with Clarissa in the field as both held the rank of sergeant, although Hope was the superior within the team. Macleod generally split them, happy to let them work either alone or to take Ross or another constable with them. Ross, however, was going nowhere. Macleod had him checking through the passenger list for any random detail that could pull out a potential killer. He'd be cross-referencing, checking credit cards, all in a hopeful attempt at trying to narrow down who had been on all four ferries.

In the back of Hope's mind was the idea that maybe this one murder had been it, maybe the other, suicides, and then someone had taken advantage, but there were too many things that were out of line. All the suicides hadn't been seen. There was no confirmation that these people had jumped of their own accord. Were they really that upset that they were being driven to suicide? Macleod, of course, had been right. You'd find it all out in the details of the people. You needed to know who they were, what they did, what their lives were. She understood why they were investigating, why the Coastguard needed their assistance. This was the murder team's bread and butter, and Hope truly believed they'd get to the bottom of it.

One thing about being with Clarissa was that Hope wasn't driving. If she was with Macleod, she automatically took the wheel, and she agreed with Clarissa's view that Macleod drove like a pedestrian. Hope didn't think he drove that well either. She didn't know if it was an age thing or the fact the man was just a poor driver. But having gone now with Clarissa and sitting in the small green sports car, half of her was wondering if maybe she should go back with Macleod. Hope had forgotten her hair tie, and her red hair was streaking out the back as they raced along the motorway south.

Clarissa seemed to be in her element, a headscarf tied around her head, the top down on the vehicle, and Hope wondered if Clarissa would turn around and start waving at every car she overtook. To give her due credit, Clarissa was a very good driver, and she knew how to handle her own car. That, however, did not make up for the fact that Hope would rather have been in a normal hatchback or saloon with the heating on and not being required to drink so quickly because the cool air meant any beverage was cold in less than five minutes.

'Not long till we're into the Derbyshire Hills. You'll see how this thing handles then,' said Clarissa. Hope wrapped her arms around herself. She could do with her man here. Could John wrap her up? Hope normally wore a leather jacket, open. She liked that with something with colour underneath to highlight the black, but instead it was zipped up tight, her arms folded around her and tucked in under her armpits. Beside her, wrapped in her shawl, Clarissa looked radiant.

Soon the motorway faded, and the Derbyshire Hills were as Clarissa had predicted, filled with curved roads that Clarissa seemed to have a sixth sense about. The speed at which she took corners made Hope wonder if she could see round them in a fashion that no normal human could? She overtook people at speed, dropping the gears often to get that burst of power. When they eventually pulled up at a house halfway up a hill in an old mining village, Hope staggered out of the car and then feigned a number of stretches.

'Just tired sitting there so long,' she said.

'See? That was more fun than driving with Macleod, wasn't it? I still remember the old pursuit driving back in the day. They said I could handle the car, then of course, I went off into art and antiques. 'Wasted,' they said to me.'

'We're off back up towards Scotland after this,' said Hope. 'I think we might do well to find somewhere and stop for the night. If Macleod needs me quickly, I'll fly.'

Clarissa shot her a look, then marched up and rapped the front door of a small cottage. She watched the curtains at the side being pulled back and then the door opened to a woman that stood almost six feet, with wide shoulders and a thunderous look on her face.

'Yes?'

Charming, thought Hope, and reached inside her jacket to pull out her identification. 'Excuse me. I'm Detective Sergeant Hope McGrath. This is Detective Sergeant Clarissa Urquhart. We need to talk to Marie Culshaw regarding the death of her husband. Would you be her?'

'No. I'm Angela, Angela Sinclair. Marie is my sister, and I don't think you'll be able to speak to her.'

'Why is that?'

'She hasn't been well since he died. She's not coping.'

'I'm afraid this is part of a police investigation. I'd rather come in and talk socially with her, but if needs be, we can go down to the station. I don't wish it to go that far.'

'You'd haul a widow down to the station? It's barbaric. Is that what they do up in Scotland?'

'Up in Scotland, we do the same as they do down in England. There's been a murder, and we need to talk to Mrs Culshaw about the death of her husband. There may be possible links.'

'If you must, wait there,' said the woman firmly, and shut the door in their face.

'You want me to kick it in?' asked Clarissa. Hope nearly reacted, put her hands out to stop Clarissa doing it, before realising the woman was joking.

'Yes, it was a bit strong, wasn't it?' said Hope. 'You might have to—'

'You're getting like him. Do you know that?'

'What?' asked Hope.

'Macleod. You're just like Macleod. Oh, here we come. Here's the difficult person in front of who you want to talk to as a witness, and guess what? Let's get old Clarissa to take them to one side.'

'Well, you're damn good at it,' said Hope, not batting an eyelid.

'You just better hope our roles don't get reversed. I give you a pleasant drive down in the car and you dump me with this?'

'It's the joy of rank or, in fact, seniority. We have the same rank.'

The door opened and the intense face of Angela Sinclair looked back at them. 'She's in the living room but five minutes.'

Hope stepped forward and held her hand up. 'Mrs Sinclair, this is a police investigation. You're not a medical doctor. You don't have a patient that you think could be compromised by prolonged questioning. If they said to me five minutes, it would be five minutes. I will take what time I need with your sister. I'd kindly ask that you talk to my colleague.'

'Your colleague? Why would I want to talk to your colleague?'

'You probably don't. She wants to talk to you. We need to get a rounded view of Mr Culshaw.'

'Well, okay, but just once I see that Marie's all right.'

'Is it this way?' said Hope, marching into the hall and trying a door. She opened it to see a woman sitting on the sofa, looking up with sullen eyes. 'Excuse me. Are you Mrs Marie Culshaw?'

'That's me,' she said in a voice that was like a church whisper.

'I'm Detective Inspector Hope McGrath, and I need to speak to you about the death of your husband. It's just routine inquiry into a different murder investigation we've got.'

'Okay,' the woman said quietly, and sat back in the seat. Hope watched as her sister sat down beside her, right on the edge of the sofa, staring hard at Hope.

'I'd like to ask you first about your husband. What sort of a man was he?'

'Andrew? Andrew was hard to live with, but he had some good sides to him. He was a loving guy in a lot of ways. I remember when we got married, and he would—'

'He used to smack her about,' said Angela. ' I'd come in and I'd see her. She'd be red around the chops. He used to humiliate her at times, pulled down her trousers, and smack her like a child.'

'Is that right?' asked Hope. 'Is your sister correct in what she's saying?'

'Yes,' came the whisper.

'Well, I'm deeply sorry for that. Did he do anything else other than—'

66

'Oh, he did things, all right. I mean he was wicked. Wicked man.'

'Don't talk about him like that. You didn't understand us. You didn't.'

'"I didn't understand" my arse, Marie. We told you before he should have got it earlier. Best thing that happened to him.'

'Did you take that trip together, alone, away from the rest of the family?' asked Hope.

'We did. You see, we'd won tickets for the trip. That's why we were on it. Andrew was actually quite excited. He'd..., well, he'd packed certain things, things that would've—'

'He packed your dirty costumes. That's what he did.' Hope glanced over at Clarissa and gave her a nod.

'I'm afraid, Miss Sinclair, I need to speak to you. The sergeant will need to speak to your sister alone. If you'd come with me.'

'I'm staying here.'

Clarissa stood up and marched over, before positioning herself between Angela and her sister. 'If you're staying here, we'll have to do that bit down the station. Better if I speak to you now. Up, please.' Clarissa put an arm under the woman, lifted her up, and escorted her briskly out through the door.

'You can speak more freely now,' said Hope, 'now that your sister is gone. Just say things as they are. I won't be shocked. You'll be amazed at how much we see in our work. You were saying Andrew won the tickets?'

'He did. He won these tickets. Then he came home with some more outfits. He liked me to dress for him, that sort of thing. He was quite generous that way, but he did use to hit me, especially if I didn't like the outfit.' The woman was looking off to one side and Hope felt so sorry for her.

'Was he getting any help for that?' she asked.

'We had gone to several counselling sessions here, there, and everywhere. I was advised I should leave him, offered refuge, women's refuge and things, but I was never going to get rid of him. My husband, he'd told me he loved me. I couldn't walk away from him. Do you understand that?'

Hope wasn't really sure she did, but she said so anyway. 'When you went onto the ferry,' asked Hope, 'what happened?'

'Well, that's the thing. We had a bit of a row. Andrew was not happy.'

'Why was that?' asked Hope.

'I'd put the wrong top on, or rather I'd worn a top that he wanted a certain garment underneath, but frankly, it was a bit revealing, so I decided to say no. He hit me. Then when we were on board, he turned around and he told me that I looked like nothing good. He was the one who could make me look better. He was highly abusive. In that sense, it was a pity because he did love me.'

It sounded like a funny sort of love to Hope, but she decided to continue with the line of questioning. 'You had counselling sessions. Where was that?'

'We actually ended up in Glasgow for a lot of them. A Dr Stevens. He was recommended to us. Dr Stevens was good. She was helping him, but Andrew was a tough case. I'm not sure he appreciated having a female counsellor to begin with. I did though. I appreciated it. It felt safer with another woman there.'

'Did the sessions help?'

'In a way, they did. You see, she had Andrew doing nice things for me. He suddenly would stop hitting me. He'd suddenly make the dinner, or he'd take me out somewhere.

Then it would go wrong, he'd buy a dress, and really, you wouldn't wear these things out and about, but he'd insist on it and I'd get annoyed. He'd then get angry. He'd end up hitting me when we came home, especially if I hadn't worn what he wanted.'

'Dr Stevens, did she tell you to leave him at any point?'

'She did. She even gave a name of refuge and places. Andrew found them and went nuts, but I didn't choose to leave him. There was good inside him. All my sister can see is the bad side.'

From the hall outside, Hope could hear some swearing, swearing referring to a man in the vilest of terms.

'Yes, she does sound like she doesn't like him,' said Hope. 'When you rowed on the ferry, what happened then?'

'He stormed off, went upstairs. That's the last I saw of him. He threw himself off the top. I'd like to think the guilt got to him. Then I feel guilty about saying that. I didn't want him dead. Never wanted him dead. I wanted him to see, to be better. I wanted him to be a proper husband.'

'When you were on the boat, was there anyone close to you? Anyone you saw looking at you?'

'Whole boat stared at me when he started rowing and he hit me.'

'Did anyone interfere at that point, especially when he hit you?'

'Some men came over and that's when Andrew went upstairs.'

'Did any of them follow him?'

'Not as far as I could tell,' said Marie. Hope continued the questioning for another half an hour but learned nothing that she hadn't learned in those first engagements. As they left the

69

house, Angela Sinclair saw them to the door. 'I'm so glad he got that ticket,' she said.

'Why?' asked Hope.

'Because that's what made him go up there. That's what made him jump. Go to his death. She's better off without him. She won't see that, but she is better off without him.'

'Are you sure he won the ticket?'

'Totally. He was too tight to buy something like that. The only thing he spent money on was stuff to make Marie look—well, look like you know what, tart, and a pretty dirty one at that.'

'We'll let you get back to looking after your sister,' said Hope. The door was slammed shut behind them. She sat down in the small green sports car, and Clarissa joined her.

'Guess it's back up the road,' she said, 'but it's interesting.'

'How come?' asked Clarissa.

'Warring couple. Everyone seems to be a warring couple in counselling.'

'Everyone except the fellow that fell off the boat in Leverburgh. His wife was already dead.'

'Maybe they were warring before that.'

'But they're all warring with each other. So what? We've got four random people just going around in boats looking for somebody who's having a fight and then bumping one of them off?'

'I know it sounds a bit wild at the moment,' said Hope. 'It's a feeling in the gut.'

'Seoras said that he had a feeling in his gut as well,' said Clarissa. 'I'm struggling to swallow that. We can't go on gut anyway. We need to find some evidence.'

'You don't think the sister could be a suspect?'

'If it was a one-off,' said Hope. 'I would. But four? Why kill off the other three? Practice?'

'You've come across practice before, I thought.'

Hope thought down to earlier times in her career when the Skye Bridge was blown up, the shooting at Fort Augustus along the line of Neptune's steps.

'This doesn't feel like that. It really doesn't.' Hope's head threw back against the headrest as Clarissa spun the car around and drove off back into the Derbyshire countryside. *Next time*, thought Hope. *Next time, I drive, even if I have to hire my own car to get here.*

Chapter 09

Ross started sifting through the statements from the passengers of the ferry. Occasionally, he would glance out of the window of Stornoway Police Station, but in truth, it wasn't the greatest view he'd ever seen. The station was tucked away a few streets behind the main Stornoway thoroughfare, if you could call it that, on a road that swept into town through Bayhead and followed the harbour round before finding its way out to the other side of town to one of the town's supermarkets. The day had clouded over and outside was cold.

Ross furtively looked up the street at the curry house on the corner, his stomach rumbling, knowing that it was lunchtime, but such a main meal was not on the cards. He looked at the reheated noodles in a plastic tub, and knew why he hadn't eaten many of them.

Standing up, he made his way out of the office. Scurrying along the corridor until he found a kitchen, Ross grabbed an apple he'd left there earlier, took it back to his office, and sat down again. He moved as if he was alone, but in truth, there were busy constables around him but to him, they could have been in a different world.

He was processing, churning through the statements he'd read. Every now and again, Ross would put another one in front of him, and his pen would shoot across to the blank piece of paper, a way of cross-referencing. He could do it on the computer, but Ross liked to see the old-fashioned pencil and pen, which seemed to connect more with him, despite how good he was on a computer.

His train of thought was broken as the door opened, and he heard a measured but firm set of footsteps coming towards him. He looked up knowing it would be the face of his boss.

'Sir?' said Ross.

'How are we getting on?'

'Well, Daphne Walsh doesn't seem to have been seen by anybody. I've gone through statements again, and the only person I can see who actually saw her before she went into the water was a child who was down on the lower deck at a window. They have these big round ones. I guess a small child can sit in them so the little girl was looking out watching for dolphins, and then she saw Daphne come past.'

'That must have been a shock for her. So, she raised the alarm then?'

'Indirectly. She paddled along and told her parents that she'd seen somebody go in. They didn't think much of it but thought they should report it, at which point, most of the crew went up on deck and could see Mrs Walsh out the back of the vessel in the water. They called the attention of the master, the boat turned around, Mayday given to the Coastguard. Everything ran from there, sir.'

'Did nobody see her up on deck?'

'No. Nobody near her. People saw her going up to go on deck, but nobody actually saw her up there.'

'What about people who went up at the same time as Daphne? People trying to go up the stairs, or disappearing out on deck?'

'Hard. You've got a couple of hundred people in this boat, and some of the steps you can go up without actually going out on deck as well. I'm not getting any consistent picture of someone around the same time as her. Most reports are very general descriptions; brown hair, maybe five feet seven, up to five feet eleven. There's nothing concrete you could pin on anyone.'

'So, what you're telling me is, Ross, that we have all these people on this ferry, and nobody manages to spot her going upstairs, and then going into the water?'

'Oh, they spotted her going up the stairs,' said Ross, 'there's just nothing after that.'

'I don't believe that for a minute.'

'It gets tricky though, sir, because she didn't go up the stairs once, she went up several times. Trying to weed out who actually saw her on the last occasion, I've also tried to see if anybody was following her up on each occasion, but there's no pattern. Although to be truthful, I'm not sure half of these people would have noticed.'

'Somebody must have.'

'Why?' asked Ross. 'Why would you? People won't recall that. They won't recall who's gone up. Some of them are struggling to recall even seeing her. Several of the people I've interviewed said they saw this person going up, and then I showed a photograph of who it was, and they said, 'Well, that's not the one I was talking about.''

'Come on, Ross. There must be something. This is number four. We know they're being killed.'

'We know one's been killed, sir. One was murdered and that's Daphne Walsh. The others, we don't know, do we?'

'Yes, yes, Ross. I know what you're saying, but four passengers overboard this close together, blast it, why? Why? What is it with this? Anyway, Ross, I need to go and speak to Mr Walsh. He's downstairs. Not going to be the most pleasant of my duties.'

'Would you like me to sit in on it, sir?' asked Ross.

'No, it's fine. I'll take it. To be truthful, I'm not sure how much we're going to learn. It's going to be a background search. Nothing more, nothing less. Nobody puts him anywhere near once she's gone up on deck, do they?'

'No,' said Ross.

'Well, in that case, you need to find the connection. You need to find out why these people have been killed. What's the key to it? I'll speak to you later.'

'Oh, sir,' said Ross, 'I was thinking, dinner tonight? Maybe we should get one a bit earlier, around teatime.'

'Well, I haven't really thought about it, Ross. I don't know where we're going to be going.'

'There's that curry house up in the corner. We've been there before, remember?'

'As I recall last time, Clarissa had me up trying to sing. I hope you're not looking for a repeat performance.'

'No, sir. Except for the biryani.'

Macleod allowed Ross a half-smile, more for encouragement than actually feeling any particular humour about what Ross has said. Macleod was too involved at the moment, his mind racing through possibilities. He never settled while the case was on, always thinking.

Ross was different. Ross could snap into a mode and snap

out. When a case was happening, it consumed Macleod. Jane had told him so, told him to go and get things done before coming back. She said she lost her partner every time a case kicked off, and he struggled to correct her on that.

Macleod walked out of the office and down the stairs towards the interview room. He knocked on the door, and a constable let him in. A man was sitting behind a desk, a cup of tea in front of him, and he was hunched over. He had black hair, clearly uncombed, and a shirt that looked ruffled.

'Mr Walsh, it's me Detective Inspector Macleod. Again, can I offer you my condolences on the loss of your wife?'

The man slowly raised his head and Macleod could see the red eyes.

'Thank you, Inspector,' he said, and then put his head down.

'I'll try and be as quick as I can,' said Macleod, 'but we think that your wife's demise may have been one of many and I need to look into her background.'

'One of many?' asked the man suddenly, lifting his face to Macleod. 'Why would Daphne be one of many? What . . .?'

'I regret to inform you, sir, that your wife was injected with a substance that would've paralyzed her, and we believed she was thrown off the ferry.'

'Daphne? Why? I mean, what did Daphne ever do to anyone?'

'Well, most people can offend someone,' said Macleod. 'I know that the two of you were rowing before she went upstairs.'

'You don't think I did it, do you?' said the man suddenly. 'I wouldn't touch her. I wouldn't . . . , I mean, yes, we'd argue, but I wouldn't . . . , I wouldn't do anything to Daphne.'

'I don't believe that you did, sir. I certainly don't believe that you were up on deck and in any way, were responsible for your wife's demise. I just bring it up to try and find out a bit of background about Mrs Walsh.'

'About Daphne; she's called Daphne,' said the man.

Macleod could feel a resentment when he said 'Mrs Walsh', something much stronger than he would've thought of. He didn't read it that the man was insisting on the woman's first name because she was somehow precious but rather as a reaction to something else. It may have seemed cruel, but Macleod thought he should press on with the point.

'Daphne, Mrs Walsh, was arguing with you about something. What was that about?'

'Daphne argued about a lot of things. An awful lot of things.'

'Such as?'

'Daphne had a problem. She never saw things anybody else's way; she could get fiery, violent.'

'Did she ever hit you?'

'Yes. Often, frequently, but we were trying to work it. We went to see a counsellor, Dr Jacobs. Although she seemed to get worse then, in a lot of ways. She didn't like to go.'

'And he called her Mrs Walsh, didn't he?'

The man's teeth clenched. 'Yes,' he snarled. 'Mrs Walsh, she hated Mrs Walsh, she was Daphne. Even Daphne Walsh would've done, but he kept calling her Mrs Walsh.'

'Why did she get upset by that?' asked Macleod, 'it seems fairly normal, a detachment, maybe, from a counsellor to his client.'

'It was her thing, Inspector. You need to understand that about Daphne. If Daphne saw something as black and white and you saw it different, Daphne was right. Daphne was always right in Daphne's mind and if people didn't change, she got

77

angry. I think Dr Jacobs wanted to try and get that anger out to then try and control it, but it didn't work. I didn't get what he was doing.'

'How long were you with Dr Jacobs?'

'We were still seeing him. We went over to Aberdeen as he was recommended to us by some friends of ours. I don't have a particular problem with him, except that, well, it didn't work, did it? She got angry. Maybe that's what happened, maybe that's why they threw her off.'

'No, I'm afraid not, Mr Walsh. Your wife was murdered. She was injected, as I said, with a substance that paralyzed her, and then she was thrown off the ferry. I need to know if there's anybody who had cause to hate her.'

'Cause to hate, yes. Daphne upset people. She was challenged in that way. Like I said, she couldn't see how somebody else could be right and she could be wrong and if it became a bone of contention, she would lit; she would go after them.'

'Had she ever hit anybody else?'

'Once, but I had to stop her several times.'

'Did you ever think you got anywhere with the counselling?' ask Macleod.

'We did at one point. We were going to move and take up a new home, out in the country; it would've been good for her, but then she ruined all that. She attacked the guy who was selling the house to us. This is the thing; anytime you made plans with Daphne, anytime you sorted something out, suddenly something would go wrong. She'd get angry, she'd get violent. It was a full-time job just trying to control that. Do you understand me, inspector?'

Macleod looked into eyes that were now streaming with tears. 'I tried hard. I tried damn hard. You can't do more as a husband, and every time, she wrecked it. Every time, that thing inside of her, that bloody, arrogant, son-of-a-bitch, festering ego wrecked it.' The man put his hand up to his chin, which was suddenly trembling. Macleod could see him physically shake.

'When she couldn't hit other people, she hit you, didn't she?'

'Yes, she did. Then she'd tell me, 'Why the hell am I Mrs Walsh? I'm not Mrs Walsh anymore,' and she'd hit me with whatever, anything at hand. On the ferry, she had a go at me because I told her that I had made another appointment for Dr Jacobs. She went up on deck because she couldn't find anything to hit me with, to attack me. With the way she was, I thought she was best left alone.'

Macleod sat back as the man began to cry again. He watched the shoulders shudder, the sobs now coming hard and heavy. As Macleod leaned back in the seat, he wondered just what the connection was between all of these people.

'One last thing, Mr Walsh. Why were you making this trip?'

'Because we won it,' he said, 'we won the trip. A couple of pairs of tickets arrived. Daphne apparently had won it, and these tickets came addressed to me. I thought it was strange, but they gave us the tickets after Daphne contacted them, so we went. That was a bone of contention too. She kept telling me she had never entered anything. It would be like her though, put it in my name and if we didn't win, she could blame me.'

'But you think she did actually enter something?'

'Well, what other explanation is there?' said the man, his eyes still streaming.

'I give my condolences,' said Macleod standing up. 'Thank you for coming in to speak. The constables will assist you in any way they can.'

Macleod left the room and picked up a telephone in a nearby office. He called direct to the ferry company asking what competitions they'd run when they were giving away tickets, and they told him none in the last year. He put the phone down carefully. Maybe that was something to look at.

Chapter 10

Derbyshire had been hills and swinging roads where Hope had hung on as the nippy green car of Clarissa Urquhart had sped along. Now they were up in the Lake District with vast views of water and quaint towns, one of which they'd stopped in for cake and coffee before driving to the home of Gerald Lyndhurst. The man was in his garden on a rather dour day, down on his knees attending to what Hope could only describe as yellow flowers. She'd been a city girl all her life and botany was something that had never interested her.

Clarissa Urquhart parked the car and she saw the man raise his head briefly before putting it back down again, focusing on the foliage before him. Hope walked along to the man's gate, thought twice about entering and shouted across, 'Excuse me, are you Gerald Lyndhurst?'

The man stood up and Hope could see pads on his knees. He must have been gardening for quite some time.

'Yes, that's me. Who are you?'

'My name's Detective Sergeant Hope McGrath from Inverness police station. This is Detective Sergeant Clarissa Urquhart. Do you mind if we have a word, sir?'

'Scottish police. This'll be about Peter, isn't it?'

Hope could see the man begin to shake slightly, but he tried to hold his bearing.

'It's probably better if we go inside. I'm just about finished here anyway. You couldn't give me a hand, could you? There's a couple of tools there in that,' he said pointing to a bucket, 'just to bring into the house. Don't like to leave them out in case I forget. They get rusty you see. Rusty tools don't help in the garden. I always like things nice and neat. Peter was the same.'

The man didn't wait, but slowly trudged off towards his front door and Hope picked up the tools. She saw Clarissa entering the garden, so the pair then walked towards the front door of a small cottage. The garden around them was immaculate. Hope wondered how somebody could keep it so well. As she stepped inside the front door, she heard a shout from the kitchen.

'I hope you don't mind, but we don't wear shoes in this house.'

Hope caught Clarissa's look of, 'The man's a nutter,' but considering his friend had just died, Hope acquiesced to the man's request, slipping off her boots before walking into the kitchen behind him.

'Would you like a cup of tea, because if you don't mind, I'm going to have one. I was trying not to think about him today, trying to just do. You've kind of screwed that up.'

'I'm sorry, but we have to investigate.'

'Investigate,' said the man suddenly. 'Why? He fell off the ferry.'

'He certainly came off the ferry,' said Hope. 'I am afraid that whether that happened as an accident or not is very much up for debate.'

Hope saw the man almost stumble and she reached out,

getting a hand under his arm and steadying him.

'Maybe I should take you through. Sergeant Urquhart, maybe you could finish the tea.'

Hope assisted the man over to a door, to what she presumed would be the front lounge. As they reached the door, the man stopped suddenly. 'No more than five minutes,' he said.

'What?' asked Clarissa.

'The tea. No more than five minutes. Milk second.' Clarissa's face was in total bemusement but Hope quickly nodded at her to just get on with what she was doing. The red-haired Sergeant assisted the man in to the sofa inside.

The living room was immaculate as well, everything in its place, a set of antimacassars on the back of the sofa, and around the walls were neatly framed pictures. Hope noticed that a few of them were wrong. The frames that were up against the wall were too small. Sun clearly streamed in through the front window and the wood panelling on the wall had faded around where the photograph had been. They'd clearly been replaced with a smaller photograph and the wood that was not exposed was a different colour than that which had been exposed the whole time.

'Can I get you anything else, Mr. Lyndhurst?'

'No, no, please just sit.' Hope sat beside the man and he placed his hand into hers. 'It's been difficult,' he said. 'Really difficult.'

'Well, it's hard to lose friends,' said Hope.

'He wasn't a friend. You have to understand that, my dear. We've kept this going for years. He was everything to me; you get that? Everything, but he wouldn't tell anyone. He wouldn't tell anyone because of me. I wanted it all quiet.'

'Are you telling me that the two of you were intimate?' asked

83

Hope.

'I guess we were in that sense a little, although we were very platonic. I mean, look at me, look at the age I am. This wasn't some sort of hot affair or anything. We just were easy in each other's company, really easy. I guess it developed out of that.'

'Nothing wrong with that though, is there?'

'You tell that to people around here.' said the man suddenly. 'There's always someone, isn't there? Always someone that doesn't like it. The way you are.'

'Have you suffered before?'

'Yes,' said Gerald. 'I lost a partner twenty years ago.'

'This is the second partner that's died on you?'

'No. The first one didn't die. I lost him. He was hounded out. We were both hounded out and then he couldn't take it.'

'Hounded by who?'

'Those who don't like men with men. This time I kept it quiet. I said to Peter we keep quiet. We'd just have ourselves, but Peter wanted…, he wanted to come out. He wanted to tell everyone.'

Hope looked up at the wall again, and noticed that many photographs contained an image of Peter Hughes. All the photographs, all the frames that looked out of place, they had Peter in them.

'You didn't have his photo on the wall, did you?' asked Hope. 'I see you do now.'

'Guilt,' said Gerald. 'That's why they're up there. It's guilt.'

'How much pressure did he put on you to open up to everyone else about your relationship?'

'He was determined to do it. I loved him but he really was forceful about it. Constantly at me. I couldn't take it. I couldn't take it. I thought, well, if we can get help, if we know how to do this. He wanted me to go to one of his counsellors, one of the ones that just…, they want everything out in the open. I said no. I said, "We go to somebody who's there just to help us both. Not somebody of any particular sides."'

'How did that work out?' asked Hope.

'We went to a Dr Greene in Inverness, one of these relationship counsellors. We looked him up. He seemed quite good, but we still struggled. Peter never changed his mind. He wanted to force, he wanted to push the issue, so we argued at times. Dr Greene said Peter was the issue. He had this obsession with wanting to be out in public, wanting to flaunt, he said. Flaunt things. Not just to have things the way they are, but to flaunt them. It's almost like he wanted the issue out there. He thrived on the issue being out there. I didn't. I just wanted the quiet life and him.'

'Who told you about Dr Greene?' asked Hope.

'I just looked him up. We liked Inverness. We couldn't go around here. We couldn't go local, and we'd made several trips up to Inverness already. There's a little haunt up there; maybe you'll know it. There's a little cottage, just beyond Beauly but it meant we could go and see Dr Greene without worrying about anybody else, knowing the man was discreet. To be fair to him, I don't believe he ever told anyone down here about what we were coming to him for.'

'What were you doing on the ferry?' asked Hope. 'Wasn't that a little bit overt, going together?'

'Yes. When we went to Inverness, we travelled apart, but Peter was always wanting us to travel together. I thought, well, if we take a trip, we can travel together. We don't have to show people that we're a couple. We can just be two friends. That worked for me.'

85

'You planned a trip?' asked Hope.

Before the man could answer, Clarissa came through with some tea. She placed a cup down in front of Gerald and Hope saw the man's face.

'Nice and wet that one, love. Get that down you. Help you a bit.' Hope saw that Clarissa's comment about the tea was not well received.

'I just don't feel like it at the moment,' said Peter, pushing the cup to one side.

'You were telling me about the trip,' said Hope as Clarissa sat down on a couch opposite.

'Well, the trip came about because Peter won it. He won some tickets in the post. He said to me, 'Have you ever been on this ferry over to Mull?' I said no, and the next thing Peter had booked some accommodation. It was a bed and breakfast. He booked a double room for us, a proper double bed. I said no, got him to change it and we took a little cottage instead. That was him, always forcing the issue. "Let's go in there and just show everybody who we are." Some of us don't want that. I'd done it last time. You don't understand the things that they say. Are either of you?'

'No,' said Clarissa, and then she started as Hope announced, 'Yes. I'm bi.'

'You see that's what I don't want.' He pointed at Clarissa. 'You haven't said anything even nasty, but you reacted with shock and it puts a barrier up. The last time it was worse than that. Threats, violence. You have to be so careful.'

'I can understand that from your experience,' said Hope. 'But back to the tickets. You said he won them?'

'Yes, they came through the post. He said he couldn't remember entering anything but clearly, he had. Peter was a bit sketchy like that. I was the ordered one. I was the one who would plan things meticulously. A pair of tickets arrived, and he said to go and use them. Then he just goes on, wildly books a B&B for the pair of us with a double room. We sorted that out. I like a bit of control on things. Do you understand that? Is that a bad thing?'

'No, it isn't,' said Hope. 'Tell me about the trip then, because you were arguing.'

'Well,' said Gerald, 'Peter had booked this double room and then I changed it. We were on the ferry and Peter came back again and again at me saying we need to start showing who we are; we need to live our real lives. We had spoken before in front of Dr Greene. I couldn't, from what happened before, I couldn't do it. It put a massive strain on our relationship because he kept forcing things. He kept saying we should do this. Do this, do that. For me, it was becoming too much. That's why we rowed. He disappeared off.'

Hope sat back watching the man stare and she could see he had disappeared into another mind. They stayed for another ten minutes asking similar questions, but it was clear the man did not know much. As they returned to Clarissa's car, Hope was aware of her staring at her.

'What's up?' asked Hope.

'You kept that quiet,' said Clarissa.

'Kept what quiet?'

'Bi. I wouldn't have put you down for that.'

'Why?' asked Hope.

'Look at you. Six-foot, red hair, turn all the guys' heads. You wouldn't need a woman.'

'It's not about need,' said Hope, 'and, like Gerald, I don't advertise. I don't keep it a secret either, though. That man's living in fear. Living in fear of something that happened to him a long time ago.'

'But he was also living with friction,' said Clarissa. 'Did you notice that? And he's been off to a counsellor. Things are beginning to line up.'

'They are, aren't they?' said Hope. 'You should talk to Seoras. See what he knows about his victim.'

Chapter 11

Ross shovelled a pile of rice and lamb tikka up to his mouth before washing it down with a swig of Coke. He would have enjoyed having a beer with his dinner, but he was still working, and had wandered along to the curry house despite the fact that Macleod had not joined him. He had been told by the Inspector he'd be there at six o'clock, but six had made it to a quarter past and Ross had ordered. Now at a quarter to seven, he was almost finished his meal, and there had still been no sign of the Inspector. Ross found it hard to do things on his own at times like these. He and the Inspector were coming into a different station, although they'd been there several times now.

Still, he felt that as a team they should be sticking together, to eat, to work. Macleod's dedication—or was it obsession?—with work made it hard for Ross to apply mealtimes in a sensible fashion, but if he had waited for Macleod, who knows when he would have eaten, maybe even not at all, and at midnight, the curry house wouldn't have been open. Ross wasn't one for a kebab, so he made sure he got to eat what he wanted.

As his plate was being cleared away, Ross saw a constable

appear at the door of the curry house and then approach the table.

'Inspector Macleod would like you back at the station soon as, Constable.'

'Thank you,' said Ross, and immediately stood up before wiping his mouth with his napkin. He paid quickly and took the short walk down the street into the police station to find Macleod sitting in front of his laptop.

'Ross, can you get this thing set up?'

'For what, sir?'

'The team, we need the team, we need to talk to the team. It's not doing it. I don't know why it's not doing it. I pressed the buttons, the ones you said last time and it's not doing it.'

'Yes, sir. On it now,' said Ross. Thirty seconds later the screen was showing a picture of Clarissa which was shortly joined by a picture of Jona. Ross said nothing more, but Macleod kept staring over at him.

'You can say it, you can say it.'

'Say what, sir?'

'The old man is an idiot. What did I do wrong?'

Ross didn't know quite how to play this. The real question was, what did he do right because he hadn't done anything correctly. Ross was trying to work out how something that should have been fairly simple was not executed correctly by a man who obviously had intelligence.

'I'll take you through it another time, sir; probably best we should crack on.' Macleod gave him a stare and Ross knew that Macleod understood what the comment really meant.

'Is McGrath with you?' asked Macleod.

'She is here,' said Clarissa, and moved the laptop slightly. Macleod could see in the background Hope bringing over a couple of coffees.

'You're the one who wanted it, Hope. What have you found out?'

'We found a couple of similarities between our couples.'

'Couples?' queried Macleod.

'Yes, couples,' said Hope, 'I was down at Uist, which you know about, learning about Fred Martin. Now his wife had committed suicide before him, but they were both in counselling. He also won a trip to go on that ferry. We then went to Derbyshire where Marie Culshaw confirms that Andrew Culshaw and she were both in counselling, because of Andrew's abusive nature. She also said that they were on a trip that Andrew had won. We then went down to see Gerald Lyndhurst. Gerald was in a relationship with Peter Hughes. It was quiet and kept under the counter, but Peter wanted it brought out to the public. It was a cause of much distress amongst the pair and they went into counselling for it. This didn't seem to work for them either. Oh, and Peter also won a ticket on the ferry.'

'So did the Walshes,' said Macleod. 'They were in counselling as well. The coincidences just seem to be piling up here.'

'Thing is,' said Hope, 'they all have relationship issues, and I could easily look at this and say they all committed suicide when nobody saw them. They all disappeared off the ferry. If Jona hadn't brought up the fact that one of them had been injected with ketamine, might have probably opened and closed this quickly.'

'It's probably all we could have done,' said Macleod. 'Unlucky coincidence, but it doesn't sit right.'

'No,' said Hope, 'It could be that lemming effect. People see it, read it, do it. They all would have had a case for ending.'

'But we have Jona's belief that Daphne Walsh was murdered. You still have that belief, Jona?'

'Absolutely, Seoras. The thing is that she was injected with ketamine and was paralyzed. You don't do that to yourself. You certainly don't do that yourself and manage to get up and off a ferry. If you were going to kill yourself, you wouldn't go to that trouble, just throw yourself into the water. Throw yourself into the water, don't struggle, you'll soon sink.

'We've got people who won a ticket to get on a ferry. Our killer knows where they're going so they either work at the ferry company or they've sent the tickets. How's that working?' said Macleod. 'The ferry tickets that you get, they're interchangeable, you could phone up and change them anyway even if they arrived as a ticket. If you take a car, you have to put the car on.'

'Do we know anybody alive that actually got the ticket, or is it the person that always died? Just a moment,' said Macleod, 'We've still got Mr Walsh downstairs. He's in with one of the bereavement constables being looked after. Let me see if I can clarify this.' Macleod stood up and departed, leaving the rest of the team looking at each other.

'You eaten yet, Alan?' asked Hope to Ross.

'I have, I just went and did it. He had to pull me back.'

'Where did you go?' asked Clarissa.

'That Indian up in the corner from here.'

'The one where I had him singing in last time?'

'That's it,' said Ross.

'How far did you get through your meal before he grabbed you?'

'Just finished. He might not even have asked for me except he couldn't work the computer to get on the screen.'

'Write it down for him next time.'

'I don't need to write it down for him,' said Ross. 'It's just the fact that he gets worked up. He's not thinking about what he's doing. He's thinking about the case all the time, the way he gets, obsessed in it. Anyway, I wasn't going to wait for him this time for the food.'

'Well, that's an improvement,' said Hope. 'Sometimes you've got to manage your boss as well.'

Ross could hear the door behind him.

'Sometimes you just have to get a hold of him, Alan. You've got to be the one that moves him about. He's got to bend to you sometimes.'

Macleod appeared on the screen from the side. 'Who's Ross managing now?'

'Sorry, sir. Just a bit of chat,' said Clarissa. 'He's got many problems getting his car sorted.'

'He never told me,' said Macleod. 'Anyway, it's not what we're here to talk about. I've just been down to Mr Walsh. Apparently, there was a phone number to call and arrange. He thought it was quite funny because it seemed to be a mobile number. Here's the number, Ross. You need to get onto that.'

'If it's a mobile number, it's probably going to be a Pay-As-You-Go SIM,' said Ross. 'That's what I would do. That way you can't trace it. It might still be active, though I doubt it. Besides, they might have given a different number to each one. Soon as they've made the call, close it off. Then they can book the tickets for them.'

'Then we need to check where they were being booked from,' said Macleod. 'This is right up your alley, Ross. Get on this one, find out where those tickets were booked, how they were booked. Check the phone number. Let's get onto the other victims' families, check with them. See if they know how the tickets were bought, and how they were sent in.'

'The other commonality here,' said Hope, 'are the doctors.'

'Absolutely,' said Macleod. 'Where are the two of you at the moment?'

'In the Lake District, Seoras. Why?'

'Get back up to Scotland. Find those doctors, get their addresses, hunt them down and find out what was happening with these couples.'

'They were all seeking counselling. What's that got to do with it?' asked Clarissa.

'If they're all seeking counselling, and if it is a common trait,' said Macleod, 'somebody's got to know they were in counselling. Somebody's got to know these doctors. Somebody's got to know these records. You need to have a look and see if there's an angle through there.'

'It's pretty wide-ranging though, isn't it?' said Clarissa.

'Yes, it is. We haven't got a lot,' said Macleod. 'Except we've got four dead people with a few similarities. These similarities will bring us to who actually is carrying out these murders. Where are you off to first then?'

'Furthest south is Glasgow. I think it's a Dr Stevens,' said Hope. 'We'll head up and see Dr Stevens. Should be up there early afternoon. I'll try and contact the rest to see where they are. We've got Aberdeen and Inverness. I just need to make sure they're there.'

'Good,' said Macleod. 'Ross is going to tidy the ticket issue up. Jona, you're kind of redundant at the moment. Probably best if you head back to the station in Inverness, in case you're needed for elsewhere. Get some rest.'

'Will do, Inspector,' said Jona, glaring suspiciously at

Macleod. 'Only a phone call away if you need me.'

'What are you going to do, Seoras?' asked Hope.

'Think on it. I'm going to get some dinner as well. Was hungry earlier, but Ross didn't invite me along.'

Clarissa near spat when she saw Ross's face on the screen. With the screens closed down, Ross stood up and made his way over to a small desk he was operating out of. Then he watched Macleod slowly wander over to him.

'What did I do wrong in setting it up?'

'You know what to do. I've told you before. It's just you don't focus at times like this, sir, with respect.'

'What do you mean I don't focus?'

'You've got everything else going on in your head. It's like the technology doesn't work when it comes to times like this because you're not focused on the technology. You're focused on doing everything else. It's okay. I'm here.'

'Sorry for disturbing your food,' said Macleod. 'I think I might go and get some myself now. Let me know if you come up with anything.' Ross watched as the Inspector left the room and then gave his head a shake. As per usual, he'd been given the task of digging up and hunting out all the information. He called up Minchlines and asked them to check through where the tickets had been bought for the four couples.

As he held the line, he pondered how else to reach into the family background? He could check through medical records because they were all there for counselling. Maybe he needed to get a better idea of what for. Of course, it would be the deceased person's records he'd go for. It took ten minutes before Minchlines came back. The representative told Ross that all had been bought at different ferry points, had been paid for in cash, and had simply been booked in the names of those who got on board.

Ross asked for the names of those who were working, and it took the rest of the afternoon before Minchlines came back with the four workers who had sold the tickets. He spent his evening trying to trace them and to speak to them, only to find out that most of them hadn't got a clue who had paid. In truth, that wasn't surprising. They saw so many customers per day. There wasn't anything unusual about the bookings either. When Macleod came to see Ross at ten o'clock that night, Ross was feeling maxed out.

'Ross, go to the hotel. Go and get some sleep and go back at it tomorrow morning,' said Macleod.

'I've still got a lot to get through.'

'You can't talk to the families at this time of night. I'm telling you, you need to wind down, relax for the night.'

'Yes, sir,' said Ross, and he found himself walking back to the hotel. It was only when he got there and entered his room, he suddenly thought that the Inspector hadn't come with him. Then it dawned on Ross. When the sergeants had talked about Ross managing Macleod, he'd sworn that the man hadn't understood that it was him they were talking about. Macleod managing Ross. He'd heard. He'd flipping heard.

Chapter 12

J enny Trimble smiled, handed over the coffee, and took a step back from the counter, watching the customer disappear out the door. Two minutes left and then she was on her break. She'd get an hour off, an hour to herself. They'd left Islay when she was on shift and now as they crossed the waters over to the mainland, she would be able to step out on deck and take a cigarette in the sea air. She perfectly understood the clash of context, but like most things in life, Jenny didn't care.

She took a look at the ring on her finger and quietly slipped it off, putting it in her pocket. She generally wore it only when the captain would be about or the senior customer officer. Whenever she was fraternising with the rest of the crew, Jenny was more than happy to drop off the ring that spoke of her marriage. Who knew, on the way out to the upper deck, she might even, well, bump into one of the guys? She quickly thought through who was off at that time. You had to be careful though; it was obviously frowned upon, that sort of thing. It was much easier to do that onshore than it was on the vessel. There were always prying eyes somewhere.

Jenny looked up as Ken MacNeil walked in.

'Coffee, Jenny love.'

Ken was in his late thirties, but Jenny thought he managed to maintain a rather impressive figure. Yes, she was ten years his younger, but maybe that would help in her attempt to seduce Ken. He was a family man; she had heard that, but she wondered just how committed he was to his partner. You could always test them, always see. She had thought that he looked at her at times. He certainly gave her a smile every now and again, but she thought she recognised the eyes behind the smile. Was there a hunger for something?

'Just about to go off, Ken. What about yourself?'

'No, I'm just in, I'm going to be serving crew in about five minutes. You can come through there if you want and talk to me.'

It wasn't what Jenny was looking for. She didn't want to talk. 'Oh, it's fine, Ken,' she said, 'I think I might go up on the deck, take a bit of the fresh air, you know? I'm very hot here, there's all these lights.' She moved her hand just inside her blouse, adjusting her strap, making sure she was facing Ken when she did it. The man, however, was looking across at a packet of crisps. *Well, that was wasted*, she thought. *Totally wasted*.

She turned, took a cup, put it under the machine, pressed the button and waited for Ken's coffee to be dispensed.

'So, what's new, Ken? Everything all right at home?'

'Fine, the usual, kids out and about doing whatever, running us ragged, but yes, we're fine. What about you?'

'I was thinking to head off, but I've got to go and do one of these counselling sessions. Robbie wants it.'

'Really?' said Ken, now taking a bit more notice. 'Why is that then? You two okay?'

'We have never been okay, Ken. Robbie just thinks everything can be fixed. I mean, when your wife disappears out to here and does this sort of job, what do you expect?'

'Well, I'm sorry to hear that,' said Ken.

'I bet your wife doesn't complain like that, does she? How many kids is it now?'

'Six. Why do you think I'm working here?'

'Oh, you get to be clear of them for a couple of weeks.'

'No, I need the money. I'd rather be at home working, but I can't get the work at the moment, so you got to do what you got to do, haven't you? Why on earth are you here though, Jen? I don't understand it. Even if things aren't going that well between you and Robbie.'

'Well, sometimes you need a bit of space, don't you? Got to look around the field again.' The coffee machine finished and Jenny took the cup, put a lid on it and passed it through the small hatch to Ken.

'Cheers for that, Jenny. Well, I hope things get better for you. You know?'

'Ken, if you ever get a bit lonely out here, you know I'm available.'

'For what?' said Ken. 'You mean like a chat?'

How gullible was this guy? How stupid.

Jenny slid round the edge to the counter, came up towards Ken and put her hand into one of his. 'Now, if you really need something,' Jenny felt the hand being whipped away.

'Well, it's kind of you,' said Ken, 'but, no that's not me, but thank you, for the coffee,' he said, picking it up and striding out of the coffee cabin.

Jenny gave a sigh, she'd have to make do with one of the others. She had grown to like Ken; he had a good sense of humour and he obviously had plenty of kids, which seemed to make him more attractive, although Jenny didn't know why. She didn't want any of her own. Robbie was always pestering her at the start about kids; now he just pestered her about where she went some evenings. Well, if he was what he should be, it wouldn't be a problem—she'd be right there.

She watched Alice come in, an older member of staff. Alice simply gave her a nod, slid behind the counter and asked was there anything that she needed to know. Jenny shook her head, walked out of the coffee cabin, and went through a crew door that allowed her to step up inside the ship and move out to an outside deck.

She grabbed a cigarette, stuck it between her teeth, and lit it.

She heard somebody clanking up the steps. Jenny turned around to see no one there. Had they stopped? She turned away again and heard the clanking resume. She had been aware since they'd left of someone watching the cabin as she served her teas and coffees. They were hidden under a hat, and she hadn't been quite able to make out who they were or what they were doing. Still, it wasn't unusual. She got checked out by quite a number of people.

Jenny was fortunate in that sense; she had inherited a heck of a figure from her mother, one she hadn't ruined yet with childbirth. If people wanted to look at her, well, that was all right. She would rather they'd have come up and said something; she could gauge if there was any use for them but if they didn't, she couldn't very well just parade out there and ask them the question.

Jenny heard the clanking again, and this time she turned to see a large hat arriving towards the top of the stairs. She turned away, puffing on her cigarette, looking out to sea.

This was crap. She was stuck working on a boat, looking

to get what she could from a load of guys who quite frankly, either were married off or working two weeks at a time on their own. She needed to do something about this, go and work somewhere else, work away, maybe down in London or Glasgow or somewhere.

She heard footsteps moving around behind her on the open deck but that was the only sound. Yes, Jenny would have to sort her life out, get what she wanted.

A hand went over Jenny's mouth and suddenly a pain went into her shoulder. Somebody had just stuck a needle in her. The person held her tight, and Jenny felt her muscles beginning to relax. Soon she could hear everything, see everything, but she couldn't move. She would shake with terror except she couldn't.

Jenny toppled forward, her shoulder hitting the rail of the vessel. What had gone wrong with her? What was this person doing? She then realised her feet were being lifted up, her shoulder tipping over the rail, and her head began to point down towards the sea below. She saw the water breaking, the white waves spreading away from the boat and then she began to fall.

* * *

Ken took his drink with him and sat down in a seat in the crew quarters, sipping it, awaiting his time to go on shift. Jenny had been at it again. She had a heck of a figure, that was true, and a part of Ken liked her, but he also would like her to be a far nicer person. She was clearly doing the dirty on Robbie and the poor guy was trying to fight for her when really, he should just let her go. *Must be hard for him though*, he thought, *to have a catch like that. A woman who on the outside looked like everything a lot of men dream of, but on the inside, she was toxic. What on earth was she doing coming after Ken? He was married with six kids. There was no way he was ever going to leave, and that whole thing with her hand inside her blouse.*

Ken did not like being come on to. He never had his whole life. Ken sipped on his coffee, looked at his watch, and knew he was going to stand up again in two minutes and start taking over the shift. He looked out the window to his left, saw the sea, as ever, churning along, a sea he knew so well. The colour didn't change often, it was more the way the light shone on top of it. Some days were miraculous. He saw dolphins jumping alongside the boat, he saw the waves roll up high, but other days were calm. In truth, calmer days were better. He'd had this fill of wiping up other people's puke as they couldn't handle the vessel's motion.

For Ken, the motion had never been a problem. In fact, he remembered the first time Jenny had made a move towards him was when she'd been sick. She hadn't long been on the vessel, and they got a particularly rough day. She'd come through towards his quarters and been sick in the corridor outside. Ken had helped clean it up and get her to her bed. He remembered quite clearly how she'd stripped off and climbed inside. At the time he thought it was shocking, but maybe it was just the more modern ways of people, ones that he didn't understand. When she threw back the blanket and invited him in, he understood perfectly what she wanted and that was when he left.

Dear Jenny, he thought, *she could be such a person. It's such a shame*. He hated to see someone throwing their life away like that.

102

Something went past the window outside. It was brief, but it was definitely large, maybe person-sized.

'Someone's just gone in, 'said Ken loudly in the crew room. 'Someone's gone in.'

'Well, run outside and have a look, see what it is, Ken,' said the second officer, and Ken stepped out from his fixed table, made a run through corridors up onto the upper outside deck. By the time he got there and looked out, he could see a figure in the sea.

'Overboard!' he shouted. 'Man overboard!' Behind him came the footsteps of the second officer.

'What do you mean, Ken?' the man shouted.

'Man overboard in the sea. I can see. I can see from here.'

'Keep your eyes on,' said the second officer and ran off, presumably to tell the master of the vessel, or at least get the helm to turn around. Ken watched as slowly the boat made a wide turn, then came back onto the reverse of track that they had previously been on. The sun wasn't reflecting off the sea and everything looked like a dull grey.

'What was the colour? What was the colour of who went in?' asked the second officer, having returned.

'White and black. It was like a white and black flash,' said Ken.

'The master's launching the rescue boats, won't be long.'

Ken tried to keep his eyes on where he had seen the figure in the water, but it was getting harder. The second officer took some details off him, and was working out timings and positions. Ken could see that the rescue boats were about to be dispatched.

'Where the hell's Jenny?' asked one of his crewmates, looking to deploy one of the boats.

'The call's gone out, she should be here. There's a bloody rescue; where is she?'

'She'd just come up to the deck, I just saw her. She was coming off shift, then going up on deck.'

The second officer turned to a crew member, despatching them for Jenny. Ken watched the water but the figure he'd seen before was now out of sight. When the despatch runner had returned, the second officer stiffened up slightly and then turned to address the crew around him.

'We're looking for Jenny Trimble. Jenny Trimble is missing.'

Ken felt the sickness in his stomach. No, this couldn't be right. This couldn't happen. His eyes scoured the water, gazing here, there, and everywhere, but it all looked the same. There wasn't anyone there. Ken continued to watch.

At first, the helicopter arrived, then other vessels and a lifeboat. The things he had seen, the time he'd seen them at were reconfirmed by the first officer but after that, Ken was left gripping his hands on the balcony rail and looking down into the sea, hoping to find Jenny. But in truth, there was little chance.

Chapter 13

M acleod had to pick up a flight from Stornoway to Glasgow as Minchlines ferries had begun to get calls from the press asking if there was a murderer on board. Macleod had instantly gone to Jona to ask which of her staff knew about the needle in the body of Daphne Walsh, but Jona defended her people fiercely, saying that nothing had leaked out.

Macleod knew Jona Nakamura; he knew she wouldn't have leaked anything. He was also aware that she'd come down hard on anyone who had even thought about it. Although the obvious place to start, Macleod also thought of those working with him. He had kept the idea of murder amongst his top team, and certainly, none of them would have given any offhand remark to involve the press. He decided he would go to the press conference to find out what the lay of the land was and to back up the ferry company who'd been particularly helpful.

On arrival in Glasgow, Macleod had been picked up by a local constable and taken directly to a small hotel. In one of the rooms, a small stage was set up with a number of chairs in front of it for the press. Macleod was taken through to another room at the rear where he shook hands with the chairman of

Minchlines ferries.

'I can't believe we're getting all this heat,' the man said. 'All tales of murderers on the ferries. Can you imagine what that's going to do for our business? I hope you'll be able to issue a full and frank rebuttal of that idea,' the man said.

'I'd like to be able to,' said Macleod. 'Truly, I would, but that's not going to happen.'

'What? Why not? You're investigating these things. We brought you in to investigate, to point out there wasn't anything wrong.'

'With all due respect, I was brought in to find out if there was anything wrong and I'm afraid there is. We've kept it close to ourselves.'

'Not close enough,' said the man, 'clearly. Why wasn't I informed?'

'Because of this. You would be panicked. A panic from you could spread to everyone else. At the moment, we believe one of the people who died in the overboard situations was actually murdered. The others are much more difficult to prove seeing as some of the bodies are still in the sea. It's a terrible situation.'

'Terrible it is. One of our own this time. Jenny Trimble.'

'Did you know her?' asked Macleod.

'Only met her once,' said the man in the seat opposite. 'Once was enough. Striking woman. Very striking.'

Macleod didn't quite know how to take that comment but instead looked to see the doors of the room beginning to open.

'If there's a murderer onboard, Macleod, should we stop running?'

'No,' said Macleod. 'Why? Why would you stop running?'

'To prevent more deaths.'

'If we had a murderer here in the city, what? We just close

106

everywhere down? We just don't do anything? No, you need to keep running. You've got lifeline services.'

'But if this publicity continues,' said the CEO. 'It's not going to be good for us, is it? It's not going to be good for the business.'

'We are working on it and we're getting there.'

'What am I meant to say when we walk out here?'

'You refer the questions to me,' said Macleod. 'I'll take care of them.'

A woman walked up to the CEO and announced that they were ready for them next door. Macleod followed the man through the doors onto the platform with a large number of camera flashes around him. He was well used to it. Macleod sat down behind a line of tables awaiting the CEO to take charge of the proceedings. The man took a moment to stand and drink some water before announcing that the press conference was open. Almost immediately, the first question came in.

'With the number of deaths on the ferry and the recent disappearance of one of your own colleagues, is it true that the ferries have got a murderer on board?'

'Now, let's not get ahead of ourselves,' said the CEO. 'There's no evidence that there is any murderer on board. There's no . . .'

Macleod put his hand across in front of the CEO. 'Excuse me. I'll advise if there's a murderer onboard or not. Please, I'll take this question.'

Macleod rose to his feet, staring down the press contingent. If there was one thing he hated, it was these vultures. Sure, they sometimes could be helpful if you were looking for a missing person, but so many of them were melodramatic with it that the actual information seemed to get lost to the general public.

'If I can just set the record straight,' said Macleod. 'First off, there have been a number of deaths on various ferries belonging to the Minchlines company. We are investigating those at this time ascertaining whether they were suicide or if some other party was at work. Currently, we cannot confirm a third party being involved.'

Macleod knew that wasn't strictly true. There was convincing evidence that a third party was involved if not confirmed but the wording made it sound a lot more vague and that the police were still investigating. The last thing Macleod wanted any potential murderer to know was that he was on to them.

'Does this mean that the ferries will be shutting down? If you have a murderer running amok, Inspector?'

'Just a moment,' said Macleod. 'That comment is loose and wild and will only lead to the general public being scared.'

'Are they safe then? Are the ferries safe?'

'At this moment in time,' said Macleod, 'we're investigating, ascertaining what has happened in these circumstances.'

'So what? In the meantime, we all have to risk being on board with a potential murderer.'

'I reiterate to you that we are investigating. At this time, I believe the ferries will continue to run. Is that correct?' Macleod turned to the CEO beside him. He simply nodded. 'I think we need a bit of calm.'

'Can you give us the odds of there being a murderer on board?' said a male journalist. 'Is it more there is, or more that there isn't?'

'I'm not at liberty to say that,' said Macleod.

'Well, we're here to try and find out for our readers whether it's safe to be on a ferry. Can you say it's safe to be on a ferry?'

'That would be a crazy comment,' said Macleod. 'Is it safe to be on a road? Is it safe to be up in a plane? What do you mean by safe?'

'It means, are we all going to get murdered.'

Macleod could feel all the hairs in his neck rising and anger seething through him. He'd given a sensible statement. All they had to do was just leave it there. *Why did the press always have to come on and go for the jugular?* Macleod was sweating but tried not to show it. *If only Hope was here. She was better at the press. Either Hope or Clarissa. Clarissa would chew them up and spit them out. Although she'd probably cause a serious incident at the same time.*

'I reiterate again the investigations are continuing.'

'Are the ferries safe, Inspector?'

'I told you, I can't answer that. It's not a question that has any level of appreciation of the situation.'

'Would you suggest that people don't go up on deck on their own?'

Of course, they'd interviewed all these passengers. Some of the questions were bound to come back. Did you see someone alone? Did you see them up there? Was anyone else about? The press would soon find out from the interviewees.

'Once again, Inspector, is it safe to be on the ferries?'

Macleod bit his lip. He wanted to say, 'Come over here and I'll give you a good clip around the ear for being such a clown and stirring up the public.' On the other hand, they were right. There was a murderer on the ferries.

'Various coincidences are being investigated thoroughly by my officers. As soon as we have something, we will brief you.'

'At some appropriate junction,' Macleod said in his head, because without it, the statement would probably be a lie. The press were the last people he briefed.

'That's a no then. We're not safe in the ferries. They've got a murderer.' The room began to break into an uproar. Macleod sat down. He hated the press. He really did.

* * *

Laura had only been on the lifeboat crew less than a month. That was when she got her qualification and was able to be part of the search crew. She stood up on the deck of the lifeboat, looking out across the water. The waves kept going up and down, making it hard to see each part of the sea as the helicopter passed over ahead. Other vessels were making way here and there, nobody seeing anything except for the blue.

In truth, they were probably looking for a body, especially in this cold water. The victim had been in for too long, although there had been cases of people surviving longer. The casualty had entered the water in what seemed like an uncontrolled fashion. They'd also had no life jacket and who knew how well they could swim.

The coxswain turned the lifeboat back as it began another straight-line search through the water, Laura and her colleagues looking out, trying to spot anything that was untoward. The vessel, now routing the other direction, became bumpier as it chopped through the water. Laura hung on with one hand when she tried to look through binoculars with the other. She'd bring them up every now and again, but most of the searching was done with the bare eye.

Laura thought she saw something in the water, something that moved. She pointed with her finger. 'There,' she cried. 'Something over there.'

'Whereabouts?'

'Turn about one hundred and thirty-five degrees.'

'Have you got eyes on?'

Laura watched the waves go up and down. She did have eyes on. Then she didn't and then she did. The lifeboat turned quickly and started to make towards where Laura pointed. As they got closer, they could see a figure in the water. The coxswain called to the crew to prepare to bring the casualty onboard, and they reached out with long poles, dragging the floating victim towards them. As they pulled her onboard, they could see it was a woman dressed in a ferry uniform.

Laura could hear the cox calling for the helicopter to drop down their paramedic while two of the team began to work on Jenny Trimble's body. However, there seemed little hope. She wasn't breathing when they brought her on and she still wasn't breathing several minutes later while the winchman above was descending. It only took the winchman paramedic less than a minute to confirm that Jenny Trimble was deceased. Within another five minutes, he was back up in the helicopter, which was now routing for its base. The lifeboat turned back towards shore and Jenny Trimble's body, placed inside a black bag, was carried down below. They would rendezvous on the shore where a coroner would pick up the body.

* * *

Macleod was back in the room behind the press stage and fending off some difficult questions from the CEO of Minchlines. His phone began to ring and he gave a silent prayer of thanks as he excused himself from the man and strode over to the far corner of the room.

'Sir, it's Ross. I think we need to get Jona on down to Oban.'

'Why?' asked Macleod. 'Something come up?'

'Jenny Trimble's come up. We just heard that they've found her. I've asked the undertaker to keep the body to one side and not to touch it.'

'Good work, Ross. Get yourself down there as well and join Jona. Quick as you can. Take some statements, find out what happened. I'm going to head back up to Inverness. Once I find out how Hope and Clarissa have gone on, we'll start to work out where to go with this investigation. In the meantime, I want all details about what happened on that Islay ferry.'

'Of course,' said Ross. 'I'll try and speak to you tonight.'

Macleod closed the call, hung his head low for a moment, and then walked over to the CEO of Minchlines. The man began to hassle the Inspector.

'Macleod, explain how this business is meant to work. What have you done by not confirming there was no murderer onboard?'

Macleod put his hand up in front of the man, stopping him in his tracks. 'Look, I've got some bad news for you. They've just found Jenny Trimble's body. The good news from our point of view is because we found it, we can find out if she was murdered.'

'Dear God,' said the CEO. 'Can you believe this? Can you believe this?'

In all his years as a policeman, Macleod knew the extent to which people would go to kill. He could believe it very, very easily. Rather than lie to the man, he simply replied, 'It can be hard to believe. That's true.'

Chapter 14

Hope gratefully stepped out of the little green sports car onto a Glasgow side street. Looking up at the tall building in front of her, she stretched. At six feet tall, she towered over Clarissa and was not designed for the passenger seat of a small sports car. The drive up from the south felt like a long one and Hope had tried to think through what had happened so far on the case. Were these doctors the answer? She wasn't sure, but hopefully, she'd find out.

As Clarissa fed some money into a parking metre, Hope walked over to the front door of the building before her and saw the sign for Dr Stevens's marital counselling. She pressed the intercom, and advised who she was, before the door buzzed open. Slowly, she climbed two flights of stairs, Clarissa behind her, huffing and puffing, and complaining about the lack of a lift, but for Hope, there were no such worries. Finally getting to stretch out her legs was a blessing, not a curse.

The door that presented itself to them on the second floor was simple enough, a brown affair with a dour plaque on it, simply spelling out, once again, Dr Stevens Marital Counselling. Hope knocked on the door and heard a, 'Come in.' Inside, a secretary offered Hope a seat saying that the doctor would be with her very shortly and asking whether they would like a cup of tea or coffee. Hope passed, but Clarissa eagerly grabbed a coffee, reminding Hope of Macleod, that the older detectives seemed to live off the stuff.

It took another two minutes before they were shown into an office with a desk on one side and a small set of sofas in the other corner. Dr Stevens was almost as tall as Hope but was of a skinnier configuration. She looked tall and elegant with brown hair that had some white streaks running through it. She wore a black jacket with a long pencil skirt and a white blouse. Hope noted the heart locket hanging from around her neck.

'Thank you for seeing us, doctor. I'm Detective Sergeant Hope McGrath. This is Detective Sergeant Clarissa Urquhart. I hope we aren't disturbing you, but we need some information about some of your clients.'

'Well, I hope I can give it to you,' said Dr Stevens. 'There is client confidentiality.'

'Said client is dead, so I'm hoping that won't be a problem.'

'Is their partner or spouse still alive?'

'Yes, they are, but we're actually running a murder investigation, so anything you can tell us would be gratefully received.'

'That's understood, but my first duty is to my clients,' said Dr Stevens.

'Andrew Culshaw,' said Clarissa, 'he was a client of yours, wasn't he?'

'The Culshaws? Yes, terrible tragedy falling off the ferry.'

'You said, "falling off,"' said Hope. 'You don't believe he committed suicide then?'

'Well, I'm just saying what I know. He fell off the ferry. Did he jump? I don't know. Was he pushed? I'm beginning to wonder because you're here.'

Hope thought the woman was fairly smart, not giving away anything, choosing her words wisely. 'What can you tell us about the Culshaws?'

'Well, Andrew Culshaw was a highly volatile figure. He believed he had a right to everything, including his wife and the way she behaved. He would constantly get into trouble because people would deny him that he felt entitled to. He would simply demand things. In some ways, he was mentally unstable.'

'You said he felt he had a right to everything; where did that come from?' asked Clarissa.

'I think he thought it was God-given and I mean that in the genuine sense. He felt that he was owed it. God had put him here. He certainly was like that with his wife, seemed to think she was property. I tried to dissuade him of that, tried to let her show what she thought, but he was a very difficult case.'

'How do you show him that side?' asked Hope. 'Forgive me, I'm not very experienced. I've had a couple of partners, not been in a marriage, and I'm quite intrigued to know.'

'Well, I knew only too well,' said Dr Stevens. 'I'm divorced at fifty-five now as well. I learnt the hard way. If someone wants to take everything in the marriage, it doesn't work. That's what I tried to show him, show him the effect he was having on his wife. It took time. It took a lot of patience from her.'

'Is she a patient person?' asked Clarissa.

'In my opinion, she is. The woman is probably free of a lot now. Though I don't know . . . She stayed with him because she really did want him. That was the sad thing, he didn't need to have ownership of her. She was there with him, but the way he went about it made her life hell, and that's why they ended up with me. Although it took a long time for her to get him to come. She came alone for the first four or five sessions.'

'You say he wrecked the marriage? It very much was all him, was it?'

'Completely, she's a decent soul.'

'Yet, he came off the ferry,' said Clarissa. 'They were both on the ferry at the time. Is there any chance that Mrs Culshaw would have done it?'

'Mrs Culshaw? Mrs Culshaw couldn't lift me out of this room. Could she throw someone off a ferry the size of her husband, I doubt it. I really do. I don't think she'd have the inclination either. She cared for him. She worshipped him. She just wanted him to change. I don't think it's really a sensible option.'

'She couldn't have snapped or anything, do you think?'

'No, she wasn't near to that point, very rational woman.'

'Apparently, they were arguing just before it all happened. I'm just wondering if she could have lost it with him,' offered Hope.

'No. No way. They argued a lot all the time. Andrew was unbelievable. If she did something, she did it wrong. It didn't matter what it was. He wouldn't have done it that way, and often, even if she managed to do it his way, he was complaining because he had never asked her to do it in the first place. It could be as little as how she set her hair. There was definitely a mental issue within the man. Definitely.

'However, it was very hard to get at because he wouldn't spend time with me. In a lot of ways, he ruined her life. She should have walked from him ages ago, but she wouldn't; she couldn't. I guess I know a bit about that, but that was some time ago.

116

'Look I don't want to rush you either,' said Dr Stevens, 'but I've got dinner arrangements and so I'm going to have to depart sometime soon. So, if you just keep your questions coming, I'll do my best. Anything I can't answer here and now, obviously, I'll get back to you.'

'She had said they were on a trip away on the ferry,' said Hope. 'Was that normal for him to take her away or for her to go with him?'

'Absolutely. For all that they argued and bickered, they were never apart. As I said, she did worship him in a lot of ways even though he made her life a misery.'

'Why on earth do people do that?' said Clarissa. 'I don't understand that.'

'I'm sure you don't,' said Dr Stevens. 'You seem like quite a formidable woman.'

Hope rolled her eyes. It was only too true. Clarissa, for all that she was, a tour de force, Macleod's rottweiler didn't have a lot of sympathy for people who didn't cope.

'We'll try and be snappy as we can,' said Hope. 'We're off to see a Dr Jacobs who's in a similar line of work as you, do you know him?'

'Yes, I do. We met at a conference but that's as far as I know him.'

'Very good,' said Hope. 'Would you know of any reason why Andrew Culshaw was being targeted by anyone?'

'What do you mean?' asked the woman.

'Targeted enough to be killed. It would be someone who had planned it.'

'Do you think he was killed?' asked Dr Stevens.

'We do think it, but we can't prove it. Unfortunately, Andrew's body's never come back to us; otherwise, we might be able to. They may have used Ketamine, large dose.'

'Well, it's definitely not Marie Culshaw then. She can't stand needles; she can't use them. She'd been a mess trying to do that. Definitely not her. And with his nature, who knows who Andrew may have annoyed?'

'How did you feel about your clients?' asked Clarissa.

'How do you mean?' asked Dr Stevens.

'Well, you see these poor wretches come in, people like Marie; do you feel sorry for them?'

'I'm sure I do in the same way that you feel sorry for people who are victims, but you also have a professional duty to do the best for everyone. I was trying to help Andrew as much as Marie. I mean, you get that, don't you? If somebody pulls a gun, you try and disarm them, you don't just obliterate them to save the innocent party standing beside them.'

'Indeed,' said Clarissa, 'but sometimes push comes to shove, doesn't it?'

'I don't know what you mean by that,' said Dr Stevens.

'I just wonder how you feel seeing all these things. Is this merely mind games to you, as something to be successfully mastered, or do you actually feel for these people?'

'I am human,' said Stevens, 'but in here I maintain a professional detachment. Now, if you'll excuse me, I really do have to get on for dinner. Is there anything else?'

'Can you let us have access to some of the notes, the times of the visits, et cetera?'

'Of course, but the actual meeting notes, I want to be here to discuss with you if you need them.'

'I'm not sure we will do that at the moment but we're just looking for possible outside connections to Andrew. Anybody else that might have had a grievance against Andrew Culshaw.'

'Of course, you just talk to my secretary; that won't be a problem. I'm sorry I have to rush you, but I really do need to be going.'

Hope stood up with Clarissa, and Dr Stevens showed them out to her secretary outside. While the pair of them stood with the secretary making notes about who had appointments around the same time as the Culshaws, Hope noticed Dr Stevens depart the building. She had a scarf around her neck and had changed her skirt and jacket into something that looked even smarter. She gave the pair a quick wave as she left the office. Five minutes later, Hope and Clarissa were downstairs about to get into Clarissa's car.

'I'm not sure what we learnt from that,' said Hope, but Clarissa tapped her on the shoulder. 'Walk with me now.' Hope followed Clarissa down a small side alley where Clarissa stopped and turned around, peering around the corner. 'For someone being off to dinner, she's coming back.'

'Are you sure? She went down the street. Is it definitely her?' asked Hope.

'Trust me, she doesn't look like she's got a happy face. Let's bump into her.' Clarissa marched back out of the alley and met Dr Stevens as she arrived at the front door to her office.

'I thought you were off to dinner,' said Clarissa.

'It has just been cancelled, unfortunately, so I thought I'd come back and do a little bit more work. Was my secretary able to get you everything you needed?'

'Yes, she did. Not a problem,' said Hope. 'I think we've got everything. I'm not sure we need to disturb you again. As I said, we've got to meet at Dr Jacobs.'

'He works out of Aberdeen; how are you meeting here?' asked Dr Stevens.

'He's stopping down in a hotel. Apparently, he's got some meetings, but has agreed to say "hello" to us.'

'Very good. Don't let me detain you,' said Dr Stevens. 'Like I say, if you need anything else, please reach out to me.'

'Will do,' said Hope and watched as the woman made her way to the front door of the office. Her feet seemed leaden; her shoulders slumped.

'She's pretty disappointed, isn't she?' said Clarissa. 'Anyway, onwards. If we're going to meet Dr Jacobs, we're going to need to get a move on.'

'That's all right,' said Hope. 'Remember, this is Glasgow; you can't drive like a maniac around here.'

'Who was driving like a maniac?'

'On the way up here put me in mind of making sure I get with Ross next time.'

'That would leave Seoras with me; that's not going to work, is it? He's petrified of me.'

'He's petrified of you in a car, and I don't blame him.'

'Enough,' said Clarissa. 'Get in. You're only complaining because of those long legs of yours. I can't believe you complain about them either. If I had legs like that, I'd happily display them.'

'You're not really women's lib, are you?'

Clarissa laughed. 'I don't need to be freed,' said Clarissa. 'I've been dominating men most of my life.'

She laughed loudly as she rounded the car and got in at the driver's side. Hope carefully stepped into the car, pulling her legs up tight, wishing she'd more room to stretch them out. It was dawning on Hope that she hadn't really worked with Clarissa much. Usually, Macleod was with her, or else, she was off with Ross. Hope was beginning to understand why

Macleod liked her. He seemed to like women who had a bit of fire in them. Jane was like that as well.

He seems to view me slightly differently, thought Hope. *Maybe that's a good thing.* Hope reached around the back of her head making sure that her ponytail was secure with a borrowed hair tie, and then quickly put her belt on as Clarissa pulled out into the Glasgow traffic. Hope nearly swore as a number of car horns were sounded, all aimed at the little green machine that was now racing across Glasgow to their next meeting.

Chapter 15

Alan Ross stared around the room where the ferry crew had gathered. They had brought in the reserve crew who should've started next week, and they were preparing the ship to depart but Ross had noticed even with them, there was a large degree of unease. The oncoming master had said there were a number of sicknesses that had come on suddenly, and Ross had the general feeling that the situation was beginning to get out of control.

Jenny Trimble's body, having been recovered, was now at the local morgue, with Jona Nakamura in attendance. She would come back with her findings soon enough, but in the meantime, Ross had taken charge of a small detachment of constables from the local area to interview the crew. Initially, they'd started with the passengers, but there was little to be found from them. They didn't know Jenny Trimble. Sure, they'd seen her working in the shop, but that was it. Nobody had been up on deck to see her, and so from the time of her going up on deck until she hit the water was still a complete mystery. Ross understood one thing, that while finding out what happened in that time may provide some sort of explanation, what was going to stop these crimes was finding out the link between all the victims, how they were being selected.

Jenny Trimble had worked the ferry for a number of years. Ross had found that out from her records, but he wanted to know what sort of person she was. A constable had been dispatched to her husband to advise him of her demise and also to see if he could find any details. She wasn't an old woman by any stretch of the imagination, just arriving to her thirties, and Ross thought her slightly different to some of the others. But then, they were all different, weren't they? There were heterosexual couples, homosexual couples, but they're always couples, he thought, and couples with problems.

Ross watched the constables begin to work their way round the room, taking aside a crew member at a time and asking questions. Ross would soon pore over the statements and verify what was being said, but he watched one woman being particularly talkative. She was diminutive in figure, but she seemed to have a mouth that made up for it and he wondered if it ever could fall silent. The rest of the crew seemed to be in shock that made them withdraw but this woman seemed to erupt because of the fright she'd had.

Ross wandered over and listened to the woman for a few moments before tapping the constable on the shoulder. 'I'll take this lady through to a different room. I want to take a full statement from her.'

The constable nodded and spoke to the woman, advising her to follow Ross into the next room.

Inside there was a bare table and Ross turned to find the coffee machine and fetch what he thought was the weakest-looking coffee he'd ever seen in his life. *It shouldn't be that colour*, he thought. But he placed a plastic cup in front of the woman who was now sitting down on a chair but still talking.

'Woah. Hold on,' said Ross. 'Let's just start over again. I'm Detective Constable Alan Ross, and I'll be taking a statement. Your name is?'

'Anna Chain. Yes, as in like what you do with a bike. You chain it up to something. Don't ask me how I married a Mr Chain.'

'And you knew Jenny Trimble quite well?'

'We've been working this ferry for three years together. We knew each other. She would come and chat to me. Pop into my quarters if she was bored.'

'What was Jenny like?' asked Ross.

'What was Jenny like?' said the woman back to him. 'You can ask anyone here, Jenny liked to put it about. Jenny liked to flirt and be adored and have a good time. That was Jenny. Don't get me wrong, she was fun to be about. Quick tongue and a funny one with it, but not a stable sort of person.'

'Did she know you thought that of her?'

'Well, I told her often enough. Probably just needs to settle down but she never did. I think Jenny regretted being married.'

'What's the name of her husband? Did you ever meet him?'

'No, but she told me a lot about him, Robbie. Very staid guy, she said. Very traditional. Liked a woman who was demure. Not in her place, don't get me wrong; the guy wasn't an ogre or anything—he was just a lot calmer than Jenny. Well, at least that's how she put it. Apparently, she found him at a wedding, and he fell for her and they got married quickly, within six weeks. After a year, she was bored of him, and she was off finding other people.'

'So, you said she slept around?'

'Yes, that's right,' said Anna.

'Okay, did she sleep around on the vessel?'

124

'I shouldn't really say this, but yes. I mean, I'd never admit it to the bosses.'

'That's fine,' said Ross. 'You just need to admit it to me. Who did she sleep with?'

'Well, there was George, but he's not on this cycle. She jumped into bed with him a few times. Then there was Sally.'

'So, she didn't really have a preference?'

'She was mainly men, but yes. I think she just liked to experiment; that was her words. Well, that's what she told me. I didn't ask too much if you understand.'

'Oh, of course,' said Ross. 'If she felt this bad though, why didn't she just leave her husband?'

'Oh, she said to me that she'd asked him several times for a divorce, but he wouldn't have it. He was afraid of the shame of it. He was almost happier to let her run around making a fool of him in some ways.'

'And Sally? Is she on at the moment?'

'No, she got off just before this run. That's the thing, if you're looking for people that she actually had been with, they're not on the boat at the moment. The other person she liked was Ken.'

'Ken who?'

'Ken MacNeil. He's got a big family, loads of kids. Lovely guy, Ken. You can't help but like Ken. I think Jenny liked him in a lot of respects. He is a funny guy; he can make good jokes, but she obviously saw the fact he had a lot of children too. I think she liked that about him. Thought that must mean something, whatever that means,' said Anna, looking away. 'She was a bit of a nutjob. I know it's probably wrong to say that of the dead, but she was a nutter, an attractive nutter. She knew how to entice; I'll give her that.'

125

'It's funny how you talk about her because you said you were friends.'

'Boat friends. I wouldn't be doing anything with her off this boat,' said Anna. 'There's no way. But here, what can we do? You sit and you natter. She wasn't interested in me physically, which is fine so, therefore, her tales and stories, they were quite fun to listen to. It does get a bit monotonous on this boat. Back and forward seeing the customers, not happy with this bit of food or delighted with this. 'Oh look, it's choppy today.' You know, you get all the normal tales and then you got what Jenny told you. She'd tell me about all her sexual exploits from the previous weeks when she was off the ship. It was fun; I was bored. I'll miss her from that point of view. Certainly, wouldn't have wanted to see her go like this.'

'Can I ask? Do you know if Jenny and her husband saw any professional help?'

'Professional help? I think they did. Jenny occasionally would be off the boat for twenty-four hours. You might have to ask the master about that. She said it was because she had to go somewhere with her husband. She never told me what it was. In honesty, she seemed nearly a little bit embarrassed by it.'

Ross nodded and began to think.

'Where were you when Jenny disappeared?'

'I was up in the canteen. It's where I work, preparing. You can ask anyone. The chef, everybody there. I was in there the whole time.'

'Okay, Anna. Would anybody on this vessel want to harm Jenny?'

'I don't think so. She got on well with everyone. I mean, obviously, there's the two she got intimate with, but outside of that everybody liked Jenny. I mean, she was nice-looking, she was a lot of fun, and like I say, you didn't actually have to go anywhere with her. We're just work colleagues here, so that was okay. I mean, to be out with her in public, I mean on a night out or whatever, I can imagine she'd be quite shocking. I'm not sure everybody here would take that. You know what though?' said Anna. 'It's really sad. She had everything, in a lot of ways. She could have any man she wanted if she toned herself down a bit or just been a bit faithful. She could've, but she just couldn't handle herself. It's a real shame. Genuine, lovely person. She actually cared at times too, but she couldn't keep her libido in check, always wanted a bit more. Maybe it was her husband. Maybe he couldn't, well, you know. It's weird talking about people like this, isn't it? I guess that's at the core of some people's lives.'

Ross took down the woman's address and thanked her for her candour before letting her depart. When he stepped back out into the main room, the constables were over halfway through the crew but Ross called the master aside, taking him into the room previously occupied by himself and Anna.

The man was in his fifties and looked somewhat ashamed.

'I know why you've brought me through,' he said, 'but it was once and once only.'

Ross sat down, his coffee still untouched to his left-hand side. 'I haven't brought you through for anything except to ask some questions,' said Ross. 'What are you talking about?'

'Well, Jenny, you know how she was. I'm sure they've told you. Well, me and Jenny at one point.'

'You had sexual relations with a member of the crew?'

'I know it sounds bad when you put it like that. Certainly don't want my bosses to find out, but it was once and once

127

only. It wasn't really me she was after; she just liked the idea of doing it on the bridge. It was when we were weather-bound for a day.'

'Does anybody else know about this?'

'Well, she'd have told somebody, but the crew wouldn't let on. Most of them probably think it's a rumour or something that Jenny just made up. She was lively and vivacious, I was having a hard time and well, she offered. Not proud of it. I'm really not proud of it, but also know I was up on the bridge. I was in sight of everyone when she went into the water.'

'Okay. What I really wanted to ask you was, Jenny took time off according to one of your colleagues, twenty-four hours at a time on occasions. What was that for?'

'Medical appointment,' said the man. 'It's a medical appointment, except she told me it was to do with counselling. Her and her husband. She had brought me a form in for the appointment just to try and prove it, which I didn't ask for. I think she was indignant about it, that's why she was giving me the form. Wanted me to tell her that she didn't need counselling.'

'Did she require counselling?'

'She required a lobotomy. She was so full-on. Jenny was nuts. Really likable girl, but my goodness, she was crackers, but good at pulling you into her way of thinking. Very full-on. Could turn a man's head as I've said.'

'Do you know which medical professional they were seeing?'

'Dr Jacobs. I remember that because I always associated it with crackers, the ones you eat, and she was crackers. I know it's daft, but it's funny how the brain sticks things in your head, isn't it?'

'So, Dr Jacobs. That's useful. Thank you.'

'Do we know who did this?' asked the master.

'Not yet. It doesn't look like it was any of the crew.'

'There's been a number of these deaths now. Our crew are worried, I'm worried. I mean, you don't expect to work a ferry and start losing members of crew or passengers. Happens once. Well, you know, people do things. They jump off ferries, there's accidents, arguments. There's too many now. This is going to scare people. Not just my crew—it's going to scare passengers.'

'I'm well aware of that, sir. We're going to try and get to the bottom this quickly.'

'It's all different ferries. That's crazy, isn't it? All these different ferries. Are they just grabbing people and throwing them over?'

Ross wanted to tell him no, Ross wanted to tell him that actually, it looked like it was couples. As long as you weren't having any problems and seeing doctors, you were probably all right, but he didn't. He simply stood up, shook his head, and advised the man that inquiries were still proceeding.

Chapter 16

Macleod stepped out of the Detective Chief Inspector's office and could feel the sweat on his head. That had been a lot of questioning, even for an experienced hand like himself, and having been involved in the conference call with the ferry company and members of the Scottish Parliament, he felt he needed to sit down for a couple of minutes. His team were deployed here, there, and everywhere for such was the nature of the crime. He didn't even have the smiling face of Ross there, building him back up, ever a protector of his boss, and one thoroughly efficient man.

Macleod made his way back to the main office where a couple of constables were working their way through some data for him but otherwise, the office was empty. None of his three colleagues were there, and when he went over to the coffee machine, he found it wasn't even on. *Some things just won't do*, he thought.

He wanted to be back out on the road with the team, but he had got pulled into talking to higher-up authorities and Macleod hated it. He liked being in charge, liked being the main dog in the office, able to send people here, there, and wherever. What he didn't like was being on the end of a leash, brought in by the DCI to answer the questions that, really, he felt his boss should be dealing with.

His boss had only entered the role, replacing a woman Macleod had seen as a competent person, but now he had no rapport with the man who was currently in that position. He was younger than Macleod and Macleod wondered just how much detecting he'd done, for he seemed to be a lot more about image and how things would play out amongst the public. Macleod had always thought murder was about finding who was responsible.

He cleaned out the coffee machine, put some freshly ground coffee into it, filled it with water, and stayed beside it as it dripped through. He listened to it gurgle, sniffing in the aroma as the water passed through the coffee, urging it on so he could pour out a cup of the liquid below.

Ross would be getting on with it. He thought of his junior colleague and realised this was the first time he'd let Ross loose since that time on the Monach Isles. The poor guy had almost ended up dead, but he'd done well uncovering a major drug operation in the most extreme of circumstances. *It was about time that Ross made sergeant*, thought Macleod. *It was about time that he stepped up. The man needed to think about his career.*

Ross was that efficient person, the person that was keeping Macleod afloat in some ways, covering all the bases underneath, the little details that Macleod would never get round to. *The trouble with people like that*, thought Macleod, *is they're too useful. They get kept there. They are never allowed to show their real potential.*

Kirsten had been very similar in the sense that she could handle all the details, but she'd gone on and ended up working for the Special Services. In some ways, Macleod thought it a success, certainly in career terms, even if he wasn't overly keen about Kirsten actually working for such a dark organisation. The woman had a good heart and a lot of integrity, and Macleod sometimes wondered just how that fitted in.

Ross was the same and Macleod really should be starting to check up on him, make sure the guy didn't need any more help. He walked into his office once the coffee had been poured, sat down behind his desk, and opened up his laptop. Now, Ross had said to click this icon over here, then to make sure that these other boxes were checked. Macleod did so, then found that nothing was opening up properly. He reached inside his jacket pocket, took out his phone, and dialled Ross's number.

'Sir,' said Ross, 'can I help you?'

'How are you getting on down there? Everything okay?'

'We've been going through all the passengers, and we've just finished the crew. It appears our Jenny Trimble was a flirt. Had issues with her husband, very similar to some of our other victims.'

'Tell me more,' said Macleod.

'Well, I've just had a constable come back from talking to her husband. He said Jenny was unfaithful to him and they were getting help. I know it's from a Dr Jacobs. That's the same person the Walshes were seeing. Jenny Trimble was sexually active with a number of people after becoming bored with her husband, but her husband wouldn't give up on her, said she needed treatment, needed to deal with what he saw as an addiction.

'She was seeing two other people on the vessel, but they weren't on board at the time the incident happened. It's looking very similar to what happened before. I'm expecting

Jona to call in a minute. Do you want to come off the phone, sir, and we'll go into the video chat and the three of us can talk together?'

'Good idea,' said Macleod. 'I was going to video chat to you anyway, but it won't open again.'

'Did you tick the second box down?' asked Ross.

'Second? Thought it was the third.'

'No, we talked about this. That's not the one, it's the second one.'

'You should write this down for me,' said Macleod, and then he saw Ross's eyes narrow. Yes, Ross was right. Macleod should write it down every time, but he felt that with regard to the computers, he'd have a book of written notes that would accompany him everywhere. He grew up in a time of typewriters for goodness sake.

Macleod put down the call and made the adjustments to the screen and was speaking to Ross again within two minutes.

'You can see me now, sir. Is that correct?'

'Yes, I can. When's Jona joining us?'

'Any minute now.' Macleod sat patiently sipping some of his coffee.

'Do you know, Ross, that I came back today out of a meeting with the DCI and there was no coffee on the go?'

'Well, no, sir, there won't be. I tend to put the coffee on. Failing that, Clarissa does it. If we weren't there, Hope would do it.'

'But I've got two constables here helping out on the case, working from the office; they didn't put it on either.'

'Well no, they won't,' said Ross.

'Why?' asked Macleod.

'It's your coffee. They know you; they don't touch your

coffee.'

'What do you mean they don't touch my coffee? They can make the coffee.'

'No, they can't,' said Ross. 'You're very particular about your coffee and to be quite honest, I think they're scared they'll get it wrong.'

'Scared they'll get it wrong? I'll give them scared to get it wrong, lazy good-for-nothings. They can make the coffee.'

'When was the last time you made the coffee, sir?' asked Ross.

'Just now.'

'But before that?'

Macleod thought back; he was struggling, really struggling.

'You don't make the coffee,' said Ross; 'we make the coffee. We know how to make the coffee for you. You would complain about the coffee if it was made by other people.'

Macleod sat back and simply nodded. More and more, he seemed to be under attack by the team over the small things. They never questioned the way he led an investigation or what he was doing, but things on the periphery: how to drive, how to make coffee, and he wasn't sure if this was them being on a different level of comfort with him, or whether he was losing his authority. The appearance of Jona Nakamura on the screen broke his train of thought.

'Good, Jona, how's Jenny Trimble?'

'Well, she's dead,' said Jona.

There we go again, he thought. 'You know what I mean, Jona.'

'Sorry, Seoras, she's very similar to our other victim, she's been dosed up with a large amount of ketamine, the date rape drug. Once again, it looks like it's a massive dose, would have caused paralysis, she'd not be able to move, but she would have been awake hitting the water. There's no physical damage to her, she simply drowned. It's quite scary, you could tip her up and over, leave her hanging off the edge of the ferry, although I doubt they did that.'

'No,' said Macleod, 'they'd want to do it quick. If you're on your own up there, you would do it quick. Would she respond?'

'Respond?' queried Jona. 'What do you mean exactly?'

'You say it puts them in a state of paralysis. Would they give a facial reaction or anything if they were hung over the edge? Would the killer be able to look at them and think, 'Oh yes, they're panicking; they're scared?''

'No,' said Jona, 'but they'd know they were awake. They could also tell them exactly why they were being killed.'

'Why don't we start looking at the ketamine side of it? We know two of them have been paralysed this way so, therefore, maybe that could be a lead,' said Ross.

'It's not that difficult to get hold of, Ross, though,' said Macleod, 'but if you think there's a chance to trace it.'

'Well, if Jona can get samples out of the body, I'll see what I can do. It's a long shot but sometimes these things are worth pursuing.'

'Indeed. How long are you going to be down there?' Macleod asked.

'We still need to wrap up, I'm not sure how long Jona is going to be here either.'

'We've been over the ferry, forensic-wise, can't find anything, I'm just about done with the body; we'll start moving back up to Inverness shortly.'

'I'll try and come up tomorrow, sir,' said Ross.

'And I'll try and have the coffee on,' said Macleod, which caused Jona to look bizarrely at the screen. 'Too long a story,

135

Jona. Thank you both.'

Macleod closed down the call, stood up from his chair and walked over to the window. He felt like he should walk out into the office, stand around and catch a bit of chat with his colleagues, except they weren't there. He didn't want to go down to the canteen either. He had played his pieces and they were coming back with information. Now he needed Hope and Clarissa to come through with something. It seemed that the doctors were an important part of this puzzle. Everyone who died had been seeing one of them, but not the same one. What connection was there amongst them? Why were they important?

Macleod nearly jumped when his phone rang at the table, and he slowly turned before picking it up. 'Detective Inspector Seoras Macleod, how can I help?'

'This is Kiera Sedwell. I'm from the Minchlines ferry company, secretary to the CEO. He's asked me to advise you that we're having a lot of problems at the moment. We're getting mass cancellations.'

'I'm sorry to hear that,' said Macleod. 'I'm not quite sure how I can help.'

'He said you were in a meeting earlier on with him and he wanted you to be aware of the extent of the issues we're having because he didn't feel that you were taking him seriously enough in the meeting.'

Macleod thought back to the meeting. They were wittering on about passenger numbers, about people coming to the islands, and would the holiday season be okay. *There are people being killed*, Macleod had thought, *people dying. That's the key bit. That's the important bit. Not whatever tourist can or can't come*, and now the man had got his secretary to ring to reinforce the point.

Macleod wanted to pick up the phone, find the man, and throw it at him. How cheeky was that? Did he think Macleod had nothing to do except worry about his passenger numbers? About whether or not he was making a profit? Macleod had enough on his plate, but instead, he breathed in deeply and answered the woman politely.

'You can tell him that I'm very sorry for what's happening at the moment, but we are working earnestly to try and bring a killer to justice, and at this time, investigations are continuing.'

'He did ask me to get an update on how you were getting on, Detective Inspector.'

'The way we are getting on is that investigations are continuing. Tell him I thank him for his concern, but that frankly, at the moment, he needs to let us get on with our job. I'm sorry that you're having trouble with your passengers and if there's anything further, he can call directly to the Detective Chief Inspector, who I'm sure will be more than happy to answer any questions he has.'

'Thank you, Detective Inspector. I'll pass that on.'

Macleod thought he could hear in the woman's voice a little touch of sympathy for him, but he had none for the CEO. The DCI could handle him. That what was he was meant to do. Lift all of the minutiae off Macleod, let him get on with investigating.

He turned back to look at the laptop and thought about pressing it to try and communicate with Hope and Clarissa. He hated this time. He wanted answers and he wanted them now, but he had to wait for his pieces to play, to come through for him. What was he going to do in the meantime? Macleod wandered over to his door, opened it, and looked out into the main office. Maybe he'd teach some of these constables how to make proper coffee.

Chapter 17

Clarissa sat on the sofa in the hotel lobby, stretching her legs out in front of her. Opposite her in a chair was Hope McGrath, who scanned the people checking in.

'You can ease off, you know,' said Clarissa; 'you don't have to keep an eye on everybody in this entire building. Just relax until he gets here.'

'He's five minutes late,' said Hope.

'He's a doctor; of course, he's late. Probably could be anything up to half an hour to an hour. You know what they're like with appointments and that. They run over all the time.'

'That's not the point. He's meeting the police; you'd think he'd make an effort to arrive on time.'

'Still,' said Clarissa, 'gives us a chance to get a coffee. Have you spoken with anyone else?'

'I got a quick call down to Ross. He's just about wrapped up down in Islay, but he said that Dr Jacobs was also looking after Jenny Trimble and her husband, so we'll have a word about that while we're here. Makes sense. That's if he ever gets here.'

'Come on, wind down a bit. You've been up to high doh like anything.'

'No, I haven't. It's just . . . '

'You're becoming like Macleod; that's what it is.'

'What do you mean?'

'Seoras, when he's on the case, can't stop. It's all about the case, constantly. It's not me. I drop off at times, tune out for a bit, take a half hour here or there. Otherwise, it will drive you insane.'

'That's all right, but I'm the senior here. I'm the one who's meant to find things out.'

'There you go. That's taking Macleod's attitude. He's in charge, he's meant to solve everything, meant to get everything done. You can only do what you can do.'

'Well, sorry,' said Hope. 'I just can't take your "don't-give-a-stuff" attitude. I can't do that.'

'It's not a "don't-give-a-stuff" attitude. I just don't have time for piffle.'

'Piffle?' said Hope. 'Piffle is not a word I would associate with you.'

'No, but it's a reasonably posh hotel. I don't like saying other words.'

'I was born and raised in Glasgow; you can say whatever words you want. It's not like I haven't heard them before.'

'Well, piffle it is. A lot of time for piffle,' said Clarissa. 'You get the job and get stuck in, but sometimes when there's nothing left to do, you have to wait, chill out. Don't start marching around, getting up to high doh.'

Hope stood up, instantly began to walk, and then stopped and looked at Clarissa.

'That's what he does as well; he does that.'

'I am not becoming Macleod.'

'No, but in fairness, a lot of men wouldn't look at him the

way they look at you.' This drew a sharp look from Hope.

'What? Well, I'm sure Seoras has his admirers.'

'I'm sure he does,' said Clarissa, almost absentmindedly. Then glanced up to see Hope staring at her.

'Really?' said Hope. 'I thought you two were at loggerheads. It's not, is it? You're not? You're actually teasing him. You are, aren't you? You're teasing him with all that.'

'Well, he's a good man. A little bit stuck-up at times for my liking, but a good man.'

'You got him up to do karaoke. You had him singing things in front of the team, but you know his type, don't you? He's tight with Jane though.'

'I didn't say I wanted to marry him,' said Clarissa. 'All I said was he'd have his admirers.'

'Well, I've never heard you say that about anyone else,' said Hope. 'No one.'

'You've got to admit though, there is something about him.'

'Well, he'd probably have to be a good thirty years younger for me,' said Hope.

'That's so ageist,' said Clarissa. 'That's an ageist thing. Why can't he be thirty years older? Why can't the boy be thirty years younger than you?'

'Because then he'd be a child,' said Hope, 'if he was thirty years younger than me.'

'You know what I mean,' said Clarissa; 'it's only the age thing holding you back.'

'It's not just the age thing holding me back,' said Hope.

'Well, what else is there?' asked Clarissa.

Hope suddenly realised she was on the back foot for some reason. How did this happen? She'd gone after Clarissa having an interest in Macleod and now she was defending why she wasn't chasing the man.

'Well, he's my boss for a start.'

'I ask you for the reasons why you shouldn't be going after him and the best you can do is "He's my boss?" I thought I had it bad.'

Hope walked around the table and sat down beside Clarissa. 'You're lonely, aren't you?' she said.

'Yes,' said Clarissa, 'I am. Not many men will take me on. I'm too dynamic for them at this time of life, too hard to handle, especially now I'm older. When I was younger, men seemed to be more up for that, but not now. They want somebody quiet, somebody they can just curl up to at night, remind them where they left their keys.'

'Well, that's not you, is it?' said Hope.

'No. It's easy for you. Look at you, you and your car-hire man.'

'Don't bring John into this.'

'Why? I mean, what did he see in you?'

'Personality. My fun nature,' said Hope.

'I'm not saying he didn't, but what was the first thing he saw in you? Well, probably those legs for a start and that red hair.'

'Stop right there. He's not like that.'

'Of course, he's like that; he's a man.'

'Okay, he is like that,' said Hope, 'but he also appreciates the other sides of me.'

'And I'm not saying he doesn't,' said Clarissa, 'but looks fade. The longer you go on, the more you're reliant on your personality and if that's hard for them to handle, well, you end up like me, wedded instead to a green sports car.'

'He's still not here,' said Hope. 'I'm going to phone his secretary.'

'Okay,' said Clarissa. 'Good idea. It's better than walking up and down there, reminding me I don't have the legs you have.'

Hope stuck her tongue out at Clarissa, picked up her mobile, and called Dr Jacobs's office.

'Dr Jacobs's office; how can I help?'

'This is Detective Sergeant Hope McGrath. I was to meet with Dr Jacobs at his hotel tonight. Is he still there?'

'No. He left over an hour ago. He should be there by now. He said he was going to go back and get a shower before he met you.'

'Well, he's not arrived. Would you call him for me, find out what's happening?'

'Well, if anything's happened,' said the secretary, 'I think it's better if you ring him. I mean, you're a police officer after all, so I'll give you his mobile. I can trust you with that.'

Hope took the mobile number down.

'What's the matter?' asked Clarissa.

'Left an hour ago, still not here. I've got his mobile. Hang on,' said Hope. She dialled the number, but the phone just kept ringing.

'Wait a minute,' said Clarissa. She stood up and made her way over to reception. When she came back, she announced that room 235 was Dr Jacobs's. 'Let's go up and see what's happening,' said Clarissa, 'we can always ring from outside the room. See if it makes any sound.'

Together, the two women approached the lift, taking it to the second floor. Scanning the numbers on the doors, they walked down through a corridor before finding themselves in front of Dr Jacobs's room. Hope picked up the mobile and redialled the number. There was no answer from inside.

'I don't like this,' said Hope. 'Meant to be meeting us; we've

143

got a murderer on the loose. I think we should check the room.'

'Do you really have cause to enter?' asked Clarissa.

'I've got the gut instinct that says I do. We'll not break in. We'll go down and ask the attendant at the lobby to come with us.'

'You stay here,' said Clarissa, 'I'll do that.' She disappeared off down the corridor and back to the lift.

Hope stood waiting, looking up and down the corridor to see if anyone approached. She rapped the door several times asking for Dr Jacobs, but there was no response. A door down the corridor opened and a couple came out wearing smart dress as if they were going out to dinner. They peered up as Hope banged the door and then the man marched along.

'It appears he doesn't want to be disturbed, whoever it is in there. I think you should go.'

'And who might you be?' asked Hope.

'I happen to be one of the local councillors so please don't take that attitude with me.'

Hope reached inside her jacket, took out her credentials, and held them up in front of the man. 'I'm a detective sergeant pursuing inquiries. Carry on to your night, please, sir.'

The man looked agitated, but he turned, made his way back down the hall, and started grumbling to his wife about what was going on. Hope resumed her banging on the door but got no answer. When Clarissa got back, she was accompanied by a woman who took a swipe card and passed it through the lock on the door of the room. Hope watched the little green light flash. She pushed down the handle and opened it gently.

'You better stay here,' said Clarissa, 'just in case there's anything untoward happening.'

The woman with the card nodded while Clarissa followed

Hope into the room. They could see a double bed stretched out with sheets that hadn't been pulled back. In the far corner there was a briefcase sitting on top of a small desk. It was opened. Clarissa took a look realising it had been rifled through. A jacket lay over a chair in the corner.

'He made it back here then,' said Hope, 'so where is he?'

Clarissa looked around the room, then marched over to the bathroom. She opened the door to see blood lying in large pools. Carefully, she stepped around it, reaching over to the bath that had a shower curtain pulled across it. With a gentle hand, she moved it back before it got caught midway. At this point, she could see a pair of hairy legs. Tilting her head so she could see the full extent of the bath, Clarissa took a deep breath inward. The man was lying there, blood all around him, his throat evidently slashed.

'We need to seal the room, Hope. Get Jona or one of her cronies down. It appears Dr Jacobs is in the bath.'

'In the bath?' queried Hope. She walked for the bathroom, but Clarissa held up a hand.

'No,' she said. 'Don't. It's not pretty.' She slowly made her way back out of the bathroom.

'You better phone Seoras with this,' said Clarissa. 'I'll deal with the staff member outside.'

Hope nodded, picked up her phone and dialled Macleod's number.

'Hope, it's about time. What have you learned?'

'I've learned that we're closer than we think,' said Hope. 'We saw Dr Stephens but we've moved on to Dr Jacobs.'

'Has Jacobs been of any use?' asked Macleod.

'No, he's dead. He's lying in a hotel bathroom with his throat slashed,' said Hope. 'Like I said, I think we're getting close,

Seoras.'

'What's your move then?'

'Well, we're going to seal off the room, obviously. We'll see if we can get forensics down. Take a look through the CCTV, if anybody came through.'

'No, Hope. I mean yes, but no. That's the basics. That's straightforward. What's your move now?'

'Well, I mean Dr Jacobs must have been important because there's two of the victims who had Dr Jacobs as their counsellor.

'But the others didn't,' said Macleod. 'You need to get hold of Dr Stephens and you need to get a hold of Dr Green.'

'You think they're in danger, too?' asked Hope. 'I mean we saw Stephens. We've already spoken to her.'

'But did she tell you everything? Whoever this is, clearly has been able to get information from the doctors. The important thing now to do is to make sure that they don't silence them or that link. Jacobs obviously knew of the person who's doing these killings. We have to assume that Stephens and Green will probably know them as well. We need to move. What's Clarissa doing?'

'She's out organising the hotel here. Shall I leave her to cover this off?'

'No. I wouldn't,' said Macleod. 'I'd send her for Green.'

'Why?' asked Hope. 'Surely it's better if I do it.'

'No. You'll guard him while being here because you'll learn more. You're a thorough detective. If Green's in trouble, Clarissa will haul him out of there, however she has to, and she'll haul in whatever force she needs to do it. Coordinate it. Don't do it all yourself.'

'Okay, Seoras, we'll get on it. I'll speak to you shortly.'

Clarissa came back into the room to a rather strange look from Hope. 'What's up?' she asked. 'I've just started to pull it together with the staff. They'll keep this room locked and marked off. She's gone off to get records and talk about where I can get CCTV.'

'You leave that to me,' said Hope. 'Got a job for you. Dr Green, find him. Put him somewhere safe.'

'Now you're talking,' said Clarissa.

Chapter 18

Hope had waved off Clarissa in her green sports car before returning to the hotel. A number of uniformed police had arrived, closing off the room, and a forensics section, at the request of Jona Nakamura, had made their way in from one of the Glasgow stations. Hope watched them go to it before taking aside the hotel staff one by one, asking if they'd seen anyone. She sat looking through CCTV as well, but she couldn't pin anyone to the room. There was CCTV in the lift, but no one had got in on that floor who couldn't be accounted for in the hotel. The hall that ran to Dr Jacobs's room had no CCTV. Hope interviewed everyone staying along it, but no one had seen anything.

Hope was in a bit of a fix, but she made sure she took images from the CCTV of everyone that was about the hotel. She sent them over to Ross who had used scanning software as well as his own eye in trying to see if anyone turned up at any of the murder sites more than once. Hope had tried ringing Dr Green's surgery, but got nowhere, and instead had rung his general practice. A constable assisted her, and after an hour and a half, they got hold of Doctor Green's home number. Although it rang, it was not answered. Neither was there any response from his mobile. Hope picked up her phone and called Clarissa who was racing up the A9 in her sports car.

'Where are you?'

'Pitlochry,' said Clarissa. 'I've got my foot down. What do you know?'

'Got his house number and his mobile. Not getting anything. Uniform popped round, but he wasn't in the house. However, I'd start there. If you're going to find anything, you're going to find it there.'

'Have uniform remained?'

'Negative. We don't know he's definitely in trouble, and they said they're not sitting there for the night. They've got plenty on.'

'That's fair enough. Where's Seoras at the moment?'

'He got called into a meeting. The ferries look like they're in trouble, cancellations left, right, and centre. They've got staff saying they're not going to work, thereby closing down all the ferries. It's a disaster for the islands.'

'Is that why the constables went round to the house and not Seoras himself?'

'Exactly,' said Hope. 'But I spoke to him, and he wanted you out there.'

'Well, I'm not that far off. I'll go direct to the house.'

'That's a good idea. He's stuck in this meeting, and he can't get out. He's not very happy with the new DCI, says he's hand-holding at the moment.'

'Well, I can see that would upset him. I'll be there shortly. I'll give you a call when I have something.'

Clarissa Urquhart closed the call and settled down for the drive through the night. She had pulled the hood up on her small sports car, the cool of the night too much to drive through, and she settled into a relaxed mode of driving. Many people wouldn't have recognised how calm she was for the car was hammering along. She hoped she wouldn't be stopped by anyone in a police car. It was always embarrassing when you had to explain you were hot-footing it to a potential crime scene.

Dr Green lived on the edge of Inverness. Clarissa drove up to the house, parking a short distance away before making her way slowly along the streets. She moved into the shadows but expected no one to be about at two o'clock in the morning.

She got closer. Clarissa stepped into the garden of a house across the street, scurried along behind some of their trees, and peered out towards the house of Dr Green. A light had gone on in an upstairs room. Clarissa wondered when he'd got back. She looked over and saw a car outside but had no idea whether it was his or not. Something caught her eye across the street and Clarissa froze.

There was a figure in the trees in the garden of Dr Green's house. She watched as the figure raised a camera and seemed to scan the lit window carefully. Clarissa crept back out of the garden into the street and edged her way along the opposite side in the shadows. When she got level with the person who was in Dr Green's garden, she stole quickly across the road, up on her tiptoes so her heels wouldn't make a sound.

As she got closer, Clarissa took a pair of handcuffs out from within her shawl, reached over the wall, and grabbed a man by the left arm, pulling it back hard. She heard a yell, and she slapped the cuffs on his wrist before grabbing his other arm and securing that wrist as well.

'Bloody hell. I'm just watching him, what's this?'

Clarissa recognised the voice. 'Well, it's been a while,' she said. 'What are you doing here?'

'Getting my arms taken off by the looks of it. Do you mind?' Clarissa grabbed the key for the cuffs and undid them as the man turned around to face her. 'I am here on legitimate business,' he said.

'Carl Mackenzie, I thought you'd given up with this sort of nonsense.'

'Not yet. I haven't got enough money stashed away. What about you? What are you doing here at two in the morning? I thought you were the high-classed, art-world detective. I see you more and more in the background of that Macleod guy. It's all a bit cut and thrust for you, isn't it?'

'I was always cut and thrust, darling,' said Clarissa, 'You just never got to find out.' Carl Mackenzie was a figure that Clarissa had run into many a time in her art dealings. If you wanted to know who was with whom, or who was cheating on whom, Carl was your man. He'd been hired by many of the richer clients simply because he was so good at exposing what their other halves were up to, but Clarissa thought he'd retired and finally got away with that package. It seemed he was still working.

'Who's hired you then?' asked Clarissa.

'My client, Mrs Green, has asked me to keep an eye on her husband, Dr Green, and a good job too.'

'What did you find out?'

'Not a lot. They came in from the rear, I think because I was out front so I don't know who's up there with him and I haven't got a photograph. I'm just going to wait until I see her emerge in the morning.'

'I'm sorry to do this to you Carl, but I'm about to go up and knock that door.'

'You can't. You can't do that,' he said.

'I'm afraid I can. Like you said, I now work for Macleod, and this is a murder investigation I'm on. It can't wait for your paycheque.'

'Well, that's just charming,' he said. 'We've all got to make a living, you know that?'

'When did they come?'

'Less than an hour,' he said. 'I got a call from my client; she said somebody had been ringing, couldn't find her husband.'

'Well then, looks like I'm responsible for your fee. That's us checking up on him.'

'Checking up him? Why? Is there something afoot? I'm not in a dangerous situation, am I?'

The man was sitting in a hedge, trying to expose another man for cheating on his wife, and Clarissa was wondering just how dangerous the situation needed to get. People under that sort of duress, especially when exposed, didn't tend to hold back.

'No, you'll be all right here,' she said. 'But I'm going up to that door. I will suggest that you go around the rear and you might be able to catch some good photographs, but I start walking in fifteen seconds.'

'You ever regret it?' said Carl, starting to walk away.

'The time you propositioned me?' said Clarissa. 'No, I don't regret it.'

'I do. Everyday. Just saying, if retirement gets lonely.'

And with that, the man was gone. Clarissa shook her head. She was lonely. She had told Hope as much, but she wasn't that lonely.

Clarissa turned and marched across the garden, up a set of stone steps to a large wooden door. There was a brass knocker and a bell, but Clarissa took the knocker and started slamming it like it needed to wake the hounds of hell. She continued for the next three minutes until a man opened the door dressed in his dressing gown, bare legs beneath it.

'What the blazes are you doing?' he said.

'Are you Doctor Green?' asked Clarissa.

'Yes, I'm Dr Green. What the hell do you want?'

'I want to come in and make sure you're okay. My name's Detective Sergeant Clarissa Urquhart, and we have been contacting you because we've been worried about your safety. Firstly, you've neither picked up the house phone nor the mobile so here I am knocking. It's a good job you answered. I'd have been forced to kick in the door. Do you mind if I come in?'

'Of course, I bloody mind if you come in; it's two in the morning.'

'You look rather out of breath,' said Clarissa. 'Is anyone else in the house?'

The man looked over his shoulder, 'No. Nobody.'

'You won't mind if I come in then? I just want to check around. I believe that your life may be in danger.'

'My life in danger? Why?'

'I take it you know a Dr Jacobs, works out of Aberdeen, similar line of work to yourself.'

'Of course, I do. It's not that big a community amongst us.'

'Found dead tonight, throat slit. May have a possible link to the murder investigation that we're looking into, one that has your name in it.'

'My name in it? What do you mean?'

'Yes, a link to clients you have. A number of them have died. I'm just going to check upstairs if you don't mind.'

Clarissa could hear something, somebody upstairs, but she didn't let on. Instead, she marched up, and spotted the main bedroom and walked into it. The main bed sheets were a mess, and Clarissa sniffed the air. There was a heavy musk perfume.

'I'm going to need you to come with me to the station,' said Clarissa. 'I'm sorry about the late hour, but it needs to be done.'

'Dead?' said the man. 'Jacobs is dead?'

'Very much so,' said Clarissa. 'I believe that could be quite upsetting for you, but that's the way it is. Please, go and get changed.'

'I'm going to have a shower first,' he said. 'Is that okay?'

'By all means,' said Clarissa.

She stood in the bedroom until she heard the man lock the bathroom door. She went over to where a range of perfumes sat on the dresser, checking out each one. They were women's perfume, but none of them actually matched the scent that was in the air. When she heard the shower still continuing, she made her way downstairs and out to the rear door of the house, stepping outside and letting the light flood into the garden. She gave a wave and Carl Mackenzie emerged from the bushes.

'Did you see anyone come out?' asked Clarissa.

'Yes,' he said and turned his camera around so she could see the LCD screen at the rear of it. There was a woman who looked like she'd been dressed in a hurry, clutching a number of bags, exiting the rear of the house.

'Do you know her?' asked Clarissa.

'Well, yes, I do. Apparently, she's a friend of Mrs Green. Close friend in fact. Very naughty, but I think I've got her banged to the rights, and him as well.'

'Hang on to it for a couple of days,' said Clarissa.

'Why?' asked Carl. 'I've done my job.'

'Indeed, but he's going to be in interview with us for a little while. Probably best to deliver the goods when his wife will have a little bit less in sympathy with him. Might get you a bigger fee.'

'That's what I liked about you,' said Carl. 'You can always see past what is going on.'

'Well, the sooner you get a bigger fee, the sooner you retire,' said Clarissa. 'And the sooner you realise that retirement without me is perfectly fine.' Carl smiled and turned away, giving Clarissa a wave.

'Text me that picture,' said Clarissa. 'I just need to make sure she's not in our inquiry.'

'And if she is?'

'That camera's coming in for evidence.'

'Well then, I hope she isn't.'

Clarissa walked back inside, and on returning upstairs, she could hear that the shower had finished. She knocked the bedroom door and Dr Green asked her to wait for a moment while he was still getting changed. She heard a beep on her phone and looked at the image that had arrived from Carl Mackenzie. It wasn't that clear. She blew it up on the phone as much as she dared and then started walking around the house, looking for photographs of friends of Doctor Green's wife. There were a number here and there of different charity functions or dinners they'd been to. Clarissa compared each one. Well, Mackenzie must have been wrong. There was no close friend here. Nobody that matched the image she was looking at.

Dr Green came out of his room. 'Are we ready?' he said. 'Let's go and get this done.'

'You sure there was no one here tonight?'

'No,' said Dr Green. 'My wife's away, you see. On my own.'

Clarissa let the statement slide for a moment. She'd take him into the interview room and soon sort him out, because the guy was lying through his teeth.

Chapter 19

Hope stood behind two constables in a Glasgow police station looking at the CCTV video footage in front of her. They had reviewed nearly all of it and interestingly, the two constables in front of her believed they'd narrowed down a certain suspect.

'If you look here, Sergeant, she comes through, hangs around in the lobby for a bit, then disappears back out. She's back in again, comes upstairs, then disappears downstairs. Here, Dr Jacobs comes in. This is after she's gone outside again, but this time when she comes in, she once again ends up taking the lift up to Dr Jacobs's floor, and she gets out. Ten minutes later, she gets back in again. She comes downstairs and disappears into the night.'

'Pause it on her,' said Hope. The woman before her never looked up at the camera once but she had red hair like Hope and a large pair of dark sunglasses on. The image was quite grainy, and Hope found it difficult to work out exactly what the woman looked like.

'I thought these CCTV cameras had gotten better these days.'

'It was quite an old one in that lift though,' said the constable. 'I agree with you; it's a bit of a disappointing image considering how long she was up there.'

'It doesn't prove anything either. It could have been some-body in the hall. Came and did it and then went back to their room. We'll need to have a look through though. Can you send that image off to Detective Constable Ross? He's got images from everywhere else. He might be able to connect that image too. See if that woman was at any of the other murders.'

'Will do,' said the constable.

Hope thanked them for their time, and she made her way down to the canteen within the station house, realising it was four o'clock in the morning. Her eyes were almost closing but she knew she'd need to take a run-out again to the hotel just to check off that everything was closed off. She'd take an image of the woman as well, put it in front of the guests, see if anybody recognised her, or could give a better description. That would require taking more of the constables with her, the last job of the night shift before they went home.

Hope sat and looked into her coffee. She was a little bit off just now. That was the way to describe it. She was out here working on her own, something she'd done before but she felt a little bit blindsided that Macleod said to send Clarissa all the way back up to Inverness. She wasn't sure how to read it. Did he not trust her to get that job done? Was she too precious to go? What did he mean by it? Or did he simply want everything done right in Glasgow, so he needed her there?

The team was spread very thin at the moment, and it had been a long time since a case had them travelling so far. Most murders occurred fairly close to the other in a particular series, especially when committed by the same person, but this killer had travelled quite happily, setting things up on different ferries. Were they trying to disguise it? Did they actually hope to get away with it? Clearly, the efforts of the investigation team had spooked them. For whoever it was, she had come, as Hope believed, to finish Dr Jacobs off.

Hope smelled the chips that were just being poured into a large canteen tray and she succumbed, standing up, and strode over to pick up a plateful. She sat down with them, ate about half of them, and then felt that she really couldn't finish that sort of food at this time of night. She picked up her phone and called through to John, her partner in Inverness, the car-hire man.

'What time is it? What's happened?' he said quickly on answering the phone.

'Nothing's happened, I just wanted to talk.'

'About what? You're not pregnant, are you?'

'No, I'm not pregnant, I don't need to talk about that. I'm just . . . , well, I don't know what.'

'Are you all right? I can come down if you want.'

'That's not going to work,' said Hope; 'we're at the tail end of this investigation, and frankly, I'm probably going to be back up in Inverness soon. It's just been an awkward one—it really has. I'm down on my own away from the team. Ross is over at Oban, Clarissa was with me but raced up to Inverness. Macleod's stuck in meetings all the time. It's just weird; we've never worked this far apart before. I haven't even seen Jona.'

'Why, where's she?'

'Last I heard, she was down with Ross, following the dead bodies around. I've had to work with the local force. They're fine, it's just it's not our guys, it's five in the morning, and I'm just sick of this at the moment.'

'Is there anything you want me to do?' asked John.

'I want you to make it all go away,' said Hope, 'I want to be back up there.'

'You sound like you're having problems,' said John. 'Are you okay? It's not us, is it?'

'No, it's not us; it's nothing to do with you. I'm not blaming you for anything.' Hope stopped instead of going on with the sentence. *That's it*, she thought. *It's blame. It's all blame; she's blaming them. It's always this side, the partner who's caused the issue, killing the cause of the problem.*

'Thanks, John, that's great, but I've got to go.'

'You called me,' he said, 'I'm not going to go back to sleep now, the least you can do is talk to me.'

'Sorry, I need to phone Seoras.'

Hope cut John off and immediately dialled Macleod's number. When he picked it up, she could hear the foul mood he was in.

'I've literally stepped out. I need the bathroom. What?'

'Sorry, I'm stuck down here in Glasgow at five in the morning as well, you know, but I got something.'

'What?' asked Macleod.

'This person, who's doing this, I think they've been shunned by their partner. I think they've been put off. Something has happened to them, they've been in counselling or something, or they've seen it up close. They're blaming the person who has done the most damage in the relationship; don't you see it?

'Andrew Culshaw, he's violent. Peter Hughes was pushing Gerald Lyndhurst to come out about their relationship. Daphne Walsh was a wild woman, Fred Martin, he was the one that caused his wife's problems, why she committed suicide. The murderer has blamed him. That's why he's dead even though she's already jumped. Then you have Jenny Trimble;

she's been running around on her husband. He's played the good guy, not getting divorced, but she hasn't. She's been the one causing the problems. Therefore, the murderer's gone for her.'

'Okay,' said Macleod, 'but what's the ferry bit?'

'I think they've thought that they can get away with it by making it look like suicide. Also, I think it's a woman. We've got a potential female who's in and around Dr Jacobs's room when he dies. Trouble is the CCTV's so poor. I'm going to have to go back out and canvass everyone in the hotel and see if I can get a better description of her. She's gone to the ferry source because, think about it, you can kill them, and they disappear below the sea. I think she's reckoning on them not being picked up or turning up so late that anyone looking won't see her as a part of it.'

'Needs to be a certain somebody though,' said Macleod, 'who knows how to use Ketamine. What about all these doctors? They're good for it, aren't they?'

'Well, it wasn't Dr Jacobs,' said Hope; 'he's dead.'

'They all know each other, don't they? In that sort of a field, maybe they talk about issues, maybe they talk about clients. Maybe that's what's done it. What do you think about that? I think it could be one of these doctors. Clarissa's holding Dr Green. He's coming in at the moment and I'm going to sit and interview him; see what I can extract from him.'

'Could be the other way around, of course; could be the partners. Who do you talk about at home, about the work, and what's going on, your partner?'

'I don't,' said Macleod, 'I talk to you about that. I only talk to Jane about how I'm feeling. She doesn't want to know about the other side, says it's too grim.'

'Yes, but we're police officers. Other people on normal jobs, it's a bit less gruesome. People love to talk about what they're doing, especially if they've got problems. Maybe we should be checking out the wives of these doctors or the partners.'

'That's a good idea. See if they can get photos of their partners. You can get a better ID, either through CCTV or with the people in the hotel, see if we can pull this together. I take it you sent the image off to Ross.'

'Hopefully, he'll be looking at it. We'll be lucky to get a match though due to the grainy quality. To be honest, I think it's a long shot at the moment, Seoras. We're going to need to get hold of him. Whittle this down. There's something that these doctors know. Somebody's got to be able to break this open.'

'Well, I hope we do soon because I've just had it in the neck from the ferry company, from the politicians, from the rather useless DCI. I'm only saying that to you. I'm sick of sitting in a room and telling them we're getting on with it and not being allowed to get on with it because I'm sat in a stupid room with them.'

Hope could feel the rage coming from Macleod. 'Easy, Seoras. Easy. We'll get this. You'll get it. You always do.'

'We'll get it. I'm just frustrated. I've been waiting for all the pieces to come to place. I've sent you all out, you've all done your jobs, and it's not there yet. Why? What are we not seeing? Who are we not seeing?'

'Maybe we don't know them yet.'

'Then we need to get to know these people.'

'Do you want me up the road tomorrow?' asked Hope. 'We can pool resources that way.'

'No,' said Macleod, 'you've got Dr Stevens down in Glasgow, Jacobs was Aberdeen, Green is up here in Inverness. I want you down there. The Glasgow contingent are good, but I need somebody from our team there to organise and supervise. You carry the rank of authority outside of me. Clarissa will only upset people. I hate to say it, but I think sometimes she needs a handler with her.'

'Well, you can tell her that,' said Hope, 'because there's no way I am. Is that why I was down here with her?'

'Well, since she came in, look at the things she's gotten into. Absolutely, you were down there to oversee it, look after, make sure nothing went crazy. She's great for tearing a place up, but you can't leave the carnage behind.'

Hope thought of what Clarissa had said about Macleod and wondered what she'd make of him saying that she was too forward, too much chaos, and not enough of the steely but controlled attitude that a detective needed to have.

'I better get organised,' said Hope, 'get back out there and interview these guests again.'

'Go at them but be gentle. It's five o'clock in the morning. We're not at our best at five in the morning.'

'Well, I'm not,' said Hope, 'I'm not my best at all.'

She closed the phone call down and thought of John before picking up the phone again and dialling John's number.

It rang eight times before a blurry answer went, 'What now?'

'Sorry, I just phoned up to apologise.'

'I just got off to sleep,' said John.

'Sorry,' said Hope, 'I don't know when I'm coming back up. Seoras has me staying down this end. Are you all right?'

'I'm fine,' said John, 'I could honestly just do with my sleep, but if you need me . . .'

'No,' said Hope, 'it's fine. You go to sleep.'

She never thought she would lie to him, but she needed him

right there and then to sit and listen, and yet, she didn't even know why. What was up with her of late?

Hope closed the call and made her way up towards the offices at the top end of the Glasgow station. There she would find the constables that she'd take with her to start interviewing more of the hotel guests. She'd print out an image, see if anyone had seen this woman, and what she'd done.

As Hope looked out of the window, the printer sending out multiple copies of the woman's face, Hope saw the red sun starting to come up against the city skyline. She realised what was up. This had been home. This had been where she'd grown up. Yet here she was working with Glasgow's finest, operating in and out of the city that had been such a part of her and right now, it felt as far away from home as it could possibly get.

Chapter 20

Macleod stretched in his office chair, trying to push away the sore bones and shoulders that were currently causing him pain at this early hour of the morning. Clarissa was sitting across from him at the small table they used for conference and he could see her eyes beginning to droop.

'Come on, up and at it.'

'Seoras, when you signed up, what age did you think you'd still be doing this kind of shift?'

'I never thought about it,' said Macleod, 'I didn't back then, then after the wife died, any time of day was fine. I can see now though, it affects Jane.'

'It affects me,' said Clarissa. 'If I don't get my head down on a good bed, when I get up, I'm achy; everything just feels off.'

'And you get grumpy,' said Macleod.

Clarissa looked up quickly, a shocked look on her face. 'I get grumpy? I'm not the obsessive one, I'm not the one that . . .'

'Can we just get on?' said Macleod. 'What is this with you? Every time I say a comment about you, you fire it back at me. I never thought I'd get to this age and somebody of a similar age would be sitting fighting the bit all the time.'

'Don't you age bit that on me,' said Clarissa.

'You were the one who was just starting to say about it,' said Macleod.

'I'm allowed to, just you remember. I'm a lady; you speak nicely.'

Macleod raised his eyebrows then pointed to the door. As Clarissa walked to it, Macleod strode round from behind her and pulled the door open.

'For the lady,' he said. She stuck her tongue out at him.

The pair walked in silence down two flights of stairs into an interview room in Inverness Police Station. Inside was Dr Green, who was looking a little bedraggled and also extremely tired. Macleod pulled a seat out for Clarissa, who sat down giving him a glare. Macleod then joined her on the seat beside and put his hands together on the table looking across at Dr Green. The man raised his head, his eyes were starting to well up. Macleod pitched him as maybe middle-aged, and he could tell a face of regret as soon as he saw one.

'I'm Detective Inspector Seoras Macleod; you've already met Detective Sergeant Clarissa Urquhart. We're going to ask you some questions about tonight. More specifically about this woman.'

Macleod took an envelope that was on the table and pulled out a sketchy image of the woman who had left Dr Green's house.

'That's Janine, Inspector. I'm having an affair with her.'

'Well, that's pretty straightforward. Janine who?'

'I don't know.'

'Well, how did you meet her then?'

'She was at a hotel down in Glasgow. I was in the bar; I remember it was quite late. She came up to me and she was wearing this rather knock-out dress. The missus had given me a hard time, has been for the last lot of years, and well, Janine was so attentive. Pretty soon we ended up talking until the small hours of the morning. She suggested that we go back up to my room, with a bottle of red. It all kind of went from there.'

'I can understand the one off,' said Clarissa, 'but it went from there. Who suggested it went from there?'

'Well, we both found out that actually, we live up round the Inverness area, so Janine said, "Why don't we do this again?" She said she enjoyed it; it was good. Told me how good I was. I said, "Yes," but obviously, we needed somewhere to go and if we were in Inverness, we couldn't kind of do it in the hotels around there. Too easy to get caught out, seen by people. Seen by my clients, even.'

'True,' said Macleod, 'so where did you go for your quiet times?'

The man bent his head forward. Macleod saw the tears coming from his eyes.

'I didn't mean to do it. Well, it wasn't my fault. It's just, she was so available, and she treated me nice. She treated me well. She built me up. My wife she just takes. Do you know what that's like? Just takes and . . .'

There came a loud sobbing from the man and Macleod sat back for a moment, giving him time to let the emotion flow through. It wasn't the time to press him. He'd speak wildly. Better to let him regain his composure. Macleod wanted accurate facts, not some hysterical nonsense. He looked over at the constable sat in the room and called him across.

'Get me a coffee, please,' he said. 'Don't go to the machine either; up to the team office, bring one down. Clarissa here will have one as well. Dr Green, do you want anything? Can we get you a cup of water, coffee, tea? Give you a moment to steady yourself.'

But the man just simply cried. Macleod waited five minutes until the coffee had returned and the constable was dismissed to stand outside the room.

'So, Janine,' said Macleod breaking the still-whimpering sobs of Dr Green. 'Janine built you up, so where did you go for your quiet moments?'

The man raised his eyes. 'I could only know of one place we could truly be safe. Well, we suggested her place, but she said no, the neighbours were too close and nosey, so she suggested that we do it at the surgery where I carry out my work.'

'Okay,' said Macleod, 'and how often?'

'Two to three times a week. Occasionally, she was going away though, but when she was about, it was two to three times a week.'

'And what? A quick hour in the afternoon. How did you work it?'

'Oh, no, at night. Always at night. We slept there. I'd tell the wife I was off with a client, or I was working late, had to stay over at a hotel. She seemed to buy it, so we managed to spend the night together. Always a bottle of red. That was Janine, always a bottle of red. I can't take a bottle of red, you see. Too many glasses and after a bit of exertion, I'd fall asleep, and that'd be me until morning.'

Macleod shot a glance at Clarissa; he could see she was thinking the same thing. Dr Green was paralytic, fast asleep. The woman could gain access to any of the records in his office.

'So, you're telling me,' said Macleod, 'that you took this woman to your office, you had sex with her, drank a lot of wine, you would pass out and then in the morning, you'd just get on with it or head off to wherever?'

'We were gone by six. My secretary sometimes comes in at eight, sometimes even earlier so we were well clear.'

'And you hold all your records there, do you?'

'My records, my notes, everything,' he said. 'Why?'

'Inside your office, are they locked away?'

'Well, we have the filing system for the handwritten notes and that. They do go on the computer, but they don't get locked away in the cabinet. The cabinet is usually open; there's no point. I lock the office door.'

'Just to confirm,' said Clarissa, 'you're saying to me that you slept in this office. You were then out for the count and this woman could have had access to any of the documents there. Would you have known? Would you have heard her move to get them?'

Green suddenly sat up and stared across the table. 'No, I wouldn't. Why? Why are you asking me about my records?'

'Have you read the news recently? I'm thinking particularly about Peter Hughes.'

'Peter? Yes, I heard the tragic story—fell off the ferry.'

'No,' said Clarissa, 'we believe he may have been murdered and dumped off the ferry, and we believe it may have been because he was trying to force Gerald Lyndhurst to come out in a relationship.'

'How did you know about that?'

'Well, Gerald told me, and we believe somebody else knew about it, and we believe it came from your office.'

The man froze and stared. 'How do you mean?'

'We believe that someone has been targeting couples that have been having problems, but especially that person in their

169

relationship that was causing the problem.'

'Peter Hughes was the problem,' said Dr Green. 'He really was; he wanted to force Gerald into coming out. He had an obsession about everyone knowing. An obsession about being clean that came from his childhood when he had to repress everything, but that was all in the notes. I mean they were my private notes where I said that, the ones that were held . . . oh dear God. Really?'

'What did you tell this Janine woman?' asked Macleod.

'How do you mean?'

'What did you tell her about your clients?'

'Nothing. Nothing. I mean, usually when we talked it would have been about me, about . . . '

'Your wife?' suggested Clarissa.

'Yes, it would have been my wife and what she was doing with me in the relationship and how it was hard because she never cared, and she always forced me to the . . . , you don't . . . '

'Where is your wife?' asked Macleod.

'She's away; she's on holiday; took a trip with a lot of her friends. She's down in England.'

'Have you got the name of the hotel?' asked Macleod.

'I do. I do. You don't think . . . '

'I don't think she's in trouble tonight,' said Macleod. 'Janine was with you. To be honest, I think at the moment you may be in trouble, because Dr Jacobs got killed for what he knew. We believe that he may have been infiltrated somehow but hid the information about his clients. Although we're not sure how yet.'

'But she was there tonight.'

'Yes, she was,' said Macleod; 'describe her to us.'

'Well, Janine's in her thirties, at least that's what she said. She's got dark brown hair. She's strong for her size. Maybe about five feet seven, can handle herself. Very energetic, but she came tonight, and she didn't kill me. We were going through our usual routine. I was surprised because she came to the house. I didn't care because the wife's away, so I thought, why not? In fact, I was quite interested to take her to the bed. That would show my wife, wouldn't it? Have somebody else in there. Oh, dear God. What did I do? She could've . . . '

'I think if Sergeant Urquhart hadn't arrived, we may have found you dead in the morning,' said Macleod. 'I don't think you'll be going anywhere quickly. I'm going to advise the local constabulary where your wife is and get an interview with her about what's going on.'

'You can't tell her. You can't tell her; she'll go crazy.'

'I think that bird's flown,' said Clarissa. 'We're in the middle of a murder investigation and we think that the murderer may even have been with you tonight. You were intimate with her. This is not a patch-up job. You need to understand, Dr Green, these things are going to come out at some point.'

The man put his head in his hands and began weeping again on the table.

'I'll be sending along a sketch artist. I want you to tell him exactly what Janine looked like so we can get a sensible image up, see if we can find out who she really is,' said Macleod. 'You can stay here at the station for a while. It's probably safest until we work out where Janine is.'

With that parting shot, he stood up, draining what remained of his coffee and walking out to the corridor outside. Clarissa followed him. Once the door was shut, Macleod turned round to her. 'Blast,' he said, 'she was there. Whoever she is, she was there.'

'But we can get a decent image now. If we get the sketch artist, we'll soon find out what she looks like and then we'll need to get that image in front of the rest of our medical professionals. Well, Stephens, at least. See if she knows who it is. Because that's the weird one, isn't it? She's clearly going to bed with Dr Green. Dr Jacobs, well, we'll see, but she got into his room. But I'm not sure about Dr Stephens. She may have played a fast one there, coming from a different angle.'

'We'll wait and see,' said Macleod. 'Modern age, you don't know who's doing what with who. I've learnt to have a much more open mind these days.'

'I stand corrected,' said Clarissa, beginning to walk back up to the office. 'Modern Macleod has told me so.'

Chapter 21

Alan Ross had driven through the night, and the morning sun felt sore on his eyes. He had the windows rolled down, trying to make himself feel better, but in truth, he was tired. Dr Jacobs's surgery in Aberdeen was right in the heart of the city, and as Ross drove through the early morning traffic, he found himself having to concentrate harder due to the sheer volume of cars on the road. He'd come up through the night when hardly anyone was about, and although he struggled to see much due to the darkness, it had been, up until Aberdeen, a very pleasant drive.

It had been a while since he'd been out on his own. He was always with Macleod or Clarissa, or even Hope. In some ways, he thought Macleod was too protective of him after that time in the Monarch Isles. It wasn't Macleod's fault he got shot, and in fact, he'd only been shot after everyone else had arrived. He always thought he had coped admirably with the situation until others had joined in, trying to round up the drug dealers.

Ross parked the car in a large multi-storey car park, took the lift down because his legs were feeling so tired, and then walked across the centre of the city until he saw a set of serviced offices high up. Ross looked up the list alongside the main door before buzzing and asking for Dr Jacobs's office.

'This is Dr Jacobs's office. I'm afraid he's not here yet. Do you have an appointment?'

'I'm Detective Constable Alan Ross. I'd like to come up and speak to you if that's okay, madam?'

'Absolutely. Of course,' she said. 'I'll just buzz you in. We're up here on the fifth floor.'

Ross pushed open the glass door in front of him, again walked over to a lift and stood in silence as he was transported up to the fifth floor. He closed his eyes due to the brightness inside, but when he heard the ping and the doors begin to open, he gave out a large yawn, flicked his eyes several times to try and take any remaining sleep out of them. He told himself to get his brain into gear for, after the long drive, the business end of his trip had arrived.

A set of large double doors had the motif for Dr Jacobs's surgery on them, and Ross gave a quick knock before opening one of them and stepping inside. A secretary was sitting behind a desk tapping away on her computer but stood up on seeing him and walked out from behind the desk. Ross thought she was older than he, dressed in a rather neat skirt, blouse and jacket, looking like the perfect professional's assistant.

'I'm sorry to bother you. I'm Detective Alan Ross,' he said, pulling out his credentials. 'When was the last time you saw Dr Jacobs?'

'Oh, that would have been two days ago, although I did speak to him yesterday during the day. I had to send him down some information on some clients. He's down in Glasgow at the moment doing some work. He'll be back up later today.'

'If you take a seat, madam. What's your name?'

'Mrs Thompson,' said the woman, starting to look concerned.

'Is there anything wrong?' she asked.

'I'm afraid there is, Mrs Thompson; your employer was unfortunately killed last night in his hotel in Glasgow.'

Her hand flew up to her mouth and the words 'Dear God' arrived.

'How? What do you mean killed? Was he in an accident or something?'

'No. I'm afraid he was murdered,' said Ross, 'in his hotel room. I need to ask you some questions.'

'I was up here. I was at home with my husband.'

'I'm not saying you're in the frame for anything, so please calm down and don't worry. What I do need to know is a little bit about Dr Jacobs and what's been going on in his day-to-day work.'

The woman looked away from Ross for a moment, but he could see her shoulders begin to shake. Then she seemed to turn round resolutely to him. 'I'll get you some coffee,' she said. 'Yes, you've come in, you should be getting coffee. I'll do that now. Take a seat. I'll tend to you now.'

'No,' said Ross. 'You've clearly had a shock. Sit there. I see the coffee and tea and things over there, I'll get you something. I think you need a cup of tea. It's clearly been a shock for you.'

The woman said nothing but simply stared over at the wall.

Ross made some tea with a lot of sugar in it and a hefty dose of milk before taking it back to the woman. He watched as she sipped it and he encouraged her to drink more of it until he saw the cup go down on the table. Ross pulled a chair around it and sat directly opposite her.

'Mrs Thompson, I need you to try to think clearly, if you can do that for me. Dr Jacobs, in recent weeks or even months, has there been anything different about him? Any trouble with his wife?'

'She's dead. He's a widower. Has been for a number of years. He needs a little bit of looking after in that respect. You go above and beyond as a secretary.'

'In what way?' asked Ross.

'Sorting him out with ties; sometimes you have to go and make sure he's got new shirts and things, organise that for him. He comes in with trousers and they're the wrong size. They're not right and you have to go and get them altered. He just . . . , well, he clearly missed someone who could look after certain sides of his life.'

'The other sides of his life, was there any change in them?'

'In what way do you mean?' asked Mrs Thompson.

'Well, he obviously lost a partner when his wife died, so has anyone come in to replace her?'

'I'm not one to gossip about my employer. I wouldn't want him to find out.' She then stopped. 'He's not going to find out, is he?' Tears rolled down off her cheeks, but Ross tried to keep her talking.

'You said you wouldn't speak out of turn; there's no out of turn anymore. He's been murdered. I need to know if anything was different, unusual.'

'She was. The client, Kerry Watson. I knew there was something about her. He said she had some sort of trauma that he was trying to work through. She would come in here always with a scarf over her head, although her blonde hair rolled out behind, sunglasses too, but she dressed that way. When you're a woman, you know how other women are dressing. You can tell when they're fishing for something or trying to entice. She wasn't incredibly overt with what she was doing, but she was trying to trap him in. Dr Jacobs had lost his wife, so I didn't feel it was my place to comment. She was taking advantage of him clearly.'

'In what way?' asked Ross.

The woman almost looked embarrassed. 'In that way,' she said.

'Sexually?' asked Ross for clarification.

'Yes.'

'How do you know that?' asked Ross.

'Well, she would come in here—it'd be the morning or the afternoon—into his office; the door would get locked and well, you hear things, don't you? You know what I mean? They'd be out of breath. You'd go in afterwards and you could tell people had been energetic in that room.'

The woman was clearly having difficulty with what she was saying and trying to put it in a fashion that didn't make it sound sordid.

'This Kerry Watson, did you ever see any ID, or . . . '

'None. Dr Jacobs said just let her come and go. She never paid anything either.'

'Do you know if he saw her outside of this office?'

'No. I don't know. I do know that they did row about it once. I wasn't listening, I was just sitting here at my desk, and I remember her saying that because of her husband, she couldn't. Said she'd been married, or was married, and she couldn't go elsewhere, it would have to be in the office, always in the office.'

'How long were these meetings?'

'Well, quite often they'd go on over lunch. I remember because Dr Jacobs used to come out and you'd look at him and you'd think, 'Yes, you've tried to dress yourself again quickly in a hurry.' He'd pop out to the off-license and next day there would be empty bottles of champagne.

'He never sent me for the booze. Never, which I found a little bit odd, but maybe he just wanted to keep all that to himself. He was a widower at the end of the day. Not my place to interfere in his personal affairs. If it affected his business I might have said, but if he wanted to spend two or three hours in there with that woman, that's his business. My job was to man the phones and organise his appointments and his work. I'm not here to deal with his private life.'

'I understand,' said Ross; 'there's no need to blame yourself.'

'Do you think that she was the one that did it then? Do you think she killed him down in Glasgow?'

'We don't know,' said Ross, 'but can you give me a better description of what she looked like?'

'No, I can't,' said Mrs Thompson. 'I really can't. She came in either with a headscarf on or a hood of some sort. She'd always have big sunglasses on, the kind you can't see through as well. As I say, it was blonde hair because I saw that straggling out the back of the hood at times, but outside of that, smallish lips, sort of a roundish nose, but very hard to tell you. Her ears I never saw.

'What about her height?' asked Ross. 'How tall was she?'

'Oh, maybe five feet seven, maybe five feet eight. I say that because I'm five feet seven and she was round about my height.'

'Anything else you can tell me about her?'

'Well, she wasn't married.'

'Why do you say that?' asked Ross.

'There was one time she came in and whatever had happened, she had got something on her hand. It was like jelly or something and she had to get it off the ring she was wearing but she came out to me still in sunglasses and the scarf, and she took the ring off to give it a wipe and clean it up. There was no mark underneath. Look.'

Mrs Thompson took her hand and put it in front of Ross. She removed her wedding ring and he stared down.

'You see the mark? Clearly, I wear a ring right there. When that Kerry Watson came in, there was nothing underneath, but I thought maybe she was trying to take him for a ride, look after his money, but then she was coming on with the marriage story, so I didn't know what she was after. He seemed to be enjoying himself; that's why I didn't interfere. That's why I didn't. You don't think I should have, do you?'

'No,' said Ross. 'You were being what you should've been, a good secretary. I'm very sorry for your loss. I'm going to have a sketch artist come along. I want you to try and remember as best you can what Mrs Watson looked like. I don't suppose there's any CCTV is there?'

'You can try the building. They might have some, but we don't have any access to that. There's none in the office. There's no way they would've got up to what they got up to with that in the office.'

'I guess not,' said Ross. 'Can I call anyone for you? You're obviously in quite a distressed state.'

'Let me call my husband,' she said. 'If you'd stay with me until he comes.'

It was half an hour later when Ross left the building. Mrs Thompson's husband had arrived as well as a sketch artist, and Ross left them to it. He picked up the phone calling Macleod but found him unavailable as he'd been pulled in with the DCI again. Clarissa Urquhart answered, however.

'From what you're telling me, this looks like the same person. I'll get hold of Hope.'

179

'The thing I don't get,' said Ross, 'is how do we get hold of this person, where they're at? We might have a face, but if it doesn't hold up on any records, how do we go after them? Where do we tail them to? Are we simply hanging around people until she comes to kill them because they know too much? Who's to say there won't be more occurrences on the ferries.'

'Well, they won't be happening for a while. They cancelled the ferries today.'

'That's not good,' said Ross. 'The boss is going to be angry at that one.'

'You better believe it. He's in his office next door on the phone. You should have heard him shout when they announced it.'

Chapter 22

What do you mean find me someone? I can't just find you someone. This is a murder investigation. You have to work your way through; we have to collect evidence. You don't just haul somebody out for it.'

Clarissa watched Macleod slam the phone down on his desk and then sit back in his chair. He was staring up at the ceiling, but his face was red with rage. Despite this, she marched up to the door, knocked it loudly, and opened it without waiting for a 'Come in.'

'Got information for you.'

'Good,' said Macleod, 'shut the door.' Clarissa turned round and closed the door behind her. 'See that man. Do you see that man? He's a . . . '

'Don't swear,' said Clarissa.

'I never swear. When have I ever sworn?'

'Well, don't start now,' said Clarissa, 'and calm down. We need to get on with this. You wouldn't let me blow my lid like that.'

Macleod went to react, but as per usual, she'd backed him into a corner. One in which he'd have to admit she was completely correct. Macleod just felt his fuse was being shortened every time he spoke to the new DCI. Generally, in his career, he'd got on well with superior officers, but this one—this one just drove him nuts.

He let out a sigh. 'Sit down,' he said. 'What have you got?'

'Just had Ross on the phone. Apparently, Dr Jacobs had a fancy woman coming in. They'd spend time in his office. He'd nip out every once in a while, go and get champagne and lunch and that; she had free access to all the files.'

'So, what does she look like?'

'Well, we got a sketch up, but the secretary said she never saw her face fully. The woman always arrived with a hood or a scarf on, glasses. It was all apparently because of her husband, but the secretary swears the woman didn't have a husband. Said there was a false ring on her finger. She'd seen underneath it and there wasn't any ring mark.'

'Would explain how she could get into his room,' said Macleod. 'The woman down in Glasgow, she was scarfed up with glasses. Do we know if they're the same glasses?'

'Unsure, but they seem to be similar. We got the sketch through from what the secretary had seen. We also got the sketch done from Dr Green. Trying to compile them together because they certainly look very alike. The boys are trying to make it into an image we can take round.

'Well, when we do, we'd probably want to get that down to Dr Stephens. See if she's seen anyone similar.'

'It's going to be hard though,' said Clarissa, 'to trace a face and a dress. Even if she does know her, will she know her well enough? How will she know her? Where will she know her from? There must be some other way of connecting in.'

Macleod sat back in his chair. 'A lot of these victims, they won a prize to go on the ferry. It looks like they were set up to be on the ferry. Now, we had our ferry worker who died as well. It's my guess that they were setting everything to look like some sort of ferry suicide or someone who'd have an issue with a ferry or some sort of angst because the ferries have just been cancelled. Maybe they were looking to push us in that direction.'

'When they got the prizes though, they had won them,' said Clarissa. 'If you got a letter through the post, you'd expect it to have some sort of address on it. If they contacted them by phone, they'd still need details. We're not quite sure how they all won. Are we?'

'But those that received it are dead,' said Macleod. 'Get on the phone, Clarissa. Phone back the partners of all the victims, those who received ferry tickets, see how they arrived. See if they spoke on the phone because we know some did, but the number it went to was an old number, but if you got a prize, it would have something on it, an initial response. See if any of them didn't contact by phone, maybe contacted in a different way—email, something else because they had to give details, didn't they? Give details so they could get the tickets. Get booked with the passenger details, cars.'

'Will do, Seoras,' said Clarissa, standing up. 'Are you okay to calm down now?'

'I'm just going to ring Hope,' he said. 'Put her in line with what's happened overnight. I think she needs to try and get her eye on Dr Stephens. She's the one doctor we've got remaining. She could very much be at risk.'

Clarissa went back to the main office, sat down, and picked up the phone. The first person she called was Marie Culshaw and asked about any correspondence that had been left behind. Andrew had picked them all up though. Andrew had done everything with the ferry; that's the way he was. She spent ten minutes rooting around the house, but there was nothing, no detail, so Clarissa thanked her and moved on to her next call. She placed a call in to Fred Martin's brother, and also to Constable Alan McNair but neither of them had any paperwork around how Fred had won his prize to go on the trip, so Clarissa decided to ring Gerald Lyndhurst.

'Hello, Detective. I did speak to you when you were down. It's been quite hard getting anything of Peter's, but I can see if I can get to his house. Have a look.'

'Was he orderly enough? Would he have kept them anyway?' asked Clarissa.

'I don't know, probably. He did like that. He did make sure he hung onto things.'

'Give me an hour.'

Clarissa twiddled her thumbs while Gerald Lyndhurst was presumably entering the house of Peter Hughes. He had a key but maybe the man was still unsure about going in. An hour later, Clarissa received a call back.

'Detective Sergeant, this is Gerald. I've been round to Peter's. Went through a lot of personal documentation and to be honest, it was quite difficult. I didn't actually find any of the tickets. I did find the initial letter, that he'd won the prize.'

'Have you got it with you?' asked Clarissa.

'Yes, I do. I don't see anything in particular. It has a phone number for him to call. I think that's how he did it.'

'Has it got anything more than a phone number? Anything you would say, like an address?'

The man scanned. 'It does say that you can send it to an address here . . . , well, it's not an address; it's a post office box.

'Can you let me know what it is?' Clarissa made a note of

the post office box. It says, 'It's Glasgow, the post office box,' said the man. 'I don't know if he wrote to that or not.'

'Regardless, that's very handy. Do you know how to scan documents?' asked Clarissa.

'Of course. Shall I send it up to you?'

'Please do,' she said and passed on the email address for Gerald Lyndhurst to send up a captured copy of the initial document. Five minutes later, Clarissa sat with it in front of her. It had clearly been done to look quite professional. It did, indeed, give the option of contacting via the post office box. The telephone number on it they had checked before, and it was a pay-as-you-go, untraceable, but the post office box wouldn't have been so easy. Hope picked up her telephone and called the Glasgow headquarters of the post office. It took her a moment to get through to the right person, but once she had, she inquired about who the post office box belonged to.

'Detective Sergeant, this is Greg here with the post office. Yes, I've looked up that post office box number for you and I've got an address, it's down in Glasgow.'

'When was it opened up?'

'Been there for about four years. I'm not sure how much correspondence comes through it, or who picks it up. I can get you through to some of the local workers. They might be able to tell you.'

'That's brilliant,' said Clarissa and she took down the address in the Bellshill area of Glasgow. 'I'll just patch you through,' said Greg. 'Just give me a minute.'

Clarissa hung on the call and could see Macleod looking out from his office towards her. She gave a wave with her hand and the Inspector made his way over to her desk. He was about to speak when Clarissa put her hand up, a single finger to her mouth indicating he should be quiet. She was aware that the other constables in the room who were helping them with the inquiry seemed to look sheepishly away, believing that this was not something you did to Macleod.

'Hello, this is Emily. Are you the detective?'

'Yes, I am,' said Clarissa, and gave the post office box number that she was inquiring about.

'Just give me a moment and I'll ask amongst the staff.' While Clarissa hung on the phone, she advised Macleod of what she was doing, and she could see the excitement rising within him.

'This is Emily again. I've spoken to a couple of our colleagues, and apparently, it's a woman that comes in for that. We know because she always wears big sunglasses, even in the height of winter and a big hood or a scarf on.

'What colour hair does she have?' asked Clarissa.

'Well, that's the thing. We were just saying that. The hair keeps changing. It can be blonde, it can be a brunette, sometimes it's red. Quite bizarre, really, isn't it?'

'Does she have a name?'

'Kerry Watson. I believe you've got the address that the post office box is linked to.'

'We do,' said Clarissa. 'If I send someone round, do you think your colleagues could describe them to them so we can make up a sort of a photofit picture?'

'Of course,' said Emily. 'Just ask for Emily at this office. I'll be aware of what's going on.'

Clarissa came off the phone and could see Macleod hovering over her desk.

'That address is a post office box on the bottom of the initial competition letter. Gerald Lyndhurst retrieved it from Peter Hughes's house. I've checked the Post Office box and it belongs to Kerry Watson. I think that's a false name, but there's an address attached to it.'

'I think it's time we get Hope round there. Where is it again?' Macleod looked at the address. 'Not the most salubrious area,' he said, remembering from his many years spent down in Glasgow. 'In fact, I think nowadays it's quite a run-down sort of place with lots of boarded-up houses.'

'Ideal then,' said Clarissa. 'If you wanted a false address or somewhere you didn't have people go very often. If you are you going to send Hope round, what do we do?' asked Clarissa.

'You're going to go and get that little sports car of yours,' said Macleod. 'We're going on a trip down to Glasgow.'

'You think it's wise to all go down there? She was just here recently.'

'Yes. There was a woman in here last night. She got scared off. She's not going to come back towards Dr Green at the moment. Too much heat around him. She'll head back to what else she needs to sort out. If she's realised we're onto Dr Green, and Dr Jacobs has just been killed, then we need to have a look at Dr Stephens. I think she's heading that way. We also might be able to catch her heading to that address for she could be down in Glasgow already. Besides, Ross can get back here. Won't take him long to get across from Aberdeen. He can hold the fort while you and I make our way down.'

'There's got to be some stronger connection though, hasn't there? What's tying it in? Why these three? Why going through people who are trying to help couples? Why were they focusing on the member of that couple who seemed to break everything up? There's a history going on here.'

'It's more than that. They've got to be able to use ketamine and use it properly. Maybe we need to start looking at it from the angle of the doctors and people who belong to them. Dr Jacobs didn't previously know the person that was coming to him so she couldn't have worked for him. Dr Green has offered nothing up, but I doubt he knew her before or he would would have said at the start of the liasions. Dr Stephens is the one that we don't know if she's been intimate with her. Therefore, she might be the one doctor that this person is connected to in a different way.'

'And this person will know that we'll have a description of her from Dr Green.'

'Exactly,' said Macleod, 'I'm banking on her going down for Stephens. Especially if the heat's on and we find her base.'

'Well, I'll get the car then,' said Clarissa. 'Make sure you bring your coat. Don't want you complaining about the hood being down again.'

Macleod shook his head and strode away. He was like a bloodhound. As soon as the scent hit his nose, he was off, the weariness of the night thrown away. Clarissa, on the other hand, was thinking about stocking up with coffee for the long drive south.

Chapter 23

After finishing her call with Macleod, Hope placed another call to Dr Stevens's surgery in an attempt to locate the woman. Her secretary announced that she was there and put her through.

'Detective Sergeant, what can I do for you?' asked Dr Stevens.

'I think you may be in danger,' said Hope. 'I don't know if you've realised or seen the news, but there was a murder last night in a hotel. Dr Jacobs, who we went to see, was killed in his hotel room by a female we're currently looking for. I've got some pictures and images I want you to have a look at.'

'Okay. I am pretty busy though. I think I'm booked up with consultations all day.'

'If you can make the time to have a look and give me a call if you think it's anyone significant.'

'So, what? You have a person you want me to look at?'

'A picture. We're trying to establish a picture of the person who killed Dr Jacobs. I want to know if you've seen this person before.'

'Okay. I'll try and take a look, but I'm just about to go in with a couple, for a couple of hours, then there'll be lunch. By the time I'm getting back from that, we'll see. Send it through to my secretary and I'll take a look though.'

Hope came off the phone call, believing that the woman wasn't taking her seriously enough. She'd have to go round after she'd visited the address acquired from the post office with regards to the PO box in Glasgow. Hope exited the Glasgow station and dropped by at the hotel just to see if there had been any more developments before departing for the Bellshill address.

The address took Hope into a street that looked almost deserted. Out of the twenty houses, she counted sixteen which were boarded up. One didn't have any boards and possibly it was a squat, for she could see some people inside with sleeping bags. The other three houses, of which one was a flat on top of another house, seemed to be occupied to some degree. She found out the flat was the address she was looking for and climbed the outside stairs up to the front door, banging it loudly. When no one answered, she pushed the door with a little force, finding that the lock slid off and the door opened.

Well, that's unusual, thought Hope. *I guess I better check there's no one inside in trouble.*

She stepped onto the carpet announcing that she was the police and was there anyone home, but there came no answer. She looked at a sofa with mould on it. It was damp, white spots running across the top of it. The whole room stank. Reaching down to the floor, Hope found a carpet that was also damp. She could see the walls had mould and the light fitting was gone.

Had people broken in? What was with that? Hope walked through the small hall to the front of the house to see a kitchen, again, smelling like nobody had been in it in a long time. There was a cracked plate in the sink. She tried the tap and found out the water didn't work. A flick of a switch filled the room with light, but the light bulb was hanging on its own with no cover.

She just used this as a drop, thought Hope, *just a random address, but if they sent it to her, she'd have to pick it up. She must have checked, whoever she is.*

Hope was glad she was wearing her boots, because she wasn't sure about the floor as she found a small bedroom at the rear. She almost vomited at the state of the bed. *Rat poo on that*, she thought, *and maybe even human excrement, and look at the state of the sheet, ripped and eaten.*

Hope saw a door with a padlock on it, at the far side of the room. She stepped back out into the main living room and tried to work out the angles to see how big the room the door led to would be. *Big enough for a small office*, thought Hope, *big enough to sit in quite easily, accommodate maybe computers, a couple of chairs, big enough to house something.*

Hope reached inside her jacket and dug out a few skeleton keys. The lock didn't seem to be particularly advanced, and she easily opened the lock, taking it off, and then opening the door. Inside was dark and Hope took out her pen torch, skimming around the inside of the room. She was right. The room was approximately three feet square and had a computer, a printer, and a number of boards on the walls with lots of pictures.

Hope flashed the light up and saw the face of Fred Martin. One of his wife as well. She could see Dr Jacobs with his wife. Marie Culshaw's face appeared, tagged in to Andrew's, and above it was Daphne Walsh. Hope scanned again and saw Gerald Lyndhurst, Paul Hughes beside him, and up above was Jenny Trimble. Many of the figures had an X on them, including that of Dr Jacobs.

Hope reached into her jacket, took out some gloves, keen not to contaminate the scene. She looked up above her with her light and saw a single bulb hanging, and then flicked her own light around the small room, trying to find a switch. A thought occurred to her. Hope stepped outside into the bedroom and flicked on the switch at the side of the room. The bedroom light didn't come on but the light inside the small room with the pictures did.

Clever girl, thought Hope. *Bypassed, made this look like a real dump. She's worked hard at this. Clearly, whoever it was, lived somewhere else, but this is where she planned things from. This is where she operated from and what a place. A house nobody would look through twice stuck on a street that was practically abandoned.* Hope placed a call to Macleod.

'Good work,' said Macleod. 'Get a forensic team down. Check it through. Can you see anything of note, anywhere else we know she could be going? Anything that refers to her home address or even who she is?'

'Not so far, Seoras. I haven't looked through everything, but there's photocopied images here of doctors' notes. Whole histories of the people that have died. There was also a red ring around faces. Usually, those to be killed. You can see from here how she set the whole thing up.'

'Is there anything that tells us who she is?' asked Macleod.

'Nothing,' said Hope, 'nothing. I'm willing to bet even when she used here, she put gloves on, wrapped her hair up, made sure she didn't leave too much of a trace. Even if you picked any DNA up, you wonder if she's even on any database. It's a sloppy piece of work, the post office box. I guess she thought we would come and look at this and think, 'No'. There was excrement on the bed. Everything to make you walk back out of this house. Part of me thinks it was planted,' said Hope.

'Well, we're on our way,' said Macleod. 'I'm with Clarissa, so we won't be long,'

Hope gave a little chuckle. 'Good, Seoras. Because I'm worried. I'm worried if she's actually succeeded in doing everything she wanted to do, or is there more?'

'What do you mean?' asked Macleod.

'Well, she rang Dr Jacobs here and I'm wondering are there any other figures? I'll keep searching and get back to you.'

Hope hung up the call and continued to look through the items. There was much paperwork, lots of photographs, and Hope worked tirelessly to go through them. At the bottom of the pile, she found a photograph of what looked like a younger Dr Stevens, maybe from ten years ago. She swallowed hard as she saw a ring around the doctor's face. Hope took a photograph of it, and she heard the forensic team arriving outside.

Stepping out of the flat in order to take a breath of fresh air, Hope called the local Glasgow station, asking that they put a plainclothes officer outside Dr Stevens's office and keep an eye on her, especially for any women fitting the picture that she was sending to them. The picture was that of the composite that had been produced up in Inverness from the various images of the woman with sunglasses.

Hope then showed the forensic team around and slowly, they began to bag everything up. It was well after lunch by the time Hope had finished searching through all the items, aware now that Dr Stevens was a possible target. She'd also seen Dr Green in an image with his face ringed. Clearly, Clarissa had done the right thing. Hope called Macleod back.

'She's definitely lined up the doctor, Seoras. I realise that now, I put a plainclothes policeman outside her office to look especially for any women that came in matching a height of five feet seven. I'm going to go round and find the doctor myself, have a word, and see if she knows of anyone who would have anything against her. More specifically, to find out if she's got a female lover. After all, that's the way this killer moved in on the other doctors.'

'Good idea,' said Macleod. 'Clarissa is breaking who knows how many speed limits; we'll be with you very shortly, but we'll route to the office as well. I want to speak to her too. If she realises she's being guarded, our killer might just cut and run.'

'Okay, Seoras. I'll play it cool. I'll just pop round. Just see if we still got the plainclothes person there.'

Hope thanked the forensic team and left them working. Getting back into her car, she drove round to Dr Stevens's practice. It was now close to three o'clock, and as Hope strode up the steps to enter the practice, she could see a man standing in the far corner. She walked over to him directly, making him rather agitated until she said, 'Detective Sergeant Hope McGrath, I placed you here. Anything to report?'

'No. The doctor was in earlier on, I'm still right here. She hasn't come out at all.'

'Okay,' said Hope, 'I'm going to go in and talk to her. Stick around in case I need you.'

The man nodded and Hope made her way into the practice approaching Dr Stevens's secretary who recognised her.

'You're too late,' she said, 'she's gone. She was a bit bothered though. I did tell her she should call you.'

'Call me? Why?'

'There's a man outside. He's been there most of the day. She was agitated about him, so she opened up one of the rear windows and went out that way.'

'How long ago did she disappear?'

'Twenty minutes. She was heading for an early dinner in a café close to here. She was going to walk round.'

'Do you have that address?' asked Hope.

'Why? Is she in trouble?'

For a moment, Hope thought about giving out too much information, but then she thought, *what the heck?* 'Yes, she's in trouble. I need to ascertain her whereabouts and get close to her as soon as possible.'

'I'll just dig up the reservation for you. Hang on.' The woman disappeared into her computer before scribbling down an address and handing it over to Hope. 'That's it. That's where she was meeting. It's like a café that serves quite decent, quality food. It's a bit posh.'

'Do you know if she was meeting anyone?'

'Yes. She said she was, but she didn't tell me who it was, just that she'd be heading off at this time for dinner.'

Hope thanked the woman for the address, turned and marched out of the centre and found the plainclothes officer approaching her shoulder. 'Do you want me to stay in case she leaves?' he asked.

'No point. She left over twenty minutes ago. Just go back to the station.'

Hope saw a look of bemusement on the man's face, but she issued the instruction again, and he walked away. Hope jumped into her car, looked up her mapping system, and input the address of the café. It was a couple of minutes' drive and she placed a call to Macleod. She could hear the rush of the wind and Clarissa must have been driving with the top down, and she could also hear noise of traffic.

'She's gone, Seoras. Dr Stevens has gone out. She's gone to have her meal and is meeting somebody, but we don't know who. I'm on my way there. It'll only take me a couple of minutes. You need to route to this address.' Hope rhymed off where she was going. Hope could hear a simple 'understood' from Macleod, who then shouted at Clarissa to drive hard. For once, there was no comeback from the woman and the call closed down. Hope turned her engine on, spun the wheel, and drove right into the traffic, racing along a number of streets to her destination.

Her mind raced. *Will Dr Stevens still be there? The killer has got to her first. Why hasn't she stayed in her office? I had her protected. I had her safe. Does the woman not realise the issues that were going on here? People have died.* But there was nothing she could do about that now. Hope simply kept the accelerator pressed and swerved in and out of traffic as she raced to her destination.

Chapter 24

Hope raced through Glasgow before parking up the car a short distance from the café she'd been advised of by Dr Stephens's secretary. Her eyes scanned the street, looking for anyone untoward outside of the café but she could see no one, so continued to walk at pace to a small set of steps that led up into the dining area. As she entered, a woman dressed smartly in black trousers and a waistcoat stopped her, asking if she required a table. Hope didn't look at her. Instead, she surveyed the room, while taking her credentials out from inside her leather jacket and holding them up in front of the woman.

'I'm here to see Dr Stephens. She's booked a table with someone. I'm not sure if it's in her name or the other person's name. The other person I don't know.'

'Well, there's no Dr Stephens dining here. Can you see her in the room?'

'Yes, I can. I'll just go directly to her if that's okay with you? She's at a table over there.'

'Is there anything else I can assist you with?' asked the woman.

'Actually, who booked the table? The one that Dr Stephens

is sitting at.'

'That would be in the name of Steele. I'm not quite sure if it's a man or a woman, but in the name of Steele.'

'Thank you,' said Hope and walked across the dining area between tables, keeping an eye out for anyone sitting at them. It was only after three in the afternoon, so it was a quiet time, and there were only four other people in the restaurant. There was a young couple who seemed deeply engrossed in each other, while an older couple were sitting looking at their mobile phones. Hope put her hand up, waving over at Dr Stephens who raised her head up from a mineral water she was drinking and smiled.

'Why did you leave?' asked Hope. 'You were safe at work; we were keeping an eye on you there. I put a man out the front.'

'Yes, there was a guy standing there the whole time. Kept watching, looking over everything. I thought it might have been the person coming after me, so I left.'

'But you should have called,' said Hope, 'if you thought that, you could have checked with me. You could have said, 'I've got somebody dodgy out here,' and we would have sent someone round, or in that case, I'd have said to you, 'That's our man.''

'Oh, I'm sorry. I didn't want to bother you, in case it was a wild goose chase, which obviously it turns out it was. I just slipped out the back, came out to here. It's only my secretary who knows I'm coming here.'

'And the person you're coming to meet,' said Hope, 'they're aware as well.'

'Yes, actually it was a call out of the blue, a bit of a surprise. Alice Steele used to work for me. God love her, she was a poor critter. Felt a lot for her. Anyway, she sounded quite upset so I thought I'd best go and speak to her.'

'When was the last time you saw her?'

'Oh, four years ago,' said Dr Stephens, 'or is it five? She used to work for me as my secretary before we got Janine, the new one. Alice, she was a good secretary, but she had a lot of problems in life. God love her, she struggled. I was kind of hoping when I see her that she might have gone on a bit, moved on.'

'Is that all she was, though? Just your secretary?'

'Well, I did help her a bit with her husband. She was a poor critter. I don't even know why she wanted him; there were rumours that he ran off, I heard a couple of years ago. It doesn't surprise me. They never seemed to get on properly. I shouldn't say anymore, you know, patient confidentiality and all that. She still is alive after all. It's not like I'm telling you something about somebody who's dead.'

'What time are you to meet her?' asked Hope.

'Any time now.'

'Good,' said Hope, 'I've been up all night. I'm actually quite hungry. I'll sit here with you if you don't mind.'

'Aren't you meant to be sort of plainclothes looking after me? Not get in the way of people's life?'

'We tried that, didn't we?' said Hope. 'You walked out the back door, or the back window to be precise. If you're going to be that slippery a customer, I'm going to eat with you.' Hope raised her hand and waved at the maître d, who disappeared off to get a second mineral water.

'Tell me more about Alice Steele,' said Hope. 'What did she do before she became your secretary? Was she in the medical profession? I heard a lot of secretaries in your work start off in medical professions before they change roles.'

'That is true. We do sometimes get ex-nurses. People who

trained up and didn't feel it was for them but still wanted or needed to get a job. Quite often the medical background can help if you're operating as a secretary.'

'Was that the case with Alice?'

'She wasn't a medical nurse. I believe she was actually in the military. That's right. She never actually qualified, was a trainee military nurse. I could never work out whether it was her husband, or if it was actually the military that she couldn't hack. You'd have thought if it was her husband she would have stayed in, but maybe it was because he was quite abusive with her, told her what she should do. Like I say, I heard he disappeared, possibly ran off with another woman.'

'Did she say why she wanted to meet you now?'

'No, not at all.'

'As your secretary,' asked Hope, 'would Alice have had any access to your records?'

'Almost all. She'd have filed doctor's notes, everything. Much the same as Janine does now. You have to trust these people; it's part and parcel of it. They work with you, they don't make comment, they don't pass out anything about anyone else.'

'Would they be able to access what's in your office now?'

'Well, Janine would of course. She has the keys to access all the locked-up material; that's because I need her to. I need her sometimes to go and get files for me. Sometimes if I'm away, she runs the office. She needs to pull out confidential information.'

'You mean like addresses, histories, things like that?'

'Totally.'

'Did Alice have access to that?' asked Hope.

'Completely. Just the same as Janine.'

'And did she have a set of keys?'

'There are two set of keys, Janine has one, and I have the original set. Prior to Janine having hers, Alice had them before she handed them to Janine.'

'You didn't feel that you needed to change the locks or anything?'

'Why? These are medical professionals. I trusted Alice for all those years. She then handed her keys in. Why would I be worried about her?'

Hope could see the picture emerging.

'This address,' said Hope, pushing a piece of paper in front of her with the address of the flat that she'd come from earlier on it, 'do you recognise it?'

'Bellshill,' said Dr Stephens, 'that's where Alice used to live. Yes. That's the old house, I think. It was a flat, wasn't it? A type of flat. Got a bit rougher now.'

'I've just come from that flat. I've just tied that flat to the recent murders we've been having.'

Dr Stephens looked up, shock spreading across her face. 'You think somebody's got to Alice? You don't think that they've got information from her?'

'No,' said Hope. 'I don't think anybody's got to Alice. I think Alice has got to a lot of other people but by the sounds of it, she was coming here to meet you. Dr Jacobs is dead. She went for Dr Green as well in Inverness, but my colleague turned up; otherwise, he'd be dead. I think she's coming for you now. Get your coat, Dr Stephens; we're not staying.'

Stephens looked agitated, but she turned around, grabbed her handbag, and pulled her jacket on before putting her handbag over her shoulder. Hope looked round and saw the maître d' bringing a woman towards her. *Approximate height,* thought Hope, *five feet seven. The hair. There's no hair, no long hair.* In fact, the woman was wearing a small beanie hat.

'That,' said Dr Stephens, 'is Alice,' over Hope's shoulder.

'Are you sure? What colour hair does she have?'

'She's got alopecia. She lost her hair quite a while ago, one of the problems with her husband, I believe—so unfair on her.'

Hope stepped across the room to meet Alice head-on, but the woman had her hand in her pocket of a jacket and lifted the jacket up pointing it towards Hope.

'That wasn't you in Inverness, was it?' said the woman, her voice was gravelly, almost husky.

'But it was you, wasn't it?' said Hope. 'Sunglasses, wigs, one minute you're blonde, then you're brunette, then red, whatever you want to be.'

'Well, I didn't get any of my own, or I did and then it disappeared. Go sit down, whoever you are. I need to talk to Dr Stephens.'

Hope edged backwards slowly into her seat as the woman came and stood a few feet away, her jacket lifted out in front of her, and Hope could see where a gun was pointed from inside the pocket at Dr Stephens.

'Alice, what is this? I thought you'd got on with things. I thought you'd changed.'

'Changed? Me? I didn't get the chance to change, did I? I came to you when I was in trouble. Could you help me? No.'

'I tried, but if the other side isn't willing . . . , and then I heard he ran off.'

'He didn't run anywhere, I just got wise to it. I just got to the point where I decided that I was having no more of it. He's gone now; he's not coming back.'

'But what are you doing? Why are you doing this? Why me?'

'Well, I was going to close off the loop. I had to move quick. You see, they started to find things out. I went wrong somewhere and suddenly there was heat everywhere. I took out Jacobs and almost Green. It was easy to get out of them all about the people they looked after. I remembered you talking about them. Oh yeah, that day at the conference, how great you guys were. How you'll solve all these issues. You solved nothing.

'You didn't solve anything for Marie Culshaw. You didn't solve anything for Una Martin—she died, committed suicide. You didn't solve anything for the Walsh man either; he suffered. That Jenny Trimble, she was playing around, same as my man, nobody stopped that. Nobody got them to turn around. I realised they're just bad eggs. Meanwhile, you people, you're just making money off us. Making money off the ones that suffer but I was able to get the real picture from their information, able to find out who was at fault, go and sort it for them, before you took away any more money.'

'And now you're closing off the loop,' said Hope. 'There's no point. You'd be better running now. Better just get out of here.'

'You can shut up. I didn't ask for your opinion. I could shoot you first. Maybe I'll have to. Stand up.'

Hope got to her feet slowly. 'Now turn around.' With her hands in the air, Hope turned. There was a hard blow across the back of her head, and she tumbled forward, hitting a chair before spinning; then everything was dark.

* * *

Clarissa Urquhart pulled the car in to a small space just down from their destination. Hope had told them where the café was and Macleod was out of the car before Clarissa had even finished switching off the engine. Macleod ran along the street, Clarissa fighting to keep up with him. Then she watched him stop dead, an arm put out.

'Easy,' he said, 'look. Look in the window.'

Clarissa looked past Macleod and could see Dr Stephens with someone behind her.

'There's a gun in that pocket,' said Macleod. 'Look at the way it's shaped. Where's Hope, where the heck's McGrath gone?'

'Stay cool, Seoras. If that's a gun, we don't want to be getting in front of it.'

'If that's a gun, and she takes her away from here, the woman's dead,' said Macleod. 'Who knows what she's done with Hope? I'm going to go in the front door.'

'Don't be an idiot. What's that going to achieve?'

'I'll talk her down. I'll talk her down and I want you to go around the back just in case she cuts loose.'

'Like the blazes, I'm coming up there with you.'

'I gave you an order, Sergeant. You do what I've just said.'

'Don't put yourself in line of fire like this. We'll call for backup.'

'She's coming out the door, there's no time. Stephens will be dead if she gets out of here.'

Clarissa looked at Macleod, and could see that he made his mind up on what he was going to do. She turned and tried to half sprint around the end of the street corner into an alley at the back. She was no runner, and she thought she could lurk at the back door in case the woman came out that way. As she made her way along the backstreet and into the rear of the kitchen, Clarissa wondered if that would be enough. Macleod was placing himself out front, putting himself into danger.

She entered a kitchen that had a lot of staff at the door, the main thoroughfare leading through to the dining room. Clarissa approached them.

'Kindly step back. I know your eyes are fixed on what's going on in there, but I'm Detective Sergeant Clarissa Urquhart, and I need to get through.'

A chef turned at her, looked at her bizarrely before turning back. She put a hand on his shoulder, 'Move,' she said, 'do it quietly. Slowly.' The kitchen staff retreated from the door as Clarissa reached it, pushing it forward, carefully stepping inside the dining room. Clarissa could see that the gun was now out of the woman's pocket and being held up to the rear of the head of Dr Stephens. Macleod was speaking, but he was doing it quietly, and Clarissa could barely hear. She cast a glance to her right and saw Hope McGrath on the ground, a pool of blood coming from the back of her head.

Clarissa wondered what to do. She crouched down as best as she could, slowly creeping her way forward through the dining room. Macleod had crept his way in, closing the door of the restaurant behind him and was standing in front of the large glass windows which he and Clarissa had looked in through just a few minutes before. She watched as the woman pressed the back of Dr Stephens, forcing her to step forward toward Macleod. The conversation seemed to be getting more heated, even if it was quiet and then Clarissa saw Macleod step in front of Stephens.

'No, you won't,' he said loudly. 'Don't do it.'

'I've killed enough already; what's another one or two going to matter?'

The woman's left hand moved towards the weapon and

Clarissa didn't stop to think, she sprang forward, running as hard as she could, shouting at the woman. The gun turned around, facing Clarissa now, but she put her shoulder down in something reminiscent of a rugby tackle. Without thought, she threw her left shoulder into the woman's abdomen, taking her off her feet and together they hit the window with enough force that it shattered.

Clarissa fell, tumbling over, her back hitting something on the ground, arms flailing out. Her wrist hit something solid as she cried out in pain. Clarissa found herself looking up at the sky, and she turned her head to see where the gunwoman had fallen. An arm shot across, grabbing Clarissa by the throat, and she began to choke, but there was a cry from above her and a foot stomped down hard on the woman's arm, causing her to release the chokehold she had.

Clarissa looked into the face of Macleod, but he was all concentration, pulling the woman's arms behind her, slapping cuffs on her and making sure that the gun was well out of the way. He kept one knee on the woman's back, looking down at Clarissa.

'Are you okay? Are you all right?'

Clarissa tried to get up, but the whole of her body ached. 'No,' said Clarissa, 'I'm not okay. The last time I went through a window, I was twenty-three.'

Macleod looked down at her. 'Twenty-three? What were you doing, woman?' he asked.

'Alcohol, Seoras. Bad days, trust me. Bad days.'

Chapter 25

'Are you sure she's all right?'

'Stop fussing, Seoras. I'm fine. It's just a little out of sync.'

'It's not a little out of sync. They said you tore something in your shoulder. It's torn. It's not out of sync. It needs assistance; it needs to be looked at. You need to be looked after.'

'If you don't shut up, I'll kick you through a window,' said Clarissa and gave Macleod a hard stare.

'I'm responsible for your welfare. You were injured on duty. We'll get you in the car and take you back up to Inverness, but you're on several weeks' rest and recuperation. What were you thinking going through that window anyway?'

'Well, thanks. She pointed a gun at you. She was going to kill you. What do you mean what was I thinking?'

'You took her out the window. You could've just grabbed her arm, put the gun up into the air. I could've run to assist.'

'Hope,' said Clarissa, 'take him away. Get him out of this room or I'm going to throttle him.'

Hope McGrath stepped into the fray with a wry smile on her face. 'Sir,' she said, trying to appease Macleod, 'I believe Ross wants you on the phone outside.'

'He's on the line?' asked Macleod.

'No. He was calling, though. I think he wants you to speak to him.'

'What about?'

'Something to do with the investigation,' said Hope. Macleod looked quizzical but made his way out of the small room in the Glasgow Medical Centre.

'Ross doesn't want anything, does he?' said Clarissa.

'Nope, but I hope he plays it. Why didn't you just tell him?'

'Tell him what?'

'Macleod, tell him why you took her through the window. You acted on impulse. It was him. You went to save him.'

'Yes,' said Clarissa, 'I did, and look at me. Look at me, the daft bird. Torn this, torn that. I'm not going to be able to drive. You realise that, don't you?'

'Yes. The streets of Inverness will be safer for a while at least.'

'How are you doing, anyway?' asked Clarissa.

'Bump on the head. A pretty big bump on the head, but a bump in the head. It was a bit of a bleeder. They put some stitches in, but I'm fine. A week's time and I'll not even know it's there.'

'Good,' said Clarissa. 'The woman was scary, wasn't she?'

'I wouldn't have said she was scary,' said Hope. 'She was someone who just had everything stacked up against her. It seems that after being kicked out from her role as a military nurse, she became a secretary but then her father divorced from her mother. He was abusive to her mother, and Alice saw most of it. It was a bad divorce that had left her mom penniless. Alice managed to come out of that, became a secretary, and then got married. She was then cheated on. They say he ran off, or at least, that's what Dr Stevens said.'

'What do you mean that's what she says? Doesn't anybody know?'

'Yes, Sergeant Urquhart,' interrupted Macleod, 'Alice said she killed him.'

Hope looked around the white walls of the room as if anything would be preferable to Macleod's face. He'd been listening.

'I think you got the wrong end of the stick, Hope. Ross didn't seem to know what you were talking about. Banging your head must have been worse than we thought.'

'Indeed,' said Hope, 'Clarissa was just asking about Alice's husband. At least, Dr Stevens said that Alice's husband, Alan, seemed to be of a slightly different vein.'

'Once we took her in, Sergeant, she told us. He's underneath the floorboards of the Bellshill flat. There were so many other things in there that stank, it didn't really make much difference. It's been a day or two of quite disturbing interviews,' said Macleod. 'I feel for the woman. She had it rough. Her husband was running around on her, her father had left them, her mother had ended up destitute, and she just snapped because those people that were meant to put the world right, the Dr Stevenses, Dr Jacobses, and the Dr Greens of this world, they didn't. Charged a fortune for it. She saw it all too often.'

'But they do sort some things out, don't they?' said Clarissa.

'Of course, they do,' said Macleod, 'but not from where she was standing. Not her situation. She lost it, but she decided other people should lose it for that. She wasn't daft. She was going to set up a cover. It would be suicides. People killing themselves off the ferries. Her ploy was good, except we recovered some bodies and we got them quickly. If we hadn't been able to realise it was Ketamine in the system, find the needle marks, we wouldn't have suspected anything. We'd have gone along with a strange state of suicides.

'Just people seeing a way out after other people have done it. After all, all those that died had plenty of black marks on their copybook, didn't they? Cheating, forcing other people to do things. That's why she went after them. You can easily see the guilty, but we got her, at the end of the day. We managed to find out. The hardest part of it was, after all of this, getting a "Well done" from the DCI. Said it was brilliant the way I've spoken to him the whole way through, kept him in the loop.'

Hope stared at Macleod, 'You didn't?'

'I did.'

Clarissa looked across, 'Did what?'

'I told him what I thought of him. I told him how badly he played this.'

'How did he take that?' asked Hope.

'Well,' said Macleod, 'have you been wanting to become a Detective Inspector because there might be an opening coming up?'

'How come?'

'Well, he basically said he was there to stay. I would have to like or lump it. Either that or get out of the station.'

'You'll see him gone,' said Hope, 'of course, you will.' She tapped Macleod on the shoulder, but she could see he was thinking.

As Hope left the room, Clarissa kept studying Macleod's face. 'Don't go because of somebody else,' she said; 'never go because of somebody else. You don't let them chase you out. You walk out on your own terms when you're ready.'

'Well, thank you for that advice,' said Macleod, 'but next time, if I need it, I will ask.

'You don't have to ask,' said Clarissa; 'it's always free as well from me.' She was sitting on a chair, and she watched as Macleod came over closer to her.

'Look,' he said, 'I just wanted to say.' Clarissa looked up and saw the man's face moving towards her. He reached up with his hand, touched the side of her head, and placed a kiss on her forehead. 'That was reckless, way too reckless, but thank you.'

'You mean a lot to me, Seoras. You mean a lot to the team.'

'And a lot to me,' he said, 'but next time, just let me deal with it. I don't put you at risk like that.'

'Then next time, don't put me out there.' She watched him smile at her.

'I did wonder when you came on board, was I doing the right thing? I think, so far, it's been a good idea.'

When he turned away, she reached to give him a slap on the back. It connected with next to no force and she grimaced.

'Just get me out of this darn room,' she said, 'I've been sat here, pushed, and prodded to be told that I don't feel great. I knew that. I knew I needed rest, so let's get going.'

'I thought I would run your car up to Inverness. You could travel with Hope, in hers.'

'You're not driving my car up. There's no way. You take Hope's car and I'll drive up with Hope.'

'You can't drive,' said Macleod. 'Doctor said, "No driving." Hope's not familiar with your car anyway. I'm more used to it. After all, you've raced me up around here, there, and everywhere recently. Better if I drive it. I've seen how you handle it. Probably best if we show you how to take care of a car.'

Macleod was out through the door before Clarissa could

reach him. She winced in pain, and she stretched for him but she shouldn't have. Racing through the room, she saw Hope look at her.

'He's taking my car. He's going to drive me to bloody Inverness.'

'What's wrong with that?' asked Hope.

'We'll be hours. Have you seen him drive?'

'He said you needed to learn the speed limit,' said Hope and laughed as she saw Clarissa in agony, running out of the hospital after Macleod, but as she saw them both go, Hope felt a shiver. They'd been lucky. She'd been lucky. All she wanted to do now was jump in the car and head home. John would be waiting, and she thanked whoever was out there, whoever helped look after her in this life, that at least her relationship was good. She'd seen enough bad ones to last her a lifetime.

Read on to discover the Patrick
Smythe series!

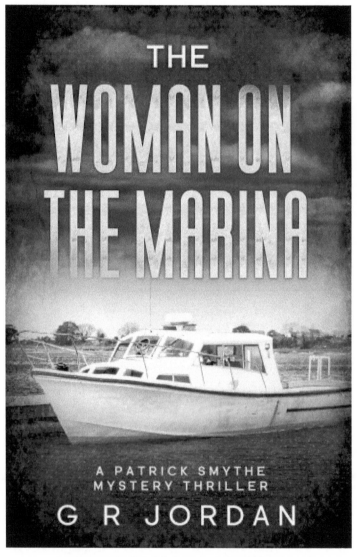

THE WOMAN ON THE MARINA

A PATRICK SMYTHE MYSTERY THRILLER

G R JORDAN

Start your Patrick Smythe journey here!

Patrick Smythe is a former Northern Irish policeman who

after suffering an amputation after a bomb blast, takes to the sea between the west coast of Scotland and his homeland to ply his trade as a private investigator. Join Paddy as he tries to work to his own ethics while knowing how to bend the rules he once enforced. Working from his beloved motorboat 'Craigantlet', Paddy decides to rescue a drug mule in this short story from the pen of G R Jordan.

Join G R Jordan's monthly newsletter about forthcoming releases and special writings for his tribe of avid readers and then receive your free Patrick Smythe short story.

Go to https://bit.ly/PatrickSmythe for your Patrick Smythe journey to start!

About the Author

GR Jordan is a self-published author who finally decided at forty that in order to have an enjoyable lifestyle, his creative beast within would have to be unleashed. His books mirror that conflict in life where acts of decency contend with self-promotion, goodness stares in horror at evil, and kindness blindsides us when we at our worst. Corrupting our world with his parade of wondrous and horrific characters, he highlights everyday tensions with fresh eyes whilst taking his methodical, intelligent mainstays on a roller-coaster ride of dilemmas, all the while suffering the banter of their provocative sidekicks.

A graduate of Loughborough University where he masqueraded as a chemical engineer but ultimately played American football, Gary had worked at changing the shape of cereal flakes and pulled a pallet truck for a living. Watching vegetables freeze at -40'C was another career highlight and he was also one of the Scottish Highlands "blind" air traffic controllers.

These days he has graduated to answering a telephone to people in trouble before telephoning other people to sort it out.

Having flirted with most places in the UK, he is now based in the Isle of Lewis in Scotland where his free time is spent between raising a young family with his wife, writing, figuring out how to work a loom and caring for a small flock of chickens. Luckily, his writing is influenced by his varied work and life experience as the chickens have not been the poetical inspiration he had hoped for!

You can connect with me on:
- https://grjordan.com
- https://facebook.com/carpetlessleprechaun

Subscribe to my newsletter:
- https://bit.ly/PatrickSmythe

Also by G R Jordan

G R Jordan writes across multiple genres including crime, dark and action adventure fantasy, feel good fantasy, mystery thriller and horror fantasy. Below is a selection of his work. Whilst all books are available across online stores, signed copies are available at his personal shop.

Anti-social Behaviour (A Highlands & Islands Detective Thriller #20)
https://grjordan.com/product/antisocial-behaviour
A youth is found dead at a children's playpark. A stolen car burnt out with the joyriders inside. Can Macleod discover the avenging angel brutally restoring the highland's peace and quiet?

When a spate of deaths indicating teenagers as targets sends Macleod and McGrath into a very public hunt for killer, they must walk in view of the hottest debate of the day. But when Hope believes she sees an angle that points the blame at those who responsible for the nation's safety, Macleod must trust his Sergeant's instincts while dodging a career ending bullet.

It was all easier back in the day, or was it?

 **The Man Everyone Wanted (A Kirsten Stewart Thriller #7)**
https://grjordan.com/product/the-man-everyone-wanted
A foreign agent goes rogue on Scottish soil. A city centre bloodbath shows the stakes at play. Can Kirsten secure the agent amidst a plethora of deadly friends and enemies?

When a shootout in the centre of Inverness ends in a mass of foreign bodies, Anna Hunt tasks recently recovered Kirsten Stewart with finding out why? When the trail leads to an agent who holds the key to a country's invasion, Kirsten must tread between friend and foe to bring the plans to light and stop a war. Will Kirsten prevail and avoid a myriad of friendly fire in the process?

You can always take a bullet for anyone's agenda!

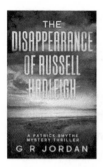

The Disappearance of Russell Hadleigh (Patrick Smythe Book 1)
https://grjordan.com/product/the-disappearance-of-russell-hadleigh

A retired judge fails to meet his golf partner. His wife calls for help while running a fantasy play ring. When Russians start co-opting into a fairly-traded clothing brand, can Paddy untangle the strands before the bodies start littering the golf course?

In his first full novel, Patrick Smythe, the single-armed former policeman, must infiltrate the golfing social scene to discover the fate of his client's husband. Assisted by a young starlet of the greens, Paddy tries to understand just who bears a grudge and who likes to play in the rough, culminating in a high stakes showdown where lives are hanging by the reaction of a moment. If you love pacey action, suspicious motives and devious characters, then Paddy Smythe operates amongst your kind of people.

Love is a matter of taste but money always demands more of its suitor.

Surface Tensions (Island Adventures Book 1)
https://grjordan.com/product/surface-tensions
Mermaids sighted near a Scottish island. A town exploding in anger and distrust. And Donald's got to get the sexiest fish in town, back in the water.

"Surface Tensions" is the first story in a series of Island adventures from the pen of G R Jordan. If you love comic moments, cosy adventures and light fantasy action, then you'll love these tales with a twist. Get the book that amazon readers said, "perfectly captures life in the Scottish Hebrides" and that explores "human nature at its best and worst".

Something's stirring the water!

Corpse Reviver (A Contessa Munroe Mystery #1)

https://grjordan.com/product/corspe-reviver

A widowed Contessa flees to the northern waters in search of adventure. An entrepreneur dies on an ice pack excursion. But when the victim starts moonlighting from his locked cabin, can the Contessa uncover the true mystery of his death?

Catriona Cullodena Munroe, widow of the late Count de Los Palermo, has fled the family home, avoiding the scramble for title and land. As she searches for the life she always wanted, the Contessa, in the company of the autistic and rejected Tiff, must solve the mystery of a man who just won't let his business go.

Corpse Reviver is the first murder mystery involving the formidable and sometimes downright rude lady of leisure and her straight talking niece. Bonded by blood, and thrown together by fate, join this pair of thrill seekers as they realise that flirting with danger brings a price to pay.

Lightning Source UK Ltd.
Milton Keynes UK
UKHW010726170622
404574UK00001B/172

9 781914 073939

When God Laughs

Steve Hawkins

When God Laughs

Onwards and Upwards Publishers
Berkeley House, 11 Nightingale Crescent, Leatherhead,
Surrey, KT24 6PD.
www.onwardsandupwards.org

Printed in the UK by 4edge Limited.

ISBN: 978-1-910197-64-6
Typeface: Sabon LT
Graphic design: LM Graphic Design

About the Author

Steve Hawkins teaches English as a Second Language in London and is part of the New Zion Christian Fellowship family in Welwyn Garden City.

Having served the body of Christ for some time, he came to see that he was bound by degrees of legalism, through a visit to Toronto Airport Christian Fellowship. Here he was strongly impacted by the Father's love and now longs to see others enjoy genuine freedom in Jesus Christ.

Previously employed in both the catering and financial services industries, he now teaches students from all over the world in a large college.

The author of 'From Legal to Regal', 'Blood and Glory', 'The Unbroken Cord: Celebrating Kingdom Sexuality', 'The Pointing Finger' and 'Heaven's Gold', he ministers today with a growing prophetic edge in leading worship, preaching and teaching.

The author can be contacted at:
steve.hawkins@cheerful.com

Steve longs to see those in the Body of Christ live in the freedom that Jesus has bought on the Cross. If you would like him to speak or minister at an event, please contact him.

When God Laughs

I dedicate this book to those believers who have falsely believed that the Father was scowling at them in disapproval. On the contrary, He revels in revealing His delight in us.

When God Laughs

Contents

The Lord your God is in your
midst, a victorious warrior. He will
exult over you with joy, He will be
quiet in His love, He will rejoice
over you with shouts of joy.

Zephaniah 3:17

Foreword by Stephan Krueger

When I first met Steve in Toronto at a month-long Leaders' School of Ministry, I knew that he was longing for the real thing. His hunger for the presence of God and his desire to allow God to bring change to his heart were apparent. The insights and encounters that flow out of his pursuit of God, together with his British sense of humour, build the foundation for this highly readable and insightful book.

The Bible tells us in Psalm 16:11 that there is "fullness of joy" in God's presence. God is in a good mood; He is not angry with us or with the world. In his love for us He gets involved in our lives, drawing us into an everlasting dance with Himself, the Godhead. In His presence we come to rest as we find ourselves in the one who created us in His own image.

I remember a time when, while leading a group of former School of Ministry students, I encountered Jesus in a very special way. As we engaged in worship one evening, I entered into a vision and saw the scene described in the Gospel of Mark 2:23-28. It was the scene where Jesus walked through the fields with his disciples on the Sabbath. While the disciples were picking the grain with their hands, the Pharisees started to challenge Jesus, asking Him why his disciples were breaking the law.

The scene continued and all of a sudden Jesus turned towards me, looking me straight in the eyes. He said, "Stephan! There are no more rules!" Then a second time he spoke: "Stephan! There are no more rules!"

After a short moment I replied and said, "Well, Jesus, that is not really true. I am involved in youth work, and with youth... well, we have a lot of rules!"

Then, with a serious but kind look on his face, Jesus said, "Stephan! There are *no* more rules! *The* rule *am I!* You follow me!"

This encounter happened years ago, but it still has an impact on my life, my thinking, my theology and, of course, my relationship with God. God did not come to bring us a list of rules to be obeyed, but to share His life with us in intimate relationship. We have become partakers of *His* divine nature, now fulfilling the law through love.

While reading this book I felt drawn closer to God, able to tune in to the heavenly rhythm of God's divine dance. In this book Steve shows us a heavenly perspective in which we can live with childlike faith that flows out of our relationship with the Father. I encourage you to read this book with an open heart, ready for the Father to draw you into a deeper relationship with Him than you have ever experienced before and to allow His joy to be your strength on this journey.

Stephan Krueger, M.A. Theology
Director, Awake Europe

Introduction

*"Our God reigns!" The praise is sung
and declared by all now our worship's begun,
"Our God loves us!" Celebration is real
and we follow it smartly with "Our God heals!"
And our God walks and our God talks,
and whatever the case, He knows our thoughts.
But one thing we seem to have missed by a half
is that our God smiles and, moreover, He LAUGHS!*

If there is one quality to God's character and personality that has surely been largely overlooked through the ages, it has to be this:

God laughs. God has fun and He is fun.

It's not that He laughs in spite of His magnificent authority, but because of it.

We laugh too, because we have been created in His image. He gets the credit for our ability to express our fun and delight in this way.

Many of us have been taught, or perhaps through experience have come to believe, that most things to do with God are of a solemn nature. He is God, right? He is the awesome, unfathomable Creator who sits enthroned above the circle of the earth. He is remote, sober, and surpassingly superior in every way, and therefore beyond our understanding and incompatible with our notions of humour and fun.

Well, yes and no.

Awesome, yes certainly. Entirely unfathomable? No, He is not. Remote? – hardly! If the remote are distant from us, what does the Bible say about Him?

> *And the Word became flesh, and <u>dwelt among us</u>, and we saw His glory, glory as of the only begotten from the Father, full of grace and truth.*
>
> *John 1:14 (emphasis added)*

The mere concept of God having a sense of humour, laughing or horsing around seems to be foreign not only to those who do not purport to know Him but even to many Christians. And yet the winsome Son of Man, who came and lived among us, was sought after by all and sundry including some of the most unlikely candidates.

We are going to see that He has a hearty laugh and a right royal sense of fun. At times He is hilarious. I mean – He made you, right? No disrespect intended, but I bet the subject of 'you' could fill a chapter or two alone, don't you agree?

Even the not overly optimistic Ecclesiastes recognized that as well as a time to weep there is a time to laugh. (Ecclesiastes 3:4)

Unfazed

We also need to see that He is utterly unfazed by even His fiercest opponents, and for those of us who have come to know Him in Jesus Christ this is especially significant. Our God stands tall, very able and with His mighty right hand very steady on the affairs of our lives. He rules over the whole of earth's creation, the universe and beyond.

> *All things came into being through Him, and apart from Him nothing came into being that has come into being.*
>
> *John 1:3*

Perhaps part of the issue is that we do not really know Him very well. We have learned much about Him, but a great deal of what we have come to understand is essentially second or third hand and amounts to little more than hearsay in terms of personal experience.

How can you really know what someone is like until you meet them personally in some context and then progress together into degrees and layers of relationship? The degree to which we do not really know Him perhaps amounts to the lengths to which we go to imagine a God in our own image, rather than know for ourselves that the truth is the other way around.

I pray that this book will, in the hands of the Holy Spirit as well as ours, bring tremendous release to our concept of who He is. The God of the Angel Armies, the Lord of the Universe, the Saviour of the world is also wonderful company. If we truly knew Him intimately, He would be first on our next party's invitation list as well as the companion with whom we would love to pass our time. To whatever point we may feel we have made His acquaintance, He is always available that we might know Him in greater intimacy and reality. At the same time, we need to remember that we approach Him on His terms, not ours.

He is magnificent in majesty and is not remotely threatened by forces spiritual or physical that would raise an angry fist of defiance to Him. Our God employs even young youths to toss a stone at boastful enemies and bring them right down to earth. Such renowned opponents have even been known to completely lose their heads... (1 Samuel 17)

Just as God is much more interested in who we really are than what we simply do, so we need to discover more of the Person who is the Cosmic Manager of all things and yet is marvellously acquainted with each of us.

Join me in this excursion into aspects of Father, Son and Holy Spirit that may, in some part, have eluded us. Perhaps our discovery will become a more permanent part of our deepening relationship with Him and with one another.

An agnostic was flustered at not being able to find a parking space in a large supermarket's car park. *I'll take a step of faith,* he thought to himself.

"Lord," he prayed, "I can't stand this. If you open a space up for me, I swear I'll give up drinking whisky and I promise to go to church every Sunday. I'll even give that Christian Alpha course a go with the missus."

Suddenly, the clouds parted and the sun shone on an empty parking space.

The agnostic said, "Never mind, I found one."

CHAPTER ONE

He Fell Off

In 2003 I spent a privileged month at Toronto Airport Christian Fellowship (TACF) in Canada. For several reasons this visit turned out to be a memorable life-changer for me – a life-*saver,* I might say.

At the time of my visit, I was a tired, over-stretched, confused and emotionally frazzled individual. Despite this, there was much in my life to be grateful for; I was part of a Jesus-centred fellowship and a busy member of the church; a ready participant in its weekly activities. It was an environment in which, over many years, I had devoured opportunities to cut my teeth in ministry and I had learned to lead worship in and through personal interaction with the Holy Spirit, as well as discover ease in hearing from the Lord, sharing prophetically and in preaching. I am grateful to the leadership of that body who so generously encouraged a free flow of the Holy Spirit among us and allowed us opportunities to learn in the divine school of the Holy Spirit.

I remember asking the pastor's wife, in those early days, if I should consider going to a Bible college. She replied, "You're in one, dear."

In retrospect, however, I was arguably too busy; a large slice of the 'core Steve' had become desolate in my multi-active participation; genuine joy was, in all honesty, in short supply in my daily experience of God.

Such testimonies as my own that I outline here appear to be growing in number in the Christian church, and our Father, I would suggest, is not impressed. He did not save us at such immeasurable cost only to then have us live lives that are so driven that we begin to internally shut down under their colossal weight. Jesus said that when we do things His way the burden is light. The Amplified Bible (AMP) renders the well-known Matthew 11:30 as follows:

For My yoke is wholesome (useful, good – not harsh, hard, sharp, or pressing, but comfortable, gracious, and pleasant), and My burden is light and easy to be borne.

Looking back, I have no doubt that I had an identity crisis. I wasn't really sure what God thought about me (I mean really, deep down in my heart), and my frequent times of ministering aided and abetted my tendency to deflect my discomfort away and push such foundational questions to one side. I assumed that as long as I was 'being used', things must be pretty much all right. Well, Father showed me that this was a skewed and ultimately unhealthy view.

Of course, He does use us. We understand what we mean by the expression 'to be used'. But it's not the best way to describe God's moving in our lives, is it? Aren't we really talking about a partnership with the Holy Spirit, at the very least?

Looking back at that time, I am still astounded and humbled that God loves me so much that He personally intervened to release me from the imbalance of the lifestyle I was leading. Sound prophetic voices spoke into my life in Canada, in the first instance, and I knew that our very personal God was about to bring a major change of direction in my life.

Of course, despite the pressures and anxieties that I was facing, my life had its enjoyments and there was laughter from time to time; I made others laugh, too, that's for sure. But I shed many tears, there's no question about that.

In 1999, having been made redundant from an eleven year career with a life insurance company, I started a new venture in teaching English as a Second Language to adults and teenagers in London. I quickly discovered that humour was going to play an important role in my teaching style; people were able to connect both with me and with each other as fun played its largely spontaneous part in my lessons.

I just couldn't help myself, to be honest! During stages of my lessons I would remember funny anecdotes, recall ridiculous mistakes that I had made along my life's path and point to miscellaneous observations about people. Students could relate to them and it enabled them to take in the learning points from the classes much more easily. Little has changed over the years, in this respect, since I began teaching. As long as they are learning, I am happy for my students to have a ball!

So, returning to TACF... I went there to attend a Leaders' School. Those of us blessed to be there were 'loved on', taught, prophesied over and generally bathed in God's love over a period of five magnificent weeks.

During one particular time of ministry, the Holy Spirit was meeting with people in various ways, as He is apt to do. One young lady (let's call her Maria), who became a sweet friend over the stay in Toronto, was 'having a blast' with the Holy Spirit! She was laughing. A lot. As I recall, there seemed to be a kind of rhythm to her expressions of delight, almost as if a comedian was telling her jokes.

Jesus – is – Joy. It is more accurate to say that He *is* it rather than He *has* it. In the same way we say that Jesus doesn't merely *have* life eternal; He *is* that eternal life. So the truth is that were it not for Jesus, there would be no genuine joy at all. "You can't have the fruit if there ain't no root." (A little local English there for you from East London!)

Maria's laughing went on for some time. When this communal and individual time with God had eased down, she told us what had been going on.

Her own hilarity was centred on Jesus' joy.

The Holy Spirit took Maria on a visionary trip, a spiritual hike. She had a very interactive vision in which she saw herself flying high over many nations of the world. As she ascended and, at times, descended in her vision to the nations of the world, she was able to 'pick up' a nation and carry it to Jesus. As she gave Him these nations, and as they disappeared into His pocket, she heard Him laugh. And as He laughed, she laughed. His expression triggered her own.

Aspects of this account may seem somewhat foreign to some of us, and yet we are probably all familiar with occasions when a baby, toddler or young child has laughed in response to their dad's humorous antics. Have a look for examples of this on a video website such as YouTube – you will find scores of clips of those very instances.

Maria laughed as her Father laughed. She, like you and me, is united with Him in the Holy Spirit, right? Just as a child is a product of the father who has raised him, so we, in Christ, now have His DNA within our being, within the new creation (2 Corinthians 5:17).

Oh – but we are talking about God. Surely He doesn't behave like that, does He?

Logic tells me that we only doubt such an aspect of His character because somewhere along the way (and probably repeatedly) we have learned to believe, and have come into an internal agreement, that God is far too serious for frivolity and horseplay.

It's understandable. Jesus went to the cross, for goodness sake. His Father required it of Him. It isn't particularly hard to struggle with notions of divine humour in light of His Son's unique, appalling suffering.

But if we have consented to such an agreement, I would suggest that it is time to reconsider. It is time to repent of assigning God a misrepresenting character that we have concocted and tied ourselves to.

There are many times in our faith walk when the Holy Spirit sheds His light and wisdom on to truths that have long become established pillars in our spiritual make up. We need those pillars; many of them are key stones in our godly foundations.

Nevertheless, our life in Christ is a progressive walk of revelation, an intimate walk with the living Christ. Christ died terribly, for sure, but equally He lived again gloriously and lives still. We need the Holy Spirit to breathe on what we have learned and on what we are learning; in this way we remain current and are better able to see the true nature of this wonderful God that we are getting to know.

As we read the Bible, too, it is good to ask the Holy Spirit to enlighten our spirits with what we are reading.

He is super-abundant. He is generous beyond words. We may have hardly started to know Him as He can be known.

We want to know Him, don't we? We are not satisfied with knowledge about Him or knowing what each other has discovered. This is a 'Him and me' thing as well as 'Him and us'. We make up the Body of Christ and my intimacy with Jesus strengthens it, as does your own.

Maria laughed and laughed as she placed nations into Jesus' hands. I believe this was an intercessory vision and that, in her childlike walk with her Saviour and Lover, Maria was free enough and transparent enough for Jesus to be able to interact with her, achieving some powerful Kingdom business.

The Log

On another occasion at TACF, a young woman who was praying saw that she was sitting on a log with Jesus. They were having fun; they were larking around, enjoying a time of sheer nonsense for the sake of it. Friends do that together, don't they? They know that they are accepted and that they can express their sense of humour and love for one another in sheer silliness!

As she and Jesus sat on the log, He fell off it. Those of us around her at the time heard her roar with laughter.

Jesus fell off a log. He did it deliberately to make her laugh. He knew what would make her laugh and He did just that. How does that sit with your theology? When did you last exalt the King of Slapstick?

Is there anything in this anecdote that you and I recognize? *Truly, Lord Jesus, we have only just begun to really know You and a wonderful path of discovery lies before us.*

One of my favourite comic and serious actors recently published his autobiography. I have so appreciated his television work over the years; I have watched a particular comic series of his again and again and it still brings me so much joy. Last year I decided that I wanted to write to him and say thank you; ideally I would have loved to meet him, to shake his hand and thank him in person.

I wrote to him twice, sending a short letter to two addresses I had managed to locate online. I received a reply from his representative, thanking me for my enquiry and kind words but saying that it would not be possible for me to meet the celebrity. Oh well! At least I had passed on my expression of gratitude.

A week or two later, I received a signed photograph from the actor himself. I was thrilled. It was a small but significant connection; a personal touch that I really appreciated.

But I was saddened as I began to read his autobiography. Of course, I had known none other than his popular characters in the television series that had so delighted my family, friends and me over the years; nevertheless he spoke of his disillusionment with Christian faith from a young age. He had been taken to the House of God and yet, in his experience, God had not been at home.

How I would love this dear man to know that Jesus is alive and very much at home among those who love Him and those who are coming to know Him in a personal way!

My own early days in my local Anglican church were quiet, whispered, generally serious occasions. Outside my involvement with the choir, I cannot recall any real fellowship at all; not that I knew Jesus in those days. I appreciate that not all Anglican churches are like this. Far from it. But I am not sure that I remember laughing even once in this place that represented His name. I expect I did, probably because I was acting inappropriately! But those visits to church were teaching me that the house of God was a serious place, a place of introspection and, for me, a place of prayers lifted to God more in semi-hope than faith. In those days, I did not know He could come so close, as close as my breath itself.

Perhaps, like I do, you want to know Him like that.

He already knows you with that degree of closeness. His very breath is in you.

> *Then the LORD God formed man of dust from the ground, and breathed into his nostrils the breath of life; and man became a living being.*
>
> *Genesis 2:7*

Here is it in the New Century Version (NCV):

> *Then the LORD God took dust from the ground and formed a man from it. He breathed the breath of life into the man's nose, and the man became a living person.*

I like that a lot. God breathed into the man's nose and he lived. Our God is about His business of getting 'up close and personal'. This has always been his heart towards us and He continues to move by His Spirit in an endeavour to draw us closer to Him – the real Him!

A man is talking to God. "Lord, how long is a million years?"
God answers, "To me, it's about a minute."
"God, how much is a million dollars?"
"To me, it's just a penny."
"God, may I have a penny?"
"Sure, but you'll have to wait a minute."

CHAPTER TWO

Joy in the Cross?

Perhaps one of the most staggering lines in the Bible is found in the twelfth chapter of Hebrews:

> *Therefore, since we have so great a cloud of witnesses surrounding us, let us also lay aside every encumbrance and the sin which so easily entangles us, and let us run with endurance the race that is set before us, fixing our eyes on Jesus, the author and perfecter of faith, <u>who for the joy set before Him endured the cross</u>, despising the shame, and has sat down at the right hand of the throne of God. For consider Him who has endured such hostility by sinners against Himself, so that you will not grow weary and lose heart.*
>
> Hebrews 12:1-3 (emphasis added)

Excuse me? "...who for the joy set before Him endured the cross..." Where do you start with this statement?

There it is, as plain as plain can be. If ever there was a case where we needed Holy Spirit revelation (the Holy Spirit's heart, His wisdom and His eyes to discern with) then it is here. Our natural minds alone are going to be very hard pressed, to put it mildly, to reconcile the concept of joy with the torture of crucifixion.

If you have not already seen the gruesome depiction of Jesus' sufferings in Mel Gibson's highly publicised and widely critiqued 'The Passion of the Christ' (2004), a few minutes of online searching will suffice to take you to a range of pages that explore many aspects concerning Jesus' Passion in explicit scientific detail. There were those who, revolted by the graphic portrayal of Jesus' diabolical treatment in

Gibson's movie, argued that a man simply could not have endured such barbaric and prolonged abuse at the hands of his haters; that the scenes depicted were just 'over the top' and that exaggerated dramatic licence had taken over. Certainly, if you compare the scenes with the pictures reeled in previous films about Jesus, they are potent beyond any of their predecessors. Several earlier movies appear to have given considerably less attention to facets of His physical treatment by his opponents.

One prominent film critic has described the film as belonging to the genre of horror rather than religion or drama. I can see his point. It's an explicitly violent movie and a spiritual one to boot.

There has been much excellent cinematic work over the years concerning the Lord's life, death and resurrection, work that has ministered enormously into the lives of millions across the globe. I say amen to all that the Holy Spirit reveals to those who see these productions. Long may their circulation continue throughout the nations across boundaries and cultures!

On the other hand, contrary views have also been expressed that Gibson's film may even have understated the treatment meted out to Jesus when the truth about Roman standards of punishment is scrutinised in greater detail.

A close look at the Gospels shows us that Jesus suffered at the hands of various religious and politically motivated groups before He actually arrived on Calvary's hill. Mel Gibson's Jesus arrives in the Jewish so-called 'court' of the priests already considerably battered and bruised. The Chief Priests have not even questioned Him as yet, let alone delivered Him to His subsequent menu of punishment at the hands of the Romans.

The somewhat ironic stipulation in Jewish legal affairs was that a man should not receive more than forty lashes of the whip in a sentence of flogging; if it appeared to be an apparent nod to a small degree of mercy it may have been more in order to ensure that the victim did not die at the whipping post. It is thought, therefore, that lashings were counted to thirty-nine so as to take into account a possible miscount of strokes administered to the guilty party.

The Romans did not, however, always place such limitations upon their judgements. Their notions of honour concerning their Roman kingdom were equalled by their concept of 'sport' in punishing and crushing their enemies. To punish the enemy, to humiliate him, was to glorify Rome.

When Pilate decreed that Jesus be scourged and then crucified, the result of the flogging was, according to the prophetic word in Psalm 129, that his back resembled a 'ploughed field'. It is unclear whether Jesus received more than the stipulated thirty-nine strokes. Indeed, many that were sentenced to crucifixion never made it to their Roman crosses; they died beforehand from blood loss and trauma at the scourging post.

Joy

It is extraordinary, therefore, when we consider our Bible's encouragement that Jesus was compelled by joy as He faced and subsequently underwent His torture. It was the joy of reconciling you and I to the Father that was so exquisite, so utterly desired and treasured, that no amount of physical or mental abuse could deter Him from following through with His mission (Romans 5:10). It was a joy that was 'set' before Him and He embraced it. Let us ask the Holy Spirit to reveal the reality of this to our spirits! Jesus saw the nations and those millions that would follow His generation – for generations to come, including you and me. He saw you and me and knew joy to the extent that He reckoned it worth enduring what He did.

And, let us remember, we are talking about the Son of God. Add into the macabre package the unique spiritual panorama of what was taking place and you have an unrivalled degree of burden that only Jesus could have endured – not because He was employing magisterial powers to offset His suffering but because His love was a unique, purposeful love that was determined to stand.

Can you even begin to imagine the scale of the heavenly battle that raged through these earthly hours in Israel? All leave must have been cancelled in hell as every available demonic authority was summoned to heap assignment after assignment upon Jesus. This was hell's moment to turn the Son of God, if He could be turned.

The Lord's own angel armies had to stand aside and allow satanic abuse its access; angelic swords, for the moment, lay asleep in their sheaths. I wonder how much these warrior hosts knew at that time about what was occurring. In these hours, mankind was being embraced in mercy by the Father; the angels could have fought off

Satan's hordes but had to stand down in order to secure the Godhead's victory. It was this embrace that had so thrilled Jesus, and the prospect of it held Him firm in His determination to see His mandate through to its epic conclusion.

This was the unseen reality, wasn't it? In standing aside, the angels were aligning themselves with the accomplishment of the Godhead's will through the shedding of perfect blood and the nailing of the Saviour.

> *In Him we have redemption through His blood, the forgiveness of our trespasses, according to the riches of His grace which He lavished on us.*
>
> Ephesians 1:7-8

Jesus saw us, as I have said, and already knew you and me. We were in His heart long before we uttered our first cry at our earthly birth. He saw that we would die if we walked the earth in a state of separation from God. Such a prospect was one that He could not tolerate; such sorrow would have been too much even for the Son of God. Rather, He saw the glory and wonder that would surround and inhabit our lives once we were reconciled to the Father's arms. This joy was unbridled, invigorating; it consumed Him.

Yes, invigorating. His goal 'in-vigour-ed' Him, strengthened Him, steeled and set His resolve to ensure that the chasm separating us from Him would be demolished. He could not deny us. His love was too strong, the joy set before Him was too great to be refused, even in view of hours of personal agony.

It would be facile, I think, for us to try to comprehend the full extent of what Jesus did for us, at least with our own understanding. But the Holy Spirit, our divine revelator, longs to bring love and life and to connect with our inner spirit man; He is more than capable of showing us life-transforming glimpses of God's great love and enabling us to taste the joy He has in being intimately acquainted with us within His Kingdom.

God gave us an illustration of how pain is forgotten once the goal is achieved, in speaking of a mother in labour.

> *Truly, truly, I say to you, that you will weep and lament, but the world will rejoice; you will grieve, but your grief will be turned into joy. Whenever a woman is in labour she has*

*pain, because her hour has come; but when she gives birth
to the child, she no longer remembers the anguish because
of the joy that a child has been born into the world.
Therefore you too have grief now; but I will see you again,
and your heart will rejoice, and no one will take your joy
away from you.*

John 16:20-22

Even in this depiction, Jesus does not focus on His own suffering
but on that of His disciples. It is a powerful passage as it shows us how
Jesus knew that His own approaching anguish would be swallowed up
in the joy of 'children born' – that's you and me. There is nothing like
the Bible to boost our sense of self-esteem! As the Holy Spirit illumines
the Word, we are staggered to discover our true identity.

Remember, too, the well-known parable of the lost sheep in Luke
15 and how Jesus is prepared to leave the ninety-nine in order to go
and find the lost one. Wow – He really must take great joy and pleasure
in us.

The parable of the prodigal son, also to be found in Luke 15, shows
us that our Father loves to party! The best beast was culled to feed the
guests that celebrated the return of the younger son. If you recall, the
older son knew that a party was in full swing because he heard the
music! Them feet must have been a-dancing!

And once back home in the fold, He shows us that the rescue was
only the beginning! The Holy Spirit continues to draw us to Him,
teaching, counselling and bringing us release and new strength. Our
journey into the destiny of God gathers pace as He reveals truth to our
spirit man; we see that we have been crucified with Him (Galatians
2:20) and have become an utterly new person (2 Corinthians 5:17); we
see that we have become part of a heavenly family (1 Corinthians 12)
with brothers, sisters, mothers and fathers, and that this magnificent
Body of Christ is also moving in its divine calling and destiny (Matthew
11:12). Flawed she may be in some respects, but the Church is engaged
to Jesus Christ with a ring on her finger, and the marriage preparations
are well underway (Revelation 19).

If you wonder why there are seasons of challenge in your life then
look no further than the approaching Marriage of the Bridegroom and
His Bride. All brides make themselves ready. We are cherished, you
and I. We are highly prized and the Son delights in His fiancée!

A burglar broke into a home and was looking around. Then he heard a soft voice: "Jesus is watching you."

Thinking it was just his imagination, he continued his search.

Again the voice said, "Jesus is watching you."

He turned his flashlight around and saw a parrot in a cage.

He asked the parrot if he was the one talking and the parrot said, "Yes." He asked the parrot what his name was and the parrot said, "Moses."

The burglar asked himself, talking out loud, "What kind of people would name a parrot Moses?"

The parrot heard him and said, "The same kind of people who would name their pit bull terrier 'Jesus'."

Chapter Three

People Make Me Laugh

I don't mean I laugh *at* them. Rather, they make me laugh when they express something of themselves that is so – well – unmistakably *them*.

God designed you uniquely. You have your peculiar quirks and qualities; your facial expressions are part of the personality that you express; there are those moments where you are, simply, unquestionably *you*. It may be to do with how you typically respond in certain stressful or humorous situations; it might be something you say and the way you express it. Perhaps there are certain jokes that you just don't get. Ever. It might be that I know what you are thinking or that I know that you know what I am thinking!

We warm to each other; when we are apart, it is often those singular aspects of 'you-ness' that are missed.

Dan

Let me tell you about Dan. In some ways, Dan and I couldn't be more unalike. For a start, I am handsome, he isn't. All right, at least Marina, his lovely Swedish wife, and their gorgeous bunch of children wouldn't agree with me on that one!

I had better backtrack. Dan and I met at our previous church and got to know each other relatively well there; we have had our highs and lows, and shared many of them. It so happens that we are once again part of the same local church family.

Don't you just love the unity of the Holy Spirit? It has nothing to do with conformity of expression or the need to agree with one another about everything; it has everything to do with our living within the intimacy of the Holy Spirit, and as you and I do just that, we are in unity in Jesus.

You may be more in unity with someone that you have parted ways with than with someone you see regularly. It's a God thing; it's a spiritual deal. Sometimes we maintain our unity by needing to say, "No, I don't agree with you there..." or, "I sense that God would have me take a different direction..." We have nothing to fear in that at all. The fear of man would have us stifled and unable to express our true views and our true selves.

As I referred to my need to backtrack, please note the pun here because, as it happens, Dan is a train driver.

He's a big bloke, a salt of the earth type; he 'says it as it is' and doesn't waste his words; flouncy expressions are not for him and rarely are heard from him, unless he is pulling your leg. He isn't one for the limelight, but when he pops down to the front of the church to testify, you know that his cockney accent is about to release revelation in transparency and power.

I can say that Dan is a man that I absolutely trust.

Dan and I 'have something'. We recognised it some years ago. We saw that each of us had strengths that the other could benefit from, particularly in what God had done in our lives. With both of us being somewhat prophetically wired, we made a prophetic statement one day at church. Out of public view, we prayed together, briefly swapping T-shirts as a symbol of divine exchange. I wanted to bless him with what God had given me, and he likewise blessed me. I would venture that both of us have benefitted from what God did in those purposeful few moments.

It's great doing things that the Spirit leads you to do, especially when they are 'out of the box'!

One afternoon, Dan and I were invited to a couple's house for lunch. I am going to need to explain this delicately. Or maybe not, I could just tell you straight. Perhaps as a tribute to Dan, I'll do that.

This lovely couple were a gentle, solid support to many in the church we were part of. I remember that God had clearly sent them to us. A little while before they had arrived, we had lost a similarly warm, parental couple that had needed to move away from our locality, and it is as if God had reckoned, "Right, this church has lost precious people; this needs to be fixed right away."

The couple (I will call them Tom and Julia) regularly welcomed church folk and others into their home, a haven where they were loved, listened to, well fed and prayed for carefully.

The thing is, Tom surprised us on this occasion in their company. To be frank, how would you react to someone blowing a stray raspberry? You think you know until it happens to you.

I mean, some people get wind (and I'm not talking about a newborn baby here) and perhaps blush slightly, apologise or give you the "I can't think how that can have escaped" look on their face, especially if the deed has been so evident that it cannot be ignored. At least in that case you can reassure your company that "it was nothing". The recognition somewhat diffuses the sense of embarrassment.

Whilst we are on the subject, and at the risk of uncovering my dear friend and brother, Dan has been known himself to demonstrate a skill or two in this arena, although, should it happen, he will immediately suggest that it was you. He does so love to share.

One thing about Dan is that I have come to know his facial expressions. I know how he looks when he is messing about. I know his face when he is worried about something. Sometimes Jesus looks through his eyes when he is talking to you with an encouraging word or two.

I also know his face when he is trying not to laugh. He may try but, I'm sorry, it's hopeless, he just makes it worse! He puts on this kind of pseudo-frown to try to compensate and make himself appear serious, when you know that underneath he is trying hard to hold back the laughter. The more he frowns, the worse it gets. The more he tries to appear serious, the more you slip down the slope to a point of no return.

So here we are, Dan and I, at the couple's house. They have fed us generously and we have spent a fine time together. Prior to leaving (and I am now grateful that it happened then and not earlier), Dan and I were standing with them in their hallway, our visit in its final moments.

Without warning, in mid conversation, Tom let one rip.

There was no mistaking it. He didn't bat an eyelid. There was absolutely no recognition of this trespassing contribution to our chatting whatsoever.

To add to the scenario, Julia didn't seem to register anything either. Did she not hear it? She surely must have done.

The complete and total lack of response from them both only added fuel to the fire that had now began to engulf Dan and me. We knew what we had heard without a shadow of a doubt. And soon we were in trouble.

I am laughing now even as I recall Dan's expression. You know what it's like when you catch someone's eye. It's too late! In that split second of eye contact, a thousand words have been spoken. The mutual understanding is palpable. This was a potent cocktail of humour and anxiety.

I knew exactly what he was thinking, and as I gingerly cast a glance in his direction, there was the trademark frown, eyes focused intently on the topic of conversation, the corners of his mouth tensed as they strained to refrain a smile from invading his face.

I was far less successful. I think I just smiled a lot and tried to add some fake humour into the conversation. I had to justify my very evident Cheshire cat grin in some manner. Dan frowned on and, boy, we were both in a pickle!

It got worse. We were now on red alert. Dan excused himself and went upstairs to the bathroom. I knew why he had gone. Talk about running from the scene! This departure had nothing to do with needing a visit to the gents'. He had fled the hallway, unable to maintain his outward poise any longer.

Dan's absence gave me brief respite. Very brief. Because I knew only too well that as soon as Dan descended the stairs, it would take only one look. A single meeting of the eyes would suffice. True to form, once back downstairs, it required just one exchange of glances between us and I capitulated. It was now my turn to scarper up the stairs to the safe refuge of the bathroom. And I laughed and laughed.

But here's the thing with a dear friend. You know that much of the shared humour is because you are sharing it together. It's an enjoyment of one another and, in its own way, a celebration of what you share in friendship.

Please understand, this was not an expression of disrespect towards our dear hosts! The raspberry was long past its sell by date in the equation. For Dan and I, this was now about our survival.

So, once locked in the bathroom, I tried to expel as much 'laugh' as possible – have you ever done that? – so that when I returned downstairs I would be 'all laughed out'. I was all out of plans.

So that's what I did. I tried to get as much laugh out in that bathroom to give myself a fighting chance once back in Dan's company.

I can't say it worked. Once back downstairs again, it's as if my laugh had spontaneously refuelled on my way back down the stairs and my proximity to Dan was as lethal as ever.

We made it outside and back to the car without major embarrassment (and none, I do hope, to our hosts) and shared the hilarity again, knowing that our futile attempts at laugh control had miserably but wonderfully failed.

Yes, wonderfully. It's wonderful that just one aspect of the personality of someone such as Dan can bring so much fun. God made Dan to be Dan; and I, with many others, am much the richer for that.

We have already noted that having been created in God's image, we only enjoy a sense of humour because He has one Himself. Moreover, when you consider the endless range of tastes and flavours of humour in one another and the gamut of things that make us laugh, we really need to see that it is because God is rich in fun that we can also experience pleasure in these ways.

To say that we have a great deal to discover about this side to God's nature is a major understatement.

Think about some of your friends for a moment; recall episodes you have enjoyed with your family. Many of us have been reduced to tears – of the hilarious variety – in welcome, unplanned incidents that have crossed and enriched our paths. Some of those occasions we will probably never forget.

Laughing with friends until your stomach aches is, I think, my favourite social experience! It communicates love to my core being; it speaks of being known, of loving and being loved, and of being safe. And although much of today's humour within the media has become tediously smutty and indecent, I prefer to recognise that God must yearn for those who do not know Him to know real joy, the joy that His presence surrounds and fuels. Many comedians do a fine job of encouraging tired, stressed people to unwind and to laugh. There are so many of them that I think that the way we were created speaks for itself.

How we all need to laugh!

CHAPTER FOUR

Joy's Adversary

If you let your fear of consequence prevent you from following your deepest instinct, your life will be safe, expedient and thin.

Katharine Butler Hathaway (1890-1942)

Joy and fun have an opposite number – a draining, energy-sapping foe. He is a liar, too, and his name is Fear.

In another of Mel Gibson's Oscar-nominated movies, Apocalypto (2006), an early scene involves the unexpected meeting of two tribes in the Mayan forest, one of them being on the move away from their home turf. The tribes are strangers to one another and both of them suspect the potential of conflict. However, the calming influence of one of the elders (Flint Sky) ensures that the unannounced arrivals pass through this particular patch of jungle without warring incident.

During the brief exchanges, however, Flint Sky's tribe learns that the travellers are seeking a new start, having been ousted from their locality by a rampaging mob's brutal force. Flint Sky's son, Jaguar Paw (JP), wants to find out more but is prevented from continuing the conversation by his father. JP, though saying nothing, takes mild offence at his father's restraining hand and a little later the elder takes him aside concerning the matter. The son is about to learn a valuable lesson from his concerned and discerning father.

He asks JP if he had noticed anything particular about the travelling party, to which his son gives no reply. Flint Sky – and I just want to add here, how we need the wisdom of fathers in the Body of Christ! – answers his own question, citing fear as the strangers' trespassing companion. He says that the fear was deep and was rotting this

31

community of people. He had discerned it as an accompanying intruder. Moreover, looking at his son, he explains that JP has already been tainted by it and orders him to strike it from his heart, lest he bring a 'fear infection' into their own village and community into which they are about to return, following the expedition.

As we walk with Jesus we learn that fear is not part of who we truly are. There can be many reasons for its presence and activity in our lives, but we can be confident that the Holy Spirit within us is greater than fear and that He has an agenda to expel it from the territory of our hearts and minds. Fear would accompany us too, if it could, but God has better company in mind for us.

Jesus says that fear is incompatible with our belonging to Him.

> *But the Advocate, the Holy Spirit, whom the Father will send in my name, will teach you all things and will remind you of everything I have said to you. Peace I leave with you; my peace I give you. I do not give to you as the world gives. Do not let your hearts be troubled and do not be afraid.*
>
> *John 14:26-27*

He doesn't say that fears will never assail us but He gives us authority to confront them assertively and to deal with them. It is not surprising that the Prince of Peace is not satisfied with our living with fear. He has given us the same peace that He is – He lives in us and He is restoring us by teaching us of the Kingdom and by exposing lies that have held influence in our lives.

Millions of men, women and children around us develop strategies for coping with fear without ever really getting to the root of the issues. Although some may attempt to break free with some counselling or so-called 'alternative strategies', many do their level best to ignore their fears, avoiding them and masking them with a plethora of activities and substances that appear to push fear to one side.

Some try positive thinking; the enthusiasm and brief honeymoon of hope may appear to bring relief but sooner or later, you cannot hide from the fact that if you are fearful, then fearful you most certainly are.

Others do their utmost to keep busy, packing their schedules with activity and volume of noise in an attempt to muffle out fear's voice. This can work quite well for a time, until sheer exhaustion or unexpected windows in the diary release fear's whispers back into the rooms of the mind and heart.

Henry David Thoreau said:

*It is not enough to be busy. So are the ants. The question is:
What are we busy about?*[1]

Substances, of course, are a common choice of self-medication. It is little wonder that addictions are rife in our communities, and for many born again believers the situation is little different to that outside Christendom. I say this not to shame anyone in any respect; but there is no gain to be had from denying what is true. Jesus isn't interested in the currency of shame; He just wants us to experience freedom from those roots and their behaviours that keep us so earthbound. We are Holy Spirit people and there is much adventure to be embraced within His realm!

Jesus' issue with the Pharisees of His day was that they were not as honest about their bondages and weaknesses as the lame, demon-bound, prostitutes and beggars were. These religious teachers, in their closet respectability, were harder to reach than the vulnerable and the outcasts who flocked to Jesus as they acknowledged their need. Similarly, some of our personal struggles and sins are possibly more respectable with their modern day labels but they are no less lethal to the life of the Holy Spirit; offence, lust, lying, boredom and hurt are just a few of the conditions that God would have us bring to Him transparently.

I know areas where I am not yet free in my own life and I am sure that you have a pretty good idea of where you need His help, too. We don't have to have the answers, but we do need to invite Him to work in our hearts in order to unravel some of the tangled string and then establish His truth in our spirits. It is His revelation that we need. We are only ever going to live and prosper by His bread, as Jesus says in Matthew 4:4.

It is worth remembering, too, that the enemy uses the currency of fear because he understands it only too well. He knows that his time is short and that even his apparent gains and victories only serve the agenda of our King of Kings. It must be a constant, painful thorn to him that whatever he tries to do to de-rail the Lord's purposes, God

---

[1] See Bibliography

simply reveals that He had already taken it all into account and superseded its purposes.

As Hannah Whitall Smith says:

> *Second causes must all be under the control of our Father, and not one of them can touch us except with His knowledge and by His permission ... No man or company of men, no power in earth or heaven, can touch that soul which is abiding in Christ, without first passing through His encircling presence, and receiving the seal of His permission. If God be for us, it matters not who may be against us...*

Jesus said:

> *...do not be worried about your life, as to what you will eat or what you will drink; nor for your body, as to what you will put on. Is not life more than food, and the body more than clothing? Look at the birds of the air, that they do not sow, nor reap nor gather into barns, and yet your heavenly Father feeds them. Are you not worth much more than they? And who of you by being worried can add a single hour to his life?...*

> *Matthew 6:25-27*

I have often thought about the last statement in the passage above; it is a pertinent comment that goes to the heart of the matter of doors in our lives that may be open to the entrance of fear.

Give Way

I believe that a core issue that can plague us is self-dependency; deep down, in our heart of hearts, we have not yet yielded ourselves, in some parts, to God's care and perhaps to His purposes. Dare we do so? The Holy Spirit can show us that this is the safest place we can be – where else could we be more secure? Fear would have us believe that it is for us to ensure our survival and prosperity. Faith, however, invites us to live very differently.

Faith says, "You do not need to strive to survive – even to the adding of another hour or two to your life (which would be so simple for God to accomplish). Yield – give way to God and let Him live His life in and through you."

Fear says, "Contain; hold back."

Trust says, "I am going to pursue doors and step out."

If you are aware of a particular fear in your life, and especially if it has been becoming more acute, be encouraged! God is on your case. He is rooting it out. It will bow to the Prince of Peace in your life in Jesus' name! The Lord knows how He is working in your life to bring you to a place of release. You can speak, too, to these trespassing fears in the name of Jesus and command them to leave your life. In this way you can partner with the Holy Spirit as He works in you to bring about freedom.

Sometimes this liberation just seems to happen, to almost overtake you. God's timing arrives and – there you go – you are free. Conversely, you and I may be more aware of a process that is taking place whereby freedom is being obtained in stages. Either way, Jesus is Lord of the process. So we can align our expectation with His word that declares freedom in the realm of the Spirit.

Now the Lord is the Spirit, and where the Spirit of the Lord is, there is liberty.

2 Corinthians 3:17 (emphasis added)

I love the assertion in this verse that the Spirit of the Lord is indeed the Lord; one God, Father, Son and Holy Spirit in perfect unity! He is so worthy to be praised!

As we begin to live and move in new degrees of freedom, we are encouraged not to shrink back to the place from which we have moved on (Galatians 5:1). Even if we should slip back into a behaviour that we thought we had left behind, let us refuse entrance to fear and discouragement, and rather persevere in faith in what Jesus has purchased for us. Let our faith be in Him rather than in our ability to be different.

Fear says, "Work harder!"

Faith says "Rest. Recover your poise and peace in Jesus because even despite you, He is working through His purposes and effecting change in you."

A Catholic priest, a Pentecostal minister, and a rabbi want to see who's best at his job. So they each go into the woods, find a bear, and attempt to convert it.

35

Later they get together.

The priest begins: "When I found the bear, I read to him from the Catechism and sprinkled him with water. Next week he might make it to my service."

"I found a bear by the stream," says the minister, "and preached God's holy word. The bear was so mesmerized that he let me baptize him. Glory to God!"

They both look down at the rabbi, who is lying on a stretcher, covered almost from head to foot in a plaster cast.

"Looking back," he says, "maybe I shouldn't have started with the circumcision."

CHAPTER FIVE

Our God Laughs

Our human senses are so attuned to, and used to, the dynamic of conflict and the 'win some, lose some' philosophy that we are very hard pushed to imagine what it might be like to be totally dominant in the sense that God is. So utterly is He the Lord, in fact, that God is able to act and withhold taking action with pinpoint, absolute, precise control.

I love that about Him.

We are so often encouraged to see strength in what people are able to do. Look how far they can go! But rarely is strength lauded in those who have the power to act but in wisdom choose *not* to do so.

> *The one who has knowledge uses words with restraint, and whoever has understanding is even-tempered.*
>
> *Proverbs 17:27*

We, raised on imperfect Planet Earth and only too aware of our flaws, have learned 'not to count our chickens' and a varied range of other such so-called wise, contingency-minded life lessons – but God is surer of Himself than that!

I concede that it isn't easy to get our heads around the fact that God apparently took several steps backwards in order to achieve His greatest ever victory. How else can a finite mind understand the Cross of Jesus at first consideration? Those carnal minds within the heads of the onlookers that surrounded His cross taunted Him and demanded that He prove His majesty by coming down off it. It was a clear cut, two-dimensional case. Jesus had obviously lost.

Actually, involving the Kingdom dimension, He was demonstrating His Kingship by remaining on the cross.

Even when we use such a phrase as "achieve His victory", as I have just done, it is perhaps somewhat misplaced as it suggests that there was a genuine matched contest in the first place. But this was no contest of strength but rather one of managed process. There was never any doubt about the superiority of God to His archenemy; but the path that Jesus had to walk in order to achieve our freedom was one that required absolute commitment, determination and endurance.

I also acknowledge that just because God always knew that Jesus' death and resurrection would re-open the way for man to live in and from heaven in relationship with Him, this does not at all diminish the battle, agony and sacrifice given by Jesus on our behalf. He had to walk and experience every ghastly step of it.

One God Only

In case we have wondered or been muddled on this question of superiority or authority, let us clear it up now.

There is only one God.

There isn't a league ranking of gods or even a competitive array of gods. There was no cosmic knockout competition whereupon a cohort of gods was whittled down to the final two. Nor does Jehovah sit in permanent first position in a kind of Premier Division table of powerful deities.

He is God; He is Lord – period. There is no other. There is only one uncreated Creator, our all powerful and everlasting God.

Now, you may say that Muslims worship God and that Hindus worship hundreds of gods. Respectfully, you would be mistaken on both counts. They do not worship God, Yahweh of Israel, who can only be worshipped and known in relationship through Jesus Christ His Son and Lord.

In the book of Romans, Paul states clearly:

> For I am not ashamed of the gospel, for it is the power of God for salvation to everyone who believes, to the Jew first and also to the Greek.
>
> Romans 1:16

The Good News Translation says:

> I have complete confidence in the gospel; it is God's power to save all who believe, first the Jews and also the Gentiles.

This is not about a religion, something concocted in the mind of men. This is about the very real power of the Most High God, a power that is able to save and deliver.

What is undeniable from the Bible, however, is that there is a whole hierarchy of spiritual principalities and powers (Ephesians 6:12), the majority of them allied to the Kingdom and a minority in rebellion to it. It is hardly surprising that if Satan himself desired and desires worship and seeks to promote rebellion against Jehovah, then he also manufactures a whole host of fake deities with which to entice empty hearts to feed upon.

The enemy is satisfied, concerning a soul, if he can work to keep it separated from Jesus – that's the bottom line in his agenda. Be the person an atheist, agnostic, Buddhist or nominal church attendee, it really does not matter. As long as the spirit of a man remains in darkness and unredeemed, the enemy retains ownership of that life, ultimately. But this dynamic does not make him a god. He requires the willing participation of the individual concerned.

I would much rather that my life were in the hands of the eternal, living God than in those of a fallen, created angel.

This chapter is not going to attempt to debunk in detail the foundations and beliefs of religions and certain philosophies in their own histories. Nevertheless, those belief systems *came into being;* their original source is laid bare in the Bible. The one who birthed them would, no doubt, be delighted to take all the credit for the deceptions that they weave, but he is no rival to our God. I say again: he is *not a god.* He is merely a discredited, self-obsessed spiritual creature that has little time remaining in which to spit and lash out at the Kingdom and its glorious Leader, King and Father.

The Bible could not be clearer on these matters; here are some lines from Isaiah 43:

> *"You are My witnesses, " declares the LORD,*
> *"And My servant whom I have chosen,*
> *So that you may know and believe Me*
> *And understand that I am He.*
> *Before Me there was no God formed,*
> *And there will be none after Me.*
> *I, even I, am the LORD,*
> *And there is no saviour besides Me.*

It is I who have declared and saved and proclaimed,
And there was no strange god among you;
So you are My witnesses," declares the LORD,
"And I am God.
Even from eternity I am He,
And there is none who can deliver out of My hand;
I act and who can reverse it?"

Isaiah 43:10-13

Here is verse 13 in The Message (MSG):

Yes, I am God. I've always been God and I always will be
God. No one can take anything from me. I make; who can
unmake it?

Two chapters later, in Isaiah 45, we read similarly:

Turn to Me and be saved, all the ends of the earth;
For I am God, and there is no other.

Isaiah 45:22

In the Book of Acts, Peter explains clearly how a crippled man has been restored to health and explains that only Jesus Christ is Lord.

...let it be known to all of you and to all the people of Israel,
that by the name of Jesus Christ the Nazarene, whom you
crucified, whom God raised from the dead – by this name
this man stands here before you in good health. He is the
stone which was rejected by you, the builders, but which
became the chief corner stone. And there is salvation in no
one else; for there is no other name under heaven that has
been given among men by which we must be saved.

Acts 4:10-12

Our God sees all men, witnesses every action and hears every word that is uttered. To those, whoever they are, who may oppose Him, His response is certainly not one of being intimidated in the slightest degree. Rather, He laughs. In essence, the notion that an opponent could at all shake him is ridiculous.

Why are the nations in an uproar
And the peoples devising a vain thing?
The kings of the earth take their stand

And the rulers take counsel together
Against the LORD and against His Anointed, saying,
"Let us tear their fetters apart
And cast away their cords from us!"
He who sits in the heavens laughs,
The Lord scoffs at them.
Then He will speak to them in His anger
And terrify them in His fury, saying,
"But as for Me, I have installed My King
Upon Zion, My holy mountain."

Psalm 2:1-6

The Message (MSG) reads, in the middle of this passage:

Heaven-throned God breaks out laughing. At first he's amused at their presumption...

God laughs. He has no competitors. He despises rebellion and yet has the heart of love that will embrace the weak and damaged. His mind is as superior to ours as He is greater than us; even so He fills us with His Spirit and we have access to His wisdom once we have come into friendship with Jesus Christ, the Son of God. Such power and such humility! Only One so strong could act with such humility.

He is The One

His roar would upset a nation and His embrace can melt the hardest heart. If you know Him in Jesus, this is your God; and if you don't yet know Him, He knocks gently but persistently at the door of your heart because you are deeply loved. Perhaps He is pursuing you because He wants you to know Him either for the first time or more deeply.

Many of you will be familiar with the following verse:

Look! I stand at the door and knock. If you hear my voice and open the door, I will come in, and we will share a meal together as friends.

Revelation 3:20 (NLT)

Fancy words are not needed to deal with a God such as this. Your own words are perfectly adequate. I want to encourage you to speak to Jesus; come to Him just as you are. Tell Him what is on your mind.

He can handle all of it and can take the reins of those things that might be troubling you; they are of no threat to Him. You can pray something like this, if you are not sure how to put it:

> *Lord Jesus, I come to You just as I am. I lay my heart open before You. I am concerned about _____ [go ahead and name those things]. Thank you that You're hearing me as I come to You genuinely. Thank you for showing me on the cross that you really love me. Thank you for being able to not only blot out my sin and mess but also to take me and my life on from here. Amen.*

If you have never asked Jesus Christ to come into your life, you can do that now, if you like.

> *Lord Jesus, please come into my life and fill me with Your Spirit. I give you the reins of my life. I can't clean up my own life but I believe that on the cross you died and took away the mess on my behalf. Thank you for doing that. I place myself and all that concerns me into Your hands. In Jesus' name. Amen.*

If you have prayed that for the first time – congratulations! It would be a good idea to find a lively church in your locality; get to know other men and women who have come to Jesus just like you did!

We will never be perfect in our own right; it is only His goodness that He applies to our account because of the cross that counts in the long run.

And coming to Jesus means that He liberates us to live in Holy Spirit life, in which you and I can express what is unmistakeably you and what is unmistakeably me.

CHAPTER SIX

Twonk

A piece of string walked into a pub and ordered a drink at the bar. The barman addressed it: "Sorry, we don't serve string in here."

The piece of string grumbled, turned around – how would you notice that? – and left.

The next day it was back.

"Look," said the barman, "I told you yesterday and I'll tell you again. We don't serve string. You have to be at least eighteen years old and preferably human. Now clear off."

The piece of string departed.

The next day it was back. It went to the bar and was about to order – don't ask me how one would know that either – when the barman lost his cool. He picked up the piece of string and slapped it down five times on the bar. He tied a double knot in it and threw it down in front of the bar where it was picked up by the landlord's Golden Labrador. The dog took it outside and left it by the door.

The next day it was back again.

The barman could barely contain his fury as he opened his mouth to remonstrate with it. "Are you or are you not a piece of string?" he bellowed.

"No, I'm a frayed knot. Half a lager, please."

"You twonk!"

I think the credit for this utterance, which is best said whilst laughing, goes to my dear friend Sarah, but I may be mistaken. It isn't remotely an expression of derision but one of affectionate teasing. I remember hearing it on those occasions when someone in my circle of friends did something that was uniquely... well... *them.*

Have you ever hoovered your lawn? I have. Three times, I believe.

I'm not talking about one of those proper garden vacuums that suck up your autumn leaves. You know, the type of accessory used by real gardeners. I'm talking about a hover mower. In case you don't know, they are designed to be lightweight to make an easy job of cutting your lawn.

As my spelling is fairly good I cannot even claim ignorance in confusing the words 'hoover' and 'hover', as useful a dodge that may have proved to be had I wished to take advantage of it.

When I moved to Welwyn Garden City in Hertfordshire and to this delightful house where I now live as a tenant, a perfectly sized garden came as part of the package. It isn't a large area and that adds to its appeal, in my view. I can hardly claim to have green fingers but I have learned a thing or two having had my first garden, albeit a cottage-style one, at my previously rented house in Cheshunt in the same county. There is a lot to be said for a cottage-style garden. I think they are nature's own expression of do-it-yourself; for an entry-level gardener, it doesn't need a whole lot of attention.

My claim to fame with my first garden was a fern tree; a bush, tree thing. I had bought two of them at a garden centre during a particularly ambitious 'wild outdoors' moment. One of the ferns lasted but a few days, succumbing to the amateur treatment of yours truly. But... the second one! She – are plants 'she'? – grew and grew, blossomed and flourished. I, Steve Hawkins, had reared a fern bush thing. A real tree! Quite why the television companies had not been thumping on my front door offering contracts for "Gardening the Hawkins Way" I have no idea. Oh well, their loss.

Here in lovely Welwyn, I have a small lawn, let's be honest, with a few appropriately positioned paving stones winding their brief way to the shed on the left at the back. Perhaps God, knowing my lack of proficiency in this area of DIY, had placed them there as a kind of guide post: "Steve, it's this way to the back of your garden..." Such are my skills that I would not have felt patronised if He had done.

I knew that I would need a lawnmower of some description and favoured the idea of something light and immediately usable, i.e. you switch it on and mow! It would also be good if it could collect the cut grass. A hover mower would be ideal.

Looking in the aforementioned shed I discovered... a hover mower! Imagine my delight! How perfect! Wanting to create a good impression with my new landlord and, naturally, desiring to look after each aspect of my newly rented home, I set about mowing the lawn not long after settling in.

Unsurprisingly, it wasn't a difficult task. I zipped around the lawn with ease and emptied two or three mower-bucketfuls to my recycling bin at the rear of the cul-de-sac's car park.

Nonetheless, I did consider that the machine's 'finish', let's call it, left a lot to be desired. I had not expected the mower to produce a world-class Wembley Stadium 'striped pitch' result, and this didn't worry me at all; I simply wanted to ensure the garden was well kept. Parallel lines across the lawn were a long way from my thoughts and ambitions!

Within a few weeks I came to learn the reason for the somewhat unkempt appearance of the grass on my lawn. Upon checking underneath the mower, I discovered that there were no blades attached.

What a lemon!

That's right. I had effectively hoovered my lawn and simultaneously managed, purely due to the mower's rotating central mechanism which was designed to hold the blades, to scramble up a couple of containers of shredded grass. A first class twonk!

Upon fixing the appropriate blades to the mower, its performance improved dramatically! Who would have thought that using cutting blades, albeit the plastic ones which this particular model takes, would achieve such markedly better results? Wembley, here we come! My contact details are at the front of the book!

The Pineapple Cube

If that was a tad embarrassing, it has nothing on the following recollection.

I used to work in a life insurance office. Don't worry; I am not going to regale you with descriptions of savings, investment and pension plans. An annuity, maybe?

I supervised a team of sales support administrators who were each assigned to a sales representative and a cohort of insurance brokers. I worked at three different locations during this eleven-year career; the second of those was in Enfield on the outskirts of north London.

The office at Enfield was fairly large; it was open plan, seating between twenty and thirty staff as well as housing a large library of files, computers and photocopiers. Let's not forget the miniature post room and a small kitchenette that housed the hot drinks machine. Twenty-seven pence per cup in those days! Hot chocolate was my usual choice and it was 'delish'.

One day, needs meant that I went to the gents' toilet.

How should I put this? Sometimes when you go to the toilet you need to do a number one, right? A quick pee. Sometimes you need to do a number two. Make a deposit. This was a number two occasion, and I can only tell you what happened because I am encouraged and reassured by the fact that you cannot look into my eyes at this moment and – it hardly needs saying – you would never dream of laughing at my expense. Indeed, we may never meet, and if we do not meet until Heaven, I am assured that there is no embarrassment there.

Having sat down on the toilet, as you do, when I had – well – finished doing business, I pulled up my suit trousers. Somehow, though (and only the Lord and those He may have shared this with know how), I managed to hook up the toilet air freshener which was inside the toilet bowl on to my trousers. You know, one of those little yellow, pineapple cube scented things imprisoned in a small, plastic cage on a plastic hook of some description.

It was only when I walked back out into the office that I realised what I had done. Except, at first, I didn't. Upon sensing an unnatural appendage to the back of my trousers, I felt around to discover the pineapple block and I removed it. As I did so, I held it up for all to see in the office, joking aloud something along the lines of, "OK, very funny, who put this on my trousers?" Someone must have been playing a practical joke on me.

I was met with blank expressions of total ignorance of the deed, and it dawned on me, in this very public moment, that no-one had the first idea of what I was talking about. I had managed to concoct the whole incident myself. That's right, I was drawing attention to the fact that I had single-handedly (no hands, actually) managed to attach myself to a toilet air freshener. Embarrassing just does not do it justice;

in fact, the embarrassment was only tempered by the good-natured humour from my colleagues that accompanied my dreadful faux pas.

What an absolute twonk!

One evening many years ago I was at Pizza Hut with a group of friends. One of our group was a quirky young lady whom we loved a lot. When the waiting staff arrived to take the order she asked for a "deep pan Pepsi". We didn't let her forget that one for years.

The Toilet Files

Isn't it somehow endearing when we do something peculiarly amusing or embarrassing?

Some years ago, I went to my local swimming pool.

There were not many people about; I don't remember why. I seem to remember that this was a weekday so it may have been a day off work. You see, after leaving university I worked as an Assistant Manager for a well-known international pizza chain. Shift work dictated that I enjoyed (and endured) some rather irregular times both in and away from the restaurant.

So, I went into the swimming pool's changing rooms, as you do, got changed and then made my way to the pool itself. I suppose I was in the water for around forty-five minutes or so. After my swim – and again I seem to recall that the pool was sparsely populated – I went back to the changing rooms.

Having got dressed with all of my things packed away, I made my way out of the changing rooms towards the main entrance. As I walked, I went past the men's changing rooms.

Hang on a minute...

Is the penny dropping or should I unwrap this?

I said I walked past the men's changing rooms. Somehow I had managed to get changed in the ladies' changing rooms, go swimming, return to the changing area and get dressed, all without being spotted by a single female. Or by a married one, for that matter.

"This can't be right," I pondered. I made my way back to the changing area I had been in and, sure enough, there was a 'Ladies' sign clearly marked above the door.

Oh... my... goodness!

It gets worse.

Many moons later, during a day's work in the insurance office, I told a female colleague, Amanda, about this faux pas, much to her amusement.

Not long after our conversation, there was an office Christmas party at a rather posh country club outside the town. During the evening, I went to powder my nose. I will share with you all of what I remember that followed.

I was in a cubicle. I did what I had gone there to do. As I opened the door to leave the cubicle, the person in the neighbouring one also left her cubicle.

Yes – *her* cubicle. It was Amanda.

I had gone into the Ladies' by mistake.

She looked at me, smiled and simply said, "Steve, you've done it again, haven't you..."

Oh... my... goodness!

Suddenly I sense the need to quote some classic poetry that might describe the acute sense of discomfort that I now recall.

On the other hand, Mel Patterson has a somewhat simpler poem that does the trick perfectly! Here it is in full.

> *Was my face Red!*
> *Mistakenly I entered*
> *the Airport Men's Room;*
> *a man saw me... oops!*

Gotcha, Mel. I know exactly where you're coming from.

Mary Boren writes, in her poem entitled 'Embarrassment':

> *In seven seconds flat, my face has turned*
> *a dozen shades of crimson. I've outclassed*
> *the planet's leading idiots and earned*
> *the title, Queen of Faux Pas. (I'm aghast.)*

Hearing you loud and clear, Mary. You and I could work together, perhaps?

You don't want to forget those precious moments when you or your friends express themselves through some amusing and possibly ridiculous incident. We love to laugh and we love to enjoy one another.

While it is right and understandable that we approach our belonging to God with a sense of awe and sobriety (and, may I add, a healthy dose of sheer relief), we cannot be around the Holy Spirit for very long without encountering His joy because He really does enjoy who He is and what He does! And yet many in the church struggle to understand that we can legitimately experience God's laughter and His excitement. The Bible says:

Splendour and majesty are before Him,
Strength and joy are in His place.

1 Chronicles 16:27

The English Revised Version (ERV) says:

He lives in the presence of glory and honour.
His Temple is a place of power and joy.

At times, we in the Church have prayed for one another, believing for one another to be strengthened by the Holy Spirit, whilst at the same time denying or trying to shut down His joy when it wells up within His people. Some of the criticism levelled at those being refreshed by Jesus in the so-called Toronto Blessing is a case in point. I am glad that God is continuing to pour out His love, healing and Father Heart on the church all over the UK and far beyond. Boy, do we need His transforming power!

In these moments of twonk-like behaviour or tendency, we see something of the fun of heaven. How our individuality must delight the Father! We have a unique smile, a unique laugh, and we have the ability to delight our friends as we express our senses of humour and join them with theirs.

Increase or Decrease?

An often-quoted Scripture is uttered from the mouth of John the Baptist:

He must increase, but I must decrease.

John 3:30

I understand the sentiment behind its popularity; the idea that as Jesus increases His influence in our lives, then He will be seen more in us and we will be less prominent. I believe, however, that the thinking is flawed and stems from a misunderstanding of how the Holy Spirit works in our lives.

We know that we have already become a new creation in Jesus and that the old man died and was buried in baptism. The new man in Christ took over; He is our life now.

John was not in this position. John the Baptist sought to become nothing so that Jesus might fully have His way in their relationship, but John was not born again as we are. Jesus Himself said that John was the greatest man that had lived but that the lowest man in the Kingdom of God was greater than John (Matthew 11:11). Why? Because a man or woman of the Kingdom is inhabited by Christ.

As such, God is looking for us to become all that He has created us to be. This work of release and liberation cannot possibly be in conflict with His own work of magnifying Christ in our lives. God cannot be divided against Himself or against His life within us.

I would say that God's desire is that we increase into the fullness of who He has set us free to be in His Son. As that work takes its course, Jesus is magnified and the Kingdom of God is established in us, through us and out to those to whom we relate in our daily lives.

I think it is a religious spirit that would seek to squash us down and prevent us from fully expressing our divinely inhabited selves.

I have found that it is always good to say no to a religious spirit!

Talking of which...

CHAPTER SEVEN

Breaking the Religious Spirit

An Amish boy and his father were visiting a superstore. They were amazed by almost everything they saw, but especially by two shiny silver walls that could move apart and back together again.

The boy asked his father, "What is this, Father?"

The father responded, "Son, I have never seen anything like this in my life. I don't know what it is."

While the boy and his father were watching wide-eyed, an old lady hobbled up to the moving walls and pressed a button. The walls opened and the lady stepped in between them into a small room. The walls closed behind her, and the boy and his father watched small circles of lights above the walls light up. They then continued to watch the circles light up in the reverse direction. The walls opened up again and a beautiful twenty-four year old woman stepped out.

The father said to his son, "Go, get your mother."

The religious spirit is a devious robber. It would suffocate us, tie us up, thwarting our unique expression as sons and daughters of the Kingdom through a veneer of reasonableness (sometimes of the religious variety) that is not sourced from God's Spirit. The Holy Spirit is endlessly creative in the weaving of His tapestries in our lives and He has great blessings for us, particularly as we build relationships in the Body of Christ.

The enemy, therefore, attempts to hinder this work, bringing restriction, insinuation and disapproval to our paths. The sooner we recognise this pernicious spirit, the better. Some have been bound by its legalism and false righteousness for years, and I was once among

51

that number. It does its best to remain hidden from one's own consciousness but it struggles to hide in the light of the Spirit of God.

Where it does bare its teeth, you will find criticism, comparison and judgement. It exercises a counterfeit self-righteousness that, in truth, seeks to work against the finished work of the cross.

I was very bound by accusation for a time. One of my leaders suggested to me that in my striving I was, in fact, trying to sweep an already cleaned room. This was such a helpful picture for me.

If you go to the root of the issue, the religious spirit can gain access to us only to the degree that we have not appropriated the freedom of the cross in our lives. To do the latter is to enter a place of divine rest in Jesus. We rest. We realise that we have been included in Christ's work on the cross and in His resurrection victory, and that striving has no place in us. Indeed, striving has become an anomaly as we have allowed the Holy Spirit to live His life through us. We are released from the work of strife to live.

> *For the death that He died, He died to sin once for all; but the life that He lives, He lives to God. Even so consider yourselves to be dead to sin, but alive to God in Christ Jesus.*
>
> *Romans 6:10-11*

Freedom flourishes in that place of resting in Him. There is no need to strain or work for God's acceptance. It is ours already in His Son. The energy that might have been devoted to religious striving is instead available for us to enjoy and re-employ productively as we relax into who God has made us to be.

The Bible describes King David as a man after God's heart. Those who love Him in His freedom are not afraid of what others think of them; they don't waste their strength in trying to please people. This is the David who worshipped the Lord in the private place of the hillsides (unless you include the sheep), palaces and Temple but had no qualms about worshipping extravagantly in public:

> *Now it was told King David, saying, "The LORD has blessed the house of Obed-edom and all that belongs to him, on account of the ark of God." David went and brought up the ark of God from the house of Obed-edom into the city of David with gladness. And so it was, that when the bearers of the ark of the LORD had gone six paces, he sacrificed an*

*ox and a fatling. And David was dancing before the LORD
with all his might, and David was wearing a linen ephod. So
David and all the house of Israel were bringing up the ark
of the LORD with shouting and the sound of the trumpet.
Then it happened as the ark of the LORD came into the city
of David that Michal the daughter of Saul looked out of the
window and saw King David leaping and dancing before the
LORD; and she despised him in her heart.*

2 Samuel 6:12-16

The religious spirit is not sourced in the Holy Spirit; it is a legalistic, controlling influence that prevents believers from receiving and expressing Holy Spirit life. Michal, who criticised David internally and also to His face, may have felt very superior and proper at the time when the King abandoned himself to the worship of his God in full public view. Sadly, the Bible goes on to tell us that she remained barren as a result of the attitude of her heart. The religious spirit offers barrenness while the Spirit of God offers us life.

I remember being in a lively charismatic worship service in Birmingham just after I had been saved. Lots of people were dancing during the worship. I wanted to join them but I couldn't. It's not that I despised them, as Michal did David, but Jesus' life had not yet been released into me through the baptism of the Holy Spirit. Actually, I received that baptism in a prayer line at the end of that very meeting! I will never forget making my way to the front of the congregation along with many others. I stood in a line and, as the preacher (Steve Ryder from Australia) lightly touched my forehead, I blacked out and sank to the floor. Glorious!

God had literally swept me off my feet!

The religious spirit resists the freedom that the Holy Spirit brings; if you feel that this spirit has a place in your life, you can deal with it! Refuse to accept its authority in your life and declare that you are free in Jesus Christ. This spirit would try to keep you weak, wooden, leaden footed and critical, but the Holy Spirit has life, revelation and adventure for you!

You are a blessing and a gift to the Body of Christ. Whatever you may think, you have a purpose in Jesus Christ to be free, to excel, to fly! Yes, there are those who may look down on us from time to time and even tell us why we 'shouldn't' express our worship as we do or try to counsel us that our simple trust in God is naive. Well, they have had their say. You and I need to continue to express our Kingdom delight with the unique flavour that God has designed us to bring.

No-one dances quite like you do. No-one worships quite as you do. Your song and expressions of praise are unique. His revelation shared with you in the Holy Spirit is communicated through you absolutely uniquely.

I bet no-one paints quite like you do if you are an artist, and you can express your adoration in dance like none other.

I wonder if there are those of you who are reading this who dance freely to the Lord in the privacy of your home but are afraid to dance in church services? God loves the private worship – absolutely. But if you feel that you would like to express your worship in dance in meetings, it could be that your ministry of worship is about to unlock some other keys in the life of your church family.

I love to see men, women, boys and girls dance to and with God! Some do it a little bit churchy! Come on, you know what I mean! That up and down, slightly shuffled, regimented bop! Well, praise God that they are dancing! Go for it! But I love to see other more personalised expressions of praise and worship too. It's just so lovely, so pure, so transparent. Gravity has fallen by the wayside and they are free! Free, free, free!

> *It was for freedom that Christ set us free; therefore keep standing firm and do not be subject again to a yoke of slavery.*
>
> *Galatians 5:1*

The JB Phillips translation (JBP) reads as follows:

> *Plant your feet firmly therefore within the freedom that Christ has won for us, and do not let yourselves be caught again in the shackles of slavery.*

These words are quite sobering. God is saying that if we are bound to others' opinions and value law-keeping above a relationship of life in the Holy Spirit, we are shackled. The verse also uses the term 'slavery'. As always, the Bible just 'says it straight'.

Perhaps the Lord is touching your heart about recognising more clearly your freedom in Him. It is an amazing privilege to hear God speak to us by His Spirit; it is also the normal way for His kids to live.

Please understand that you are dearly loved and that God wants to reveal His thoughts and plans to you. Just a word or two from Him can outweigh hours and hours of reasoning and rehearsing the 'what if' scenarios, especially if we are thinking of doing something new!

A painter was hired to paint the exterior of a church.

His practice was to thin the paint so that he could make a larger profit. He felt a bit guilty about it, what with this job being a church and all, but he went ahead anyway.

As he was painting the church, torrential rain began to fall and it washed all the paint off.

Then, as quickly as the rain had started, it ended, and the sun came out and shone beautifully.

The painter gazed skyward, realising that he was at a turning point in his life, and he heard a voice from above saying:

"Repaint! Go, and thin no more."

Chapter Eight

Turnarounds

Many of you will be familiar with the account of Abraham and Sarah, and the pair's response to an angel's news – in fact, it was the Angel of the Lord – that Sarah would bear her husband a son in their old age.

> Then God said to Abraham, "As for Sarai your wife, you shall not call her name Sarai, but Sarah shall be her name. I will bless her, and indeed I will give you a son by her. Then I will bless her, and she shall be a mother of nations; kings of peoples will come from her." Then Abraham fell on his face and laughed, and said in his heart, "Will a child be born to a man one hundred years old? And will Sarah, who is ninety years old, bear a child?" And Abraham said to God, "Oh that Ishmael might live before You!" But God said, "No, but Sarah your wife will bear you a son, and you shall call his name Isaac; and I will establish My covenant with him for an everlasting covenant for his descendants after him."
>
> *Genesis 17:15-19*

And a little later we read:

> Then they said to him, "Where is Sarah your wife?" And he said, "There, in the tent." He said, "I will surely return to you at this time next year; and behold, Sarah your wife will have a son." And Sarah was listening at the tent door, which was behind him. Now Abraham and Sarah were old, advanced in age; Sarah was past childbearing. Sarah laughed

to herself, saying, "After I have become old, shall I have pleasure, my lord being old also?"

Genesis 18:9-12

As one might expect, Sarah is embarrassed and afraid that she has been heard to laugh at the news. Nevertheless, one might be forgiven for understanding her response, in view of her age and that it is also a rather amusing suggestion...

I don't think that admitting that there is humour in the prospect of Sarah becoming a mother at this stage of her life demeans the words of the supernatural visitors at all. It's not as if the Bible stipulates that Sarah is mocking the Lord's declaration; she may be doing so, but perhaps it is rather that she sees some amusement in the natural unlikelihood of such a life change at her advanced age.

Similarly, her husband has responded in the same manner. Despite the humour, we see that he quickly clicks into a 'how to' mode by suggesting that Ishmael would surely be the vehicle of God's blessing to Israel.

Of course, events unfold just as the Lord has spoken. In Genesis 21 we read:

> *Then the LORD took note of Sarah as He had said, and the LORD did for Sarah as He had promised. So Sarah conceived and bore a son to Abraham in his old age, at the appointed time of which God had spoken to him. Abraham called the name of his son who was born to him, whom Sarah bore to him, Isaac. Then Abraham circumcised his son Isaac when he was eight days old, as God had commanded him. Now Abraham was one hundred years old when his son Isaac was born to him. Sarah said, "God has made laughter for me; everyone who hears will laugh with me." And she said, "Who would have said to Abraham that Sarah would nurse children? Yet I have borne him a son in his old age." The child grew and was weaned, and Abraham made a great feast on the day that Isaac was weaned.*

Genesis 21:1-8

We see that on this occasion Sarah laughs again, but she laughs in a very different manner. Not only that; she announces that this miraculous event will birth joy and laughter widely amongst others.

The later verses state that her husband gives a significant celebratory feast. What has previously been a promise to Abraham with no obvious avenue of fulfilment has now become displayed reality in God's purpose. Laughter crowns the events for the couple and their community. *Lord, You are good – You are a miracle worker. I am sure that You laughed greatly as You witnessed and were among the people's celebrations!*

Our God is the God of the turnaround. We have already considered what is surely the greatest turnaround in the history of mankind: Christ died, Christ rose and He is coming again. We were destined for a lost eternity and have been transferred into the Kingdom of God to live the life, now and for all eternity. How thrilling! How awesome!

As we pray, we can expect to see the Holy Spirit assert Kingdom authority on earth. Each of us can pray and anticipate seeing God move in our circumstances and within our spheres of influence. God's people are praying and communities are being affected and touched as 'one meets one' with the love of God. Marriages can be healed; bodies and emotions can be healed and restored; abuses can be swallowed up in God's healing and redeeming love; carnal lives are buried in baptism, then new creations stand up in the designated authority of Jesus Christ.

The gospel has legs: yours and mine and those of the Holy Spirit, who walks through walls and who responds to the Father's will from Heaven.

We recently prayed in our church for a minister of another church in our wider locality. He had been diagnosed with cancer. The name of Jesus has authority and he was healed.

A Hertfordshire family had an encounter with Jesus not so long ago. They fell in love with Him. As a family they are an accomplished worship band. He has raised them up to be stewards of thousands and thousands of tons of food, clothing and an extraordinary range of other goods in a complex of warehouses, with which they are blessing not only their local town but also communities in Eastern Europe (twice a month) and beyond. Recently they have also set up two farms!

God is moving in these days.

A local man who had come to Jesus while studying at university after years of abuse at school, and who had subsequently been involved in church ministry for many years, recently had the Lord speak to him in the middle of the night. Instantly he knew he was going to write a book, and the following day nine thousand words poured on to paper. This happened about a year and a half ago. He has since written seven books and is having them published in the USA and the UK.

You're reading the seventh one right now! God is moving.

You know, walls do not intimidate God. It doesn't matter how high they are, how long they have been there or what authority appears to have pinned its name to them. At Jericho, God proved the scripture in Zechariah:

> Then he said to me, "This is the word of the LORD to Zerubbabel saying, 'Not by might nor by power, but by My Spirit,' says the LORD of hosts. 'What are you, O great mountain? Before Zerubbabel you will become a plain; and he will bring forth the top stone with shouts of "Grace, grace to it!"'"
>
> Zechariah 4:6-7

I just have to let you read that in The Message Bible (MSG)!

> Then he said, "This is GOD's Message to Zerubbabel: 'You can't force these things. They only come about through my Spirit,' says GOD-of-the-Angel-Armies. 'So, big mountain, who do you think you are? Next to Zerubbabel you're nothing but a molehill. He'll proceed to set the Cornerstone in place, accompanied by cheers: Yes! Yes! Do it!'"

I would say that the Holy Spirit has done a sensational job with the verses from Zechariah! They are widely known in the midst of the wider international Church; they are widely quoted, widely preached on and, I am sure, widely prayed into concerning an inestimable plethora of diverse situations!

The premise of the verses is clear: that we are of ourselves unable to effect desired change in many varied predicaments, some of them personal, some of them local and others national and international. We have come to understand that own efforts, wisdom and strength are not the keys to unlocking the barred gates of persistent, acute or immediately desperate situations. No, it boils down to the fact that we need saving from them or in them. And only our God is able to do that; only He can intervene and bring turnaround because only He is Lord. Only He has the power, the intelligence and the miraculous touch that can restore, heal, renew and create. Our might and power are insufficient, but the Holy Spirit who oversaw the creation of all things is able. He is Lord of the turnaround.

In the presence of God, the U-turn is possible, and it is going to be seen again and again. Figures in authority change their minds and reverse policy decisions. Negative outcomes become positive ones. Permission is granted where once it had been refused. Gifts are given to God's agendas, and at times the givers are hardly aware of why they are blessing the Kingdom of God. Depression has to slope off as people are strengthened in the joy of the Holy Spirit. Those bound by curses can be released from them as the authority of Jesus' name is brought against these usurping, controlling influences. Turnaround means joy, ladies and gentlemen! We already know from Jesus' words that heaven itself rejoices as a single son or daughter comes home to the Kingdom of the Father. That's right, there is rejoicing! How does your dictionary define the term?

In the Book of Esther in the Old Testament we see a turnaround of monumental ethnic and national proportions. The King's main man is Haman – his Prime Minister and also enemy of God's people, the Jews. He has been spiritually hijacked by a satanic plot to destroy God's own possession. He is so full of rage and offence that he tricks the King into signing off on a decree that the Jews should be annihilated. The forces of darkness appear to have the upper hand. A nation's authority has effectively signed a death warrant for thousands of people on the word of a liar.

I love the way that the story is woven together in Esther, and I would encourage you to read it if you have not done so recently. It isn't a long book but it is enthralling! If you are unfamiliar with it, you will find yourself wondering just how this appalling state of affairs can be redeemed; it seems that all hope has been lost.

Isn't that the point, actually? Whatever our 'back against the wall' scenarios may be at this time, please hear me: God is not unaware and He wants to take the reins of our situations and work through His purposes. We may not know where to start whereas He is the Alpha and Omega, the beginning and the end.

God's intervention for His people in Esther could not be more complete, as I am sure many of you are aware. As events unfold, the miraculous takes place. Even a common occurrence, such as someone not being able to sleep one night (as happens to the King in the book of Esther) is evidence of God's hand at work. Justice and favour rain where previously there had been no hope. Even today, Jews celebrate the Feast of Purim that recalls God's greatness in this very story.

Rejoicing is about delight! It is about being filled with delight and joy, with pleasure and satisfaction. It means 'to exult', to celebrate in an ecstatic way!

God's work is about joy and laughter and the impossible becoming possible.

CHAPTER NINE

The Lie about the Fun

Halloween is just around the corner.

Apart from the more sinister activities that may take place during annual Halloween celebrations, our children of all ages are encouraged to dress up as vampires, ghosts and witches, and revel in the notion that 'wicked is fun'.

When I say 'wicked', I mean, of course, the traditional meaning of the word. More recently, its definition has been turned inside out. Perhaps that in itself is a fairly potent illustration of upturned values that seek to knock our children early on in their lives from a healthy course.

In today's society, black is white and white is black. Nothing is right or wrong; values are just different. Really? Follow that premise to its logical, godless end and you find yourself on Nightmare Street. Just don't blame the one who steals from you or beats you because they just have 'different' values to you! Don't complain if I treat you unfairly because that's just me, pal!

To those who would protest that Halloween is "just a bit of fun", I would say that a not-too-deep delve into the facts is sufficient to expose the spiritual activity which seeks influence in our neighbourhoods, schools, councils and higher seats of authority. These issues are real, although I am happy to confirm that Jesus is, and unchangingly always will be, magnificently Lord in His advancing Kingdom of Glory; it is the enemy's jealousy and panic that are revealed in his attempts to show off his nature from time to time.

My principal focus in this chapter is on the inherent misunderstanding among many, that God's business is pleasure-less and that the kingdom of darkness holds the rights to fun and enjoyment.

We cannot blame people for these misconceptions. Consider what they may have heard and have experienced, much of it at the hands of so-called 'church people'. What they have seen of the church has been tame in comparison with the delights that the world apparently has to offer.

For many, their only contact with 'church' has been a rare visit at Christmas or Easter, or perhaps at a wedding or funeral. Some may have been jumped upon by tract-bearing Christians at outreaches during the Saturday morning shop. There is a sense for some that although the church is there, it is not really for them. It is seen as largely irrelevant. It appears to reaffirm that the God that the church represents is either absent or largely disinterested in what matters to them.

I do not doubt for a moment the significant impact that many church communities have amongst their local people. Whether it be the running of food banks or practical helps in the neighbourhood, or visiting the elderly, or providing one-on-one care in times of need, these kinds of support are happening widely and helping considerably. But in terms of an experience of the supernatural Jesus who lives today and is alive in His born-again children, many would profess ignorance that such a God is really in the locality. "You mean, a God who delivers from addiction and sickness and despair lives here?"

Many professing believers that they may have met have been "I don't" people. "I don't drink; I don't smoke; I don't have sex; I don't go to nightclubs; I don't gamble." Yet it is precisely activities such as these that are sought by the masses to bring them warmth and comfort, those who, without the presence of Jesus in their lives, have no access to Love's treasures in Heaven. It is as if starving people have approached the church and been told to drop the few crumbs of comfort they have managed to scavenge and been given little lasting sustenance in return.

Allow me to alter the analogy a degree or two: thirsty people are desperate for a drink and the only water that they are aware of is salt water or a source from poisoned wells. When you are desperate enough, you will drink, even if the greater consequence is self-damage and an increased thirst for relief. Promises of future change do not comfort for long when the dire need is right now.

This is, of course, the nature of the addiction cycle; desperate thirst leads to temporary relief in which one's thirst re-boots to an even greater level. It's a tough cycle to break free from.

But not unbreakable, no sir!

There have to be, for those that live and work amongst us, points of access to that discovery that there is living water, as Jesus described to the Samaritan woman at the well in John 4. God's heart is to reveal Himself, and His Spirit is moving through His church in deep, deep ways so that the sons of God – that's you and me – will be revealed to a groaning world, as Romans 8 describes. The New Century Version (NCV) reads like this in verse 22:

> We know that everything God made has been waiting until now in pain, like a woman ready to give birth.

God will have, and is having, His way in our lives. He has called us to bear fruit, to exhibit His character and His love, and He will strip us down – even whilst generously gifting us in many ways – so that Christ, the hope of glory, is seen in our sphere of influence. And as He shows Himself as Lord through our lives, He expands the realm of influence so that more hungry fish may be drawn to the bait of His exhibited nature.

I say this respectfully: people aren't stupid. They know when they taste the real thing. You and I knew, didn't we, when reality had touched our lives? Others are as we were then. They are not going to warm to rules and regulations, dos and don'ts and churchy judgements. My goodness, most people are doing their level best to cope! Rather than judge the pubs and clubs and entertainment venues that believers may tend to steer clear of, I would rather pay many of them tribute for their efforts in bringing people together in at least some vestige of family and sense of community. As we begin to see the reality of those 'lost sheep' around us, Jesus births His compassion in us. Rather than criticise them, we start to embrace and to love.

Although it appears to be going out of fashion, I don't think there is anything wrong with a spot of hellfire preaching – when the Holy Spirit is behind it! Hell is a reality right now for many, but heaven is too and can also be experienced as we partner with God's Spirit. We, the Church, can be part of that revelation to those around us. Perhaps it will be a smile, a hug, a word of knowledge, some shopping paid for, a car washed, or a prayer for deliverance or healing. It may be a meal, an evening with a movie, or a coffee invitation. I love the Bible, but this 'God contact' with those around us does not have to involve one. The Bible is not God but He who lives in us is.

Love is supremely powerful. 1 Corinthians tells us that it is the greatest power. Love is full of joy. Love allows masks to dissolve and deeply twisted foundations to be exposed. The work of the Holy Spirit in our lives brings 'Joseph' fruit; where we once may have responded to others' trials with, "I told you so!" we stay silent and simply reach out, knowing that it is only because of His grace that we are still breathing God's air ourselves.

Years ago I was out of the office in northwest London, getting some lunchtime air in the town. I met a tramp. We got talking. He told me that he had once been in love but that things had not worked out. His relationship had failed all those years ago and he had simply gone downhill afterwards and evidently never recovered.

Countless others must have had a heart-jarring experience of this nature, but this guy's path had taken him to drink and a park bench.

You and I might have been spending time on a bench were it not for Jesus.

Such discoveries of Jesus' embrace begin to turn the tide. Religion cannot do that; it may temporarily promise change and its early momentum may bring some brief respite, but sooner or later, the truth becomes evident: there is no Life with a capital L in its vaults. What its values promised, its storehouse could not provide.

Jesus talked about the religious spirit and he despised it. He called it 'whitewash'. In one description he said that it was as a cup that was clean on the outside but grimy on the inside (Matthew 23). In the same chapter, He describes the peddlers of religion as whitewashed tombs. We all know what's inside a tomb. Hardly complimentary, is it?

The Lie has been unmasked and is unravelling. Tired eyes touched with love begin to see that the frothy, hyped, frantic pulse of the world's search for pleasure has been beating a fruitless beat. Religion, likewise, has promised peace and fulfilment but has not delivered.

It has been said that a fair definition of insanity is to repeat the same actions or behaviours and yet expect a different result. We don't learn quickly, though, do we?

The spirit of the world will continue to drive the lost along its mantra-strewn highway, filling the ears of desperate, hungry people with as much noise and propaganda as it can. Keep that noise going; keep banging the beat. Don't give people time to reflect or the opportunity to begin to sense the lack of life that drives their quest for sensation. They are hungry for reality. They need nourishment but are continually offered little more than a regular diet of ice cream.

It's a well-worn cliché, isn't it, that religious people are seen as killjoys? Perhaps they are, in truth. I think religion does kill joy, in all honesty.

There is no need, however, for Christians to find themselves in such a role. Nobody, it seems, ever accused Jesus of not being generous, of not being good company, or of being dull, tame or empty.

Here is a good way to end a chapter entitled 'The Lie':

Jesus answered, "I am the way and the truth and the life. No one comes to the Father except through me."

John 14:6

CHAPTER TEN

The Cosmic Dance

We all know that monkeys can provide much comedy and show more than a little intelligence.

Pedro works at a zoo in Panama. He has been especially impressed with one particular monkey whom they named Cheeto.

One day the zookeeper noticed that Cheeto was reading two books – a copy of the Bible and also Darwin's 'The Origin of Species'. In surprise he asked Cheeto, "Why are you reading both those books?"

"Well," said the monkey, "I just wanted to know if I was my brother's keeper or my keeper's brother."

I once heard evangelist and 'man of the supernatural' Bob Edwards speak during a prophetic weekend in Hertfordshire. He shared something with us that I have never forgotten.

Perhaps it is due to negative personal experiences of authority and its misuse that we can find it difficult to disassociate it from notions of control or overbearing behaviour.

Unlike many of those that we may have grown up with or met, God is supremely secure in His position. He has no need to manipulate, coerce or repress in any way in order to secure His wishes. He just is. I AM.

We are liable to add a dose of reasoning in our efforts to supervise and direct others. We might put on a mask; we may act and decide to behave in a certain way as we attempt to, shall we say, *massage* people towards our desired conclusions! We have misunderstandings about what effective authority looks like. Perhaps we just confuse authority with over-control, at times.

Not that all such deliberations are unworthy. As a teacher of adults and teens, I do assess how I am going to approach my learners, especially at the beginning of an academic year. I want to set the right tone. I tend, especially with the teenagers, to start a little strictly; then, once a healthy work ethic has been established and embraced, I loosen the strings a little. After all, learners need to breathe if they are going to be free to express themselves and grow as individuals as well as achieve qualifications.

Bob Edwards opened our eyes to the glory of Proverbs 8:30. Here it is in the New American Standard Version:

Then I was beside Him, as a master workman;
And I was daily His delight,
Rejoicing always before Him...

The Voice (VOICE) says:

All this time I was close beside Him, a master craftsman.
Every day I was His delightful companion, celebrating every
minute in His presence...

Here it is in your favourite Bible version, the well-known Douay-Rheims 1899 American Edition (DRA):

I was with him forming all things: and was delighted every
day, playing before him at all times...

From what I understand, the latter version is probably the most accurate rendition.

This really is an unearthed golden nugget. We are provided with a photograph, if you like, of creation: Father, Son and Holy Spirit are at work in an atmosphere of unbridled celebration. The Spirit (the "I" in the verses) says that He 'played' as the master craftsman created; the original sense of the word 'play' is 'to spin or twirl gleefully'. In other words, our beloved Godhead was having the work party of all work parties! This was an energetic, thrilling expression of love within the Godhead as their objects of love and creative goals were brought into being.

Supreme authority was at work in a heart and an atmosphere of pure joy, play and freedom. He has not changed His nature since!

We would do well to remember that Jesus' first miracle occurred at the most joyful of events, a wedding! (John 2)

Some of us perhaps need to humble ourselves before our Lord and be willing to turn our minds from misconceptions that we have held about Him, regardless of how they came about. We may know why we have kept Him at arm's length or perceived Him to be a faceless, severe authority but, frankly, we will be held back in our Kingdom adventure unless we move on from these stained glass moulds and instead embrace His true heartbeat. God is a Father of passion, and the Holy Spirit wants to express His exuberance, generosity and joy to us and then through us to touch others.

Perhaps we could imagine this passage from Proverbs as a piece of newsreel. Have you ever seen those clips on television, perhaps as part of a historical or political documentary? A rarely seen passage of film emerges from a nation's forgotten vault, showing a respected but personally unknown leader of the nation in an unusual setting; he is not at work surrounded by a team of advisors and comrades, but in a domestic scene, perhaps playing with children or enjoying himself with friends in the countryside. The formal setting has opened its windows to reveal a personable personality residing within.

Proverbs 8 shows us such a clip of our God. He rejoices in His creativity and it is not surprising, in the light of what we are seeing, that throughout the creation account in Genesis He finishes each day with a summarising statement that it is good.

Except, of course, after He had created man. This work of art earned the approving description of "very good". When you were fashioned in God's heart and then in His hands, he described you as "very good".

For a long time I heard that in us "there is no good thing". This is taken from Romans 7:8. But the context here is crucial. Unless we grasp what Paul is saying and also remember that God will never condemn us in Christ Jesus, we open ourselves to accusing lies and damage to our understanding of who we are in Him.

If you are struggling with sin or simply finding a passage of life difficult, you need to know that God is for you. He is rooting for you! He will never tell you that you are not good enough, because in Christ your Jesus was absolutely enough!

Paul is saying that we have nothing within ourselves, within our old nature, that can attain to the life of Christ. In other words, we need to be redeemed and changed from within by receiving Jesus' nature and

His righteousness. It does not mean that we are worthless or unworthy of His love. After all, the cross demonstrates the extent of His love for us!

On the contrary, that sin that we were born with was not 'us' but an unnatural attachment that His blood has dissolved. Picture a grubby mirror that really needs a good polish. The mirror is sound, isn't it? There is nothing wrong with the mirror itself. It's the dirt that needs to be removed.

Jesus has removed our dirt and replaced the corrupt nature with His own. We have participated in His initiative and engaged with the ultimate divine exchange: our corrupted nature for His incorruptible, eternal nature!

It strikes me that we have such a generous God. He created in a spirit of joy and generosity, lavishing love and detail into what His hands formed. We see through much of the Old Testament the generous heart of God in how He dealt with His people Israel; despite their frequent lapses and rebellions, He was faithful to them and heard them each time they called to Him in desperation.

In the New Testament we see God's generosity in the expression of His grace in His Son and in the moving of the Holy Spirit through the Book of Acts. Paul's letters describe His nature to us, and the Book of Revelation is a stunning, cinematic finale to the cosmic dance through time and into eternity.

This truly awesome God delights in us. He rejoices over us. A playful Father loves us with strength, compassion and an enduring commitment.

And He is Lord of the dance!

CHAPTER ELEVEN

Joy Beyond Fairness

A guy gets in from work and slumps into the sofa.

"What's wrong darling?" asks his wife. "Bad day?"

"Well," he replies, "this new fellow started in our office today. He's ten years older than me but he looks ten years younger."

"What do you mean?" she asks.

"Well, he has a full head of dark brown hair, smooth skin all over his face and arms, and he's so fit that he plays tennis three times a week. I'm not good-looking like him; I'm flabby, I've got a crooked nose and I'm really wrinkled."

"At least your eyesight seems to be spot on then, dear," she replies.

God delights us by showing that he delights in us.

We are familiar with some of the grudging attitudes around us, whether in the arena of political comment, in commerce or in the media. So we are likely to find God's take on generosity hard to comprehend, let alone accept. Moreover, when He aims it at us, personally, we may experience an inner confrontation, a conflict. The God of the universe reveals this side of His nature to us, and we find ourselves humbled and yet esteemed beyond our wildest dreams.

You see, we don't deserve it but He chooses to bless us abundantly anyway. This is how we are changed on the inside; we see how He is with us and we are won over. It truly is the kindness of the Lord that enables us to be transformed (Romans 2:4).

The revelation to our hearts of what Jesus accomplished on the cross supersedes our natural understanding of fairness. The Holy Spirit

71

touches our spirit man to reveal divine truth; this truth outweighs what we have learned to be 'true' from life's experience.

Quite rightly, we bring up our children to respect what we deem to be fair. We endeavour to give each of our children an equal opportunity to grow and develop; we provide them with enjoyment and openings to progress with both natural and learned talents. We also teach our youngsters to understand that they are unique and that this will mean, on occasions, that we treat them differently. It's not that we prefer one to the other, as a rule, but it may be that on occasions it is right to favour one of them in a particular way.

As a child I was scolded by my mother once because I sought exactly the same treatment as my brother concerning some biscuits. Oh yes, biscuits can really matter when you are a nipper! I think this might have happened at a party. Both my brother and I had enjoyed eating some biscuits but I had been keeping count! When I realised that Simon had taken three more than me, I asked Mum for three more biscuits, a request that offended her and brought me a telling off.

In retrospect I can understand her irritation. My complaint was really lodged in a lack of trust, wasn't it? Rather than trust my mother to do what was right according to me, I was taking it upon myself to try to make sure that I was not being overlooked or sold short.

My concept of fairness was, of course, flawed. To expect identical treatment to another individual is a twisted notion of fair treatment. The fact that I demanded it might be understandable, bearing in mind my young age, nevertheless, it was insecurity that provoked me to seek what I thought belonged to me.

Jesus, of course, was a master at turning people's thinking on its head. As an example of how the Kingdom operates, He described it in terms of a day's wages, amazing His listeners by explaining that a manager decided to pay all of his workers the same wage regardless of when they started their day's labour (Matthew 20). How is that fair, they reasoned?

> ...they grumbled at the landowner, saying, 'These last men have worked only one hour, and you have made them equal to us who have borne the burden and the scorching heat of the day.' But he answered and said to one of them, 'Friend, I am doing you no wrong; did you not agree with me for a denarius? Take what is yours and go, but I wish to give to

this last man the same as to you. Is it not lawful for me to do what I wish with what is my own? Or is your eye envious because I am generous?'

Matthew 20:11-15

When we think of fairness, so often we are thinking in the realm of boundaries. Jesus operates *beyond* fair. He operates in the realm of grace, favour and generosity.

The Spirit of the Age

As the world continues to reveal its bankrupt, broken nature, the clamour for fairness and 'my rights' takes on an almost pathological fervour.

Society is so desperate to balance its moral books – a futile exercise, if ever there was one, outside of Jesus' cross – that the pursuit of equality and fairness has almost become a religion in itself. I would wager that as many people feel patronised by such efforts as they do supported and looked after.

Political correctness is a desperate attempt at self-righteousness. I don't doubt the motives of many who seek to care for those who may be deemed to be vulnerable or unfairly treated, but this is probably the best that a broken world can muster in view of crippled human nature. We change our vocabulary so as not to offend others; in so doing, we often offend the very people that we are supposedly standing up for by pointing out or emphasising that they are, apparently, different enough to warrant special consideration.

We ensure that promotional material has a healthy mix of black and white faces, male and female faces, young and older faces; we may have to take this a lot further! Surely we should endeavour to have equal numbers of blonde heads and brunettes with a smattering of red heads too!

I wear glasses. I do not see a sufficient representation within the world of advertising for the visually challenged! I demand equal rights for those of us who are visually impaired to any degree! Why are there not more spec-heads modelling designer clothes? It's not fair. I am being discriminated against!

Please hear me! I think it's fantastic that disabled people and those that especially care for them campaign for healthy respect and for tailored facilities but that does not mean that every marketing image need include a disabled insert.

Such advertising scores an own goal, in my view. It has attempted to support a group of people that it has reduced completely to one dimension.

The clamour for perceived fairness is the ache of the world, actually. It is a cry for identity. The Bible describes it well:

> For the anxious longing of the creation waits eagerly for the revealing of the sons of God. For the creation was subjected to futility, not willingly, but because of Him who subjected it, in hope that the creation itself also will be set free from its slavery to corruption into the freedom of the glory of the children of God. For we know that the whole creation groans and suffers the pains of childbirth together until now.
>
> *Romans 8:19-22*

As the Lord rolls time along, His purposes will exercise the revelation of His nature through His Church. The exhausted world is gasping for life, it is panting in its thirst for reality; it wants to come to a place of rest – in essence, it wants to come home. The need to belong and be safe drives the politically correct agenda. Jesus takes us all the way home. Without Him, we hit cul-de-sac after cul-de-sac.

And, of course, it is also the Church that can be seen as a threat to that desired rest. She speaks words of life, words that separate soulish reasoning from life spirit. She rocks the boat as she proclaims that it is only in Jesus that Home can be located and accessed. The world system, set by itself and Satan against God's purposes, cannot find a place for a gospel which lauds dependence on God rather than self-sufficient righteousness.

Political correctness seeks to divert focus away from my own shortcomings and rather shine it on others', or on working for others, or on fighting and campaigning for others. It is busyness in place of transparency. Hear me clearly; I am not saying that we should never campaign or speak up for the vulnerable in our society! Of course we should do so! But there are different motives at play here.

God's people, Israel, frequently lamented their position of separation from Yahweh, although it was their own independent spirit that placed them there. Hardened by sin, they would rail against God, and then when it was too difficult to bear, they would admit their shortcomings and rebellion and would cry out to Him to save them. In those moments they knew that God was right and fair and that they were undone in their own ways; and save them He did, time and time again. But as soon as the proverbial heat was off, they would once again return to their independent, sinful ways.

Often it was the hounded prophets who would stand in the gap for the population and nation, and acknowledge that God's dealings were right and that the people were wrong. They would need to change their ways; change their minds.

Today, too, intercessors come before the throne of God in Jesus' name and petition Him for deliverance from evil and for a move of the Holy Spirit across the land and among earthly authorities. There is a difference to the spiritual dynamic in that we can come as reconciled children through the Blood of Jesus. Paul said that we are to approach the throne of grace boldly (Hebrews 4:6). We have been accepted in Christ and therefore do not need to fear rejection or judgement.

In Christ we have been judged already and found not guilty. Hallelujah!

Not Fair

And that just isn't fair. We are grateful, of course, but it isn't fair that the Innocent One has been punished on our behalf that we might walk free of all charges and condemnation.

The need for a personal revelation of the cross is crucial to our growth in Jesus and in the Holy Spirit. An intellectual understanding alone will not suffice as we participate in God's dealings not only with us but also with those around us.

It's an eye opener, don't you think, how often we believers demand fairness for ourselves yet fail to extend the same standards to others? We tend to forget, too, that Jesus has very unfairly favoured our lives.

Our blessing is unfair, though entirely welcome and enjoyed! As we receive a personal understanding of Jesus' love and favour, the Holy Spirit does some something deeply internal within us: He supersedes our demands for natural justice and enables us to respond from a different place; He enables us to draw from a new source. That source is the 'new creation' that the Bible says that we have become. We draw on the life of Christ and on the mind of Christ that He has given us.

We lay down our demand that 1 + 1 = 2. Sometimes in Jesus' economy the answer to the sum is simply better – it is superior to the natural total.

"An eye for an eye" (Exodus 21:24) has been satisfied with a greater law, the law of love (Matthew 5:38). Something greater than justice is achieved; a transformation happens.

We discover the effect of our walking in the power of the Spirit on those around us and on circumstances that we encounter.

This isn't about fairness as the world judges it and as we have previously done. This is about abundance sending the blessing spikes off the charts. This is about Jesus blowing all records. This is about Kingdom influence operating in a completely different realm to that of the world. This is about heaven's values working on, and being seen on, earth: "I am not going to give you what is fair. I am going to give you something hugely better than that. The result of what I give you will not only enhance you but also change you; God's face will be revealed to you through me. Fairness balances the books now whereas grace biases the books massively in your favour and actually does an eternal piece of work in both of us."

Sale or No Sale

During the summer of 2014, I went to a leaders' conference in Harrogate, UK. It was a fine time in the company of such speakers as Bill Johnson, Kris Vallotton and Danny Silk.

As well as being a conference delegate, I also co-hired a stand in the exhibition centre, near a bookstall. I shared the stall with a talented and anointed artist from my church; she displayed and sought to sell her art whilst I displayed and hoped to sell copies of my first two books, 'From Legal to Regal' and 'Blood and Glory'.

The table even provided the sustenance of jelly babies. A masterstroke.

Within minutes of setting up the stall, I sold my first book. I was thrilled. But the thrill didn't last long. I think I only managed to part with two or three more copies throughout the whole of the rest of the day. Well, that's what can happen when you are a new, unknown author and there are piles of new titles from excellent authors a few metres away!

Boy, this was hard work and not a little frustrating!

I fully appreciate that you and I are very alike and that I do exactly what the dear conference delegates did in that exhibition hall. It generally goes something like this:

1) Approach stall.
2) Carefully, perhaps gingerly, pick up a sample from the table. Eye contact may or may not be made with the stallholder. I must be careful because I certainly don't want to 'have to' buy it through damaging it.
3) Have a closer look.
4) Ponder.
5) Look.
6) Ponder.
7) Smile at, and maybe exchange a few words with, the calm, welcoming stallholder, who by now has put down his packet of crisps and stopped chewing. Dare he get a paper bag ready?
8) No, because you *leave*.

In case you hadn't noticed, an important step is missing between steps 7) and 8) above.

You didn't buy the item. Enjoy the jelly baby!

As you depart into the marketing throng surrounding you, you leave behind a stallholder whose emotions have just jiggled their way three times up and down the walls of the hall.

As I awoke on the second morning of the conference, I spoke to the Lord about this and told Him that I wasn't enjoying the bookstall experience very much. It was lovely to meet people, of course, but something just wasn't right.

My focus wasn't right. It had become skewed, somehow. And He spoke to me.

"It was never about the money."

Oh, of course! Thank you, Lord! And, gloriously, I was free and I knew what I was going to do.

I would give all the books away. That would be a wonderful privilege.

I did exactly that, and – you know? – I had an absolute ball. Many were surprised at the offer of a free book or two, and some asked me why I was giving them away. It was a joy to explain! Some people blessed me in prayer and I blessed them. One lady, after I explained what one of the books was about, asked me to pray with her that the Holy Spirit would work the book's contents into her life. What a complete honour to partner with Him and her in that.

I have since had contact from abroad concerning the book and I am so grateful to Jesus.

Was it fair that I gave my books away on that occasion? I should add, I did not do this to set a precedent but simply to follow His leading on the occasion in question. It wasn't fair that I should not be paid for the books, was it?

Rather, I was favoured well beyond fair. I was recompensed by Kingdom values that are superior to those of this world, and at the same time God had an avenue through my stall to bless others in His grace.

The Unfair Cross

On the cross, Jesus took our sin and gave us a clean new nature. As we live as this new creation in Christ, He does not count any of our sins – past, present or future – against us. That may appear to be a very unfair exchange in our favour but it is the good news of the gospel.

At Calvary we were crucified with Christ, and when He was raised, we were raised with Him.

He has taken our sicknesses and paved the way for us to live in divine health. He takes our infirmities and illnesses and, in their place, He gives us Kingdom health.

From being under the power and authority of Satan, Jesus has placed us far above all rule and authority in Christ Jesus. We have become partakers of the divine nature and heirs of the Kingdom.

In this Kingdom, we have become supernaturally alive; we can pray and decree in the authority of the name of Jesus. Our prayers are not limited by earth's time because we are now citizens of heaven.

God would encourage us to seek Him for revelation of these realities. We have been blessed miles and miles beyond fairness.

Wages are supposed to be fair, but gifts can be as extravagant as the giver wishes them to be. The gift reflects the giver. Gifts are not about what you and I deserve; they are about the nature of God who enjoys blessing us and enjoys seeing us grow in the knowledge of Him.

CHAPTER TWELVE

Created to Laugh

Here is a traditional tale involving an Irishman. So, you already know who the butt of the joke is going to be, right?

A Londoner, Welshman and our Irish friend have just arrived in heaven.

"Nothing is impossible here," explains the escorting angel. "God's Kingdom is one of glory, majesty and endless creative possibility. And you are going to have so much fun. Let me show you the slide. We love to give our freshers a turn on the slide when they arrive."

The angel takes the three new arrivals to a park in which is the largest, highest slide you have ever seen. At the base of the slide there is a large pool of gleaming, sparkling liquid. The gantry to the top of the slide is three thousand steps, but as the men begin the climb they find themselves effortlessly ascending to the top.

"Get ready for sheer exhilaration!" says the angel. "It'll be all the way down at lightning speed and then into the pool! And guess what? You choose what you'd like the pool to be full of! Just say the word!"

"You mean, I could dive into a pool of warm, frothy cappuccino?" asks the Londoner.

"Just say the word!" replies the angel.

The Londoner steps on to the slide and hurtles towards the pool. As he accelerates he is filled with joy and exclaims, "Champagne!" As he plunges into the pool, the liquid has become finer champagne than money could buy.

The Welshman, having seen what happened to the Londoner, begins his descent and in a moment of exhilaration cries out, "Cider!" Seconds later he disappears under the surface of the pool that has now become a reservoir of the fruitiest, most tangy apple cider that one could taste.

Next it's the Irishman's turn. As he gathers pace down the slide, the angel covers his eyes as our friend exclaims in thrilled excitement, "Weeeeeeeeeee!"

Divine Health

I understand that it takes the human face considerably more effort to grimace and frown than it does to smile. Apparently it is harder work because more muscles are used. It seems that we were created to enjoy ourselves rather than to live our lives in a state of anxiety.

Laughter is an infection that none of us really minds catching. I am not talking about the fake version, however.

The business world is one arena in which fake laughter abounds. I remember a particular sales consultant who worked in one of our offices when I was employed in the insurance industry. He had perfected his fake laugh although... perhaps he hadn't done such a great job in view of the fact that it could be identified as such! Actually, it *was* quite funny, ironically, when he 'did' his fake laugh because we knew *why* he was doing it. It was his way of cosying up to some of his corporate clients. Perhaps it was an effective tactic, too, as he had been in the sales role for many years.

Real laughter, however, is altogether different because it genuinely connects people to people rather than to a personal goal. The sales consultant was endeavouring to win business through demonstrating a winning personality. The 'real thing', however, is about an altogether superior dynamic.

Laughter is about communication and shared love. Friends who laugh together have already made the eye contact that precedes the laughter. Laughing is the consequence of enjoying closeness with valued friends. The Bible is right when it says that God places the lonely in families (Psalm 68:6). He has not designed any of us to live truly alone, although, of course, we differ in how much time we may prefer to spend in our own company and with others.

I think that laughing with a close friend, or friends, is one of life's true highlights. It isn't easy to describe it. The experience of it far supersedes mere words.

Physical Health

And it's really good for us. We all appreciate a good laugh, especially when we may have been walking a challenging or precarious path in an area of our lives. A good belly laugh brings release and relief.

Laughing relaxes our muscles, the benefit of which we can apparently enjoy for around forty-five minutes after the event. It decreases stress hormones in the body and actually increases immune cells and antibodies that fight off infection; it helps to resist disease. In addition, endorphins are released when we laugh; these chemicals contribute to the sense of well-being that we enjoy.

Did you know, too, that laughing contributes to the effectual working of our blood vessels, resulting in a healthy blood flow, thereby strengthening our physical heart?

Bonds

Laughing bonds people together. As that is the case, we had better understand that God intends us to do it a lot. He laughs, He rejoices, He enjoys being God and enjoys blessing the work of His hands. The Source of all blessing blesses us because it is His nature to do so. It would cause Him strain and discomfort not to bless; therefore, He blesses again and again. And He does so with outrageous generosity.

The following verse has greatly impacted my life. I mentioned it a little while earlier:

> *Or do you think lightly of the riches of His kindness and tolerance and patience, not knowing that the kindness of God leads you to repentance?*
>
> *Romans 2:4*

The New Living Translation (NLT) says:

> *Don't you see how wonderfully kind, tolerant, and patient God is with you? Does this mean nothing to you? Can't you see that his kindness is intended to turn you from your sin?*

I have been learning that repentance (change in my life) does not occur successfully when I try to mend my ways in my own strength; I include praying harder or setting myself goals in that. I am not saying that it is never a good thing to set oneself goals. I am saying that although I might feel better in doing so and may even convince myself that this is evidence of an inner change, I have usually come to see that this is not the real way forward. Indeed, by setting up the goal I have imposed a law upon myself – a law to keep – and we should know that keeping laws does not change our nature or reduce its propensity to sin.

The fact is that our old nature that was crucified with Christ is dead. Dead things rot. They putrefy. Our old nature is never going to recover so we might as well leave it in the grave and reckon ourselves alive in Jesus Christ.

> *For you were called to freedom, brethren; only do not turn your freedom into an opportunity for the flesh, but through love serve one another. For the whole Law is fulfilled in one word, in the statement, "You shall love your neighbour as yourself." ... But I say, walk by the Spirit, and you will not carry out the desire of the flesh. For the flesh sets its desire against the Spirit, and the Spirit against the flesh; for these are in opposition to one another, so that you may not do the things that you please. But if you are led by the Spirit, you are not under the Law.*
>
> Galatians 5:13-14,16-18

Here are verses 16-18 in the New Century Version (NCV):

> *So I tell you: Live by following the Spirit. Then you will not do what your sinful selves want. Our sinful selves want what is against the Spirit, and the Spirit wants what is against our sinful selves. The two are against each other, so you cannot do just what you please. But if the Spirit is leading you, you are not under the law.*

I have come to see that as I run into Jesus with my failings and receive His affirmation, acceptance and love, something supernatural happens within me. You see, I am turning from sin on God's terms and His ways work! I receive His confidence in His victory on the cross and somehow His extraordinary kindness touches my core being, turning my desires towards Him and away from sin. To repent is a joyful act when His way is followed.

My own efforts to grit my teeth and think differently are based upon my natural resources. In fact, they focus upon the problem, thereby magnifying it, and not on the One who liberates. His resources, however, are effective to touch the heart and to 'speak into' the core of the issue.

I am learning that when I struggle with sin, it is because I am not walking by the Spirit, the Spirit who declares that my old nature already died. Am I calling Him a liar by saying that it is still alive? I sin when I believe the lie that I have to live that way; I am like a dog that demands its bone and will not let go. Of course, show the dog a lamb chop and it understands that it didn't need the bone at all.

When we touch something of His kindness, the love that we touch reveals the dead weight of those things that would bind us.

God has no desire to see us bound in any respect:

> *Now the Lord is the Spirit, and where the Spirit of the Lord is, there is liberty. But we all, with unveiled face, beholding as in a mirror the glory of the Lord, are being transformed into the same image from glory to glory, just as from the Lord, the Spirit.*
>
> *2 Corinthians 3:17-18*

The Scripture acknowledges that there is a process at work: we are being transformed. It doesn't say that this happens by the sweat of our brow or by self-imposed religion but by *beholding*. In His generosity, He wants to show us glimpses of His glory!

CHAPTER THIRTEEN

A Joy-Killer

Dave is enjoying his engagement party and sees his grandpa sitting there without a drink. He goes over to him and fills his glass.

"Grandpa, your marriage to Grandma is legendary. Everyone talks about how you two get along so well and never fight. What's the secret to your marital success?"

"Well," said Grandpa Joe after taking a deep gulp of his favourite tipple, "it all started on the way home from our wedding. We hadn't gone but a mile when the horse started giving us trouble. I gave the horse a little tap with the whip and that's when I heard your Grandma say in a low voice, 'That's strike one.'

"A bit later the horse stopped again. 'That's strike two,' she said. The third time it stopped she moved like lightning, grabbed my shotgun out of my holster and shot it in the head. I was numb with shock!

"So I protested to her, 'What in the world was that all about? What were you thinking?'

"'That's strike one,' she said back to me. And that is what I owe our marital success to."

Therefore you have no excuse, everyone of you who passes judgment, for in that which you judge another, you condemn yourself; for you who judge practice the same things.

Romans 2:1

This is a tough verse and it's an important one. If there is something that might tame our joy and cause us to encounter spiritual heaviness, it is when we judge others.

I would wager that we do it more often than we think we do.

We have been considering the kindness of the Lord that brings about real change in our hearts. I have already said that this premise has been a real eye-opener for me, personally. Equally, however, I am aware that this 'change' can take time, and in this area of judging others, I am finding that the Holy Spirit is, shall we say, *on my case.*

It's a little bit like what Paul says in Romans 7, when he explains what it is like to live in the flesh: we don't do what we want to do and the very thing that we don't want to do, that's what we do. Remember that passage?

This very morning, I was out on the road in Cherry, my 'wicked red' – yes, really! – Citroen C3. I have been known to get a little irritated with other drivers for a series of critical offences, among them being: not indicating; not switching on their headlights at dawn, dusk or in bad weather; and, thirdly, not having the first clue about what to do at a roundabout. I mean, just what is wrong with these people?!

This morning, I had to leave the house early, in order to get an estimate for Cherry's dent – damage caused by my failure to see a moving car in front of me in a recent accident. Then, when I eventually arrived home, I realised that I had made the return journey without any lights on!

I welcome the Holy Spirit's gentle but focussed light on my attitudes!

As Romans 7 describes, I do not want to judge others but I find myself doing it a lot more often than I am comfortable to admit. Those thoughts just rise up from somewhere; words follow in my mouth; and then I hear myself saying them – usually, thankfully, for my ears only. That 'thankfully' is only the smallest of consolations because the point is that *this is happening* and I cannot deny it. I, Steve Hawkins, sit upon the high seat of judgement and cast my decisions upon the earth.

Well, not quite. But it doesn't give my Lord pleasure and doesn't really give me any, either. I need to heed the parable:

> *The kingdom of heaven is like a king who decided to collect the money his servants owed him. When the king began to collect his money, a servant who owed him several million*

dollars was brought to him. But the servant did not have enough money to pay his master, the king. So the master ordered that everything the servant owned should be sold, even the servant's wife and children. Then the money would be used to pay the king what the servant owed.

But the servant fell on his knees and begged, 'Be patient with me, and I will pay you everything I owe.' The master felt sorry for his servant and told him he did not have to pay it back. Then he let the servant go free.

Later, that same servant found another servant who owed him a few dollars. The servant grabbed him around the neck and said, 'Pay me the money you owe me!'

The other servant fell on his knees and begged him, 'Be patient with me, and I will pay you everything I owe.'

But the first servant refused to be patient. He threw the other servant into prison until he could pay everything he owed. When the other servants saw what had happened, they were very sorry. So they went and told their master all that had happened.

Then the master called his servant in and said, 'You evil servant! Because you begged me to forget what you owed, I told you that you did not have to pay anything. You should have showed mercy to that other servant, just as I showed mercy to you.' The master was very angry and put the servant in prison to be punished until he could pay everything he owed.

This king did what my heavenly Father will do to you if you do not forgive your brother or sister from your heart.

Matthew 18:23-35

Gloriously, we know from Romans 8 that there is no condemnation remaining for any of us who are in Christ Jesus, but I think you would agree that this passage is sobering. It tells us that there are consequences to our judging behaviours.

It's quite ironic when you think about it; when we judge, we really do undermine ourselves. As we judge we impose upon another a standard of our own that we may or may not actually adhere to. Romans 2:10, at the top of this chapter, says that we do not practise what we preach. As I judge, I make a demand of you, and I have no right or authority to do that.

Can we see that in essence we are setting up a law on someone else's behalf? If communicated to them, it may cause them distress, but the truth is that it has already caused us distress. Why? Because we have acted contrary to the nature of the Holy Spirit. He has not appointed us to make such laws that we would then slap down upon the heads of others.

Who Do We Think We Are?

I know that I am probably not going to suddenly stop judging others overnight. In fact, I know that my behaviour changes in various arenas of my life as I walk in the power of the Holy Spirit and receive God's affirming love. But on the basis that we reap what we sow, I know that I am liable to reap judgement when I sow it.

If I inwardly or outwardly curse another driver on the motorway for his moronic standard of driving, I run the risk of reaping in the same domain. It may be true, completely true, that the idiot – oops, there I go – is driving like a moron, but I have to learn to guard my heart. Plainly, I know nothing about this fellow human being and have no knowledge whatsoever about his life and circumstances.

You may judge a fellow passenger on the train in the morning rush hour because she is talking loudly on her mobile phone; or because he has a serious issue with body odour; or because he has a pink tie with his turquoise shirt; or because she is wearing a skirt, the length of which you consider to be inappropriate for someone who looks no older than about thirteen. Perhaps she looks no younger than sixty three.

When we judge, we write ourselves an invitation to prison, according to the passage in Matthew. Having decided that the law is appropriate for another, the same measure enters our own experience. Now that is no fun at all, nothing to smile about.

Jesus, having set us free from law and having placed us into a new covenant of grace, has not designed us to then live in this manner of counting others unworthy of the same treatment. The punishment described in Matthew's passage is a description of the unease and lack of peace that will afflict our lives if we place ourselves under the nature of the old covenant.

Do you and I really want to go back there? No, I thought not.

A friend of mine has shown me how some of this works in practice. She has testified how difficult people have changed their responses to her when she has remained in the flow of grace despite their rude or thoughtless behaviour in her workplace. One particularly difficult individual, whom I also know personally, went to her office to apologise concerning her behaviour. Such an initiative was, I can assure you, somewhat out of character!

We've all probably heard of, or used, the expression, "There but for the grace of God go I." Maybe we will never know, for sure, how God's grace has kept us from calamity and worked to keep us on track. But we all understand what it is saying. When we sow grace – in other words, when we walk in the Spirit – Kingdom principles, values and motion are on our side. We allow the Holy Spirit to inhabit what is going on.

Outrageous!

Some time ago, I experienced a rather unusual train journey. At one stop, a young person held up the train for a few seconds because he had impeded the closing doors. I happened to be sitting in the carriage behind the driver's door.

A stocky and aggressive female driver emerged from her cabin to berate the passenger who was now safely on board. Well, he might have thought he was safe until he met her. She demanded that he get off the train and announced that she would not get us all moving again until he did so. This was simply outrageous, unprofessional behaviour; she was aggressive and almost thuggish in her manner.

There was a brief standoff. The guy would not get off the train and she wouldn't return to her cabin. I thought that this was ridiculous.

Perhaps unwisely, I entered the fray, telling the driver that she had made her point but that we needed to get moving. I got a mouthful from her, but soon after, she returned to her cubbyhole and off we went: *chug chug chug.*

At some stage later that evening, I decided I was going to complain *big time.* I was going to reveal all concerning this disgraceful affair to the local newspaper!

I emailed them the story and had a speedy response. Having confirmed what happened on the train to the reporter, I was told that the paper planned to run with the story.

And then God kicked in.

It was a straightforward and releasing thought. I was to show grace. Leave it alone. Let her be. I had an opportunity to release the woman from her position as guilty party. My one and only basis for this was a moment's recognition that I could offer her what she did not deserve as I had, so many times beyond counting, received from Jesus' hand what I did not deserve. I contacted the paper and told them that I had decided to "show grace" and asked them not to run the story.

When we walk in the Spirit, He does something in the unseen that is far, far more significant than what may be at issue in the natural realm. In the heavenly places, weightier, lasting matters are being wrestled over; without them even having the slightest inkling, people can be drawn into the work of the Holy Spirit as we walk in Him.

Grace. Oh yes! It would take reams of paper to relate the occasions when I have been shown grace by others either because they made a choice to do so in Jesus, or because Jesus fixed things that way more directly.

The Safe

Have you ever left an office safe open, one that contained money and other valuables? As a manager on duty, you would be expected to treat the oversight of a safe responsibly and reliably.

Well, I left one open. All night.

My superior spoke to me the next morning to reveal my serious lapse; this could have been a sackable offence or, at the very least, worthy of a formal warning. The safe, Hawkins!

But God had given me favour with this man; he knew of my faith in Jesus and, although not a believer, he was an amiable guy who was not overbearing.

After telling me what I had done, he smiled and simply said, "Don't do that again, right?" And that was it. Stunning grace. I don't know what he had reasoned in his response to me, but God was on the scene.

It's not that God 'let me off'. "Phew! I got away with that one!" That isn't it. It's that I recognised His kindness to me, and it was so significant that it remained with me and became a building block, a Kingdom brick if you like, in my own life. Christ in me, the hope of glory; Christ in me, asking me to one day be a conduit of grace to others.

On another occasion I was driving to work one dark morning without my seatbelt on. I entered a residential area and began a descent down a hill. At the bottom of the hill, just around a sharp bend, a police squad awaited with their speed cameras. Slam dunk.

Latest score from Chingford: Police 1 Steve 0.

Hear this! I actually skidded to a halt in front of an officer who was standing in the road to order me to pull off to the side. "Man, I am in trouble!" was the general theme running through my head at this point.

The officer got into my car and asked me what the speed limit signs were at the top of the hill. He then told me that my answer to his next question would determine 'how he would deal with me'. He proceeded to ask me if I had been wearing my seatbelt. Oops! This was going to be points on my licence, surely? A fine?

I answered him honestly concerning the lack of seatbelt. He said that because I had been honest, on this occasion he would simply give me a written caution. No points, no fine. A slap on the wrist. A kiss of grace.

Grace gives. Grace relinquishes the right to apply the law that is demanding a balancing of the books. Grace says, "I have balanced them on your behalf. Your debt is cancelled; you owe me nothing. Go free." Not only does the perpetrator go free but also he or she grows through the experience.

When we show grace, we invest in someone. It's a supernatural act, a supernatural transaction.

We walk on earth in physical bodies, but an even greater reality (increasingly revealed to us through the Holy Spirit) is that we live essentially spiritual lives. Ephesians 2 says that we live from heaven and there are spiritual forces vying for authority around us. We exercise that authority as we walk in grace.

We sometimes talk about there being 'an atmosphere in the room'. Of course! We are discerning what is going on in the unseen realm. Perhaps it is an atmosphere of anticipation in which hope and faith mingle to provide an environment in which the Lord is going to demonstrate His love and power. Perhaps, on the other hand, it is one of tension and unease; a couple have been bickering or work colleagues are not seeing eye to eye. We discern a lack of peace, sensing unforgiving heart attitudes and competition between people. It's a spiritual deal.

The woman caught in adultery in John 8 was not 'let off' her sinful act. She was, essentially, ministered to by Jesus, and His kindness to her caused her to change internally. If the purpose of the law was to punish her, to right the wrong, or to communicate holy standards to the population, then Jesus' act of grace superseded what the law may have been able to achieve and did something truly radical and supernatural.

Let me repeat that. Grace supersedes what judgement may be able to achieve.

Grace goes far further. Grace spoke to the woman before Jesus and showed her what really was at stake. Jesus was showing her that life and relationships were designed to be about love and solidity rather than the vacuous version that she was experiencing.

Kindness changed her. And the ripples went far and wide as others learned of her encounter with Jesus. It is the kindness of the Lord that leads us to real repentance.

CHAPTER FOURTEEN

Real Holiness

A man went to heaven. When he arrived he was escorted to a large auditorium where there was a throng of people.

To one side of this great hall, there was a wall. As the man approached it, he saw that there was a long queue of men, young and old, winding its way from the wall into the distance. On the wall, in front of the queue, there was a notice in bold letters that read:

HEN-PECKED HUSBANDS WAIT HERE.

A few metres along, there was another notice on the wall, in front of which stood one solitary man.

ASSERTIVE HUSBANDS WAIT HERE.

The new arrival approached the lone figure, impressed that he must have been especially proficient in managing his family and domestic affairs. Reaching him, he asked him how he had managed to qualify to stand at the head of this, as yet, unformed queue. How had he succeeded in loving his wife in such a way that they had enjoyed such harmony together?

"I don't know," the man answered him. "My wife told me to stand here."

In 'The Unbroken Cord: Celebrating Kingdom Sexuality'[2], I discuss the wonderful gifts of sex and sexuality that God gave us to enjoy.

Despite the media's best efforts to convince us otherwise, it is our heavenly Father's mandate for holiness that promises to fulfil and delight us, not the vacuous version of selfish, me-centred sexuality so widely peddled outside of the Kingdom.

Let me say this – as a bloke. Ladies, you are truly beautiful. I have an inkling as to Adam's reaction when he saw Eve as she approached him. *Oh... my... goodness! She is incredible.* We are all unique, as I champion in this book, but there is an indescribable 'something' about the beauty of a woman that is to be honoured and celebrated.

Not that holiness is limited at all to the important arena of sexual purity. To be 'set apart' for Jesus is about a lifestyle that has Him as the central fulcrum. It is a life that is willing to have Him express Himself through every part of who we are, wherever we are; and for this to be a reality, we need to live our lives in close relationship with Him, as discussed in the previous chapter. I hope that we are a long way past the tendency to categorise life into spiritual, church and secular boxes; our life – all of it – is now a new creation in Christ and it has no such subdivisions in the Kingdom. Holiness is about my heart. It is about the Christ life I have received and about the space I give to Jesus on a day-to-day basis whether I be in school, at the office or factory, or in the car, or relaxing in the park.

Set Apart

> But even if you should suffer for the sake of righteousness, you are blessed. *And do not fear their intimidation, and do not be troubled,* but sanctify Christ as Lord in your hearts, always being ready to make a defense to everyone who asks you to give an account for the hope that is in you, yet with gentleness and reverence...
>
> 1 Peter 3:14-15 (emphasis added)

Perhaps we have a good summary right there in those verses: we are to set apart Jesus as the Lord of our hearts. Scripture also says the "issues of life" flow from our hearts (Proverbs 4:23). As He is

---

[2] Creation House (2015); ISBN 978-1621367970

established as Lord in the core of who we really are, life's issues can be aligned with Kingdom purpose.

How the world misrepresents notions of holiness! The enemy paints holiness as unachievable, drab and only for a select few. Even the term 'holy' is rarely mentioned outside the context of monasteries or, perhaps, a bizarre figure connected with an eastern or ancient religion. Moreover, much of God's heart has been missed by the church or reinterpreted 'in our own image', resulting in form and law taking precedence rather than the freedom for which Christ set us free (Galatians 5:1).

I think we have, at times, misunderstood the concept of being set apart. Whenever we fail to grasp what God is really saying we are liable to establish an order or lifestyle that substitutes poorly for the real thing. We reason with our minds, seeking to gain some kind of control over the concept and, as a result, institute a way of living that misses the Kingdom's mark, its quality and its blessing.

We read the Scriptures but are liable, as Jesus warned the Pharisees, to miss the very gospel liberty that they profess and proclaim.

> *You search the Scriptures because you think that in them you have eternal life; it is these that testify about Me; and you are unwilling to come to Me so that you may have life.*
> *John 5:39-40*

As the Pharisees did, we can grab hold of a principle but leave Jesus Himself on the doorstep rather than have Him express its reality to us and through us.

"Be holy, for I am holy" (1 Peter 1:16) is the Spirit's call. So we are adept to 'try' to live in a holy way, perhaps placing restrictions and yokes upon ourselves. In so doing, we miss God's goal by about five hundred miles! If we had understood that it was Christ living in us and through us that enabled us to live as 'set apart to Him' we would not have erected manmade stipulations and walls, and surrounded ourselves with a plethora of rules, the majority of them most likely beginning with the word 'don't'.

God has much better for us than this! Jesus came to enable us to live abundantly in the power of His Spirit – that is holiness. There will always be times when part of that journey will require decisions from us not to deny the Spirit life by walking in the flesh. The tempter will come; he has seen where we have failed in the past and will try to probe for weak spots.

Actually, I appreciate the value of God allowing him to do so. It reminds me, too, of where I am especially vulnerable and that I need His grace to stand firm. In all probability the right response is to keep our eyes on our Lord rather than grit our teeth and try not to want to yield to temptation. The enemy would have us enter into a fray of hand-to-hand combat with sin, to try and prove that we can overcome. Well, that isn't God's way!

> *Flee immorality. Every other sin that a man commits is outside the body, but the immoral man sins against his own body. Or do you not know that your body is a temple of the Holy Spirit who is in you, whom you have from God, and that you are not your own? For you have been bought with a price: therefore glorify God in your body.*
>
> *1 Corinthians 6:18-20*

I love these affirming verses! The imperative is clear: flee! The English Revised Version (ERV) says, "Run away." The New International Reader's Version (NIRV) tells us to "Keep far away."

White Lines

Have you heard the tale of the chauffeur's interview?

A rich, retired businessman lived at the top of a steep hill. His mansion was surrounded by beautiful countryside that included lakes, rolling land and some unusually craggy sheer drops.

The narrow road down to the village was in the region of four miles long, and the middle section was especially dangerous. Here, the road bended around back on itself two and a half times, and white lines at the edge were regularly repainted as an indication of the respect that the route demanded, especially as it was unlit.

The previous homeowner's wife had died tragically when negotiating the road one particularly wintry evening. Her end had been swift as her vehicle plummeted into the dark depths on that calamitous night. The lesson was learned. The businessman, such was his financial comfort, had no intention of driving himself anywhere. He would hire a chauffeur. His shortlist had three names on it.

Arnold, his first applicant, began his descent of the hill, his host sat in the back of the car. The car had not been rolling more than ten seconds when the businessman told him to stop the car.

"You checked your top button in the mirror as we left. That was unsafe. Thank you for coming. Good day." And Arnold's interview was over.

Don stepped up next. His CV was impressive – he had three advanced driving qualifications to his name. He set off and accelerated down the hill. He took the corners beautifully, the ride was smooth and the car's tyres never once crossed the white lines as the host, gripping his seat in the rear, caught glimpses of the houses further down the hill.

Once arrived at the bottom, Don flashed a smile. But the businessman did not return it.

Finally, Edward had his turn. He took the driver's seat and started up the hill. He drove steadily and kept the vehicle as near to the middle of the road as he could, such that the businessman could see only tarmac either side of the car.

He started work the next morning and Don's self-confident smile was a distant memory.

Though I have failed on many occasions, I have been learning that there is a cost to appropriating this amazing life that Jesus has bought for us and has placed us in.

I have a responsibility to 'drive' carefully; to keep as far away from the perimeter edge of holiness as possible. It can be fun and enticing to draw near to the sides and look down at what is on offer. But the cost of doing so could be devastating. No thank you! The life of the Holy Spirit is not found at the outer boundary of holiness.

A Jealous Loser

The enemy is a loser; he has lost you and me to Jesus and can only resort to telling lies and trying to deceive us into living in ways that are contrary to who we have become in the Kingdom of God.

When we are tempted to sin and to believe that what is on offer is worth the taking and worth a moment of forsaking our experience of Christ, we would do well to remember that the one making the offer is callous, spiteful and has only one agenda in mind. He is insanely jealous of God and of us too. There is no Spirit life in what he offers – he is cut off from it. His wares are designed to harm us or, at least, distract us from the One in whom we have now been called to "live and move and have our being" (Acts 17:28, AMP).

In essence, pleasure seekers have set themselves a course of self-destruction.

That's right. The very fulfilment that they seek will elude them because they have failed to understand a fundamental principle of the Creator, namely that it is in giving that we truly receive.

You have no doubt heard the expression that "the grass is greener on the other side". Well that is why God placed us on the other side of barrenness and darkness, into Christ! The holy place is Him, and He is Joy!

CHAPTER FIFTEEN

Your Design

Here is a joke that I remember from my younger days. It's of the 'shaggy dog' variety. If you don't know what a shaggy dog story is, then you certainly will do by the end of this. So please, pull up a chair and I shall begin.

There was once a man who lived in a lighthouse. Ben had been married in his earlier years, but now, in his retirement, he was happy to occupy the South Tip Lighthouse on the British coast.

One particularly stormy evening, Ben was just settling down with a mug of cocoa and a good movie, when the bell rang in his circular living room. In those days there was no such thing yet as an intercom, so Ben began making his way down the one hundred and ninety seven steps to the large, panelled front door.

Upon opening up, he saw a dishevelled-looking fisherman.

"Sorry sir, but I run aground on the rocks!" the fisherman moaned. "Got a bed for the night?"

Being a decent sort of chap, and having recently watched a Christian television programme, Ben let him in, and the two of them slowly wound their way up the one hundred and ninety eight steps. That's right; I had forgotten one previously.

Ben sat the fisherman down – his name was Walter – and set him up nicely with a blanket and a mug of cocoa. The two of them made themselves comfortable, and it just so happened that a James Bond movie was beginning.

No sooner had the two gents supped on their warm chocolate drinks when the bell rang again.

"You gotta be kidding me," thought Ben. He began the descent once again and a few minutes later was at the front door. Pulling the panelled, weathered door to himself he saw a storm-assaulted woman standing before him.

"Ah yes, good evening, my name Carmelita. Me having big prob-i-lims and is because I no find hotel and raining big bad. Yes?"

"Come in," growled Ben.

They trudged up the one hundred and ninety eight steps and entered the living room, where Walter had nodded off to sleep, a half drunk mug of cocoa settled in his lap. He was snoring loudly.

"Sit down over here and I'll sort you a drink," muttered Ben.

"What, you saw me and think?"

"No, I'll... oh, no problem. CHOCOLATE, HOT!" he half-spoke, half-mouthed.

Having boiled the kettle, Ben returned to the living room to find his two guests dozing. But they were awakened moments later by the bell. Again!

"For the love of all things fish, who is this NOW?" cried Ben.

Weary though he was, he bounded down the stairs this time, partly because this joke is starting to get rather long. He arrived breathlessly at the front door. Pulling it hard open, there stood a tall man in a military uniform. Three other faces peered forward from just behind him.

"Sir, sorry to disturb you!" barked the leading man. "We have been on an exercise this very night but the weather's closing in. Looking nasty, sir. We're looking for a place to bed down."

Soon the five men were making their way up the spiral stairwell. Arriving at the top they greeted the bleary-eyed Walter and Carmelita, and released their packs from their backs.

This unusual collection of people then settled down to enjoy what remained of James Bond's adventures. As the credits rolled, Ben thought he would offer his guests a final bedtime drink. Carmelita gave him a hand with the hot drinks and the evening turned to night. And night turned to day.

In the morning, the party hoped for a spot of breakfast and Ben, hospitable to the last, did not disappoint them.

"Ladies – well, *lady* and gentlemen – listen up. I've got cereal and toast, all right? Cornflakes here, or I can do porridge."

Four hands went up for porridge and one for cornflakes.

Which just goes to show that in some places cornflakes are more popular than porridge.

The End.

A Shaggy Dog Story is a plot with a high level of build-up and complicating action, only to be resolved with an anti-climax or ironic reversal, usually one that makes the entire story meaningless.

You could have a lot of fun making up your own 'shaggy dog' stories! This is a good suggestion, keeping in mind the title of this chapter!

I can think of several occasions over the years when, during a time of prayer ministry, the Holy Spirit has encouraged me to have fun.

It's interesting when you think about it. We desire to love God, serve Him, and affirm our commitment to Him and to yield our lives to Him. Sometimes it seems that His response to that is to give us a helping hand by showing us that it is isn't strain and effort that are the main keys, but getting to know Him; and this does not have to be hard work.

As has been said to me, the soil of hearing God clearly is divine rest.

I think there are times when the work of God within us is such that we may face challenges and need to very soberly consider how we are living and Whom we are living for. We may sense, too, that there are occasions when the Spirit of God is asking us to take steps that, were it not for His word to us, we would have preferred not to take.

But I do not believe that the life in Christ is designed to be an endless trudge of self-examination, self-denial and self-sacrifice.

I can think of occasions when the Holy Spirit has corrected me – perhaps in an area of my life where I need to change my attitude. Here's the thing. When He does it, it's a joy and a privilege. It's a relief when He puts his finger on something and I feel a sense of gratitude. This is a very different dynamic to legalistic self-examination.

I see it like this. We have become the sons of God! This is what the work of the Cross has achieved for us and in us. I do recognise that in the outworking of Calvary in each of us, there are times when difficult choices may need to be faced and made. There are also likely to be seasons in which the Holy Spirit majors on certain aspects of our hearts and lives; it may be about our marriage, or how we spend our money, or how we interact with others.

Perhaps we have rather a different face around church than we do at home. Why is that? Do we ever belittle our spouse or our children in public? Why would we do that?

Perhaps you are seeking solace from the compartment of your refrigerator or a fantasy emanating from your TV screen. Perhaps you are involved in a relationship with someone that is really an integral part of your life, and yet you sense that elements of it are unwholesome, or are not helping your desire to walk more deeply with Jesus. These times of focus are real for all of us.

Nevertheless, we have been designed to walk in the comfort of the Holy Spirit. Let us never forget it. Sometimes we can find ourselves living a punishing season, but it isn't He who is punishing us. We have become over-introspective or succumbed to a religious provocation to belittle ourselves or deny ourselves blessings.

He Laughed

I once heard an amazing testimony about the laughter of God. Our personable, rich-in-personality God drew near to one of His children (let's call her Joyce) who had been seeking Him concerning His place in her church's meetings.

Enjoying the presence of the Holy Spirit is a special privilege, one that is available to all of us. Life was always meant to be this way – the Church living in, and enjoying, the presence of God; seeing the fruit of it in others as they are drawn to know Him and to receive healing in their bodies, minds, souls and spirits. When the Church is in the midst of a community and God is in the midst of the Church, there is going to be impact. There is going to be shaking, for sure, and individuals and families are going to become very aware that the living God is among them.

So, this lady was asking the Holy Spirit about their meetings, sensing that some things needed to be turned on their head if they were going to truly experience the Kingdom realities that they were hungry for. The Lord was with them, for sure, but to what degree was He central to their times together? Was He very much in the midst and having His way, or was He somehow confined to the outer edges of their activities? Perhaps the Church was having fun in His presence, but was *He* having fun?

How wonderful that her heart was touched in this way, that she would have the desire to ask Him the question. I mean, we ask those that we love a question like that, don't we? You wouldn't even think twice about doing so. "Are you enjoying yourself?" You must have asked and have been asked that question many times over.

I'm not sure that the Holy Spirit is asked, however, very often. Sometimes, even when we invite Him to have His way, it may be that we have pretty much decided what that is going to look like.

We may be on to something here. The Holy Spirit is a person, with a personality, emotions and feelings. Do we box Him in our own image or give Him freedom to express Himself? He is unique and deserves our worship, love and attention.

Joyce asked Him the question and told the Lord that she wanted to hear Him laugh. Really laugh. She wanted to know that He was at home and enjoying Himself among them.

Having discussed the matter with her fellow leaders, they felt to wait on the Lord. As they did so, they became aware of their own restlessness; oh, how easy it was to 'fill the space' of their times together; the need to 'do something' was tangible. They decided to resist. In fact, they decided that they were not going to give up on this one. They wanted to know what it was like when God takes over. Joyce wanted to hear Him laugh.

They met each week at the usual time but simply waited on the Holy Spirit, holding hands (or I seem to recall that at times they actually physically sat on their hands as a reminder to themselves not to try to orchestrate the meeting). Nothing seemed to happen. They waited and waited. Nothing. But they weren't going to give up.

One week, as they met, the presence of the Lord was among them in a new intensity. Something very supernatural was going on. As they waited once again, Joyce experienced a breeze around her feet. It was brief, but it had happened. A few moments later, it happened again. And then again. What was going on became apparent to her. The Holy Spirit was running around the room. She was feeling the wind as He ran past her.

And then it happened. As He ran past her and towards the back of the room, she heard the audible laughter of the Holy Spirit. The presence of God was intensifying and people began to fall under the power of God.

God had His space and was enjoying Himself. And His unhindered power was moving upon the people.

At one point Joyce sensed that He was right in front of her. He was close – really close – and into her spirit He spoke two words to her.

"Thank you."

Let us remember that the Holy Spirit is the Lord. He is God. He is a person and He has a personality. And He thoroughly enjoys meeting with us!

Unique

As God is a unique individual, so is each of us. Well, we were made in His image!

I believe that the teaching of the theory of evolution has damaged millions. It has been a satanic strike at the core of 'made in the image of God'. It has been a spiritual stab at human identity and at people's sense of worth. It has lied that to take God out of the picture is liberating. On the contrary, it has reduced many to living beneath their human dignity – visionless and drifting.

We were made in the image of God and to purpose. How is that for your self-esteem?

Do you like people-watching? I do, from time to time. Perhaps sitting on a bench with a coffee or at a coffee shop. Here they all come: dawdlers, those in a hurry, couples entwined, other couples moving in haste, perhaps sharing a few cross words. And my favourite: seeing kids with their parents. Physically, at least, they make me smile. They are just so similar! My mum recently told me that I have never looked like my dad as much as I do now.

Sometimes you can just see it, can't you? At other times, it's not so easy; just who does that kid really take after? And babies! Now that is hard. I have a problem with working them out. "Oh, she's really got his eyes and her mouth…" Really? You can actually see those resemblances?

The fact is that we have each been wonderfully designed, created and planned for.

No God-to-man or man-to-God relationship such as yours will ever be repeated. That connection is unique. It is an opportunity for us to invest in and maximize. How we express ourselves to the world and how He expresses Himself to us are tailored to be special, remarkable, peculiar and extraordinary.

It's a question of identity, in essence. Whose are we? To Whom do we belong?

We have been extraordinarily designed, made and provided for by heaven. It is ours to discover and seek out. Our willing, generous God is about the business of revealing it to us.

A Very Special Groan Joke

The floodwaters have receded and the ark has landed on Mount Ararat in modern day Turkey. The boat's occupants have made it out on to soil and rock, and a beautiful rainbow has greeted the relieved and thankful party.

And the Lord has spoken, promising that the spectacular colour show that they are now witnessing across the sky is the sign of His promise that He shall never again flood the earth.

So you could forgive Noah for being surprised the following Friday morning when the Lord spoke to him as follows:

"Noah! Noah!"

"Yea, Lord, I listeneth."

"Pardon?"

"I mean, yes, Lord, I'm listening!"

"Noah, I want you to build me another ark."

"Pardon?"

"Yes, I want you to build me another ark, only this time the specs are going to be a little different. I know the future, Noah."

"Well... sure, I know that you know all things, Lord, but you promised about the flood and..."

The Lord interrupts Noah. "Noah, I always keep my promises. But I want a second ark. Only this time it shall have fish in it. Just fish."

"Excuse me?"

"Yes, that's right, just fish. In fact, only one type of fish. Carp. And it shall be a mighty ark with fourteen levels."

"Lord, I shall do as you command. May I ask why?"

The Lord replies, "Times are changing, Noah. You will need a multi-storey carp ark."

CHAPTER SIXTEEN

The Power of Rejoicing

Sometimes we are required to dig deep.
It's a spiritual deal. Remember Paul's exhortation:

Finally, be strong in the Lord and in the strength of His might. Put on the full armour of God, so that you will be able to stand firm against the schemes of the devil. For our struggle is not against flesh and blood, but against the rulers, against the powers, against the world forces of this darkness, against the spiritual forces of wickedness in the heavenly places.

Ephesians 6:12

God has bestowed on us all that we need to live this new life that He has placed in us. Our ability to live it well and to live it successfully depends on our 'reckoning' of what He has already done for us and in us. To 'reckon' on something is to agree with it; to consciously decide that it is right and true. It is to trust it as reliable in one's life.

You may know people who appear to live out a genuinely, joy-filled experience of their salvation in Jesus, and perhaps wonder why your own experience lacks the verve and sense of celebration that they have.

I have come to see that the Holy Spirit loves to reveal to us the truth of the Bible but then take us into a personal sense of it, so that we can own it for ourselves.

If, for example, I do not really know, deep in my heart, my identity in Jesus Christ and that I now walk this earth as a forgiven son, my experience of God's forgiveness is likely to be hampered and dulled and depend on my personal sense of how well I am doing.

If I doubt the truth that the Holy Spirit within me is the very same Spirit that raised Christ from the dead, I may live a hampered prayer life, relying on my own sense of how well I am doing spiritually, rather than on the facts relayed in Scripture.

On the other hand, if I 'own' the scriptures that clearly state that my sins and my sin nature were dealt with at Calvary and that I was included in that unique work of the cross, my experience has to fall into line. It would make no sense for me to continue to strive for what I already have; I have it because God says I have it, but I have it to purpose when I cooperate with the revelation, when I participate in it. I make it mine by a definitive decision. That word, once only a truth in print to me, has now become flesh to me and has become part of me. I have chosen to walk as the person and as the new creature that Jesus says I already am.

Holy Spirit, You are the same One that rose Christ up in the tomb. I praise You because You want to, and are going to, express Your power in and through me, too.

The paradox is that as we put in this modicum of 'reckoning work', we enter into His rest.

It's that 'deep sigh' rest – you know that kind of sigh you give when you slump back into an armchair having finally completed a chore or task that had been hanging over you for a while? *Phew! It's done. Let's bask in it for a moment.*

Actually let's bask in it for a lifetime. Take a moment to just consider the reality of your position in Jesus Christ. It is something mind-boggling that we can choose to rejoice in!

Jesus has transferred you out of the kingdom of darkness and into the Kingdom of Light. He has made you to be a new creature. Are you listening? That has already been done, and you and I would do well to take it on, believe it and allow it to work its glorious truth in our spirit man. Your sins have been erased; they dissolved in the blood of Jesus and they are no longer allotted to your account. Not only that, but should you commit any further sins – and this may happen when we forget that we have been given a new nature which does not sin – they have also been included.

Therefore, any judgement that might have applied to your account has been cancelled, having already been activated against Jesus Christ at Calvary. As we have previously said, it isn't fair but it is gloriously true.

I'm not even sure that we have a sin account any longer. I believe that Jesus closed it down, satisfying its full demands. There is a Kingdom account that tracks our progress because God is looking to reward us!

Moreover, our standing with God will continue on this basis for the rest of our earthly lives. Despite you, despite your flaws and failings, every angle pertaining to your right standing with God has been covered. So rather than waste effort and energy on trying to manufacture any right standing (righteousness) of our own, we would do much better by accepting this gift that we have been given and get on with deepening the relationship established for us by Jesus.

We can but praise our God and thank Him for an all-encompassing salvation such as this that we have received. If life is tough just now, I can rejoice in what I know has been accomplished in Jesus.

To consider ourselves unworthy of it, I would add, is a cop out. If He has made us worthy, who are we to say that we are not? This is actually pride of the highest order, and we need to deal with it, refute it and distance ourselves from its lies and accusations. Grace is not fair, it is outrageously biased in our favour, and that it how God has so designed it. It is so far above and beyond what we may have managed to achieve for ourselves, we can only stand up, marvel and say thank you.

It's rather like when someone does something for you that you would not have managed to do yourself. Gestures of recompense or reciprocal favour seem pointless. They *are* pointless. You are not supposed to be trying to match the action of which you are a blessed recipient. You are simply meant to be receiving it with a heart full of gratitude. Pride would deny you that joy and privilege. God does not enjoy our sullen, self-centred response when we decide that His outrageous grace is not for us.

God gets pleasure from our simple receiving of His love, His grace and His gifts. God says that it us better to give than receive – and He certainly models it well. It's not that receiving is bad, but it does come second to giving. God gives and then enjoys the fact that we receive. This is how He operates so we had better get used to it. As we do so, we find that we, like Him, enjoy giving generously to others and, in the same way, take pleasure as our giving is received and enjoyed by them.

Even the last bastion of death has been overcome in Christ; in Christ you are part of that. The Holy Spirit wants to take us beyond the theology and into a living reality that we are never going to die. When our earthly body ceases to operate, our new nature will continue right on, more at home than it has ever been before. Just as you and I live from heavenly places, we will continue to do so, except that we will have a new spiritual body that will no longer be subject to the contamination and natural order of decay that pertains to life on earth. This is not fantasy; this is truth.

I am going to share more about heaven a little later but here are just a few thoughts...

Heaven! HEAVEN! It is real!

I remember speaking about the reality of heaven on one occasion to my church. I took with me a holiday brochure and asked everyone to consider how much planning we are likely to put into a two week vacation. We look at the photographs and read the descriptions of the resorts and their facilities; we consider where we would like to be and what activities we would like to be involved with. We imagine it all, we look forward to it and tell our friends about it. The prospect excites and encourages us. All this for a two week holiday!

How about a destination that for certain cannot disappoint and will simply be more wonderful than we can ever ask for or imagine? How about a destination where every conceivable need and delight has been reserved for us? The most perfect Host awaits us there, as do millions of people whom we will know in an intimacy barely describable. Moreover, we will not come back from there; we will be there forever and ever, knowing that we are perfectly at home.

It's interesting in the Book of Acts that, as the power of the Holy Spirit invigorated the growing fledgling Body of Christ, the believers had all things in common. They were getting 'blessed out of their boots' by the manifest presence of God, and the fruit of this was that they had no real desire to hold on to anything for themselves. They wanted to give and give; *what is mine is now also yours.* What a tremendous testimony to the reality of God among those communities! No wonder the church was growing so fast! No wonder they were a rejoicing people.

It was an environment of the Holy Spirit; free and full of joy.

Heaven is holding a reception for new arrivals. Despite the increasing trend on earth of believers mixing outside of their denominations, several groups have separated to different parts of the hall.

An angel arrives on the scene to take a drinks order.

"Thank you, thank you, listen up please! We'd love to offer you something to drink. Baptists? Hands up for coffee? Okay. Catholics? Hands up for coffee? Right. Strict Bretheren? Oh, of course... you'll all want decaf. Methodists? Hands up for coffee, and yes, we add the cream after. C of E? Hands up for... oh, right... tea all round."

One group remained.

"OK, you cuddly charismatics, hands *down* for coffee!"

CHAPTER SEVENTEEN

Dark Light and Distraction

No wonder, for even Satan disguises himself as an angel of light. Therefore it is not surprising if his servants also disguise themselves as servants of righteousness, whose end will be according to their deeds.

2 Corinthians 11:14-15

There is the real and there is the counterfeit.

Most of us are aware of the obvious no-no temptations that we need to steer clear of. They are plain to us. Not all temptations are quite so easy to spot, however.

I recall participating in the organisation of a church quiz night. One of the rounds that we devised involved tasting and identifying different brands of cola-flavoured soft drinks.

We bought the famous brands – you know which ones – and included some less well-known and less expensive ones. Being careful to remember which plastic glass contained which brand, the samples were presented on a tray to members of the quiz teams. They simply had to match the brands to their respective samples.

It appears that we had a cola expert amongst us that evening. When we shared the results of this particular round and the answers to the matching activity, this individual assured us that we had made a mistake. Our protestations that we were sure that we were right soon lost their authority as this persuasive team member confidently identified which drinks were in the glasses of contention.

He knew which one was the "real thing".

I expect you know that this multi-million dollar industry guards its secrets jealously. The giants shroud their recipes with mystery as they seek to promote, grow and protect their commercial interests. Some of you reading these words now will not really care about which can or bottle of fizzy cola you buy, except that you perhaps draw the line at the ultra-value cheap ones. Yes, should you drink, it you recognise a cola flavour but it really might as well be engine cleaner. Yuk!

You might also, perhaps like our Mr Expert whom I referred to earlier, be able to confidently distinguish between the two – two, is that fair? – major brands. Putting the sugar free varieties to one side, I happen to think that one of them tastes noticeably sweeter than the other – that's just me. No disrespect intended, I would be hard pushed to down a glass of thirty-pence-per-litre cola.

Our spiritual enemy has a range of ploys to try to seduce us with counterfeit light. I'm going to call it 'dark' light. Because it is a *form* of light, or at least it *looks* like real light. Our spiritual enemy, a being that is ruled by sin, filth and rebellion, can morph into visions of apparent beauty where it suits his desire, to deceive and capture the undiscerning amongst us.

The mere notion of the existence of a devil is mocked by those who are already blinded by this angel of darkness. He is perfectly content for them to take such a view; as long as they stay away from the revelation of the Holy Spirit who reveals Jesus Christ as Lord, he is unfazed even at their refusal to recognise his existence. He has them exactly where he wants them. If he cannot get people to worship him, he will settle for the fact that they are not worshipping Jesus. This is how the spirit of antichrist operates. It opposes Christ and Kingdom agenda.

For those of us in the Kingdom of Light, however, a very different dynamic is operating. As sons of God in Christ, we are identified by hell and its operatives as archenemies. Our destination has been settled, our ownership has been finalised; we are now part of heaven's family and its army. The enemy has but one ploy left open to him, namely to attempt to deceive or distract us from fulfilling our Kingdom call and destiny. In other words, hell's only mission concerning us is damage limitation for its part. The Blood of the Lamb has triumphed and Jesus has won us for all eternity. Hallelujah!

God would have us feast on heaven's delights. He would have us grow and mature on a diet of the pure Word of God; this includes the Bible but I really mean Jesus Himself. He is the Word of God. Nothing that heaven would feed us can harm us or sidetrack us. The Holy Spirit is working Christ in us towards a firm purpose. A guided missile could not be more centred on achieving specific aims than the power of the Holy Spirit in our lives. And regardless of how we may be feeling, God is supremely confident about what He is doing in our life's journey. The Lord of lords does not waver, and He is able to steady us, stabilise us and further our progress in the Spirit life even when we doubt our own faltering steps. We have been born again to be agents of transformation to one another in the Body of Christ and to those who have not yet met Him.

We would do well to remember that the flesh life counts for nothing (John 6:63). God is not saying that bodies are irrelevant or that our lives on earth lack significance – completely the opposite, in fact. The Holy Spirit in our redeemed, life-activated spirits is life itself; He acts within us to move us forward in Kingdom purposes.

Our spirit man has been designed to live in relationship with the Holy Spirit. Some of us can be very task-oriented – that is why there are those who prefer religion to relationship with the Lord. We will hear Him speak with us as we walk closely with Him.

Because He has said one thing does not necessarily mean that we are to stay in it for life. We do not want to assume; we want to hear Him.

I remember talking to a dear friend about a business venture that he took on. It was a 'God thing'; he entered into the venture and all was well. Motivation comes easily as we start out on an endeavour knowing that we have the backing of heaven.

When times get tough, it is especially reassuring to recall Who endorsed the venture in the first place. He will surely guide and provide.

And yet, as He leads, we need to move with Him. To his own admission, my friend did not really continue to involve the Lord in the outworking of his affairs and a while later, he became aware that he was out-of-date with God on this issue. He had begun to take the business along a path that God had not intended and the initial fruit from it had turned to barrenness. What had begun in blessing had now become a distraction.

Sometimes the process of developing intimacy with God involves some internal unravelling and in areas where we may still be relying on the crutches of addiction and other bondages, we may have to undergo some Surgeon's work as He operates in us to release us from those damaging holds in our lives.

At these times we need to push into God, seek Him, draw upon the life of the Spirit. We have already seen this from Scripture. Where we have, or have had, a stronghold of sin, it is important to replace the substitute with something of God, something real and sourced in the life of the Spirit. The tempter would have us remain in our dark places and would even promise us an easier ride, but the truth is otherwise. Only the Spirit life will progress us in our Kingdom walk.

The Bible warns us that we live in days when people are looking to have their ears tickled.

> *For the time will come when they will not endure sound doctrine; but wanting to have their ears tickled, they will accumulate for themselves teachers in accordance to their own desires, and will turn away their ears from the truth and will turn aside to myths.*
>
> *2 Timothy 4:3-4*

I think that a key reason why the Holy Spirit wants us to know Him well is so that He can have access to us to bring us healing. Hurt people are susceptible to deception. Church people are not exempt from this. Sometimes it is as if a smoother ride is on offer but it can be the enemy's counterfeit light. It can attract us but there is no joy in it ultimately.

As an example, I have heard from two or three sources recently of individuals and even churches embracing 'new' theology or revelation concerning salvation. I am sure that they use the word 'revelation' as it sounds more progressive! Revelation from the Holy Spirit will never contradict His word! In this teaching, people are 'discovering' that God, in His abounding love, has included all people in Christ already and that no response is required from them to what Christ has done. This is counterfeit light because it denies the word of God. I understand the heart of those who are teaching an alternative gospel that seeks to embrace everyone, nevertheless, it is ultimately an anti-Christ spirit that would propagate belief that counters what God says in His word.

There can be warmth and a buzz about being part of a group that makes and shares discovery! I believe that we need to be solid about our true identity in Christ so that we have no need to seek other approval or commendation.

People with unresolved hurts, especially in the area of abuse or rejection, can confuse sympathy with love. God's love is not at all diminished because of the real existence of an eternal hell. On the contrary, His love has already demonstrated its wide, wide embrace in the sending of His Son to the cross on our behalf. But the Word of God clearly says that we need to appropriate this for ourselves, each one of us.

> *Yet to all who did receive him, to those who believed in his name, he gave the right to become children of God.*
>
> *John 1:12 (NIV)*

These are days in which we in the Church need to keep the main thing as the main thing. The Holy Spirit has promised to direct us and to supply all our needs from Christ's riches. We are not going to miss out. Let us seek Him closely, and in so doing we will avoid time-wasting tangents and the enemy's cul-de-sacs that would distract us from the simplicity of walking with Jesus.

CHAPTER EIGHTEEN

But He Means It

A truck driver gets an unusual call one morning.

"Jed, this is an odd one, but we need you to transport a consignment of penguins to the zoological park. The zoo's regular provider has let us down. I know it's short notice but there's £200 in it for you if you can take it on."

Jed sees the bundle of £10 notes in his mind's eye and the decision is made. "Er... all right... I'll be right over."

Having had the penguins loaded into his truck, Jed heads for the zoo. On the way there, disaster strikes. He gets a puncture in two tyres at the same time. He barely manages to get his truck off the highway to the side of the road.

But help is at hand. A pickup truck, passing on the other side of the street, stops and a guy calls out, "Need any help, mate?"

"Yeah, I've a real problem," Jed shouts back. "My truck's crippled and I've got a consignment of penguins on board for the zoo! Could you get the penguins to the zoo for me in your pickup? There's £50 in it for you!"

"No worries, mate!" He pulls round to the back of the truck and fifteen penguins shuffle up the ramp and on to the pickup.

"Aw, thanks pal, you're a saint!" Jed says. "You know where you're going, right? You're taking them to the zoo!"

The pickup pulls away leaving Jed with his empty truck.

Jed sets to work on his flat tyres, and after a lot of effort with a couple of spare tyres, he manages to get his truck back on the road. "Not bad," he thinks to himself. "I've still got £150 towards new tyres."

He sets off and immediately has a shock. He sees the pickup truck on its way towards him on the other side of the road and, to his horror, the penguins are still on board. He flashes his lights at the driver and both vehicles slow to a halt. They wind down their driver's windows.

Jed splutters: "Mate! What are you doing? Where are you going with m' penguins? I gave you fifty quid to take them to the zoo!"

"Yeah, yeah, I know, I've done that," came the reply. "But I had cash left over so now I'm taking them to the cinema."

Sometimes misunderstandings can occur and they cost! It can be difficult to discern, at times, whether people really mean what they are saying or are truly saying what they mean. I want to look at an example or two from the world of sport for a moment and then share some good news!

The world of football in England is in crisis – again. This week, as I write, major controversies have arisen concerning comments made by high profile figures in the game. Any suspect behaviour in the arena of the country's national sport is guaranteed to attract keen and lengthy attention, and the current coverage is fully representative of that tendency.

In one case, a professional footballer, recently found guilty of a rape charge, has been permitted by his employer – his football club – to remain on the books and use the training facilities. There is little doubt in my mind that this decision was taken as a first step with a view to retaining the player and later incorporating him back into the team squad once the attention had abated somewhat.

However, as events turned out, such was the public outcry at the club's decision and its apparent disinterest in the severity of the player's crime, it has now had a re-think and rescinded its decision. If it imagined that it would receive plaudits for the U-turn then it may be disappointed. Rather, people are asking why the club was apparently so indifferent to the realities of the controversy in the first place.

The second situation involves a recently appointed football manager whose personal electronic communications somehow leaked into the public domain. His comments were deemed to be of a racist nature, and although the individual has apologised, one wonders if the apology is genuine or perhaps a last ditch attempt to keep his new post.

Ironically, the third scenario involves the owner of the club who had appointed our manager in the second story. Having defended his new recruit to the hilt, the elderly gentleman then gave an interview to a major national newspaper in which he made comments that, shall we say, *supported* a well documented stereotypical criticism of a particular ethnic and religious group. He, too, has since apologised for his comments and for any hurt that they may have caused.

As I considered these news reports I had a wonderful thought. God tells us what He really thinks of us. He never lies and… what He thinks of us is really marvellous. No, I am understating it. He thinks we are *spectacular.*

This is worthy of our focus because we can become very used to statements being made about all sorts of situations in the public eye only for them to be retracted or amended or qualified at some later date.

It can be a bit like reading an advertisement for a deal that immediately catches your attention, excites you and then bursts your bubble when you read the small print:

FREE flat screen TV to every customer*!

Offer for 3 days only!
Simply spend £50 or more in the store!
Genuine offer! Free TV worth £499!
Come inside!

* You must be 110 years old, a serving submarine commander and born on the 29th February to qualify.

You know what I mean.

Listening to the news accounts this week, I have been struck not so much by the nature of the protagonists' original comments but by their responses, subsequent 'edits' and excuses.

In the first case I described, the footballer has challenged his original conviction – and as the law allows it, who am I to criticise? It is concerning, however, that the only public statement made by the player appeared on his website, where he read a prepared script, apologising to many but not mentioning at all the woman that he had been convicted of abusing.

Please understand, I am not making judgement on the individual. Although I believe it fine to have an opinion and to express it, I prefer not to judge anyone. Rather, I am highlighting what was and what was not included in his public statement.

The newly appointed manager in my second scenario admitted to making a mistake. What does that mean? What was the mistake? He has not explained at all. Was it that he got caught? Was it that he had held a certain view and that he has now realised that his view was wrong?

It's as if admitting to a mistake (of some nature) sweeps the real issue under the carpet. Because I would suggest that the real issue is this: what do you really think or believe about the people group that you admit you smeared?

The same goes for the new boss's new employer. He, too, has admitted to making a mistake, but what does that mean? Again, my question above applies.

Were I in the public eye, and if I was heard to say that I believed all people bearing a particular nationality or characteristic should go and jump off a cliff, what would that mean as far as my character was concerned? If I believe what I have been heard to say, I might think it wise to explain the comments. If, however, I simply apologise and say that I made a mistake, I am not really revealing anything at all except that I would like the adverse publicity to go away. Did I mean what I said or not?

I have lost count of the number of occasions when someone in public office or in a key position of responsibility has been excused his or her inappropriate behaviour on the grounds that such behaviour has nothing to do with the job role. This is nonsense.

Would you hire me to offer academic support to your young children on a weekend morning if you knew that I beat my wife? Or if you were aware that I smoked cannabis socially? "Oh yes, no problem, as long as your behaviour doesn't influence my kids." Seriously? "No problem, as long as you do your job..." I beg to differ.

The leader of an increasingly successful and influential political party in the UK has recently made it very clear how far he would go to achieve his political aims; he said that he would do a deal with the devil if it meant he would get what he wanted. If that is the kind of leader you are, sir, then you are not going to get my vote!

"Oh, but I didn't mean..." So what *did* you mean? Who are you, really, out of the suit or the uniform?

Who we are is highly relevant in what we do. Today's society seems to pick and choose, however, depending on how much it may gain from its moral or amoral decision. It will make a stand against a footballer who has been convicted of rape and applaud itself for its morality. On the other hand, I wonder what the decision would have been if the footballer had been one of the country's top players whose absence at national level might seriously affect the potential prospects of the country's team at a significant tournament. Am I being cynical? Maybe. You are free to make up your mind and, of course, you don't have to agree with me!

The Bible is clear on why we say what we say and do what we do:

> *For there is no good tree which produces bad fruit, nor, on the other hand, a bad tree which produces good fruit. For each tree is known by its own fruit. For men do not gather figs from thorns, nor do they pick grapes from a briar bush. The good man out of the good treasure of his heart brings forth what is good; and the evil man out of the evil treasure brings forth what is evil; for his mouth speaks from that which fills his heart.*
>
> *Luke 6:43-45*

The Contemporary English Bible (CEV) renders verse 45 as follows:

> *A good person produces good from the good treasury of the inner self, while an evil person produces evil from the evil treasury of the inner self. The inner self overflows with words that are spoken.*

There you have it. I would suggest that we say what we mean. We might not communicate well or clearly what we mean, but I do not really see how I can affirm a view today and then, apparently, completely reverse it tomorrow unless I have good reason for having changed it.

But God

But God is gloriously transparent. He always but always says what He means and means what He says – even when He is talking in parables! He doesn't speak with an angle or with a hidden agenda. In fact, His agendas – though not many of his ways! – are very open and plain to see.

Read the verses below and as you do so, dwell on the fact that God absolutely means what He says.

The LORD appeared to him from afar, saying,
"I have loved you with an everlasting love;
Therefore I have drawn you with lovingkindness."

Jeremiah 31:3

Be strong and courageous, do not be afraid or tremble at them, for the LORD your God is the one who goes with you. He will not fail you or forsake you.

Deuteronomy 31:6

God is faithful, through whom you were called into fellowship with His Son, Jesus Christ our Lord.

1 Corinthians 1:9

Your ears will hear a word behind you, "This is the way, walk in it," whenever you turn to the right or to the left.

Isaiah 30:21

And these signs will accompany those who believe: In my name they will drive out demons; they will speak in new tongues; they will pick up snakes with their hands; and when they drink deadly poison, it will not hurt them at all; they will place their hands on sick people, and they will get well.

Mark 6:17-18

The glory which You have given Me I have given to them, that they may be one, just as We are one; I in them and You in Me, that they may be perfected in unity, so that the world may know that You sent Me, and loved them, even as You have loved Me. Father, I desire that they also, whom You have given Me, be with Me where I am, so that they may see

My glory which You have given Me, for You loved Me
before the foundation of the world.

John 17:22-24

Blessed be the God and Father of our Lord Jesus Christ, who
according to His great mercy has caused us to be born again
to a living hope through the resurrection of Jesus Christ
from the dead, to obtain an inheritance which is
imperishable and undefiled and will not fade away, reserved
in heaven for you, who are protected by the power of God
through faith for a salvation ready to be revealed in the last
time.

1 Peter 1:3-5

God speaks words of life. His words contain the power of life, the light of life and the action of life at work. He means what He says.

Even in the few lines quoted above, we see with clarity that God promises us His declaration of love. The awesome God loves you and me – the Creator of the heavens and the earth feels and participates on our behalf. He is with us, He assures us, and promises never to leave us. How glorious!

He assures us of His faithfulness. His nature is faultless and He favours us. He has promised to lead and guide us. Sometimes we think that we are beyond hearing Him, but in His declared faithfulness He knows how to reach you, even despite you! It helps if we can slow down at times and allow Him space to speak to us!

He says that He has given us His glory. HIS GLORY! We, rightly, are engaged in glorifying Him, honouring Him and declaring His greatness and majesty. But He then responds by bathing us in His glory! As He does this, He says that He gels the Church together; we see that we are part of one another. We see that the Holy Spirit is about much more than blessing your or my church with His presence, as wonderful as that is; He wants us to have Kingdom vision, to see that we are part of one glorious, holy Body of Christ.

The glory which You have given Me I have given to them,
that they may be one, just as We are one; I in them and You
in Me, that they may be perfected in unity, so that the world

may know that You sent Me, and loved them, even as You
have loved Me.

John 17:22-23

The Message (MSG) says:

The same glory you gave me, I gave them,
So they'll be as unified and together as we are –
I in them and you in me.
Then they'll be mature in this oneness,
And give the godless world evidence
That you've sent me and loved them
In the same way you've loved me.

We are about Kingdom business. Our desire is to see the nature of
Jesus Christ expressed wherever we are: in our church services, in our
homes, in our workplaces, in the shopping centres and at leisure
venues.

Doesn't this sound like an adventure? He takes great joy and delight
in involving each of us. I may be flawed, but He is for me!

We have an inheritance that is waiting for us in heaven. Those lines
in 1 Peter also say that our salvation is ready to be revealed in the last
days. I don't think we can fully grasp the wonder and magnitude of
such a promise, but we can absolutely believe every word of it. God
has said it and we can trust Him to fulfil what He has spoken.

I am sure that there are many other wonderful truths that we could
draw from the verses above, such as Peter's affirmation that we are
protected by God's power, something that I would say we take for
granted at times. But we can certainly enjoy the transparency of God's
Word.

Of course, we should add a key additional point. God has never
had to apologise for anything He has said. He has never misjudged a
single word. He has never spoken or acted with questionable motives.
He has never had to step aside from His position of authority or
responsibility due to a conflict of interests.

As we grow up in our faith, we may leave behind some of our
childish immaturities but we are not to leave behind our childlike
approach to the Lord. Children largely take what you say to them at
face value – unless they know you are prone to pulling their leg! We,

too, can expect God to speak plainly to us and take what He says as reliable, trustworthy and solid.

CHAPTER NINETEEN

Lose Your Life and Win

I will also rejoice in Jerusalem and be glad in My people;
And there will no longer be heard in her the voice of weeping
and the sound of crying.

Isaiah 65:19

Moses has a spot of time free, as you do in Heaven, and says to Jesus, "Lord, do You fancy a round of golf?"

"Sure," replies Jesus.

At the first hole, Moses and the Lord take their first shots and both of them manage to land their ball down the middle of the fairway.

Moses then takes his second shot and skews the ball to the left towards some water. As the ball hits the water, the water parts and forms a bank on one side, sending the ball in a curve back towards the green. It rolls to a stop just three centimetres from the hole.

Jesus takes His second shot and He too slices it, sending his ball towards the water. But his ball merely skims its surface and a gust of wind pulls the shot high towards the green. The ball then dips, bounces twice on the short, crisp grass and rolls plumb into the hole.

At that moment, a ball soars over Moses' and Jesus' heads. It arcs to the right, straight into the mouth of an incoming eagle. The eagle carries the ball for a few seconds before dropping it. It lands on the back of a rabbit that has hopped on to the green. The rabbit flicks the ball into the air with its tail and the ball loops into the hole.

Moses says, "Lord, this always happens when your Dad plays too."

You know, I'm going to play some sport with the Lord in heaven. I wonder how that works; do you think He'll let me win?

Jokes aside, I want to remind us of a hugely important premise that Jesus has taught us about living productively.

> *...you must help the weak and remember the words of the Lord Jesus, that He Himself said, 'It is more blessed to give than to receive.'*
>
> Acts 20:35

St Francis echoed the same exhortation when he said that it is better to give than to receive.

The Amplified Bible (AMP) reads like this:

> *...we ought to assist the weak, being mindful of the words of the Lord Jesus, how He Himself said, It is more blessed (makes one happier and more to be envied) to give than to receive.*

Blessing is the touch of God. It is the interaction between God and us; it is His initiative towards us in all that He thinks about us, does on our behalf and produces in and through us. Blessing is that relationship that God, through Jesus, activates and grows within our spirit man. It is His lordship, His friendship and His fathering. It is what He works in us which partners with His revealing of the Kingdom of God on earth.

It is very much about Him being present in us, around us and in the expression of our lives with others. We are the ones who are owned by Jesus – we belong to Him. The Holy Spirit would have us live lives that are anxiety-free, lives that rest in a cradle of 'God trust'. We grow in Christ and strive less; that rest is the soil in which joy can flourish.

C.S. Lewis reminds us in his famous 'Screwtape Letters' that we truly find who we are as we yield ourselves to the Lord. Wormwood counsels his minion demon:

> *When He [God] talks of their losing their selves, He means only abandoning the clamour of self-will; once they have done that, He really gives them back all their personality, and boasts (I am afraid, sincerely) that when they are wholly His they will be more themselves than ever.*

The prophet Nehemiah told the people around him who were working in God's purposes that the joy of the Lord was their strength (Nehemiah 8:10). It is difficult not to suffocate joy if you are in striving mode. Striving is born from fear, from a mentality of lack and distrust. Striving says, "I am relying on myself." Rest says, "I am relying on Him because that is how I was designed to live."

The 'easy yoke' and 'light burden" that Jesus speaks of in Matthew 11 is the perfect illustration. Are there burdens (challenges, work) in life? Yes, but in the power and presence of the Holy Spirit, we can experience them as 'light'. Is there a yoke to God? Absolutely! The blood of Christ has united us with Him, but not to a life of strife and anxiety born out of a sense of threat. On the contrary, Jesus calls the yoke 'easy'. It was never meant to be difficult or punishing.

I sense that God would encourage us to trust Him at new levels, ones which will mean letting go of the reins in some areas of our thinking. Do you need to do that? Can you see aspects of your life in which you are tired from striving to control the tiller? "If I take my hands off the controls, everything is going to fall apart," whispers a threatening voice.

Today, you can move in the opposite spirit. Dare to rest and to place your worries and overstretched sense of responsibility at the foot of the cross. There is a different way to live! Jesus didn't complete his mission in order that you and I might live our lives in tension and stress. Perhaps it was these Bible verses that drew you to Him in the first place:

> Come to me, all you who are weary and burdened, and I will give you rest. Take my yoke upon you and learn from me, for I am gentle and humble in heart, and you will find rest for your souls. For my yoke is easy and my burden is light.
>
> Matthew 11:28-30 (NIV)

The fruit of living in this manner is joy. Joy relaxes, it breathes, it rests. Joy is our participation with what God is doing through His Spirit rather than our attempting to manipulate God and others through our own efforts and with our own understanding. I like what Steve Mariboli has said:

> You must learn to let go. Release the stress. You were never in control anyway.

It is worth investing in living according to those verses in Matthew 11. We cannot change ourselves but we can allow God to do His transforming work. Sometimes that process involves heavy struggle. We would all say that we have had our fair share; which probably means that conflict is a natural part of God's working in us. Sometimes we face challenges in which we feel utterly out of our depth; we may be promoted in the workplace and feel like a fish out of water until we learn to adapt and to develop new skills. We may suffer an injustice and it appears that God is not on our case.

I am learning that it is especially when I feel that God is not on my case that something in me is being pricked by the Spirit. Oh yes, Father is on to something. He has a target. He has my freedom in mind and it is on the way.

He is the Alpha and the Omega (Revelation 21, 22) – He sees the beginning and the end seamlessly. This also means that He sees everything in between! We have, if we can see it, come into a place of rest already because we have committed our lives and the purpose of them to Him. That's right – we died with Christ and were raised with Him. Our struggles are often about our laying down of our own wearying agendas so that we can live freely in His that will bring blessing and also further the Kingdom.

Sometimes we can discover more of this will by taking time to wait on Him prayerfully. Free of agenda or requests, we can take a little time to invite His presence and to soak in it – to just be. He may just drop something very significant into our hearts.

Let me leave the last word in this chapter to Allyson Felix who has said:

> The most important lesson that I have learned is to trust God in every circumstance. Lots of times we go through different trials and following God's plan seems like it doesn't make any sense at all. God is always in control and he will never leave us.

CHAPTER TWENTY

Happy Ending

Blessed are you who hunger now, for you shall be satisfied.
Blessed are you who weep now, for you shall laugh.

Luke 6:21

Since the early days of my life in Jesus Christ, I have had a solid assurance of the reality of heaven. We are going to spend a rather long time there, so it is a great place to end this book.

During a particularly traumatic time during my final year at university, I heard the sound of heaven. It sounded like a trumpet call and I heard it twice. It was real enough at the time for me to have asked my shopping companion whether she had heard it too. I have never forgotten that moment, and in my subsequent growth in faith over the years it has remained bedrock.

Heaven is real. Not only are those of us who have come into relationship with Jesus going there but also our eternal life has already begun. As I write to you today from heavenly places in Christ Jesus, I sincerely hope that you are reading from the same location and position. If you are in relationship with Christ, then you are.

I have walked through a lot of hugely uncomfortable phases of earth life. Those episodes, I would imagine, fall into many of the categories that have involved challenges to you too. I do not want to spend time describing them because my aim here is not for us to hold a mutual group hug. (Not that hugs are a bad thing; they are great, come to mention it!) Rather, I would like us to have one of those biblical 'Selah' moments. You find these scattered throughout the Psalms, where David (or one of the other songsters) ponders something of God's truth. He chews on it for a moment; he allows his mind to 'reckon as right' what He is declaring about God and a particular facet of his power, love and faithfulness. 'Selah'. Pause for a moment and just think on that.

You see, Holy Spirit perspective does help. He is the Truth. He is God. Nothing that He reveals can harm us or discourage us. He declares and reveals divine possibility, progress and advance.

We are assured of God's presence and care throughout our days on earth, and also we have to recognise that there are major challenges to be faced. God takes every step with us and even carries us on occasions. He walks through walls of impossibility and promises that each and every circumstance that we face is absorbed into the divine mix of His will for our lives. He is the Redeemer. This does not mean that He always intervenes as we may ask or demand. Sometimes His apparent inaction or silence can be hard to bear, but nevertheless He has promised what He has promised, and He has never lied once in His eternal existence and being. Indeed, He is the same yesterday, today and forever (Hebrews 13:8).

We may, if we are film buffs, be used to periodic flights into the fanciful world of the moviemakers. There anything is possible, right? Worlds exist beyond our imagination – though apparently not beyond the imagination and design of the film producer! It is but a short escape into a distant land of 'other realm'; but the credits roll, the dimmed lights of the cinema illumine again and a blast of cold air from the overhead air conditioning slaps us back into the reality of the world in which we walk.

We walk here on earth, true. But it is in Him that we live and move and have our being.[3]

I want us to take this moment together to ponder an astonishing reality: you and I belong to Heaven, and after our earth excursion has completed, we will continue there forever and ever and ever.

It is good to suck the marrow from life in the here and now. We want to fully enter into its joys, and a consequence of living abundantly is that the pains are also keenly felt. It can be of little comfort that Paul describes them as "fleeting" or "brief" in the Bible's book of Romans; he is right, but when you are pressed into grief or into pressure's corner,

---

[3] See p.96

the reality of 'momentary-ness' can seem a more distant encouragement.

So, perhaps we might consider the extravagance of eternity for those bought back to heaven's company and family by Jesus' finished work.

> *Then I saw a new heaven and a new earth; for the first heaven and the first earth passed away, and there is no longer any sea. And I saw the holy city, new Jerusalem, coming down out of heaven from God, made ready as a bride adorned for her husband. And I heard a loud voice from the throne, saying, "Behold, the tabernacle of God is among men, and He will dwell among them, and they shall be His people, and God Himself will be among them, and He will wipe away every tear from their eyes; and there will no longer be any death; there will no longer be any mourning, or crying, or pain; the first things have passed away."*
>
> Revelation 21:1-4

The New Living Translation (NLT) gives verses 3 and 4 as follows:

> *I heard a loud shout from the throne, saying, "Look, God's home is now among his people! He will live with them, and they will be his people. God himself will be with them. He will wipe every tear from their eyes, and there will be no more death or sorrow or crying or pain. All these things are gone forever."*

"Forever." We are so used to the beginning and ending of things – the hope experienced as something looked forward to draws near or something not enjoyed comes to an end. We feel excitement and we feel anti-climax. We might even dupe ourselves into thinking that we have a grip on how timing works in the seasons of our lives. But in my experience of my own life, and in what I have observed in others' lives, we are adept at misjudging them. We can often be surprised when God is in the mix too, working through purposes that we had not really had a handle on.

Forever. There will be, I can guarantee you on the authority of God's words, no sorrow or pain in this place where we are going to continue to live forever. God's presence will be a tangible constant, habitual, always around us and in us. There is fullness – completeness – of joy in His presence, and this is going to be our lot forever and ever.

Joy, fun, laughter, fulfilment, warmth, love, unity, delight, wholeness, clarity and peace. Forever and forever. Really.

I expect your imagination can fathom a few possibilities as to what this might look like. We have the Holy Spirit who loves to reveal reality concerning God's nature and order of things. In any event, why should Hollywood's producers have all the good ideas?!

It is wonderful to recognise, though, that whatever notions we are able to perceive concerning this reality that approaches us closer day by day, we can only see in part.

> ... *"Things which eye has not seen and ear has not heard, and which have not entered the heart of man, all that God has prepared for those that love him." For to us God revealed them through the Spirit; for the Spirit searches all things, even the depths of God.*
>
> *1 Corinthians 2:9-10*

The Message Bible (MSG) puts the first part in this way:

> *No one's ever seen or heard anything like this, Never so much as imagined anything quite like it – What God has arranged for those who love him.*

To say, therefore, that we are in for pleasant, sensational surprises is clearly a massive understatement.

God has promised us that, even now, preparations are being made for his sons and daughters. Think about that for a moment. As you live here on earth, involved in your various enterprises, heaven is preparing your place. You will not be simply 'one of the crowd'. You are well known, loved and very much valued even as your dwelling place is being arranged.

The Bible says that we are going to reign with Christ. To reign! Those who reign have authority and oversight. We are going to be marvellously involved in Kingdom business. An eternal business.

I encourage you to ask the Holy Spirit to show you aspects of heaven. I do not believe for a moment that this diminishes the significance of our lives now. On the contrary, perhaps we need a larger dose of heavenly perspective as we embrace our courses here.

He may show you something that no one has ever seen.

He may show you the streets of heaven and places that are there; perhaps someone who is there. A single revelation from Him could breathe new life and hope into your anticipation of heaven and of its reality.

People praying today are seeing glimpses of heaven. Some are experiencing its reality as they pray – and I'm not talking about an immediate end to their days on earth! Remember what Jesus said to John when he was exiled on the island of Patmos: "Come up here!" You can read what he saw in Revelation 4.

We are learning more about the role of the angels in Kingdom business. They are not to be worshipped but are our valuable allies and servants. We can involve them in our intercession as we pray in the Spirit. Angels enjoy being around God's people and play important roles in enforcing Spirit-filled prayer as the Holy Spirit orchestrates it.

I made you a guarantee and I want to make you another one. Heaven is going to be much, much more wonderful than you could ever imagine!

God laughs. God laughs with unfettered joy, and we are part of the Kingdom of this God. We are going to 'have a blast' in heaven. Its atmosphere is almost unspeakable; it is otherworldly and yet home. You simply could not wish to be anywhere else because it is where God's home is.

As I bring this chapter to a close, I would like to share a testimony with you – one that will perhaps astonish you (as it did me).

Put your seat belt on…

It concerns a young teenager who died. That's tough. She had been involved in a skiing accident. I don't know if she kept a journal into her teenage years but she had done so when she was a young girl.

Her name was Maurissa. A short while after Maurissa went home to heaven, a minister who had experienced a number of spiritual adventures in heavenly realms happened to hear of the tragedy.

Subsequently, on another one of these heavenly visits, the minister saw a girl in heaven whom she knew to be Maurissa. She saw her as she was on her way to a fun park with a young man. This young man, the minister discerned, was her great grandfather (in his new, ageless heavenly body). At the amusement park there were roller coasters just like the ones that we have here on earth. The Holy Spirit spoke to the minister and told her to encourage Maurissa's mother that all was well with her and that, moreover, she was positively living out her heavenly destiny.

How's your theology doing?

The minister duly wrote down what the Spirit of God had shown her and, to cut the story short, she later met the girl's mother. Maurissa's mum later corroborated all that had been shared in the conversation and confirmed that the girl that had been seen in heaven was certainly her daughter.

A short while later, the teenager's family came across an entry in a journal that Maurissa had written six years previously when she was just seven years old. It was a precious discovery.

In the entry, part of which is quoted below, she wrote concerning a dream in which she had died early and gone to heaven. When you read it for yourself, I imagine that you will be as amazed as I was. How good God is, and what an astonishingly gracious intervention!

I have left young Maurissa's spelling as it appeared in her journal.

Journal, 10/3/95.

Once I dreamed ... that Jesus took me up to heaven early. And I got to see my greatgrandfather earlay. I got to ride all kinds of rollar coasters. I did see tons of manchines. It was wonderful. But when Jesus took me up he only gave me a peek...

May the LORD bless you and keep you.
May the LORD show you his kindness
and have mercy on you.
May the LORD watch over you
and give you peace.

Numbers 6:24-26

CHAPTER TWENTY-ONE

Final Thoughts

She turned to leave and saw someone standing there. It was Jesus, but she didn't recognize him. "Dear woman, why are you crying?" Jesus asked her. "Who are you looking for?" She thought he was the gardener. "Sir," she said, "if you have taken him away, tell me where you have put him, and I will go and get him."
"Mary!" Jesus said.

John 20:14-16

How are you doing with God today?

In the passage above, Mary has yet another life-changing moment in the company of Jesus. She had met Him before. He had touched her with grace and forgiveness and He had won her heart. But since His death and the indescribable trauma that had accompanied it, where was hope now?

Hope was standing right in front of her. He knew her name. He knows yours too.

We all have our ups and downs, our challenges and areas of life that we prosper in more easily. But I wonder if the trend for you, were you to have a chart, is a positive line or one that has been dipping? There is never a wrong time to come to Jesus just as you are and talk to Him. There is never a wrong time to sit and listen to the Holy Spirit and to engage with Him in a transparent heart-to-heart. I am not talking about navel gazing. That kind of introspective analysis has its roots in fear and it is unnecessary in our relationship with God.

The truth is that we are already fully known by Him.

> *For now we see in a mirror dimly, but then face to face; now I know in part, but then I will know fully just as I also have been fully known.*
>
> *1 Corinthians 13:12*

The Contemporary English Bible (CEV) says:

> *Now we see a reflection in a mirror; then we will see face-to-face. Now I know partially, but then I will know completely in the same way that I have been completely known.*
>
> *1 Corinthians 13:12*

It's not that we haven't met Him, for we have. We have received real revelation from the Spirit of God. We have touched Him, we have come to know Him in part; and as much as we may enjoy and even revel in His presence and in intimate exchanges with Him, the Bible says that in comparison with how things will be in the next world, our experience is dark. I am encouraged by that, not discouraged! It must mean that there is so much more to discover about Him and, of course, His heart is to reveal Himself to those who will seek Him out.

I love the fact that my relationship with God – with Father, Son and Holy Spirit – cannot be compared with anyone else's. It is as unique as you and I are unique. We are very good at identifying those whom we believe have a 'close thing' with Jesus and, yes, Kingdom fruit is evidence of that to a degree. At the same time, no-one else in all history has lived your life up until this point, and no-one else is going to step into your shoes. Jesus Christ is fully committed to you and to the expression of your mutual love, friendship and service that cannot be equalled by another person on the planet.

We are in 'potter's wheel' territory, not systematic, machine-driven manufacture.

I love the picture of the potter at the wheel. All of the potter's attention is given to his task. All his faculties are engaged. He turns the wheel with his foot as his mind pictures the finished article a long time before the clay has been through its full process. A hand scoops water on to the clay as the other steadies it and begins to form the design. His eyes watch precisely as the shape develops, and his mind alerts his hands to the need for pressure here, shaping there as progress is made.

Two hands cup the newly formed item as the sides are smoothed and perhaps raised a little, or reduced a little, or balanced into line. This is an original creation in the making.

You are an original creation in the making. You are a work in progress of unique specifications that the potter takes delight in bringing to being. That's it, really, isn't it? In Christ Jesus, we all were lost and have been found. We were broken, damaged, deceived. Now, on the Potter's wheel, something supernatural has been placed into us and that the Holy Spirit has begun a determined and progressive work in forming the life of Christ in us. How wonderful that He – He *personally* – is expressing Himself through you.

Yes, you may have 'messed up' on occasions. Join the club! You may have done things that you should not have done and omitted to do what might have been done. But this was never about your own efforts to make yourself into a new person; rather it was always about recognising that you have been made new already and that from a position of rest in God's ability, He is acting on your behalf to ensure that your life bears the fruit that its roots were created to produce and that this expression should be undeniably you-flavoured.

He loves that – your flavour. He loves the body He gave you, the mind and its sometimes odd ways, the level of intelligence he blessed you with, your sensitivities and your unparalleled, receptive spirit. You are truly a one off and He rejoices in you.

He gave you a sense of humour and enjoys it. He smiles as you progress in the Spirit life. He rejoices when you stand firm in faith and refuse to be bowed down before criticism, unfair treatment or a difficult challenge. He laughs when the enemy threatens you – as if this bedraggled, fallen angelic enemy could derail you from your glorious inheritance in Christ! The battle for you and me and for our future has been won – let us just stay in our seats, firmly strapped in with the belt of truth.

That seat is not in this earthly realm. It is in heavenly places, where our home is and to which we belong. Heaven laughs a hearty roar as Kingdom citizens grow and mature to recognise their true identities and their true citizenship. The enemy is forever accusing us that we are unworthy of God's love and of His gifts, but he in turn forever misses the point. He despises us as the dust we were formed from and is revolted when he perceives such dedicated, delighted love stream our way from our Father in heaven. This love has rescued us and redeemed us and is doing miracle work within and through us.

We bear His name; we bear the mark of Christ; heaven celebrates us and joy reverberates through the corridors, streets and halls of heaven, sending echoes of praise across its domain.

> *Mighty your acts and marvellous,*
> *O God, the Sovereign-Strong!*
> *Righteous your ways and true,*
> *King of the nations!*
> *Who can fail to fear you, God,*
> *give glory to your Name?*
> *Because you and you only are holy,*
> *all nations will come and worship you,*
> *because they see your judgments are right.*
>
> *Revelation 15:3-4*

O God, the Sovereign-Strong! Amen!

Bibliography

19   http://www.laughfactory.com/jokes/religious-jokes

31   http://www.brainyquote.com/quotes/topics/topic_fear3.html

33   http://www.brainyquote.com/quotes/keywords/busy.html#X9q6cxwZDxtHLaG

34   The Christian's Secret of a Happy Life – Hannah Whitall Smith – 1985 – Barbour & Co

43   http://www.crimperman.org/2008/12/02/long-jokes-shaggy-dog-stories/

48   http://allpoetry.com/poem/6949682-Embarrassed-by-Meter-Maid# sthash.jFJxTvKI.dpuf

48   http://allpoetry.com/poem/10292519-Was-my-face-Red--by-Mel-Patterson# sthash.ptBOBN8Z.dpuf

51   http://jokes.christiansunite.com/Amish/A_Miracle_Transformation.shtml *accessed 18/10/14 – adapted*

67   http://jokes.christiansunite.com/Creation/The_Monkey.shtml

92   http://www.greatcleanjokes.com/jokes/marriage-humor/marriage-jokes/

100 http://tvtropes.org/pmwiki/pmwiki.php/Main/ShaggyDogStory definition

104 http://www.yuksrus.com/religion_noah.html

125 http://jokes.cc.com/funny-god-jokes/b1ej8z/jesus-and-moses-play-golf adapted

126 The Screwtape Letters – CS Lewis © 1942. From 1998 edition, Fount Paperbacks

127 http://www.goodreads.com/quotes/tag/control

128 http://www.brainyquote.com/quotes/keywords/control.html#gDeylvaTBW4FYZQ3

134 Revealing Heaven – Kat Kerr – 2007 – www.xulonpress.com

Also by the Author

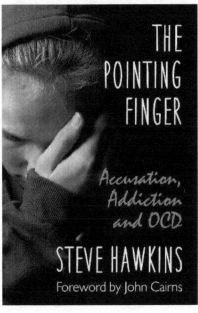

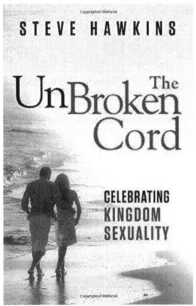